ADEN'S SUDDEN DECLARATION OF LOVE CHANGED EVERYTHING. . . .

Kit gave him a hard look, then pulled away and resumed walking at a steady pace. Inside she was reeling. She'd thought she wanted this to happen, had woven daydreams on nothing else since that fiercely beautiful night in his bed. . . . But something had gone haywire. She'd begun to detect it in the way Aden was looking at her, speaking to her, touching her. It was shy and fiery all at once. Gone were the bandying of insults, the unpredictable almost-come-to-blows quality of their relationship that had kept her on the tip of her emotional toes. From here, romance looked like a prison.

Why did he have to spoil everything by falling in love with her?

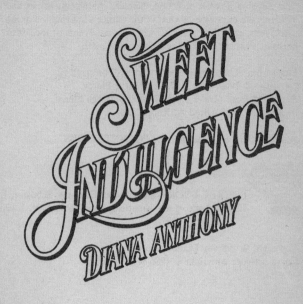

SWEET INDULGENCE

DIANA ANTHONY

PUBLISHED BY POCKET BOOKS NEW YORK

This novel is a work of fiction. Names, characters, places and incidents are either the product of the author's imagination or are used fictitiously. Any resemblance to actual events or locales or persons, living or dead, is entirely coincidental.

Lines from "Unlearning How to Speak," on page vii,
copyright © 1969, 1971, 1973, by Marge Piercy.
Reprinted from *Circles on the Water* by Marge Piercy,
by permission of Alfred A. Knopf, Inc.

Another *Original* publication of POCKET BOOKS

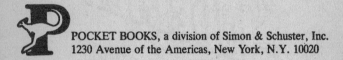

POCKET BOOKS, a division of Simon & Schuster, Inc.
1230 Avenue of the Americas, New York, N.Y. 10020

ISBN: 0-671-83449-5

First Pocket Books printing August, 1986

10 9 8 7 6 5 4 3 2 1

POCKET and colophon are registered trademarks
of Simon & Schuster, Inc.

Printed in the U.S.A.

For
My Sweet Indulgence

"She must learn again to speak/starting with
I starting with We/starting as the infant does/
with her own true hunger/and pleasure/and rage."

MARGE PIERCY

Prologue

Society Editor
Ronnie Hazelton
in *Ladies Wear Weekly*

June 17

NEWPORT, R.I.—On Saturday, *LWW* went to see Kit Daniels, only daughter of Whitney Daniels III of Southampton and Palm Beach and Marva Chance Daniels of Rome, marry Jonathan Cantwell of Newport, R.I.

For the socials, it was to be the wedding of the year—and *LWW* has never seen its like for surprises.

The bride wore black. At least, the tissuey silk-taffeta skirt was midnight black, drawn in at the knee for a bubble effect. The bodice with its rare Caen lace and ivory beading was a more traditional off-off-white.

Mallory Daniels' sketch—*sans* color—for the wedding had been printed in *LWW* (March 15). But on the willowy bride it was even more striking. Once again, Daniels outdid himself in the fabric and beadwork for which he is famous, but then, as he said, "Kit Daniels' body was a dream to work with." I guess we'll just have to take his word.

The bride's hair was loose and wild, apparently in its natural ruddy chestnut state, twirled round with Queen Anne's lace to piquant effect. At her approach, they murmured that she was a walking Botticelli—all of Newport did, that is, for no one would dare to miss the half-million-dollar wedding.

But the day held more surprises. No sooner had the bride come into the church to *Lohengrin*'s strains than there was a flurry of confusion. The next thing the guests knew, she had gone bounding back up the aisle, leaving Whitney Daniels III in her dust—not to mention Jonathan Cantwell himself, and half of the *Bluebook* staring in silence. No family member was later available for comment.

As promised, it was a wedding we at *LWW* shall not soon forget.

And you thought Newport was boring.

PART I

Maiden

Chapter 1

A<small>T LAST</small>, K<small>IT</small> Daniels' debutante ball.

A hush, as if at the first sight of love. And then, balloons, twelve thousand pink and white balloons. With airy hearts and thin skins of acrylic, the sweet dreams incarnate of three hundred debs. It's a hot summer's eve, here in Southampton-by-the-sea.

Balloons, in a gush, in a cloudy jet. Here, bounced to the floor in a pastel clutter. There, buoyed by all good wishes to the crown of the bright, white tent at Maregate. Forty balloons, or forty dreams each for the dolls of the debutante ball.

Oh they were hot, these girls of summer, a few with the consummate nerve to come punked out in leather, flaunting ankle bracelets that spelled the magic names of their lovers: "Tink," "Micki Lee," "Dallas" . . .

Their young men showed bright shocks of hair and jackets cut taut as they leaned forward to catch something in their arms, a girl or a pleasure as yet undefined by the summer night. Rich, easy, they prowled the tent in attitudes of grace.

Others swayed and swooned to the disco beat. Barely dining off gilded plates, they held their long-stemmed crystal to flashing fountains of champagne. Waiters in white passed among them like ghosts.

Outside on the front lawn, the local police were camping out. Holding their torches aloft, they saluted waiting Mercedes and Rolls Royces that stood backed up to Broadway.

This is what the police guards heard and saw: a car door popping open with the sound of a holiday cracker. Another pair, in summer whites, alighting on the lawn. Soft giggles together, touches as they follow a breezily swaying trail of balloons, always balloons, into the floodlit Tudor mansion neatly set inside its border of boxwood and clipped cones of yew, like a perfect painting of a house.

Everyone said the grand manner of the Daniels' ball had not been seen since eighty years ago, when the grandmothers of the young officers on the lawn had read about one James Paul of Philadelphia. A rich man too, he'd flown in some ten thousand Brazilian butterflies, "the hair ribbons of the angels," to grace his daughter's party, only to have the creatures succumb to the heat of the chandeliers and pour down their crazy rainbow brilliance upon the festive throng.

Imagine the cracked rainbow, the flash of jungle in the deluge it made. Imagine the beating-winged assault of dying butterflies, a dry rain falling soft as paper roses upon the startled faces, a ghostly whir as thousands of innocents floated to their beautiful deaths, against the white lace and bosoms of the young beauties of their day.

Tonight, Whitney Daniels III had no need for imported fauna to lace the evening with color. A rare windfall of drama was already being provided by his own bright, beautiful, but blatantly overweight daughter, Kit. She'd refused to come down.

Her debutante ball had been doomed from the start when Princess was not invited to "come out" by any of the venerable New York charity balls. It was, in addition, slightly off season and overdue; Whitney Daniels III had waited as long as he could for her to get in shape.

She never had.

6

Even now, it was something of a shock to come upon "Princess" in her current, overblown condition. Like any unpleasantness that managed to slip through the golden nets of his charmed life, this overnight ballooning, this sudden, fleshly opulence of his once-perfect "little" girl had taken Whitney Daniels very much by surprise.

No matter. The child remained his ideal companion, his solace, his sweetheart, as Marva had never cared to be. It was only baby fat that had caused Kitrin the years of adolescent agonies. No doubt it would pass, by and by, like the once-awful bogey of the braces on her teeth.

After all, there was no time he could recall when Kitrin had disappointed him in anything essential, what with her golden grades, natural beauty (not like Marva's—more robust, more real, actually), and athletic excellence. Some time ago, in the pitch of bitterness, he'd decided that blame for their family troubles must fall exclusively on the white shoulders of his wife. For hadn't Marva, over the last few years, kicked away from them both, aimed for the allure of foreign shores, foreign men? Without formality of divorce?

Indecent. Whitney frowned. He should have guessed at some profound disjunction between mother and daughter when the infant had first rejected Marva's milk.

An allergy, the doctor had said . . . hah!

An allergy to selfishness, to spite.

But then, what young man loves a woman like Marva with clear sight to the future child, his greater love for that child?

For Kitrin's sake he'd invited his wife here tonight. For Kitrin's sake, they would act like friends.

With habitual grace, he stepped over to a nearby table, draped in pink and ringed round with young girls. By the time he left, they were all a little bit in love.

Still a sky-eyed charmer at seventy, Whitney Daniels was accustomed to being courted by younger women. (Kit's little friends were always crazy about him). And why not? The Daniels men were known for their butterfly brilliance.

Like his sire before him, Whitney Daniels III had been educated at Groton, Princeton, and the Académie Julian in

Paris. Before the war, this most obviously gifted of the Daniels men had maintained a duplex on the ninth floor of the Hotel des Artistes, where he turned out fine post-Impressionist landscapes and still lifes, some of which now hung in the library at the new Maregate, rebuilt after a 1939 fire.

It was there, in the gusto and glitter of Paris, that he had launched his legendary career as playboy and dilettante extraordinaire.

But if the adult Whitney Daniels best epitomized the hero of drawing-room farce, his early life had run more in the mode of domestic tragedy. The central fact, the suffering core of his youth, was the untimely loss of both gay, beautiful parents in a hotel fire on the Riviera. He'd doted on his socialite mother, and her death had been a devastation. Although Whit and his brother Julian were well cared for by a great uncle, the younger Daniels heir had soon become suspicious of the whole world of strangers who'd let him suffer so early and so crippling a blow. Anger made a deep home in him, settled in to stay.

Then, a young girl named Marva Chance had walked into a candlelit Paris drawing room and taken his breath away. For a brief, intoxicated time, she had cleft through the stone ringed round his heart. For once in his life, he was able to put vengeance aside.

Until she too grew restless, and began, in little ways, to leave him . . .

Kit had been his only solace then. With "Kitten" by his side, he'd heaped up a universe of dreams, raised a psychic castle for two, sealed off against a world that had betrayed him once again, in the cruelest way a man can be betrayed: through a woman.

A waiter offered a silver tray. "Telegrams, sir."

"Thank you." Daniels unfolded the first message, sent by a Madeleine Lefkowitz, from abroad. One of Kit's fat friends. Impatient, he turned to the next one.

"Congratulations, darling. Sorry to have missed your Big Day. Write me at Rome address. Ciao. Mother."

He tore the telegram in two. Damn the woman! She'd

dumped this whole embarrassing affair into his lap—and now she wasn't even going to show up!

Kit would take it hard.

As he scoured the festive tent for his only daughter, he could sense the line of his paternal power beginning to go slack.

For some reason, it was getting harder and harder to keep track of his women these days.

And tonight, for Whitney Daniels III, at his fat daughter's debutante ball, the reason why seemed more elusive than ever.

The girl too big for the cheval glass is swathed in white, like a postulant or a bride. The dress, a pale flowering of batiste, is sugared over with lace appliqué. The neck is high; the waist dips gracefully into a skirt cut for fullness. White-clothed buttons flow down the back, while pink freshwater pearls, set in Grandmother's antique gold, glow in her ears. A pearl choker pulses like a chain of light around her throat.

Tonight, on the eve of her twentieth birthday, Kit Daniels' life would finally begin. She hoped.

With a critical eye, Kit posed before the mirror that reflected back her high-ceilinged bedroom: the powder-pink walls, the counterpane bed fit for a Spanish infanta, the hi-tech interlock of her complete entertainment system. She never had to leave the room.

"So what do you think, ladies and gentlemen? Is it *Portrait of a Lady* or more *Porky the Pig?*"

There was no discernible answer from the audience of old dolls who sagged in a bedraggled row along a petit-point loveseat. Snookers, Annie Laurie, and Badlands, a Raggedy Andy type with one beady black eye to his name and an eruption of orange yarn atop his trapezoidal head. The only response she did receive came from Admiral Byrd, the family's prize-winning malamute, who took the opportunity to nuzzle her palm.

"Ah, so you like the way I look, huh boy?" He gazed up at her with his wolfen eyes. "Hell, what do you know, Byrd? Your taste is for the dogs!"

"Mine's not. You look sensational." Her immaculately dressed, potentially handsome cousin, Mallory Daniels, appeared at the door to her room, a bottle of Dom Perignon hooked under his arm.

"Mallory, you creep!" Kit kissed him on both cheeks. Her motion stirred up the talcumy scent of little June roses. "You came!"

"As promised. What are you doing up here anyway? The party's already cookin'."

"I'm seeing my whole meal flash before me." Kit pinched off one of the bumpers on her body where there was more of her than there ideally should be. "I mean, when the *Gazette* said I'd be coming out tonight, I'm sure they didn't have this much of me in mind."

As she said this, there was a hint of tears in her eyes. With one hand, she took a swipe at her reflection, while with the other, she ravaged a hidden stash of Zabar's chocolate fudge brownies, each one stuck with walnuts as big as fangs.

After a while, she offered the bag to Mallory, who shook his head. Then she lay flat on her back upon the enormous pink bed, staring up at the ceiling and crunching away.

Oh God, another binge! And tonight of all nights!

Mallory thought once again how stunning Kit would be if she'd only refine and polish her beauty. She was certainly tall enough, had a fine pair of eyes—a full, electric volt of blue, like her father's—and a queenly crown of auburn hair, played with heavenly lights.

But he didn't bother to say so, as she was blind to the goddess in herself.

Cast in lifelong eclipse by her high-fashion mother, tied dangerously by the heartstrings to her matinee idol of a father, Kit had suffered humiliation upon humiliation along the bumpy road of adolescence.

Convinced of Kit's inability to cut herself down to a maidenly size by the many disappointing summers of fat farms, the failed psychiatrists ("rapists," Kit called them), the cheated-on weight-watching programs, and the mixture of hoodoo and hypnotism thrown in for good measure, Kit's parents had thrown the big party in defeat. And Mallory was sure that no one felt the defeat more keenly than the debutante herself.

Oh, the nightmare of fittings! The photographers' patronizing leers! Kit had died a little every time they let the dress out.

Gay, and no stranger to pain himself, Mallory had registered each social shock with her.

Then, to top it all off, the poor girl had gorged so greedily last night, she was unable to squeeze into the lustrous new dress dreamed up by that French designer. Forced to leave the first ten buttons open, Kit now hoped to hide the gaping V at her back with a mantle. Mallory knew all about it because he himself had come up with the solution during the panic of this morning's phone call.

Of course, the problem of wearable clothes was nothing new. Kit's body had waged a running battle with the small-minded fashion industry for years now.

Mallory could almost sense the soft explosion of garments in her wall-to-wall closet, which held the three separate wardrobes of the "fat" girl: "Before Diet," "After Diet," and what Kit dubbed "Lifejackets and Tarpaulins."

She hated all three.

He was about to suggest, delicately, that he sew her into the rest of the dress (he had this gift with a needle—not very macho, but there it was) when Kit rolled the now-empty brownie bag into a sphere, lobbed it into a wicker wastebasket, and flopped back onto her overstuffed pink pillows, scented, like herself, with essence of tea rose.

"Marva here yet?" She licked the last smudges of brownie off her fingers. Milk chocolate was such a comfort, harkening back to her days in the sun-dappled white nursery, when Marva's eyes were still kind. The dark easement, the psychic spaciousness of chocolate was fine indeed, but it didn't end there. Although she may not have been consciously aware of the method behind her madness with food, Kit had evolved a kind of science of binging, so that there were prescribed feasts set aside for specific moods.

Take, for example, bread and butter, for bad family "trips." The leavening made her feel expansive, yeasty, as

11

though she could fill the whole of her father's house with her willfulness.

Then, there was pizza for cramming before exams. All those sharply salted colors on a wheel, the geometric shapes, they anchored her to the here and now, helped her to concentrate.

Ultimately, of course, there were sweets: ice cream, pastries, cakes—and chocolate of all kinds.

They were the goodly portions, the ambrosial goo reserved for lonely times, the hell of being left out. Whenever there was no love, no discernible sweetness in her bitter life at home, Kit Daniels fed it to herself in stealth, in silence—a secret, life-shattering ritual. Of course, if you observed her in public, like many secret eaters she seemed to subsist on cups of cottage cheese and fancy mineral water. But oh, when she was finally, blessedly alone in her room, and didn't have to impersonate the perfect little girl for Daddy—and Mommy, wherever she was . . .

It would break upon her like a divine summons from some exiled goddess, an elemental hunger of such fearful passion and demonic power that it possessed her to the girlish core. The vacuum inside unfilled by parental love, by peer acceptance, by a simple sense of womanly value, must be filled by food. The anxiety stuffed down by food.

It was a chronic madness, as she experienced it. She didn't know where the brilliant scholar, Daddy's biddable girl went, once the primal darkness seeped poisonously into the stomach part of her soul. In the end, it was making a mockery of her life. With all that perfection locked away inside a bloated body, she'd become a parody of herself: her features distended to a rubber mask, her body distorted into a grotesque image of undigested womanhood. And only when she was alone, on a binge like last night's, did the discrepancy between her high ideals and her basest instincts come screaming out at her, until she too wanted to scream and scream with the breath of the beast . . .

No matter how many times she'd come under the sway of that beast, it was terrifying to let go, and at the same time, such a voluptuous surrender . . .

Just then, Admiral Byrd sprang onto the bed. Kit's attention snapped back to the here and now. "You didn't answer my question, Mal. Is Marva here yet?"

"Not yet."

A shadow flickered over her pretty moon face. "Where is the fabled Marva Chance Daniels tonight?" She put on a newscaster's overbright voice. "Monte Carlo? Cap Antibes? Disney World?"

Mallory felt sorry for her. If she were joking about Marva, the pain must be bad. It was no wonder that a ruinous kind of bond had sprung up between Kit and her father, a species of "eternal boy" in search of a sweet madonna to take care of him. For a "daughter-of-the-father" like Kit, there was scant chance of living out her own womanly life, in touch with her female instincts, when she must perform brilliantly for *him*, in school, and later in her career (Kit wasn't sure what it would be, only that it would be).

According to Kit, Marva had never really wanted to play mother in the first place. Right off, she'd suffered a dramatic nervous breakdown the day after her daughter was born. Kit worried that Marva had never forgiven her for that. Then there was the matter of the Brilliant Career. It was said Marva Chance had dieted so severely during her pregnancy with Kit, that the baby girl was born at a perilously low weight. But then again, as she'd intended, the model had soon won back her figure and was flying off to another shoot in record time.

A subsequent magazine article quoted the international beauty as claiming she'd rather "go over Niagara Falls in a barrel" than have a second child because "I've worked too hard for a great body to waste it all on another daughter."

Even now, Kit often dreamed of feeling her way in the dark, when Marva lets go of her hand . . .

For these reasons, Kit and her father had come to share an uncommon intimacy. It had been a mode of survival around Marva, the magnificent, volatile creature they each were terrified of losing, on whose account they both secretly raged.

Helplessly, Mallory watched Kit lounge against the high pile of pillows. Her lace-stockinged feet rested against Byrd's silky flanks. "Why don't we just party here? We can order some more brownies. Believe me, no one will ever know the difference." She ran her palm over the curve of her belly, mole-eyed and dreamy as a pregnant woman.

At first, Mallory held his peace. Kit was probably right. The last time he'd looked, all the dishy men were crowding around the bird-boned things in strapless taffeta. She would never be missed.

But when Kit actually began ringing up a local gourmet shop, he slapped at her wrist so that the receiver flew out of her hand. "This is no time to be discovering a new major food group!" He heaved her up by both hands. "Tonight, you're going to glitter!"

"I can't," she said in a small voice. "I don't even fit into this damn dress anymore, after last night."

It did seem to be getting worse; her body was surging out of control. The more she consumed, the emptier she was. After meals, she would secret a loaf of bread, a half-moon of cake that she could bring up to her room and wolf down, in a ritual of guilt.

And how she hated the stigma of being a compulsive eater: the chafing thighs, the unwearable clothes, the insulting stares of perfect strangers on the street!

"Here, drink this." Mallory had uncorked the bottle of Dom Perignon, '72. He held it up to her lips like a prairie doctor with a patent medicine, not sure it was going to work but willing to bluff.

"Mal, you know I can't drink."

"All the better to numb you with, my dear."

With much reluctance Kit took a swig. The wine burned sweetly at the back of her throat. The bottle swung up again, and again. Admiral Byrd whimpered. An existential warmth began to lap up from Kit's toes.

The bed seemed to sway gently, like a boat on the blue sound outside. "You know something"—she giggled—"I do feel numb."

"I bet you do," Mallory said.

"But I also feel like a candy bar. Any Snickers on you, Mal?"

"God, when are you going to get into a sane relationship with food?" Mallory's voice zigzagged at her from someplace across the sound.

A sane relationship to food, she thought, in a bright champagne fog. The last time she'd had one of those was when she was fourteen and Grandmother Ilona was still alive . . .

She'd counted the days to each visit . . . the Park Avenue penthouse, which always seemed so female, dark, and perfumed, after the white-stone brightness of midtown Manhattan. The heavy antique Persian rugs that Gran called her "rags." The fringed, rose-velvet lamps, fished out from dusty stalls on Pimlico Road. The spellbinding stories of old Budapest. It all had a witchy quality for the little girl who loved to be with Gran even more than she loved ballet class, or riding her brand-new two-wheeler.

Yes, Grandmother Ilona must have been a witch, with her healing hands. She had a shelf full of labeled bottles: balms, soothing demulcents and salves; herbal lore (bay leaf for stomachache, paprika for sore throat), and the starcluster of magical-sounding gemstones: fire opal, adderstone, bloodstone.

And her botanical knowledge didn't end with herbs. When Grandmother Ilona lived in England, she'd caught that country's passion for gardening and was full of floral esoterica. Tidbits like the fact that the common rose first drifted over from exotic Persia. Or that gooseberries had names like graffiti artists: Early Green Hairy, Slaughterman, Bang Europe, Hot Gossip.

The willful widow of an English naval officer, whom she'd met and married during the First World War, Grandmother Ilona had come from Portsmouth to America after his death in 1960. This to be with her only daughter, Marva, who, even as a child, never cared to eat her mother's nourishing meals but subsisted on a diet of parsley tea and carrot sticks.

"Be kind to your mother," Gran would tell Kit, all curled around a teacup in her rose-velvet easy chair. "Because she doesn't have a clue."

On special days, Gran would prepare their best recipes

from memory . . . peppery goulash (an entrée, not a soup) served up in an envelope of steam, a generous dish in which to lose oneself on a raw winter's day . . . *mohyaros sertesszelet,* a potato fritter with peppers or pork, spiced with the ubiquitous Hungarian paprika (no wonder the gypsies were thought to be hot-blooded; that wonderful, fiery paprika could raise the devil in anyone). A fluffy pillow of chocolate cake, light as a dream on your spoon.

Funny, while Gran was alive Kit could be content with just a taste of these wonders. But once Gran left this life, and the enchanted penthouse on Park Avenue became a childhood memory, Kit couldn't seem to taste enough of anything, ever again, couldn't climb back into the lap of well-being, or find the joy to be had in a dish of hot soup and an old woman's stories on a rainy afternoon.

Mallory put his hands on Kit's shoulders and aimed her down the mahogany staircase.

"Wait!" Kit struck a pose, and Mallory bumped up against her.

"What!"

"Mal, I think, I mean, I'm not sure—but I might be stinking drunk."

"You should be. You polished off almost half that bottle of champagne. Shall we move on?"

Uncertainly, Kit peered down the spiral of staircase.

Then, in what seemed like the blink of an eye, she was peering up.

Kit took a deep, steadying breath, while Admiral Byrd watched from his superior position at the top of the stairs. He barely lifted his head from where it rested on the velvet line of his paws.

"Byrd thinks we're bizarre."

"We are," Mallory replied. "Are you ready?"

"No."

"Never mind. Let's go."

In companionable silence, they moved out the French doors onto the deck, with its pots of red geraniums. The sky was pricked with stars, like sequins on a fine, dark blue silk. The evening air, soft on their senses, gave hope.

Inside the tent, the debs were dancing away, into the night. Long ago, their pumps had been tossed clear of the dance floor, their hair thrown back with a savvy smile. What seemed like billions of balloons were swaying in time. Wine was flowing. The musicians rode their bucking guitars like mounts.

With a sharp, sudden ache in her heart, Kit wanted to dazzle the world like all the other girls, to dance without shoes and still look like grace itself, to make men mad with her silvery brightness, like a fine, full moon on a summer's night. To be daring, and light-headed, free of encumbering flesh . . .

Oh how she wanted to be all these things for her father . . . for Madeleine Lefkowitz, her fat friend, for all the other women in all the other midsummer dreams, who would wake up tomorrow morning and dress in what amounts to sackcloth and eat nothing but ashes, because their souls were too big for their bodies, their bodies too big to fit into the cramped roles they'd been cast by others to play.

Yes, the big girl in white promised them all, as she stepped inside the tent, this night would be perfect for them.

Chapter 2

Princess?"

"Yes, Daddy?"

Out of the blond haze of candlelight, and what might well have been loops of marijuana smoke, Whitney Daniels materialized before his daughter. "Mallory." His eyes were cold blue stones.

"Hello, Uncle Whit." Mallory stared down at his shoes. In his distinguished uncle's presence, he was always five years old.

"Your guests are expecting you, Kitrin."

Kit smiled up at her father sweetly, foolishly, so Mallory answered for her.

"Kit was waiting for me, Uncle Whit."

As was his custom, Whitney Daniels ignored his nephew. "That was sweet of you, darling." He spread his fingers against Kit's vulnerable, white cotton-clad back, as though they might help absorb the imminent blow. "Princess, there were telegrams. One from Madeleine, and the other . . ."

". . . from Marva." Kit's eyes were intensely bright. "Does she say when she'll be arriving?"

Two words: "I'm sorry," and Kit had the props knocked out from under her.

"What's the matter, couldn't Marva afford the dollar eighty-two for a minute on the phone, eighty cents thereafter?" The bitter words broke from her as if against her will. She tried to catch her balance, but the alcohol was like a pane of funhouse glass set behind her temples, refracting the sights and sounds of the night into furred, nightmare fragments. By now, the sweet buzz of summer had faded to a dull hum.

Her father's handsome face held that blank look that set in whenever his gadabout wife was mentioned. "I'd prefer you called her Mother."

Kit was hurt by the rebuke, but bound to forgive him, as she always had. As she always would. A man, he was at sea in the female psyche. There was no sure map he could follow to bring him home. But Kit was almost a woman now; she had the right, even the duty, to seek out Marva, to expose in her all female faults, ambitions, vanities. She must continue to nurse this dark bloom of rage in her heart, hold it dear. For it was all she had left to connect her to her beautiful witch of a mother.

The next thing Kit knew she was standing alongside her father on an eternal reception line, pumping a file of hands, and swaying to her own inner music.

"Who's that?" she heard someone whisper from far down the line. "Petunia Pig?"

"Shh, that's the guest of honor." A male voice rode high over the electric whine of guitars. "Now I know why they rented a circus tent for this party . . ."

Kit continued to shake hands as she'd been bidden, even as she withdrew, thankfully, into that floating blue space that hung between her inner self and the outside world. As the night stretched on, all the girls appeared to merge into one heartbreakingly beautiful deb in a perfect size five, and all the boys seemed to have their soft, pink tongues in their cheeks as they kissed her, with many congratulations. Kit would rather take chocolate kisses—or those pastel candy hearts with the mottoes on them like "Hubba-Hubba" and "Be Mine." The sentiments were just as real.

Oh, if only Maddy were here, she could bear it with more patience! Maddy—her angel of the fat camps. They had met when Kit was sixteen, at Camp Beech Tree—or "Beef Free" as the overweight campers privately called it. There she and Maddy, daughter of a Larchmont rabbi and his psychologist wife, had suffered the ministrations of Miss Hilde, the Swiss sports counselor who began each day by putting a malicious disc called "Chicken Fat" on the staticky record player.

According to the telegram, Maddy hadn't made it to the party tonight because she'd been trotted off to yet another of those pricey foreign health spas, where she'd be spoon-fed on wonder diets and pummeled and steamed into slenderness. A sheep being carded and sheared for the ring came, unbidden, to Kit's mind. But she could just see Maddy, submitting to each new operation with a smile, the angel on the rack.

Oh, she could probably learn a thing or two from Maddy—like being nice for a change. She'd have to ask about it, the next time she saw her friend.

For Maddy knew all about being nice. It was Madeleine who'd first interested Kit in the Care for Children Program. Kit sent money out of her own allowance and did mailings, whenever she could. It was especially distressing to her that any child in the world should have to go to bed hungry.

At the first sight of her lofty face, Kit had sensed she could learn the beatitudes from Maddy, who had a stillness about her, a feminine sweetness. Kit herself was too hungry, too proud, too big, too loud—too full of ambitious dreams to fit the day's shrunken image of woman. It seemed she was always out of step, shadowboxing, locked in a no-win battle with every rule, every other thing around her, including her own burgeoning body.

Like the time Maddy was down at Maregate for a summer weekend and they'd dropped into a Hampton Bays supermarket to buy the Spartan staples of a new diet. Kit had only to catch the scathing looks they were drawing from the other shoppers and she'd begun to load their cart with three "Baby Watson" cheesecakes, six "Mama Celeste" frozen pizzas, and three pints of Frusen Gladje ice cream. A far cry from the crunchy vegetables, tofu slabs, and melba toast on her original shopping list.

Just to make a point. Just to hit back at those staring faces, the superior smiles . . .

"Mercy, who's that?" Mallory roared in her ear, above the electrified din.

Kit turned her face. The most beautiful man at the ball had just taken her hand. "Golden-hair" she named him, in the way Adam named the first, sunlit creatures of Eden. He stood there carved out of her dreams, illuminating the world with a pair of eyes tinted even more fiercely blue than her father's.

"I'm Jonathan Cantwell. We met at your Aunt Eliza's bon voyage party on the *QE II*."

"That was a hundred years ago." Kit didn't realize she was still holding his beautiful hand. He had the kind of beauty that soothed. In his impeccable evening clothes, he carried it like an honor. "Let's see—I must have been all of ten years old."

"If that. In braces and pigtails as I recall. We had a race on the main deck, and ate tons of those awful little hot dogs wrapped in dough. Then we snuck some champagne to see what it was like to be grown up, remember?"

"Did we ever find out?"

He gave her the grace of a smile, and Kit felt overwhelmed with gratitude.

"I never did."

"Kit . . . " Mallory nudged her in the ribs with his elbow.

Kit dropped her eyes to see that she was still clinging to Jonathan's hand. "I'm sorry . . ."

Again, Jonathan's face brightened, a sunburst in which she might happily bask for the rest of her days. "It's a lovely party," he said.

"Oh yes," Kit breathed, "you are."

"And this time, I didn't even have to sneak the champagne." He tugged on a lock of her hair, the way he had those many years ago in the glittering stateroom of the great ocean liner.

And then he was gone, caught up in the restless shimmer of guests.

"Cantwell of the Newport Cantwells?" Mallory raised his eyebrows.

"That's the one." His hair was streaked by the sun, layered with astral colors, from rich saffron to pure gold. If she loved him, she would number the hairs on his head, every one. "Oh Mal, I'm in heaven!"

"Me too." They looked at one another.

Whitney Daniels took this moment to make his excuses.

"Well, darling, I'm off to find a cozy carrel."

Without hesitation, Kit defined the word for him. "A place for reading." Her father was quite the connoisseur of obscure and eccentric words. So much so that on more than one public occasion, Kit had been sent running to the OED laid out on the great stand in his Pompeiian-red library.

This powerful vocabulary was just another badge of her father's aggressive superiority, and she was bound, out of love, to respond.

"I am impressed. Now I'll leave you to your duties as belle of the ball." He'd kissed the top of her head and made his retreat.

"What would it take to make this your night of nights?" Mallory asked, breathing more easily now that Uncle Whit was gone. He settled into the white wicker chair next to his cousin and waited for her answer.

"That's easy. A dance with Jonathan Cantwell."

"Go for it then, Kit! Ask him to dance."

"Me? Ask him? You must be dehydrated, Mallory. He's about as interested in dancing with me as he would be in dancing with you."

"Thanks a lot!"

She rested her hands on her ample hips. "Why don't you go ask him to dance if you're feeling so plucky?"

"Hey, as Uncle Whit said, you're the belle of the ball. I'm only here for moral support, not social suicide."

Just then, the waiters wheeled out the dessert: a baker's

magnificat of chocolate mousse cake, with a sugary surf of Oreo ice cream on the side.

Kit was asked to cut the first piece.

She lowered the silver-handled knife. There was a smattering of polite applause. The disco music rolled over them like a blue wave to the Newport shore.

Cake was being served.

"He's looking at you," Mallory egged her on.

Kit contemplated the remarkable Mr. Cantwell for a moment, the prince of her debutante ball.

Any contact with him would be a grace.

Some of the sweet anticipation of the earlier evening came flowing back. Love seemed near. Life seemed dear.

Up till now, love had been on hold, to be rescheduled after she lost twenty-five pounds—after the holidays, after death . . . As for life, she'd kept longing for it to snap in two, like a party favor. The glittering prizes were supposed to be waiting inside. Well, Jonathan Cantwell glittered.

And, extraordinary as it seemed, he did appear to like her, drawing her down into those deep blue seafarer's eyes . . .

It was a shot at the moon.

She decided to take it.

Before she knew it, she'd lifted a fork and a plateful of chocolate mousse cake and was traveling in the young man's direction. He was, at the moment, holding forth amid a daisy chain of debs whom Kit only vaguely remembered from Miss Parker's. A Clairol blonde with spectacular cheekbones. Perky Lauren Something-or-other, who flew her own Cessna, with style. And Mary Beth Beaudine, the wundermädchen whose claim to fame was a very, very short story published in the *Atlantic Monthly* when she was still in high school.

At Kit's approach, Jonathan apparently lost the thread of his conversation.

Oh God. She looked from face to face. They were all standing there like a garden of statues.

But it was too late to retreat; there was no place to hide.

She would have to speak to him. Now.

She thrust out the plate, as the fork, like her confidence, teetered back and forth on the gilt-edged rim. "I brought you a piece of cake." Her face felt hot as a griddle, and she was a fat, unregenerate fool. "There weren't any awful little hot dogs in dough . . ."

Now polite and distant as an ancestral portrait, Jonathan's blue eyes drilled invisible holes into her. As usual, she was fair game, everybody's fool. Here was a stranger, a perfect stranger, and she had laid herself open to his disdain: she wanted to die right then, to sink down in a pool of white batiste and give up the ghost . . .

Then, to make matters worse, the unstable fork finally slipped off the edge of the plate and fell downward onto the grass.

In an ecstasy of embarrassment, Kit dropped to her knees.

Still tipsy from the champagne, she lost her balance altogether and tipped over onto her face, coming to rest, on all fours, at Jonathan's feet.

No longer smiling, Jonathan held out his hand.

Kit flailed out blindly with her own, but as she was heaved up in an awkward lump, she stumbled onto her emergency mantle and yanked it cleanly off her shoulders.

Now the expanse of her perspiring white slip and back were exposed to all. Kit felt an imaginary breeze flit across her back. She froze in a kind of adolescent horror.

Rather than risk toppling over again in an attempt to retrieve her mantle, Kit backed into an unoccupied table set up against one billowy side of the tent.

The pink and white balloons, which surrounded the high tapers of the candelabra, tumbled all about her, as Kit leaned back on the heels of her hands and threw her face wildly skyward, imploring the trickster gods of fools and fat people to swallow her up in a clap of thunder, to end her social martyrdom under the gaze of the most beautiful man in the world, the man she had dared to woo . . .

Instead, she heard a crackle and smelled the stink of creosote.

Here on this hot night, in the midst of the hot debs, Kit had become the hottest of them all. For she was on fire, her glorious hair blazing in streamers of light . . .

"Get out of my way, goddamn it!"

Mallory, who'd taken a discreet stroll on the beach so as not to put too much pressure on Kit, had only reentered the tent to see what the commotion was about.

Thinking quickly, he rushed forward and dumped a pitcher of ice water onto his cousin's flaming head.

Kit gasped, and cried, and gasped again. Ice water ran in rivulets down her décolletage. It spread across the bodice of her beautiful dress, a lizard-shaped patch of shame, as the delicate white cotton stuck to her skin.

The ball rolled on into the wee hours of dawn, wafting about the forty balloons, the forty dreams, for each hot deb. Upstairs, the guest of honor lay curled under bandages, in her little girl's bed, her gorgeous hair shorn off, like some victim of a war she didn't know was being waged, unable even to weep tears for herself, a female fool, a burlesque, a fat woman who'd dared to imagine she deserved to be loved by a man like Jonathan Cantwell . . . that she deserved to be loved at all.

—————— *Chapter 3* ——————

T<small>HE DRAWING ROOM</small> of the Protopopovs, a shadow box, plated in amber light. A young girl rushes to her lover's arms. In tears, she has her first kiss from him, then another, and another . . .

The curtain fell on the first act of Chekhov's *Three Sisters* to a house ringing with applause. And Kit Daniels swished off the stage in her long skirts, in a daze, in a dream.

They were applauding for her. They had been applauding all year, it seemed, for the most promising student actress ever to grace the stage of the exclusive Laura Pierpont Academy for Women.

Kit had often scoffed at the hushed tone certain actors assumed when speaking of the theater. But now she understood their reverence. To step on stage is to enter a sacred *temenos,* a field of magic, where a different kind of time takes hold and miracles routinely come to light.

Now she knew how it was that actors could speak of losing all sense of ordinary space and duration, of walking about on injured limbs without pain, of emptying themselves of personal ego, so as to be filled by the strong psychic stuff of another human being, and, if the magic is sturdy enough, to inhabit for a brief, inspired time, a soul that is not one's own.

In this way Kit Daniels had "become" Natasha, the vulgar and voluptuous woman who sweeps through the trembling world of the three sisters, with a primal female force.

In the intense six weeks of rehearsals, Kit had shed twenty-five pounds. Her appetite was no less ferocious, but she now had a new passion on which to grow happy.

His name was Marcus Heller, a fifty-one-year-old doctor of theater arts, and he was all of a piece with the brilliance of the lights and the quietly joyous birth of the actress within her.

Her love for him—the patient, green, disappointed eyes, the still-handsome face, the once-athletic body that was beginning to let him down—was all tangled up with her passion for the play they were about to pull out of the air.

Full skirts rustling, Kit moved into the backstage shadows. There, in the close darkness, a man's arm slipped around her waist.

Grown weak at his touch, she rested her head against his shoulder.

"You're a beautiful, splendid woman, Natasha," he whispered. "I'm so proud of you." And she could smell the sweet cherry pipe tobacco he carried on his breath, and in the leather pouch inside his coat pocket.

He lifted her hand and pressed it to his lips, his full beard grazing the fingertips so that they burned gently, every one.

It was never supposed to happen, this unwieldy attraction between student and professor. All his academic life, Dr. Marc had been so careful to avoid the clichés. As an actor, he'd been attracted to the genius flash of innovation. An autographed glossy of Samuel Beckett garnished his small but well-traveled rooms, high in an old Victorian house, on the outskirts of the upstate New York college town.

Those rooms, in which he rested his handsome professional laurels—he was, after all, one of those rare professors at Laura Pierpont who had actually cut a swath in the theatrical world outside of academe—had become a kind of weekend mecca for the monied girls of the Pierpont drama department as well as their male counterparts from neighboring Ashton.

For years, Friday evenings had been a flurry of pan pizza, Dr Pepper, and Chekhov or Shaw or Shepard. All agreed there was enough creative energy in that shabbily furnished apartment, tucked away in a hundred-year-old turret, to run some of them straight through to Broadway, and drive every last one of them to a partisan love for Dr. Marc.

For he had his detractors too. Jealousy ran rampant as ivy over the campus.

He was held to be too radical in his vision of a "poor theater."

His directorial metaphors were too weird: he'd let Hamlet dress like a punk rocker and deliver his monologues from a giant video screen suspended over Gertrude's bed.

He'd made the upstart Natasha the heroine of *Three Sisters,* extolling her as the symbol of proletarian energy sweeping away the effete world of the Russian aristocracy.

And he'd chosen a blatantly overweight, shockingly sensual young student to do it . . .

There were rumors.

Unsubstantiated, of course. For all his cat-eyed magnetism, the attractive widower of ten years had been careful to separate his business from his pleasures, knowing the dean of liberal arts at Laura Pierpont was delicate on the point of fraternization with the student body. Dismissal would be swift and sure.

And Dr. Marc, untenured, needed the job.

For Dr. Marc had big dreams—of starting his own off-Broadway repertory company, run his own way. He had the connections. He just lacked the money. That was why he ate macaroni and cheese out of a box three times a week. And wore jeans and a workshirt to class. Taught all summer. Lectured and took on tutorials all year long, wherever in the world they beckoned . . . One day, when the time was right, he'd light out from Shakersville and make his way to Manhattan, where he belonged.

It was what he dreamed of, at night, in that turret near the stars. It was all he desired since his wife, Kathy, had died.

All, that is, until he auditioned a brilliant new talent named Kit Daniels for his Acting I class, and got his dreams entangled with hers, losing his heart, if not his mind. She was a woman of unruly appetites, and it wasn't love precisely. *Coup de foudre*, the French call it.

In any case, it wasn't supposed to happen at all. But on that rainy Sunday night when she'd come to his rooms because she "couldn't sleep" she'd seemed so young, so lost really, under that patchwork bravado, that he couldn't, in good conscience, turn her out. So she'd told him about her matinee idol of a father, her absentee mother, the debutante ball where her illusions of being like other girls had finally died. Older and wiser, he'd listened to the tales of loneliness that struck like some chronic illness down to the bare bones—the mad frustration of the woman's life she had not yet lived but had the courage to want to live.

From there, it had seemed so easy, so natural for him to put his arms about her, to rest her head on his chest as though she were a child coming to the end of her day, coming home.

The softest of kisses were natural too, and the tender stroking and cradling. Her hair, loosed and shining, moved like water through his fingers.

The wellspring of passion caught them both by surprise.

Who would have guessed at the depths of his own loneliness? He had been so busy with other things.

They had shared their passion, solemnly, as the starved share a meal. Love was a role they played to the hilt as they huddled all winter under the prop Victorian blanket in the big old brass bed that creaked and gave beneath the autographed photo of Samuel Beckett—"To a friend."

That semester, Kit was on fire, in love, off guard.

Taking a lover had begun to pull her free from the fortress of fat, unzipped her from the body of the past. She felt light and tender and new in Marc Heller's arms.

When it was over that first time, she'd thought he was angry with her. He was so silent, so grave.

"We can't let this happen again," he said.

She had begged and pleaded, given a million different reasons why they should love again.

He had withstood all of them, for her sake—and for his own.

But the time came when he'd had to surrender. Those who knew them both sensed the transformation.

Possession blazed in their eyes whenever they looked at one another, which was often. Strong feeling flew between them, hemming them in with invisible cords, charging the air around them with fiery little atoms of desire.

Like all fine actresses, Kit used this energy, the energy of her own passionate being, to drive her through each performance. Onstage, she moved like a fin in the water. It was as if her body had jumped awake after a profound sleep; in Marc Heller's presence her whole being snapped to attention.

For his part, Dr. Marc grew cunning and proud whenever his leading lady was around, even though he took meticulous care never to touch her in public.

Not to touch her tonight, this final evening of the play, when she electrified his audience with her vibrant beauty, every inch the passionate heroine he himself had crafted—it was too much to ask of a man in love.

"Are you sure you want me to join you and your father for dinner tonight?" He'd tried to control the fever running through him by concentrating on other things.

"You must!" Her eyes flashed. "I've told him so much about you. Besides, I want you there when I tell him I'm switching my major from comp. lit. to theater."

Kit knew her father envisaged her settling after graduation into some cozy situation in ivy-covered academe, a new volume on Proust falling from her pen as easily and seasonally as the leaves from the campus maples. Theater was a divertissement, not daily bread for a Daniels. His studious absence from her other performances had made that crystal clear. He would not be pleased.

"I'll come then," Dr. Heller said. "I wasn't too sure about meeting Mallory and Maddy last time. But as it turned out, I liked them very much."

"They loved you." Kit's friends had turned out in force to see her on opening night, with Madeleine bearing her mother's homemade cheesecake to celebrate. For once, Kit had been too excited to eat. Even the extended absence of her mother, who had settled more or less permanently in Rome, couldn't pull her spirits down.

Dr. Marc gently withdrew his hand from where it was imprisoned in hers. "You'd better hurry now. You have a costume change to make before the next act."

She looked at him with that mixture of defiance and despair that had taken up residence within her since the first night they made love. "I'd rather stay here with you. There's so little time to be together."

He grew short. "They'll be missing you down in the dressing rooms. Do you want to get me fired?"

Just then the blue-jeaned stage manager came up behind them. He cleared his throat. "Dr. Heller, light cue twenty-five still isn't working. I think you'd better take a look . . ."

Without another glance at Kit, Dr. Heller followed the young man to the lightboard.

Kit watched him go.

"I love you," she whispered, fiercely, into the dark, not caring who heard her. "I love you. I love you. I love you . . . And Daddy will love you too."

The restaurant they'd chosen was called La Plume Rouge. It had fancy red velvet banquettes, a French chef, and the best reputation in Shakersville.

Kit knew the evening was doomed from the instant her father sat down at the table, across from an anxious Dr. Heller.

"A trivial cellar," Whitney Daniels had declared, flinging down the foot-long, red-leather wine list with distaste. "Under the circumstances, I shall skip the wine altogether. And I suggest you do the same."

"Yes, Daddy." Kit smiled encouragement at Dr. Marc, who always drank house wine with the naive contentment of a child at milk and cookies. Theater people traditionally took their meals as they found them, when they found them.

By the time the wine steward had been dispatched with insulting haste and the dinner menu damned as an "exercise in sterility," Kit was on to her father's game.

Coldly, methodically, he had been challenging Marc Heller in a dozen different ways, digging here, probing there for the flaw in the crystal. He had a positive gift for humiliation.

"I can't wait to see this mirabiliary—'wonderworker'—of yours," he'd told Kit over the phone last night, when she'd first suggested he meet her mentor. "We'll kill him with kindness."

For his part, Dr. Marc was trying to keep the dinner party afloat.

"Did you enjoy the performance then, Mr. Daniels?"

"A weepy, effeminate play, *Three Sisters*. The lachrymose enskied." He paused. " 'Enskied,' Kit?"

Her cheeks burned. "Immortalized, Daddy."

He nodded. "The Slavs are full of tears."

"Breadstick, Daddy?" Kit thrust the woven basket of bread at him.

"Thank you, no, darling." He waved it away with his long conductor's hands. "Of course, Kitrin was charming in it. She always did like dressing up and parading about. Just like her mother. I remember the time she had the German measles and took the opportunity to adorn her face with added scarlet lipstick. She was a sight . . . dots on top of spots!"

Kit flinched. Was he actually equating her childish pranks with her finely tuned, not to say, impassioned performance tonight?

Suddenly, he looked bloodless and fussy as he perched there, with his maidenly hands templed before his face. Had he always been so sly?

With a jolt, Kit realized that she and her father were not of one mind, one heart in all things. Not anymore. The emotional cord binding them had frayed to a diameter dangerously thin . . .

"But in my directorial concept, Natasha is the beating heart of the play, and if I may say so, your daughter has carried it off with extraordinary distinction for such a young performer . . ."

"I've always thought"—Whitney Daniels cut as gingerly into his boeuf bourguignon as a first-time surgeon in the operating theater—"that Chekhov heroines have more to do with costume than craft . . ." He set down his cutlery and pushed the plate away.

Kit's heart was cleft in two. For the rest of the endless evening, the two men she loved most in the world did battle for the pieces while she sank further and further into herself. By dessert, she was nowhere to be found.

"Ah, at least they did not spoil the coffee!" Her father was twinkling, gracious. Pouring for Kit from the silver pot, he winked in the old conspiratorial way. "Dr. Heller?"

"No more, thank you." Dr. Marc seemed exhausted. His patient green eyes wore a look of bewilderment she'd never seen there before.

Her father had won the day. He had made the man she loved look like a callow boy. Sunk him in her eyes. She began to see that Daddy would never, never share her.

Kit felt depressed and tired. She wanted to go home.

"Of course, darling," Whitney Daniels said with gaiety. "But what a delicious idea it was to meet here!" He twisted the knife, charmingly. "I am so impressed with your little town, Dr. Heller. Provincial life can be a breath of fresh air."

You little man—Kit could read her father's mind—*how dare you love my daughter?*

The next time she'd seen Dr. Heller, in the halls of the theater department, he'd looked so very much older, and her grateful love for him, still raging inside her, was now all mixed up with a kind of pity.

In the fall, at the start of her junior year, she declared her major in comp. lit.

The banker's office was all varnished wood and gleaming brass. Old money gleamed in the leaded windows and stood solid in the mahogany desk, cleared of everything but a bill-green blotter and a crystal ashtray from Rosenthal.

A gift from his brother, the Supreme Court justice.

"Whit! What a surprise to see you!" Harold Turnsfield moved out from behind his antique mahogany desk. There was a gold Phi Beta Kappa pin stuck in his Italian silk tie. Just like the one in Whitney Daniels's . . .

"It's been, what? Since that PGA open three years ago . . ."

They clasped hands. Harold F. Turnsfield rested his fingers on Whit Daniels' back and guided him to a comfortable seat between the swooping leather wings of an armchair.

"Be right with you, Whit." He made a show of buzzing his secretary. "Miss Connery, I'm not here for any calls."

As a further sign of deference, he did not take a seat behind his desk but settled in an identical armchair across from Whitney Daniels. "How is Marva?"

"Beautiful as ever."

Turnsfield nodded. "And Kitrin?"

A fraction of a pause. "Kitrin is fine."

In what might have been called a fidget in a slighter man—he was well over six feet—Turnsfield picked up a brass humidor from a butler's table at his left and offered it to the multimillionaire. "Cigar? They're my father's private stock. From Havana."

"Havana? In that case, I don't mind if I do."

Turnsfield went through the ritual of clipping the end of the cigar. He lit it with his monogrammed gold-plated table lighter.

Whitney Daniels sniffed delicately at it, as if at a rosebud, then took a satisfying series of puffs. Smoke swirled from the orange tip. His eyes were medieval, hooded.

In the silence, Turnsfield seemed to strain forward, waiting for a signal that would explain the man's visit to his offices. Whitney Daniels III had been one of the prime benefactors of his brother's political career, in addition to being a trustee of his own bank and liberal contributor to a hundred different organizations on whose boards he himself sat.

"I have a small favor to ask of you."

There was an almost audible sigh from between the wings of the chair. A small favor. That was all . . .

"Anything within my power, Whit. You have only to ask."

"You asked about my daughter before. There is a slight wrinkle in our plans."

Turnsfield searched his mind like a card file. "Let's see, she's in college now, isn't she?"

"Top ten at Laura Pierpont."

A light switched on in the banker's long, humorless face. So that was it, the mysterious locus of his power. He was a trustee of Laura Pierpont Academy. His body relaxed. A family favor: even better. "Fine school. Excellent academic credentials," he said, almost sportively.

Whit Daniels leaned forward to flick an ash into the crystal bowl. He balanced the cigar on the rim. "There is a teacher . . . I understand he's up for tenure this year. I don't think that would be a good idea, Harold."

"Well, Whit, can you tell me a little more? I mean, I've got to give them a reason."

"Then give them this . . ." Whit Daniels drew himself up from the chair. He paced before the desk with his hands in his finely tailored pockets, the picture of righteous indignation. "Tell them there is an old man, not a bad teacher, really, who up till now has only been guilty of mediocrity"—his voice was peaking in anger—"but who has recently exhibited a proclivity for seducing young girls."

Harold Turnsfield turned ruddy. He pulled up from the chair and held out his hands, as though he would fan back the anger he had seen billowing toward him. "Say no more, Whit. I'll see to it that the man is disciplined."

"I don't want discipline. I don't want scandal. Just deny him tenure. Do you understand? The rest will take care of itself."

"Done."

"See that it is." He rose to go.

Suddenly, Whitney Daniels' face broke into a smile. He paused at the mahogany-paneled doors. "Harold," he said, "your father keeps an excellent cigar."

———— *Chapter 4* ————

Two extraordinary things happened that rainy November. One was the storming of the American embassy by Iranian "students." The other was that Dr. Heller's bid for tenure was turned down.

These two facts had nothing to do with each other, really, except that Kit Daniels felt as though her little corner of the universe had suddenly been invaded by hostile forces, her heart taken hostage by the callous whim of a board of trustees.

She could hardly make herself believe it. The world dumped upside down in a day.

Dr. Marc planned to leave at the end of the semester.

"Take me with you . . ." She'd lain in wait for him after class at the big old willow tree outside the theater arts building, where they'd so often met and talked, almost touching . . .

It was raining. There always seemed to be rain that autumn, pelting the withered leaves with a hard, cold force, blurring the mellow russets and golds of the season into a dull gray wash of days.

He was dressed like an old man in a black raincoat. His hands looked very white, blue-veined. They were cold when she touched them. "That's ridiculous, Kit. You know you've got to stay here and finish your education. You've a splendid future ahead of you . . ."

"You are my future." She wasn't sure if she was crying or if it was just the sting of rain blowing down through the green sway of the willow tree . . .

"Kit, stop. You're not on stage now." He was trying to be patient, but every day it was the same thing. The confrontations. The declarations of love. She was going to have to grow up. A plane passed overhead, like a shark above a diver in the sea. He was drifting . . .

This break was probably not the worst thing ever to happen to him. Now, at least, with the platform of tenure cut out from under him, he would have to make the jump into the blue that he'd been putting off all these safe, soft years. The jump off to Broadway and his own repertory group . . .

Heedless now of curious eyes—the campus was busy with people hurrying to class—she curled her hands against his chest and clung to him. The coat was slippery with rain. "Please, please, don't leave me behind . . . I know I'm still too fat, but I can lose it, believe me—just give me a couple of weeks . . ."

"Kit . . ." His voice had a sharper edge to it now. He was already gone from this place, this love. "Listen to me." He clasped her hands, and pressed them, hard, to his heart. In the wind, her long, shining hair moved like a wing. His heart went out to her, and he remembered what it had meant to him, that first night in the turret, to have her youth and warmth aglow in his arms. "Tomorrow is the last day of class before the midterm break. I want you to say good-bye to me now."

She turned pale. "But, Marc . . ."

"Shh. Just listen. I want you to know that you have been more than a lover to me. You have brought back the best part of me, the part I thought I'd left behind, in the pain of losing Kathy. Because of you, Kit, I'm going to get back to the world and do what I should have done in the first place. All this—because you loved me, Kit Daniels."

Speechless with tears, she shook her head, denying herself comfort.

As gently as possible, he moved her hands back to her. "Now, I want you to say, 'Good-bye, Dr. Heller. Someday, I'm going to make you very proud of me.'"

"Good-bye, Dr. Heller," she said softly, with a bitterness new to them both. "Someday, I'm going to make you very proud of me."

For once acting on impulse, he threw his arms around her.

Then, without another word, he spread open his big, black umbrella and hurried out into the falling rain.

Despair can take many forms in a woman.

The sorrow that follows a loss of love has a weight, texture, and shape that is sometimes visible to others who share an intimacy with pain.

It can, for example, surface obliquely in a woman's eyes, as you pass her on the street, or can be carried on the skin, as a waxenness, a luster of white roses.

In the case of Kit Daniels, who, from that rainy day beneath the willow tree, had put on the airs of comedy, it was dragged around in the weight she had gained back. And doubled.

Then again, those extra pounds could have been her unlived life, the heft of love she would never have, the ball and chain of her unborn dreams. Oh, she was riddled with dreams!

He had, somehow, betrayed her. His life had turned a quiet corner without her. Love had slipped away, under a black umbrella.

She would never show herself, unarmored, to a man again, but keep her back to the wall.

And so she grew clever, and brittle as the frost angels on her windowpane. She lost her little-girl starriness somewhere in the middle of the cold winter night he'd left for New York. With study and seclusion, she rose to number one in her class. The best graduate schools courted her. Like a serious student, she cut off her beautiful hair. She shone with a hard, new brilliance.

She couldn't bear to pass the theater arts building anymore, the willow tree where they'd become strangers, suddenly, in the rain.

Someday, I will make you very proud.

Why, Daddy? Why, Dr. Heller? Why must I make you proud?

The question asked, the taboo broken, she felt something give inside, as though the invisible cords binding her heart to the men in her life, had begun to loosen, to set her free.

From now on, it was she who would demand. She who would be proud.

It was a matter of survival.

Graduation day. A spring sky blown clear as the blue glass of Lalique. Sun pours down on a champagne toast to the Laura Pierpont senior class. Black robes and mortarboards as far as the eye can see. Rows and rows of folding chairs crisscrossing the greenest lawn. Wistful speeches and applause all afloat on the balmy air.

Marva is on safari in Kenya. Later, Kit and her father will exchange ritual postcards over dinner.

He is sitting there, in the front row, with the trustees, a white rose lighting up his buttonhole. This morning, he'd sent her a wicker basket thick with long-stemmed roses, so that the whole house vibrated with their scarlet fragrance.

This, because she is the valedictorian, and has made him proud.

She gets up to make her address. Her glance strays to where the calm professors sit, like a Greek frieze, relieved at the shuffling off of yet another year. It is where Marc Heller would have been sitting, if only he'd loved her enough.

Now all eyes are upon her. But it's all right. In these robes she looks stately. Unencumbered by fashion, she moves well.

She tells the graduates to trust their instincts and to cherish their freedoms. Her address is well received. She takes her seat once again, turning over in her mind the way in which she will tell her father that she is not going to Yale Graduate School in the fall, that she is trusting her instincts, that she and Mallory (Maddy, a year younger, is still in attendance at Syracuse U.) are running off to New York to find an apartment and a real life in the theater.

When does life start anyway?

Father and daughter dine together afterwards, having been transported by the white Rolls to the chic ambiance of a private Manhattan club.

"Happy?" He gave her the benediction of his million-dollar smile.

"Kind of."

"Dean Claymoor was quite impressed with your address."

"Thank you." She shifted nervously in the leather depths of her chair. It was cool and dim in the dining room, the bronze-colored taffeta at the windows shutting out the heat and light of the day.

Then the champagne came, chilled, in a silver bucket. Her father tasted it on his tongue and nodded. The waiter hurried over to fill up Kit's flute.

Father toasted daughter. "Here's to your brilliant career . . ."

She sipped her sparkling wine. It was cool going down, and she was starting to feel reckless. It would be good to tell him, to get it over with at last.

"Oh, I almost forgot." She lowered her glass, then rummaged through her linen purse. "I have something to show you." When she handed him the latest postcard from her mother, their fingertips grazed slightly, and she withdrew her hand as though she'd been singed. It struck her that the chemical balance between them had been subtly altered—ever since the dinner with Marcus Heller. Kit put her palms together and rested them in the white V of her skirt.

"Very nice." The blue eyes were shaded. "As it happens, I have something to show you . . ."

Kit waited patiently to see his card.

It never came. Instead, he reached into his jacket pocket and drew out an envelope, which he pushed across the table.

Still innocent, Kit picked it up. An ordinary clean, white envelope. Heavy vellum. She opened it and read the heading at the top of the paper. "SUMMONS."

She looked up at her father, uncomprehending.

"Your mother and I signed a separation agreement a year ago, Kitten. This is the summons to a divorce hearing."

Kit blinked as though, in the dark, a high beam had suddenly been trained on her eyes. "But you never told me . . ."

"I didn't want to upset you. I suppose I thought it might not be necessary, that somehow she would regain her sanity and come back to us."

"But Daddy, I don't understand, aren't you going to contest this?"

He looked beyond her, to that exquisite world he'd made her believe in too. "I think not. After all, why should I still love a woman who doesn't want me?"

Do you have a choice . . . ? He was just across the table, a million miles away.

An ancient panic reared up inside her, a cry of denial, a cradle cry. *Don't leave me to walk in the dark, alone . . .*

"She'll be coming to the States for the hearing. I'm informed that she would like to see you at that time."

Kit pushed the panic back down with a pull at the wineglass.

"Really? How interesting. I don't think I want to see her."

"Kitrin, are you all right?"

"Those were the most beautiful roses you sent me this morning. The most beautiful, ever. Thank you, Daddy." Her eyes were bright now.

Whit Daniels sat back, relieved. She was going to be all right.

The next time he heard from Kit, a week later via a postcard that showed two cherubs taking a bite out of the "Big Apple," she'd set off for the trash and flash of New York City, with her imbecile costume designer of a cousin.

Twenty-odd years ago, Whit had known they were in for it

when his misguided brother had named the boy Mallory against his own good counsel. Mallory—a time bomb of a name. A name for pantywaists, Buster Brown haircuts, and ballet tights! For benighted boys who ran off to New York with your daughter.

Oh, he would never forgive Marva for doing this to him. Or Kit—for being a woman just like her.

PART II

Amazon

——— *Chapter 5* ———

Here's how to tell the arrival of autumn in New York: the first smack of pretzels and chestnuts on the street. The Great Plains thunder of holiday traffic. Crisp Canadian winds above, and wilted yellow leaves below. Bonwit tweeds and sables at Saks.

Auditions for the new theater season.

Once it arrives, it loses no time settling in. Within a matter of hours, autumn filled Kit and Mallory Daniels' pied-à-terre on York Avenue and East Sixty-third in the old, faded-yellow tenement with the sleigh ride of a staircase.

It blew in through the barred windows, open just a crack, a salt-sharp wind off the harbor that quickened the blood and freshened the hallways. Slightly soiled, it smelled of big city hope.

For Kit Daniels, it was a welcome sign that the ordeal by fire New Yorkers call "summer" had come to an end. For this year, air-conditionless, cut off without a penny by her father, Kit had been forced to take the full blast of summer in the city. Take it on the chin.

Kit had been to Manhattan many times before, but it had always been a trip cushioned in privilege, one long smooth glide from limousine to Lutece to air-conditioned penthouse in the sky. Now Kit Daniels was *of* the city. And it hurt.

Only odd jobs had kept the cousins afloat that first five months, once Kit had stopped telling customers that she was really an intellectual in disguise and not a lowly waitress at all.

"Okay, you love it now," Mallory, her partner in penury, had warned, when she'd first flown into the apartment, charmed by the "quaint" clawfoot bathtub in the kitchen and the single "cozy" bedroom, no bigger than the second linen closet at Maregate. "But you'll curse it in June . . ."

It did take some getting used to . . . the superheated gumminess of what passed for air, the Dutch oven of a top-floor apartment, the midnight chorus line of cats in the alleyway below. New York City in August, she discovered, smelled like an old damp sponge.

Somehow, the cousins managed to pull through . . .

Kit made out her last bill and pocketed her last tip—not bad—for the day, then set down the round metal tray with a groan. The muscles in her right arm were starting to bulge. They'd cried out with pain for the first few weeks she'd worked the venerable Schrafft's on Fifth Avenue. The job had become more tolerable as time went by. But she'd never again behold a smiling waitress with anything but awe. Dealing with the hungry public, with a steam table manned by tatooed women in hair nets who never heard the desperate scream of your order, with the fickle nature of the "quiche du jour" was no laughing matter.

Small wonder they assigned you a "mother" to guide you through the fog of your workday, until you somehow got your bearings among the vats of vichyssoise.

Over the last five months, the blue peace of Southampton had come to seem very far away. Trust funds and perfumed gardens, quite hard to believe in.

Kit undid her frilly white apron and blue uniform. She yanked off the hated hair net that made her look like somebody named Gladys who spent her days sleeping amid pigeons in the park.

On the way home, she bought a bunch of daisies. Then she stopped at the chestnut stand on the corner of Thirty-fourth Street and Broadway, a few feet away from the crowds gathered around the fast-talking "Three-Card-Monte" man.

As usual, after a day at work, she was famished, her yeoman lunch notwithstanding. She could barely wait for the elderly man in front of her to be served, and commenced to tap her foot like a horse stamping the ground before nosing into her bucket of oats.

Surprising even herself, she threw down some silver, snatched up the man's bag of hot chestnuts, and, curling them into her black glove, dashed off to her bus stop.

"Hey you, girlie!" the man hollered after her. "What the hell do you think you're doing!"

She gobbled down the chestnuts before they stung her fingers through the gloves.

Out of embarrassment and high spirits, Kit began to laugh. A few tendrils of chestnut-colored hair, now grown silky and long again, escaped from under an oversized, silver-sequined beret. Her cheeks were stung pink by the wind. It was Friday night, she was an actress in New York City (via a stint at "Clown World" and a Non-Equity, Greenwich Village production of *Luv*), and everything was coming up roses.

And daisies.

"Hi, honey, I'm home!" Kit flung her beret onto the thrift-shop couch, where Mallory lay stretched out like a Maja.

"Oh God, Kit, I'm done for," he said. "That madman Crockmeyer made me pull out all the seams the girl before me had done. Do you know how many seams there are in a Ciello wedding original?"

"Migraine?"

"Of course."

"Oh poor baby. Hang on a second. Help is on the way." After fanning out the daisies in a vase on the kitchen table and shucking off her coat and gloves, Kit came to rest on the edge of the couch. She pressed her fingers, still cool from the outdoors, against his temples.

"That's heaven, pure heaven!" Mallory sighed his thanks. "You did know I'm leaving you everything in the will?"

"It's the least you can do, Mal."

"By the way, the tapwater has that interesting color again. I think we should exorcise it or something before we use it."

"Thanks for warning me. Anyway, what's for dinner?" She sniffed the air for clues.

"Salad niçoise. It's all done. Except we can't afford anchovies, so I put a paper fish in for the centerpiece."

"I saw it. Very attractive."

"You did suggest salade niçoise?"

"Uh-huh. It's Maddy's favorite on the current diet."

"Forgive me, but I thought everything was Maddy's favorite."

"Mal!" She hopped off the couch. "Try a little Robert Young, please!"

"I do try. You know I adore Maddy. It's just real hard to get pleasure cooking a meal for someone who takes less time to devour it than it takes me to devise it."

"We all have our crosses to bear, Mallory dear." Kit vanished into her crackerbox of a room and reappeared moments later, attired in her favorite beat-up blue jeans and a huge buttercream cotton-gauze shirt.

"That's what Crockmeyer says." Mallory let out a groan. "God, how I loathe that man . . . do you think we have a karmic tie or something, Kit, like we were born again to hate together?"

Kit flopped down in a ramshackle old armchair they'd spotted at a flea market and combed out her long, flowing hair. It was a soothing ritual she'd carried over from nursery days when it was Marva, with her set of silver-backed Art Nouveau brushes, who did the honors. "I don't know, Mal," she said from under the waterfall of hair. She whipped her head back up. "Could be. Have you tried finding something to like about him?"

"There is nothing . . . unless you count that he's good with plants. He has a schefflera in his office that I would kill for . . ." Mallory hiked himself up by the elbows. With the pointed nose and full shock of blond hair overhanging his narrow face, he looked like a cartoonist's rendering of an angry bird. "But really, Kit, you'd think they'd have a law to protect us failing artists from the crass and unshaven Crockmeyers of this world. After all, we're a rare breed. Have you ever heard the way the high school kids talk these days?" He put on an adenoidal voice, reminiscent of any number of student science fairs. " 'When I grow up I'm going to work with computers because that's where the money is!' " Now he was Rod Serling . . . " 'Imagine, if you will, a future nation of R2D2s chasing the buck as fast as their clanking little legs can carry them.' I mean there were the Eisenhower years for those who were still awake, and now the 'find-me-a-tax-shelter' eighties. Didn't we lose a whole generation in there somewhere?"

"You make it sound so noble to be one of us!"

"There is something intrinsically noble about being the last of anything. And hell, we're an essential part of Americana in this penultimate decade of the twentieth century. Without us starving artists, how would anybody else know whether they'd made it or not? I mean, there's got to be some reliable index of failure for the Yuppies."

Kit lobbed a bright green round of pillow at him, narrowly missing his head. "Don't cry too much, Mal. Just remember: one day all this poverty will disappear, and success will turn you back into the poor little rich boy once again."

"Hrumph. In my heart, I'll still be starving."

"I bet."

Just then, the bark of the downstairs buzzer cut off all further conversation.

"Maddy's here!" Kit ran to the door to let up her best friend, the angel in the size-sixteen dress.

And then she was being dazzled . . . "Maddy?"

The fine-boned stranger at the door took two dainty steps forward, then put down her Vuitton suitcase and threw her arms around Kit.

In some miracle of subtraction, 190-pound Madeleine Shana Lefkowitz had turned into the Thin Woman of their girlhood legends. Like Atlantis rising from the sea, cheekbones had surfaced from their hiding place in the depths of her being. Hipbones thrust out like a dancer's where once there had been nothing but the soft white rise of flesh.

Kit's head whirled. Imagine, Maddy could wear whatever she wanted—tight jeans, halter tops; do whatever she wanted —seduce men, eat in public; go wherever she wanted—rock clubs, beaches, sunny locales of all kinds.

Her life could now officially begin.

And all Kit could think of was, "Maddy, what have they done to you? Maddy, where is the rest of you?" She mourned for the sudden loss of her friend.

Soft-eyed, thin-skinned, seductive, Maddy was clad in a suit of buttery chamois. Her Dim panty hose from Paris had little brown dots all over them. Her shoes were twin arrows of suede. She was utterly, mysteriously lovely, like some slim-necked beauty you'd catch staring out from behind the gold frame of a two-million-dollar Modigliani.

In the meantime, Mallory stepped forward to kiss Madeleine on the cheek. "Happy birthday! You look smashing."

"I wanted to surprise you." She looked from one to the other of her friends. "It happened at that Japanese spa."

Kit's heart turned over; it had started to sink in. From now on, the mirror would be Maddy's best friend. Where would that leave Kit Daniels?

Shrugging off her uneasiness, she showed Maddy to her room and urged her to wash up and relax from the trip.

Mallory caught his cousin's eye. He put his hand on her shoulder. "Don't worry, Kit. This won't change a thing."

But all during the birthday dinner, Kit felt less and less sure of who Madeleine Lefkowitz would turn out to be.

Had she ever really known this ravishing young woman with hair the "color of a Santa Fe sunset" (her last "affair" had been a poet), who spoke so facilely of rival lovers and aerobic Zen? Did she know a Madeleine Lefkowitz who never once touched spoon to dessert—carob yogurt pie—with her cool, thin fingers?

Was it envy that plagued Kit all through Maddy's tales of romantic triumph and calories unbound? Kit searched her soul for traces of its taint. No, it was something more subtle, a kind of millennial fever, on a microcosmic scale, of course.

An old world was crumbling for Kit. A new one was whirling into view.

Before this evening, it had never occurred to her that Maddy and the millennium might leave her behind . . .

"Seaweed and soybeans, that's what they give you to eat at the spa." The witness to a miracle, Maddy was bubbling over with the news. "They had these volcanic mud-pack things that they wrapped us in. And every day we had to look at our bodies for a half hour, in the mirror—really look hard. You know, when you're fat"—(Fat, Kit thought. That was a new word for Maddy. She had never been so objective, so superior to her body before!)—"you don't really see yourself as you are—just what you dream you'll look like someday. Anyway, I got so disgusted at the sight—the jello jiggle at the back of my thighs, the pomp and circumstance around my hips, the fullback's padding that rested on my shoulders, the risen soufflé, ugh, of my stomach zone"—(Had she ever been so rhapsodic, so engagingly poetic in her hatred of the flesh?)—"that my will power grew very strong. It took over. Then, for six months after I lost the weight, I kept talking about myself in the third person: 'She did this' and 'She ate that.' I just couldn't make myself believe the vision in the mirror was Maddy Lefkowitz, the blob who ate Larchmont."

"Coffee?" Kit picked up the white ceramic pot, hopefully.

"No thank you. I don't drink coffee."

Simple words. But Kit was devastated. No more shared meals, no more breaking of bread! Madeleine was an island, a perfect paradise of female willpower cut off from the rest of mortal womanhood by her extraordinary metamorphosis into a deity of self-deprivation.

For the rest of the long, overcast fall weekend—the Broadway show for which they copped half-price tickets (Maddy's treat), the Madison Avenue galleries they ran through, the talks that kept them up till the crack of dawn—Kit struggled against feelings of abandonment, of rupture, of disappointed dreams.

But when Sunday night rolled around and she was kissing Maddy good-bye on the platform at Grand Central (a blind date had brought her in line for a "major affair," as she put it, and she was very anxious to get back home) Kit felt as though it were really the other way around, and was sad.

Kit lost her job in October.

Soon the earth was flying farther away from the sun so that the windowpane in Kit's bedroom darkened earlier every day. Frost blew in and it was winter.

Then the holidays brought a manic glitter to the city, and for a brief time, it was possible to lose oneself in bowls of cheer and storms of baker's sugar. Daddy was still officially "displeased" but he sent her the softest cloud of a sable coat for Christmas. Her mother must have somehow known of this because she came up with a fetching Russian hat to match. Kit wept over the dead Christmas trees, left out with the trash. The coat was two sizes too small.

There were so many New Year's resolutions to make that year, Kit sensibly resolved not to make any at all.

Hibernation goes well with winter. Girlish ambitions can slip away so easily under the blanket of frost and fog in January, through the gray stretches of February and March.

But April is another story. April demands an answer, an act of faith. The gray sky cracks open and lets in the light.

It was time to move into the world again.

It appeared that all the out-of-work, overfleshed actresses in the city had been struck by the same bright idea, at the same hour, on the same uncomfortably warm day in April.

The suite at the Appolonia Hotel was packed to overflowing with them.

That very afternoon, the word had come down the grapevine. Wanted: a fleshy woman with a pretty face for a diet-pill commercial.

In the waiting room, everyone composed their features into the nicest possible configurations and tried to look bulky in a photogenic sort of way.

A copy of *Show Business* tucked under her arm, Kit Daniels was one of their anxious number praying outside the battered rehearsal room.

Although it was only late April, summer went beating

through the air, with its saps and scents. In her chair beneath the window, the leaf-green ribbons of her float dress fluttered in the breeze, and made her think, suddenly, of home.

She just had to land this job. It wasn't fair to lean on Mallory for much longer. His little job at the costume company in Long Island City was barely enough for his own needs. Besides, she'd been out of work for six months now, ever since she'd spilled a plate of hot navy-bean soup into the lap of a businessman, on the very day a vice-president of Schrafft's had come for his visit.

And Mallory said there was no such thing as bad luck.

"Miss Daniels?"

Kit shot up from her folding chair, a tad overeager to please.

"This way." The director's assistant, a slim young woman with a thick orange plait hanging down her back, led Kit into the mirrored rehearsal hall.

Three identical men in aviator glasses sat in wooden chairs, facing the mirrors. Kit was left with her back to the wall.

I must look like a right whale heaving into view, Kit thought to herself. Although in this case, I suppose it's just as well . . .

The AD handed Kit a script from her clipboard. "Just relax. They're looking for a 'real person' feeling."

Kit smiled a weak thank-you. Rushed and harried, auditioners weren't usually that forthcoming with kind words.

"You may begin, Miss Daniels." This from one of the male trio, a bald man in a denim jacket, with his blue shirt cuffs rolled back.

"'Rite-off' . . ." Kit closed up the fourth wall. She dug deep into herself for an emotional hook to hang the speech on. All the sacred Stanislavski principles chased around her head, like Keystone Cops . . .

"I wonder if it really works?" She ended on a high note.

"No, no, Miss Daniels, you're not doing Aeschylus now. Just make it seem like a real person."

"Try it again," the AD urged, the clipboard clasped to her chest.

"'Rite-off'..." This time, Kit emptied herself of all thoughts, lest she not be real enough for them. "Hmm? I wonder if it works..."

The script now called for "going to the testimonials." Then Kit was supposed to be "convinced" to buy the product.

"I guess I'll just have to try it and see for myself." (Hold up package.) "Right on, with Rite-off!"

The three heads merged together in conference. When they turned back to her a bored voice (she didn't know from which of the Tweedle Dums it came) said, "Very nice. It looks good. We start shooting Monday."

"I beg your pardon?" Kit dropped the script from before her face.

"You're in," the AD told her with a grin. "Have you got an Equity card?" This had been an open call because they were looking specifically for a "real person."

"No..." Kit felt immediately guilty.

"You'll get one now. How about an agent?"

"No." She was an imposter. They'd shoot her at dawn.

"I know someone who can help. Just step outside and we'll set up an appointment."

When it finally fell in on Kit that she'd bagged a commercial stint, an agent, and the almighty Equity card in one sublime spring afternoon, she jumped straight up in the air.

The three bored men looked up.

"Oh thank you, thank you all so much!" Kit went by, pumping their hands. "You won't regret this. I tend to look very much like a real person. You'll see. I'll do a bang-up job for you."

The discreet AD took her by the arm and guided her out of the room.

As it turned out, the agent she'd had in mind was a woman named Joan who wore lots of jangly gold jewelry and had a voice that could cut through glass. She said Kit had a "hot look" and took her on.

Now that Kit had fallen down the rabbit hole into the warrens of New York show business, Joan sent her for a raft of other commercials.

As miracles multiplied, Kit was even cast in a few plays.

She sent the occasional donation to Care for Children. Fine wines began to appear on her table. A lively host of artsy new friends brought cheap grass and cheer to her and Mallory's drafty little apartment.

A delirious Maddy was now engaged to her love of a lawyer (the blind date). Crockmeyer left for greener pastures and Mallory's own clever costume designs were being used, on a limited basis, by his company.

It all would have been heaven if it were not that the roles for which Kit was cast were invariably "fat lady" or "comical friend of the heroine" parts.

Time and time again, the classically trained Kit Daniels was disappointed, her considerable talent wasted. How she yearned to play Ophelia, even Cinderella, any ingenue at all!

Like many overweight women, Kit didn't really see herself in the mirror. She saw instead the ideal image of the woman she "should" be, could be.

The one she would never be . . .

"Go to the audition, Kit. What have you got to lose?" Joan had called her early that damp and drizzly morning, as usual, when Kit wasn't focused enough to put up any resistance.

"Cape Cod? It's the sticks!"

"Kit," Joan said in her flat, guitar twang of a voice, "you haven't worked in six months. You keep turning everything down. Kit—you're making me nervous, Kit."

"I know, I know."

"So go to the audition. Call me and tell me what happened."

"Joan, it's not what I—"

It was too late. As usual, the agent had dampened all discussion by hanging up abruptly.

In a black mood, Kit showered, dressed in one of her tarpaulins, and drank her orange juice on her feet, like a fighter, too angry to sit down.

With a heroic effort, she passed up Mallory's home-baked croissants, which lay snuggled in the basket under the blue gingham cloth, for a hefty dose of B vitamins and one-third of a bowl of granola.

Maybe it wouldn't be so bad . . . the B was working on her

already, pumping optimism through her blood . . . Cape Cod had a certain flair, a faded blue glory. And it was a classical repertory group she was up for. Lord, she'd been so busy hawking diet pills and playing the jolly sister she'd almost forgotten the exhilaration of pasting the classics, big and bold, across the stage.

Dr. Marc had once had such hopes for her. But like any man, he'd had greater hopes for himself.

On the way out, she thought better of the croissants and tossed one down for good measure.

Today, she needed her strength.

Outside, in the stultifying summer sun, Kit took care not to catch sight of herself in a shop window, avoided even the polished bumper of a parked car so as not to lose her lift.

She stood in the subway train all the way down to the sagging building on Fourteenth Street and Broadway; it was impossible to gauge whether she could sandwich herself between the man in the gray trilby and the rat-haired musician. In the meantime, she'd busied herself with the "beats" in the monologue from Molière's *The Misanthrope*. In the end, she'd decided to do one of Celimene's speeches. Kit had always favored Celimene, a fantastically beautiful woman with a tongue like a blade. No man ever got the better of Celimene.

After a few seconds' pause for unkinking herself after the subway ride, she went up to the desk in the anteroom to confirm her appointment.

With an appraising eye, she watched the other auditioners come and go.

Then the inner door opened one more time, and one more actor shuffled out, a man in a navy pea jacket.

Kit turned to stone. For a moment she'd thought . . . She had the heartbreaking impression that if she hadn't forced eye contact on him, he would have passed out of the office, and her life, without a word.

Even though her first instinct was to run away too, the loving woman in her cried out to him.

"Dr. Heller?"

He regarded her from out of her dreams, shopworn now and battered, but still the man of fire she'd once loved.

She stared into those cat-green eyes.

"I don't think they liked me," he said in a brittle voice, that was not his voice, as she remembered it, at all.

Kit could see the strain he was under, having to face her defeated like this, but she couldn't move a muscle, was forced to watch—and judge.

"It's been hard. Things haven't panned out . . ."

All of a sudden, Kit wanted to weep with disillusionment, cry out against his pathetic failure of courage. She'd wanted him to be her champion, the bulwark against her father and his works.

And now he'd blurred their beautiful past together, forced her to see him ugly and needy and not the hero of her love at all.

How could I have loved him so? she wondered at one moment, then knew the answer, all at once, in the next. It was the insight, confidence, and yes, sheer kindness that had led him to cast a grossly overweight young girl in a crucial role in his play. Marc Heller had been the first man to make her feel like a desirable woman, if only for a brief, enchanted time.

"God," she said under her breath, "you didn't have to leave me."

His face paled. "Please, Kit, you don't understand."

"No. No, I don't understand!" She hadn't realized her face betrayed so much emotion.

Everyone was watching them.

And then she was being called to audition. "Miss Daniels?"

Kit hung there, unwilling to let him go from her again.

He looked at her with those patient eyes, and her heart broke for him. On impulse, she reached into her purse. "Here," she said, scratching out a check for three hundred dollars. "This is all I have in the world right now. Take it." She pressed it on him.

He stared down at the check in his hands. He shook his head in wonderment. "I can't take this."

"Kit Daniels?" The casting director barked out her name.

"Go on. This way you can buy yourself new clothes. See some backers. Start your company. Make me proud."

He was looking at her as though she'd pointed a gun at him and pulled the trigger.

"No, Kit, that's not the way . . ."

As he'd torn it in pieces, something he'd once said came to mind: "Real kindness has to be learned. It takes years . . ."

Kit turned her back on Marc Heller so that he couldn't see the tears shining in her eyes, as she'd seen them in his.

Later, she couldn't tell how she ever got through the audition, didn't even care when the paunchy man with the Mickey Mouse watch thanked her in the middle of her carefully prepared speech.

Joan called her early the next day.

"You're in. They want you as understudy for the female leads in the Shakespearean review—oh, and"—Kit heard the rustle of notepaper—"as extra on various productions."

"Do you have a cast list?" Kit had asked then.

"Yeah. Why?"

"Is there somebody named Marcus Heller on it?"

Joan was quiet as she scanned the page. "No. No Heller."

Old dreams died hard. All in one day. She let out her breath. "When," Kit asked, "do I start?"

──────── *Chapter 6* ────────

Aᴅᴇɴ Lᴀssɪᴛᴇʀ ʜᴀᴅ just walked into one of his favorite places in the world—a theater.

No matter that this was a shoestring-budget company all the hell the way out on Cape Cod. They were putting on a Shakespearean review, and tonight, at his elbow, Geraldine's beauty glowed like southern nostalgia.

A postgraduate fellow of the Juilliard School in New York, Aden had early on been seduced by the theater, via his late actress mother, Vita Jones, a Texan of multiple gifts and a well-documented alcoholism that had shadowed his childhood.

Today, Aden was hailed as one of the most promising new playwrights in America. As a student, he'd won every available plaudit and prize for his passion, his labor of love; he'd been so wrapped up in his work, there'd been no time for wine and women (with one notable exception). Already this dedication had borne fruit. An assortment of his pieces had been performed by one of the more innovative off-Broadway theater companies. The next play, it was rumored, would eventually be moved uptown to Broadway.

Following this time in his father's footsteps, Aden Lassiter was also a leading agent of "serious" literature in New York publishing circles. Understanding the passion for perfection, he was good with authors, reminding them of what they were capable.

In the beach-damp, great wooden block of a theater, Aden handed Geraldine Cutler her program.

Their arms brushed, and Aden's desire sprang to life. He may have come late to the garden of women, but he was making up for it now. Geraldine, "the poet of lost innocence," had satiny skin, the color of a magnolia blossom. His hands were mad to stroke the fine white hairs along her arm, finger the delicate plait of bird bones up her spine. She sat, outwardly cool and cerebral, in the lake-blue summer dress that pooled around her ankles. He tried not to stare at the shifting blue points of her knees, under the dress, or imagine the paradise that lay between them.

It never failed. She inflamed him. At first, the Louisiana-born charmer had also confused him with her outward indifference. He was so new to it all.

But now that he knew of her sinew in bed, the aura of self-involvement that clung to her like a thin, bright cloud of perfume no longer daunted him. Then too, the powerful words of her poetry pointed to someone broader, deeper, than even Geraldine fathomed.

Inside her, Aden believed, sat the soul of a tigress, powerful tail switching to and fro. Aden liked strong, self-loving women and would go to great lengths, use every last ounce of his patience, to win their friendship.

For despite the urban patina, he was tenderhearted, and in need of woman's love.

He'd discovered this years ago, on his first direct encounter with an angel.

Her name was Gwendolyn Sweet, a sugar blonde, a girl as quaintly lovely as her old-fashioned name. She laughed him out of his brown studies. She made a shy sensitive teenager look up from his books and see the sun in her eyes.

The two youngsters had grown up together during sleepy summers on Martha's Vineyard, while the brotherly feelings he'd harbored toward her, among the scrub pine and beach plums, had slowly, sweetly ripened into first love.

In the fevers of his sixteenth year, Gwen Sweet had seemed destined to take her place in his life . . . as soulmate, inspiratrice, perfect love.

It hadn't turned out that way.

Gwen never made that delicately calibrated adjustment from summer friend to sensuous lover. Even worse, she had fallen for his best friend, Peter, a teenage ladykiller who could never cherish her as he himself would have done. In the dreams he sometimes still had of her, he asked her, again and again, to tell him why, when they had had the chance for happiness in their hands, she'd let it slip away . . .

What made women slip away?

In the seat next to him, his new love, Geraldine, looked up from the program through which she browsed, as if she'd felt his eyes on her. Full of art, a work of art herself, she smiled in the very way he remembered from their last love-making.

In some ways, Geraldine reminded him of Gwen. Both of them were so achingly beautiful. Both, on the surface, seemed to be cruelly oblivious to the riots they caused in the rash biology of men. Both had minds of their own.

At least, Aden thought, there was the one enchanted year he'd managed to get Gwen Sweet to meet him, the last Sunday in October, for the "Head of the Charles Regatta" between Princeton and Harvard. Armed with a picnic basket and a warm blanket or two, they'd staked out a cheering spot along the Charles River.

Aden would never forget the casual feast of Hibachi-grilled burgers, fat bags of Doritos, French cheese, and iced jugs of wine. To this day, it remained the best damn food he'd ever tasted, the table d'hôte at Lutece notwithstanding.

There, in the midafternoon chill, they'd nestled together and cheered on Aden's alma mater, Harvard. Aden could still recall the smell of damp wool from their cocoon of blankets and the feel of Gwen's hair, a spill of cornsilk through his fingers. With Gwen Sweet beside him, his team in the lead, Aden was camped out at the gates of paradise.

It was the last time he would get anywhere near them for many years to come.

With Gwen's departure from his dreams, Aden had learned not to trust his more emotional inner voices. He continued to like women, and they from all appearances continued to like him. But the wound did not heal.

Then, many years later, in that way life has of confirming our worst fears, Aden ran into Gwen Sweet.

It took place at one of his father's shimmering summer parties on the Cape. By then a successful and even celebrated New York literary figure, Aden hadn't immediately put a name to the popcorn blonde in the plummeting black Halston. Not that she'd lost her bon-bon beauty. She was still the dreamgirl under that summer shower of white-gold hair, but there was a brassy glint to it all now. The woman who had been Gwen Sweet, his first love, his fantasy, now held herself as though a fine wire were being pulled up through her spine. Her face had thinned out with nameless tensions. Gone was that delectable, slightly off-center way she had of carrying herself, as though at any felicitous moment, she might tumble into his waiting arms.

Before Aden could recover from the first full shock of collision, Gwen Sweet had introduced her dud of a fiancé, with yet another newly acquired expression on her face: a sad and premature boredom.

To look at her was to break his heart a second time.

It had taken him only a moment to decide to ask for her number. It took her only one touch of his hand to give it.

Forsaking the party early to wander the streets of downtown Hyannis, he watched, red-eyed, as the sun came up from behind the docks.

Now he knew. He had never really released himself from the woman. He still carried her like a golden icon in his heart, an adolescent shrine, untouched by time. He had to see her again.

And he did. The shine came back to Gwen's eyes. She grew

warm and showered him with praise. He was strengthened, his life made over by her long-ripening love.

They were going to be married. Three months to the day of the party. They commuted between Boston and New York with the exuberance of eagles.

He could still remember the look on his father's face when Clayburn told him about the phone call and the chartered plane to Boston that had gone down that morning. Gwen was on it.

By the end of that sad, bewildering day of her death, Aden, although he didn't know it, had resolved never again to let any woman close enough to cause such intimate damage.

Throughout his five years in New York, it was a vow he had not been seriously tempted to break.

The houselights dimmed. Geraldine leaned her paper-doll beauty against his shoulder. For an instant, he thought it was Gwen . . .

Then an announcement was made from in front of the midnight-blue curtain. A switch in actresses playing the role of Desdemona in the scene from *Othello*. Someone named Catherine or Christine . . .

Aden was too busy inhaling Geraldine's vanilla-flavored perfume to notice the gleam of gates in the distance.

For Kit Daniels, the shining horizon of summer rep in Cape Cod had shrunk to a pocket-size dressing room shared with a cast of thousands (actually twenty) in the hot murk of July. Monotony by day. Mosquitoes by night. And all for a speechless series of walk-ons and the misanthropic hope of sudden calamity striking down one of the principals so that she, the understudy, could at last go on.

Daily, Kit cursed the hour she'd left New York for the sluggish backwaters of Mashpee.

It was bad enough, she penned, in her passionately unhappy letters to Mallory and the lovestruck Maddy, to be a virtual nonentity in the company, but she'd also been domiciled in a communal house where she could never eat in front of anyone but had to sneak into the creaky-floored old kitchen late at night for surreptitious gorging on peanut butter and Saltines. In spite of this, she'd already lost ten pounds.

Worse still, it hadn't rained a single blessed drop for the past two weeks of an unendurable heat wave.

Then, the plot twisted and turned her way.

Lettice Court, the actress who played Desdemona with the wiggle of a chorus girl, weighed her chances of someday starring opposite Lord Olivier's Lear, as opposed to, say, being known all over the dinner-theater circuit as the oldest living gamine to play Maria in *The Sound of Music*. Using her head, and her wiggle, she ran off with Truro's most prominently rich banker.

Kit was asked to step into the part.

Elation—even though Kit knew they'd only offered her the role because she'd be buried under a soufflé of bedcovers, where only her head would pop free.

In a happy confusion, Kit watched the director, Harrison Dupree, pad over on his hush puppies that fateful half hour before curtain, when the news about Lettice had just hit the little company like a bomb.

"Hon . . ."

"Kit." She was aglow from head to foot. The classics! Desdemona! Life was good.

"Kit, hon, it's not a big deal, all right?" He laid his avuncular arm around her shoulders. "Don't worry. We'll start later in the scene, right before Desdemona kicks off. You won't have to learn more than three lines."

Kit's face fell to the floor. Three lines! She'd kill him . . .

The director checked his Mickey Mouse watch. "Okay kids, time for just one quick run-through with"—he thumped Kit's shoulder—"hon, over here."

During the comically rushed rehearsal, Kit persisted in imagining that a giant rodent had usurped the place of the pudgy director: a mammouth mouse in a bow tie and short red-velvet pants, who kept consulting a wristwatch on his arm, a wristwatch that bore the sour-pickle face of none other than Harrison Dupree.

Still fuming, Kit dressed herself in Desdemona's loose white gown. By some theatrical magic, it fit.

She waited in the wings, trying to concentrate on the character, but inwardly, she was fast superheating.

After the Falstaff monologue, the lights blacked out.

In the dark, Kit slipped under the lacy covers of the huge carved bed, which was canopied in a chestnut-stuffing color, but not without first stubbing her big toe along the way.

"Oww!" she said in character. The actor playing Othello in Egyptian 3 makeup, and Mandy Lee, the production's Emilia, were already positioned onstage. The lights came up.

Kit had the first line. "O, falsely, falsely murdered!" she cried as loudly as she could from beneath the baleful pillow.

"O Lord! what cry is that?" Emilia swished closer to the bed.

Othello, who was, in fact, Richard Claremont, the most vainglorious and least favorite of Kit's colleagues in Mashpee, sawed his hands in the air, much against Hamlet's injunction. "That? What?" His bogus Gielgud accent set Kit's teeth on edge. It would, she knew, have vanished by the end of the scene. Richard was originally from New Jersey.

"Out and alas! that was my lady's voice. Help! help, ho! help! O lady, speak again! Sweet Desdemona! O sweet mistress, speak!"

"A guiltless death I die," Kit sighed.

"O, who hath done this deed?" Emilia laid her hand on her heart.

"Nobody—I myself. Farewell. Commend me to my kind lord. O, farewell."

In the script they were working from, Desdemona was to die here.

Thus, Kit's brief hour upon the stage was ended. Or at least, that was how Harrison Dupree and the Bard of Avon would have it.

But Kit Daniels had made other plans.

In a slow, majestic cobra rise from her deathbed, she rested her bare feet on the floor—and lived! "Nay, nay my lord," she spoke extempore, "and yet thy sweet Desdemona lives to love thee another day . . ."

Richard Claremont's jaw dropped open. Emilia blanched. There was a buzz of surprise in the audience.

"Why, how should she be murd'red?" The hapless Othello was still trying to follow the script.

Emilia shrugged. "Why, who knows?" she asked, with more conviction than she'd ever been able to muster at rehearsals.

Backstage, Harrison Dupree was in a frenzy of gesticulation, signaling wildly to his leading man, squeezing the air with his fists, as though it were the neck of Kit Daniels.

Claremont thought quickly. "Uh . . . what noise is this? Say you, not dead? Not quite yet dead?" he improvised lumberingly. "I that am cruel am yet merciful; I would not have thee linger in thy pain, but must kill thee yet again . . ."

He lunged for Kit on the bed, but, surprisingly nimble, she rolled away, leaving him to topple facedown on the coverlet.

"O serpent heart, hid with a flow'ring face!" Kit raised a regal hand and pointed at her "husband," who was at the moment disentangling himself from the linen bedclothes. Her eyes burned like coals. "Did ever dragon keep so fair a cave? Beautiful tyrant! Fiend angelical! O, that deceit should dwell in such a gorgeous place!"

By the time Othello hurled himself off the bed, his makeup lay smeared all over the pale green coverlet, and he was weirdly bi-complected.

In the wings, Harrison Dupree went mad. "Oh my God," he muttered to himself. "Now she's doing Juliet . . ."

A titter ran through the audience. Somewhere in the front row, Aden Lassiter growled with laughter.

"I'll kill her," Dupree said with an unnatural calm, and proceeded to move out to the stage. It took Iago and two tech people to subdue him.

"Get her off!" he cried, *sotto voce*. "Get that crazy woman off . . . There are New York critics here tonight. We'll be a laughingstock."

Cassio, still bleeding from his stage wound, edged against the flats at stage right near where Kit was wandering. She was spouting snippets of different Shakespearean plays with which she was familiar, making it up when memory failed, having a ball.

"Shall I speak ill of him that is my husband?" In a flash, she was Juliet again. "Ah, poor my lord, what tongue shall smooth thy name, when I, thy three-line wife, have mangled it?"

Then Kit got too close to the man who was hunting her. He clamped one hand over her mouth and one about her waist, and dragged her like a fallen sandbag offstage.

"At last, she is dead!" Richard Claremont spoke triumphantly. Emilia picked up the scene.

"O, the more angel she and you the blacker devil!"

"She turned to folly." Othello was staring at the spectacle of Kit being heaved out of the backstage area by three stagehands. "And she was a whore . . ."

Behind the scenes it was pandemonium.

Kicking and windmilling her arms about like a madwoman, Kit was forcibly ejected from the stage door by the burly tech people. Harrison Dupree was still being held by concerned parties at stage left.

Clad only in the pristine whiteness of Desdemona's nightgown, Kit bolted for the sanctuary of her attic room in the nearby communal house, a yellow rise of gingerbread with a widow's peak. Curious tourists in plaid shorts stared in her fluttery wake.

Safe in her room, its sloping walls papered with stained and peeling bunches of dogtooth violets, Kit collapsed against the door. Her heart was scatting like a drum.

It was time to ask the question: *what had she done?*

Her behavior onstage tonight had been insupportable—a sacrilege in the temple of the theater. She burned on the grill of self-reproach.

And yet . . .

How delicious! How satisfying!

She could still hear Harrison Dupree choking in the wings. Her moment in the sun had been brief but hilarious. She brushed her damp hair from her neck with her fingers. Yes, she could see it now. Tonight was one of those ionically charged midsummer eves when a girl such as herself could go mad with the smell of freedom in the air!

There would be no sleep for her tonight. How could there be? She had destroyed all chance of a life in the theater. Once these shenanigans of hers got back to New York, she'd be blackballed for sure. Everything she'd been working for these past few years, up in a puff of smoke from Harrison Dupree's ears.

Although Kit liked eccentric spaces, the attic room suddenly seemed close as a tomb. The "peine dure et forte" of old English dungeons came to mind. Being pressed to death, day by day, the weight growing heavier. Yes, that was what made it so hard to breathe these days, the cumulative weight of her unlived life, growing heavier and heavier against her heart . . .

Hiking up her gown, she shook up the flight of stairs to the ancient roof that sagged over the old yellow house like a bulldog's brow. As she climbed, painted flakes, like yellow snow, floated to the floorboards below.

The moon was just sliding up, beaten and grayish as old pewter plate. A damp breeze rose from the dark salt bay.

With care, Kit climbed out to the widow's walk, then stood staring out to the foil crinkle of sea and fog that rolled up against the moon.

Her hair flew behind her as she hugged her arms to her body. It had been easy to break out onstage as Desdemona. There'd been no thought behind it. She'd only needed to ride on the powerful shoulders of her instincts and feelings. But now, as Kit, she was aroused by her own daring in a wild new way she'd always been afraid of acknowledging. She wasn't quite sure what she was supposed to do next. She wished Dr. Marc were here to tell her.

There was a low rumble of thunder. The wind took a sharp vertical turn, lancing up from the fog-hung bay below. Across the navy belt of water, a ship's horn bellowed twice. Staffs of lightning cracked the sky in two, and rain slithered out, onto the rooftops of the little town that had been, for so long, spellbound by summer.

Kit's full skirts whipped around her legs. Her hair spread

out like a Chinese fan. The bay waters leaped and spit, a bonfire in a high wind, as the rain made a sound of distant cannons against the docks.

Kit never did know how long she stood there, being drenched to the skin, buffeted by sea winds, clinging to the narrow railing of the widow's walk, crying into the teeth of the storm.

But she slept well and deeply that night.

And dreamed, prophetically, of her city home.

Next morning, she was bound for New York.

──────── *Chapter 7* ────────

Lᴉᴛᴛʟᴇ ʜᴀᴅ Aᴅᴇɴ Lassiter known when he booked his two-on-the-aisle seats the day before that an indestructible Desdemona onstage would fire his imagination as had no woman since Gwen Sweet. Especially as his taste normally ran to beauty on a smaller scale.

But this unscheduled resurrection was the most uproarious thing he'd seen in a long, long time, and Aden Lassiter put a premium on honest laughter.

His own mother, rest her soul, had been like that. Big, beautiful—born to be outrageous.

Maybe it was the actress's quite beautiful face, the cloudy fountain of hair that put Aden in mind of fern—ostrich, maidenhair, lady.

Maybe it was the fluid grace with which she moved, as though she really didn't belong in that overfleshed body, but was somehow trapped inside. Maybe it was the charming sense of vulnerability she threw across the footlights, to the winds. Or the sensuous thrill of her voice.

Like most men, Aden had never conceived of an overweight woman as a maiden in distress, buried deep inside a tower of her own making. She had a dignity and originality that Aden found most appealing. Here was a lively presence indeed.

My God, yes! Aden shifted in his seat, intrigued by the prospect that had just shown itself. With a few changes in the script, this hilarious actress spouting Juliet's lines in a scene from *Othello* would be perfect for the part of Germaine in his new comedy! (Damn, if only he'd paid more attention when they announced the understudy at the top of the show! He didn't even know her name.) He'd just have to take himself backstage after the play and meet the woman.

Of course, what she'd done had been crassly unprofessional. He'd sack her if she tried anything like that in one of his own plays.

At the fall of the curtain, Aden hurried Geraldine around to the stage door. By this time, the storm was in full swing, and Geraldine, looking like some caryatid stepped from the *Porch of the Maidens,* had only the poor paper playbill to hoist over her head.

"Aden! Honey! What are you thinking of? It's wet out here!"

A small dainty brunette, she ran alongside him in her blue summer dress.

"Is it?"

"All right. That does it." Geraldine stood stockstill in the alleyway between the theater and a big red antiques barn. A breeze gaily lifted her off-the-shoulder ruffle. "I'm not taking another step until you beg my forgiveness. On your knees."

"Gerry, Gerry . . ." Aden laughed and shook his head. He ran his thumb along her cheekbone, gently. "I'm sorry."

"In Louisiana, we've got sweetwater, not this nasty codfish rain." She pouted him into a pleasant remorse, even as he watched her performance with a clear, unprejudiced eye. At parties, Aden had never known the prize-winning author of *Winter Chill* to pass by an opportunity of parading her "downhome roots." Invariably, she neglected to add that her father had been the wealthiest man in New Orleans, her mother the leading belle.

"But I thought you left Louisiana at two years old. How could you remember the taste of the water?"

"It's in the genes." She waved away his objections with a silky hand.

He laughed. He couldn't help it. He didn't mind knocking down her paper tigers, her little lies and artifices. It was like an elegant Egyptian game with etched ivory tiles that represent the progress of the soul in the underworld. He would get to her underworld, to the fires below. And then there would be bliss.

In the meantime, Geraldine Cutler was possessed of more accessible splendors: an incandescently white oval of a face with the kind of cheekbones that pass for beauty these days, the black silk hair of a silent-film vamp and eyes the smoky indigo color of an Impressionist lake. Most importantly, she sometimes wrote like an angel, if still without heart.

It took his breath away, the way she glittered and changed colors in the rain. Of course, he knew that like some fine faience pottery, Geraldine's more subtle colors were produced with acid. But he was not alarmed.

"Aden, dear heart," she sang in that Piccolino voice of hers. "You still haven't told me what we're doing here in the deluge without an ark." Geraldine's bee-stung lips were curly. A pert violet headband of raffia further contained the precision cut of her hair, swept clear to one side. Her eyes were shaded in pink and lavender. Her mouth was tinged with gold. Aden kissed it, passionately.

"Patience, darling. I'm trying to cast my play."

"Oh Aden, in your soul you'll probably always be twenty-five."

Geraldine had already brought out her Papermate pen and pad and was recording her emotions for posterity. Aden felt satisfied that she was just being an artist and was not hurt at all.

He collared the first man who appeared at the stage door.

"That young woman who played Desdemona . . ." Aden began.

Harrison Dupree tugged at the tufts of hair behind his ears.

He smashed on a fisherman's cap. "Kit Daniels, may she rot in hell!"

"Well, yes." Aden hadn't expected the invective. "But can you tell me where I can reach her?"

"I don't see how it's any of your business, but I can tell you she's been drummed out of this company, and no one knows or cares where she's wandered off to . . ."

"Wait a minute."

But Harrison had already shouldered past him and off into the storm.

"Damn!"

It was Geraldine Cutler who finally invaded Aden's thoughts with her soft, wandering hands, while jealously suggesting that he pay more attention to her rather than to that hyperkinetic hussy of an actress who had gone to a richly deserved oblivion.

Bowing to circumstance, needling rain, and Geraldine's magic hands, Aden could only oblige.

They left for his snug rooms with the Jacuzzi, where Geraldine changed into something silk and read aloud from her latest slim volume of poems, in which, even more than usual, he recognized the "bright triangle" of his own face, late into the rain-swept night.

———Chapter 8 ———

KIT LOST HER bearings shortly after sunrise somewhere on the New England Thruway. It wasn't a question of physical direction, but of some internal, psychological compass going haywire. Her mood, her very being seemed to have changed in texture and lights; her psychic molecules reassembled in some radical new pattern. Or maybe it was just the aftereffects of the ionic charge from last night's storm at sea. Yesterday, she was going to live the ordinary life in a nonordinary way. Now she couldn't even get the car radio to work.

She had been driving relentlessly since sunup in a rented compact that, true to its nature, broke down, and had to be serviced at a lonely Mobil Station where she chain-drank Coke and gnawed at a Three Musketeers bar from the candy machine. She watched the moths climb up the screen door of the station house until her gurgling machine was set to rights.

Back on the road again, she tried to take joy in the memory of the sound that had come out of Harrison Dupree when she rose from the dead. But today, in the white-hot glare of the morning after, this thought just didn't have the tonic effect she'd expected.

After all this hoopla, she had no career to speak of, and her damp back seemed permanently soldered to the upholstery of the car on this muggy day in July.

Then, punchy from the long trip back and the bad break of the night before, Kit was welcomed into city limits by the mayor, from off a big, green sign.

Still drowsing under its blanket of rose-colored smog, the city looked magical and MGM-ish. She felt unusually glad to be home.

Toting her suitcase, Kit tiptoed with shoes in hand into the quiet apartment. She didn't want to wake Mal, who, she knew, liked to sleep late on Saturdays. Her unannounced entry surprised a young stranger in his birthday suit who had just woven his limbs into the ancient glyph of a yoga position. He sat on what looked to be a prayer rug.

"What are you doing here?" Kit blurted.

"I live here. What are *you* doing here?" the lithe young man asked from the space between his legs.

"I live here too." And then it all came back to her. Mallory had written some time ago, asking permission to sublet their apartment since he'd moved in with a guy named Rock who had a great place of his own.

"Hey." The loose-limbed intruder had tipped over onto his haunches like a praying mantis. He waved his hands in indignation. "Hey, like I'm sorry about the bad vibes, but you can't stay here. There's like too much yin in here already."

She would have to get some sleep. She was hallucinating.

Kit held her hands over her eyes. This wasn't happening. When she opened her eyes, she'd be back in Mashpee, safe in her sky-top room. She'd get up and count her breakfast calories, and later she'd be an extra in selected scenes from *Henry IV*, Parts I and II.

But no, when she looked again, the subletting tenant was still very much there, blinking up at her with his bright, insect eyes . . .

"Oh, don't bother to get up," Kit said, even though the tenant hadn't moved a muscle. "I'll show myself out."

Somehow, she made her way down the four flights of stairs. At the foot, she tried to catch her breath. It was becoming clear that she would have to get some sleep or risk further hallucinations from which she might never emerge. She would be doomed to wander inside her bad dreams forever, like the bag ladies of Penn Station.

Too much yin, indeed!

Kit had already returned the car, such as it was, to the car service. She couldn't very well walk in on Mal's affair. She had nowhere to go. She felt around in her purse for her "Happy Days" address book. Mal had given her an emergency number to call.

In the meantime, the Saturday streets were beginning to stir. Young men toted laundry bags full of trendy clothes. Old people in hats took the air. Tourists got an early start spending their money in well-stocked card shops and plant-hung cafes.

Kit harbored in the glass alcove of the telephone booth. She set down her suitcase. The quarter tinkled merrily going down. She dialed. After three rings, someone grouchy picked up.

"Hello, Mal? It's Kit. I'm back."

"Kit?" His voice was fuzzy. "What do you mean you're back? What happened? I thought you were supposed to be on the Cape all summer."

"Mallory . . ." She was interested to find that her own voice was shaky. She'd always fancied herself good in a crisis, crumbling apart only when the worst was over. A *Cosmo* questionnaire had confirmed that.

"Oh, Mal, I was sacked last night. I guess in a way I deserved it—I mean I did something really crazy." The words tumbled out in a rush. "I don't know why I did it. Just that I had to. And now I have no more money, and no car, and there's a praying mantis in my living room." Her head was aching with the strain of explaining it all to him.

"Slow down! Cool off, girl. I don't know what the hell you're talking about."

Kit overheard an interrogatory rumble in the background. Rock, no doubt.

"Hello? Hello, Kit?" Mal was back on the phone. "What the hell did you do to get fired?"

"I was dead, strangled, you know, on the bed, and then I . . . I just got up, and started talking." She gave a slight giggle. "Actually, it was kind of fun."

"You mean you were supposed to be doing Desdemona," Mallory decoded her words, "and you wouldn't die?"

"Yes, that's it."

"Oh my God!" Mallory sounded awed. "You're lucky all they did was fire you."

Just then, the operator came barging on and demanded more money to feed the phone.

"But I don't have any more change."

"Poor baby," Mal crooned. "Quick, tell me where you are, and I'll come and get you."

Kit's eyes narrowed. A plan was taking shape in her head. Leaning on a friend and moving in with a guy named Rock had no part in it. "Uh, that's all right, Mal. I'm going to a green place, to think green thoughts."

"What's that supposed to mean?"

"Got to go, Mal. Be happy. As for me, I'm going to eat my heart out."

"Kit, no, wait!" Concern rang in his voice.

But jobless, apartmentless, hopeless, Kit Daniels was already wandering down the street, suitcase in hand.

The phone dangled from its cord in the booth, as some homing instinct guided Kit's steps to E.A.T. on Fifth Avenue. She stepped inside the air-cooled shop.

An hour later she emerged, the last dollar in her checkbook spent on a fortune in gourmet foods: salmon pâté from the cold waters of Canada, eggy breads, braided as smooth as a woman's hair, savory chains of sausage, scented with fennel seed and anise, bottled kumquats and cherries: sweet things to the mouth of the virago, the one who couldn't get along with anyone, who must speak out of turn, move out of line.

She cradled them like a child with a brace of babydolls. The sun steamed in the July sky as she walked on. This afternoon, the city seemed to swim in a wave of auto exhausts, manhole steam and smog. The air was dense and hard to punch through, as in a flying dream.

But then it began to smell greener. Trees popped open in the sun like kernels of corn in a popper, and there were bicycle paths and skateboarders in neon shorts. Children's laughter floated up to Kit, storytime voices around the statue of Hans Christian Andersen.

How many times had she and Mal and Maddy sprawled under the big old oak tree with the carved hearts of "Sam and Cookie" on it and dreamed out loud about making it big in the city?

There was, at least, the illusion of cool in the shade of Central Park. She spread a blanket from the suitcase over the grass and set out the food she'd purchased, slowly, solemnly, hieratically, as befit a sacred meal. A healing meal. A meal of the psyche's gods. Ambrosia could have been distilled from kumquats. Olympus must have been very green.

She started out calmly enough, with some cherries, crushing their sweetness, red as blood, on her palate. Beyond the stenciling of the treetops, she could see cutouts of blue sky as though she were sitting inside the borders of a child's crepe-paper picture.

Next an entire box of eclairs was consumed. The chocolate licked. The cream sucked out, as though she would suck out some of life's very marrow, the life that kept passing her by . . .

In the hot green thick of the afternoon, she went on with her sacred gluttony, tasting nothing, seeing no one, fighting to fill the black hole that opened up inside her and threatened to consume everything, including her miserable rich girl's failure of a life.

She saw her debutante ball twinkling at the bottom of a cherry jar, the night's passage of events, pouring dreamily down her throat.

Jonathan Cantwell and the darling debs danced on the edge of her plastic spoon. She ground them to dust with her grinders. And Dr. Marc, dear Dr. Marc, leaving her again, not loving her enough because she couldn't grow small and charming, but needed to rise and push up through the layers of her frustration, to rage and swell up with the life of her dreams, which were more vibrant, more real to her than any man's love.

Even Daddy's. Especially Daddy's.

He was there too, and she gulped down the bitter pill of his betrayal with the coiled custard of her eclair, to sweeten it.

Before long, she began to feel sick, and then there was that wall that runners talk about. The feeling receded. She was ravenous, miraculously empty again. The cavern mouth of the earth opened to receive . . . what?

The treetops began to swirl like points in a kaleidoscope and she was flat on her back, the smell of dirt in her nostrils, her hair tangled in with the grass, as she stared up at the undulating darkness that had flowered from a seed somewhere inside her and was now about to fill up the sky.

─── Chapter 9 ───

ALARMED BY THE sound of her on the phone, Mallory had combed the streets for Kit, stopping in at all their old haunts.

Finally, near dusk, he'd come upon his cousin in Central Park, passed out on a mildewed blanket, her suitcase standing beside her. She was circumscribed by the litter of a major binge.

He dropped to his knees and held her cheeks between his palms. He rolled them gently. "Kit, wake up."

Her eyelashes shivered. She lifted the back of one hand to her forehead, then tried to push him away.

"Kit, it's Mallory. You've got to get up from here."

He helped her to a sitting position.

"What happened?"

"You must have passed out." He whistled. "Just look at this stuff! What were you trying to do, be the first woman to spontaneously combust from caloric heat?"

Kit tried to laugh, but with the tangle her emotions were in, she ended up in tears.

"I know, I know. Every once in a while, life is a real bitch."

He put his arms around her. "You're just having one of those days."

Now she really did laugh. "One of those days, Mal—I'm having one of those lives!"

"Look at it this way," Mal said with a smile. "If half the world is right, you may get another crack at it."

"That doesn't make me feel any better. But, oh, it's so good to see you!" She threw her arms around him. "Thanks." But then the tears pushed up and out again. "I'll probably never work again."

"What's done is done. You should have thought of that before you got cheeky."

"I did think about it. I'd do it again. But right now, I feel so hopeless. It's just too hard to push through."

"Poor little girl! Poor little victim!"

"Victim?"

"That's right." Mal stood up in one fluid motion, slapping the twigs and leaves off his pants. "Let's really get into the old female self-hatred. I mean, when the wind is right, you can smell it all the way from Third Avenue."

Kit sat with bent legs and rested her arms on her knees. "Honestly, Mal. What's the point?"

Mallory walked over to a pile of gourmet litter. He didn't look up from where he was crouching in the grass, cleaning up the empty boxes and wrappers from the glut of Kit's feast. "The point? That's up to you, Kit. There's got to be a reason to get out of bed in the morning. Even if it's just feeding a damn canary. But if I were you . . ." He cast her a sidelong glance. "I'd stick to my guns. You still want them to say, 'Atta baby! Atta girl! That's the ticket.' You've got to stop wanting that. Like I did. It never comes."

"I know that."

"Then what is it, really, that's got you down? I mean, I've been watching you for years now, and I get the feeling you think you're too good for this world, too pure or something. Well, I have news for you. We all feel that way when we're young. You're not too pure. You're just not trusting life enough. If you did, you'd see how much it really is on your side."

Kit shook her head. "I don't know if what you say is true. But I can tell you one thing, Mal: you're better than any damn canary."

"Come on then," he said, in a voice that brooked no opposition. "I feel partially responsible for your dereliction. I'm taking you home."

"Oh really? Where's that?"

"East Seventy-third Street."

"You know what I mean."

"God, you drive a hard bargain. Okay. It's where there are people who love you."

"Bully." Kit smiled. "At this point, I'm not in a position to refuse your offer. But it's only temporary till I can move back into our old apartment at the end of the summer."

"Only temporary," Mallory repeated, while rolling the blanket into a neat cylinder and tucking it under his arm. "Of course." He tried not to show his immense relief.

For what was left of that emotionally humid summer she spent with Mallory and his lover, Kit Daniels was reminded that misery-in-splendor is still misery.

Skin stretched taut over a surge of muscles, roped with tendons, mahogany-eyed, Rock the football player lived in a Fifth Avenue townhouse co-op among early Corots and Dalis (Mallory's choice), low-key Moderne, Art Deco furnishings, and the bloom of green inside a glass-walled solarium, set smack in the center of Manhattan. Paradise East.

So Mallory was riding high. Besides the affair with Rock, his career had exploded. With Crockmeyer's departure Mallory had taken the job and begun to wow the industry with his original designs. And now Rock was financing Mallory's own theatrical costuming company.

Kit still worried about living with Mallory and his hulk, but as it turned out, Rock was as spectral a host as Kit was a guest, the latter known only by the tip-tap of heels on her way to the kitchen, the former by a lingering, spearminty trace of liniment in the air. Kit imagined his muscles were so stretched out, they'd pop without it.

Most of the time, Kit sheltered in her grandiose bedchamber with the silken bed hangings dyed the uncommon shade of persimmons. She crept out of bed only to snatch a loaf of semolina here, a Boston cream pie there, for all of which she insisted on keeping a tally. Almost nightly, she vowed to repay Mallory and Rock for the food she was consuming and the space she was taking up. In the meantime, she ventured from the co-op only to do charity work at a children's hospital to which she'd already committed herself before the depression hit.

She was enormous. Too embarrassed to look for a job.

For Kit, it was one of those times when her dream life held more light and interest than the dark span of hours when she was awake.

As a result, Kit slept clear through most of the hours of daylight. Upon awakening, she looked forward to when she would fall asleep again.

Mallory continued to plead with his cousin to stop her obsession with food. Kit only smiled a secret smile and grew larger by the day. She didn't even make the pretense of stepping on the scale anymore. She loved Mal, but he didn't understand. No man could.

Once she was swallowed by the darkness, she was beyond human help. The beast inside her unhinged its jaws, and she just wanted to devour everything—her wrath, her despair, her broken heart—swallow them down whole, like a serpent in its coils. But the hunger—the hunger never ended.

It was a possession of demons, a haunting of the witch. The more she ate, the more she needed to be filled by something more. She was terrified, because she no longer tried to check the compulsion at all. She who had hidden behind her intellect, used it as a weapon to keep the world at bay, to make her father proud, was at the mercy of a force of instinct that belonged more to the reptilian brain than to the mind of a twentieth-century woman.

Mallory loved her. But he couldn't give her the kind of love she pined for. Food was the only black magic that could fight off the pain of her life. The most she hoped for, each day, was an exhausted sleep of satiety, when she could slip away from that body, that ugly rock she'd been chained to, and drift on her bed of dreams . . .

During those three hot sullen months after her dismissal from the theater troupe, she thought she would go mad with picking at the knot of her petty troubles.

She found the only way out of this trap was to write her way out.

At first the spiral-bound notebook was full of "serious" thoughts and maunderings, but then Kit's true nature asserted itself, and she began to lose herself in laughter.

It was, of course, only doodling in words, but it consoled and distanced her enough to make it possible to sleep without the sin of gluttonizing first.

And then, on one of those fall days of perfect brilliance when the air has the cool bite of a green apple, and new seems absolutely right, the call came from Maddy. She was in town with her fiancé. Lunch. La Grenouille. Now.

Like every other woman at the change of season, Kit had nothing to wear. She'd long ago outgrown even her most commodious garments.

She ended up throwing on a dowdy float dress in a polka-dot print.

It had a Puritan collar in stale cream that would have suited Mamie Dowd Eisenhower in her time. All Kit needed was a pillbox hat to complete the picture, and, indeed, the woman in the thrift shop where she'd bought the dress had coyly urged her to try one on. Kit, however, knew with a sinking heart that she was way too big to look "retro."

From the moment the housebound Kit had walked out into a sun-dazzled September afternoon and caught a taxi to La Grenouille, she'd come down with a bad case of culture shock.

She felt drained and disheveled, after all these cloistered months. Being taken away from her private stock of forbidden foods made her cranky. She was sure that everyone in the city could tell what she'd been up to, like an adulteress just emerging from her hotel room.

Worst of all, she hadn't been prepared for the uptilted perspective of the giddy bride-to-be.

Maddy had on an up-to-the-minute studded minidress in fine, feline stripes of lilac and gray. Kit just knew it had been yanked still hot from the racks of that new Scandinavian boutique in SoHo.

Below the plucked-to-precision eyebrows, a thin silver bar of eyeshadow and cheekbones brushed with a ruby dust gave her face a carved and cunning look. Her smile, outlined with soft peach lipstick, seemed to glow at Kit like a fluorescent tube. But one's attention kept returning to the eyes. There was something gorgeously eccentric about them, the highlight of her face in a way they'd never been before.

Of course, Maddy had got herself seated centrally beneath the new tricolored ceiling at La Grenouille. The pink linen, crystal bowls of flowers, and petite fluted shades lent a pastel shimmer to the room.

With a sure instinct for self-preservation, Kit denied herself a glance into the mirror that sparkled along one wall. She knew, next to Maddy, she must look like an elephantine Minnie Pearl.

"Jared's coming later," Maddy said. "It's so good to see you!"

The two friends embraced.

"Are you happy, Maddy?" Kit asked, in that shorthand of friendship.

Maddy blinked. "I'm terrified."

Interrupted by a waiter, they ordered mineral water with lime.

Maddy's eyes seemed enormous, brilliant, as she stared at Kit over her frosty glass. "You and I always talked about getting thin and getting married, as if they were one and the same. We never said anything about what happens next. What I mean is, am I supposed to be like my mother now? That's one of the reasons I wanted to see you today. I've got to know: what's next, Kit?"

At a loss, the two friends stared at one another.

"So this is Kit." Jared London smiled intensely into Kit's

face, as though he wished to brand her with his charm. "I've heard so much about you."

At the same time, Kit felt measured and dismissed as a possible sex partner by that smile. "Same here," she replied, and set about making herself smaller against the chair back.

"What's good for lunch?" He sat down beside Maddy and stroked her arm, then draped his own around her long, vulnerable neck.

As they perused the menu together, Kit took the opportunity to survey Maddy's true love. Handsomely attired in an all-business suit of French gray and a maroon tie, he had dark, darty eyes and a full head of shoe-black hair, coiffed like a movie star, or a pope. Kit had the feeling that the young attorney could just as easily have been something else. He looked upwardly mobile and bored. But his attentiveness to Maddy could not be faulted.

So this was the next stop on Maddy's journey to "womanhood."

First, the end of female communion: "I don't drink coffee." Now the giving over to the male of her very essence. Why was it that in novels, the most interesting women were unmarried? Was it that once the wedding rites take place, the young girls go gently into oblivion . . . their great energies sacrificed without a murmur to the fortunes of young men?

Kit would never let that happen to her.

Not that she would ever get the chance.

And yet . . . Maddy seemed so happy. Or was it, more, overwhelmingly relieved?

Was it this way for every thin woman when she found her man?

"I'm just jealous," Kit accused herself inwardly, looking for the blemish. "See how loopy in love they are!" But for the next two unquiet hours, all she could think of was getting back to her gorging at home, they made her so nervous.

Dessert finally came: a pale green Limoges plate topped with lime sherbert and strawberry coulis, cool as the shade of a desert palm.

Jared lay his papal hand on Maddy's. "You don't really want that, do you, Madeleine?"

Maddy fumbled with apology. "I'm sorry, Jared. I wasn't thinking." If he'd had on a ring, Kit suspected, Maddy would have kissed it.

"If you need a caterer," an embarrassed Kit said, endeavoring to change the subject, "my father has the best caterer in the world. And they do kosher too."

"Oh Kit." Maddy looked with pity at her friend, as at the unenlightened. "Jared and I don't believe in all that ritual. We're planning to have a civil ceremony."

Maddy, the rabbi's daughter, a civil ceremony! Kit bit back the questions on the tip of her tongue. It took her a moment to realize that no hint had been made of her taking part, even in the civil ceremony.

Kit glared across at Jared London now, sitting there so self-possessed, so ecclesiastical in his pinstripe suit, with his patent-leather hair, a man who had commandeered Maddy's life and would drive her out of the bounds of friendship, family—self-knowledge.

Maddy, doomed, perhaps, to be loved in this way, took her jailer's hand and kissed it. "What do you think Miss Hilde would say about this 'dumpling' now?" Her eyes were sparkling like little stars.

"Miss Hilde and the fat camp . . . that all seems so far away now, doesn't it?"

Jared shook his head. "Not really. For someone like Maddy, it's never possible to let down your guard."

So now Maddy's body was to be patrolled by psychic police dogs, scrutinized for any signs of encroaching fat cells—for the rest of her natural life . . .

Kit spooned the sorbet into her mouth, feeling more nervous by the minute. Eating sherbert was like eating sugar water. But there was a Black Forest cake in the freezer at home—if she got back now, it could be defrosted by dinnertime.

"Well, babe." Jared consulted the black wristband of his Rolex wristwatch. "I think you'd better kiss your girlfriend good-bye. We have a few more stops to make in the city today."

"Be happy for me," Maddy pleaded with Kit, as Jared

attended to the bill. "You must be happy for me!" Her eyes—wells of aquarmarine—seemed unnaturally intense, like those of a heroine in a Disney feature-length cartoon.

"Believe me . . ." Kit kissed her on the cheek, then hugged her with both arms. "Maddy, I can't help it, your eyes . . ."

Maddy giggled in that new way she had. "They're not mine." She touched her index finger to her right eye and shoved an aqueous blue disc in front of Kit's nose. "See. Cosmetic contact lenses. They were Jared's idea. Don't you love them?"

Slightly sickened by the sweetness of the dessert, Kit let herself be embraced by her best friend for what would be the last time before she was changed forever in the pure, mysterious flame of matrimony.

"I love them," Kit lied.

She cried, real tears, all the way home.

"Hello, Kitten." Tan and fit, Whitney Daniels welcomed her back to the penthouse splendor of Rock's living room.

"Daddy! What are you doing here?"

"I'm in town on business. Mallory let me in." He paused. "At least pretend you're glad to see me."

Of course I am. I love having my emotional legs out from under me, twice in one day.

Whitney Daniels ushered her into the co-op as though he owned it. "We're lucky. They left soon after I arrived." He patted her on the back. "Would you like a drink? Apparently, your cousin's pet Neanderthal keeps a good bar."

"No, thank you, Daddy."

"Then I hope you won't mind if I have one myself." After shaking himself a martini, extra dry, he eased himself onto the banquette sofa along the bay window. "Admiral Byrd misses you. He sits by your bedroom door and whimpers."

"Byrd is Marva's dog, Daddy. He just adopted me when she wasn't around."

Kit gazed off to the distance, where the East River, she knew, would be churning in a soft, blue autumn mist. She'd rather be there—anywhere but here. It was sure to be touch-and-go tonight, and after Jared and Maddy, she wasn't ready to cope with her father, or the ghosts he brought with him. When would she ever be free?

"Kitten, I'd hoped you wouldn't be bitter about the money. I admit I was too hasty, cutting you off like that. From now on, you can have whatever funds you need."

Kit eyed her father. As ever, she could feel the pulse of his anxiety, as though it were her own. "What's wrong, Daddy?"

"Sit down, Princess."

"I'm comfortable here." She'd keep her back to the wall.

"Very well. In light of your new bluntness, Kitrin, I too will be blunt." He sipped at his martini. "I want you to come home with me. Tonight."

Kit looked at him steadily, her instincts sharper than they'd ever been in her life. They had to be if she was going to survive.

"No."

"What did you say?"

"No, Daddy. I will not come home with you." *Please don't do this to me, Daddy. I can't bear it. I don't have the strength to carry you anymore . . . two people can't live on one heart.*

"For God's sake, why? What is so alluring in your new life"—he stabbed at the air—"that you can't leave it? From what Mallory tells me you have a shabby apartment in a poor part of town, no job, no prospects, no man to love you. What does this city offer you that I and your own home at Maregate, can't?"

Freedom, Kit wanted to shout. *Room to breathe. God, I can't breathe with you near me.* She caught herself.

"I have to get on with my life, Daddy. Not go backward."

"I don't know what you're talking about, Kit. Family comes before that. I come before that." His voice was like cream. "You and I, Kit, we are more than father and daughter, we are partners of the soul. We're dream artists, Kitrin, and no career can come between us. I thought you understood."

"Why now, Daddy?" Kit asked. "Why are you asking me to go back with you now?"

Suddenly, he looked a hundred years old; his smile crumbled away. "All right. I suppose you must know sometime, Kitrin. Your mother and I are officially divorced."

Without a word, Kit wandered over to the sofa, absorbing the news. Her father took her hand and gently drew her down until she was sitting beside him. He was still cupping her hand when a chill wind blew over her heart. It was as though she were poised on a mountaintop, being shown the temptations of her childhood: the stars, the crescents painted onto the curtain of a puppet theater by her father's fine hand; the library at Maregate done in Pompeiian red like the rooms of an emperor; the kind lies he'd told about Marva for the sake of his sad little girl on many of her most sacred days . . . She remembered it all. Her spirit rang with the memories of their mutual care, their pact of loneliness, their steady love. Still, she beat back the overwhelming urge to collapse into their dreamworld once more, to float selfless on the endless stream of his needs, a fragile Ophelia, father-ridden, guilt-drowned, unable to love any other man the way she should, for the love she bore her wifeless father.

He must have sensed that she was wavering, for he grew reckless. "Kitten, there is no other life for you. No home, with any other man. I know you didn't always understand that. That's why I had to do what I did about Marcus Heller. I know you so well. I could see you were getting confused about him. You thought he had power."

"You spread those rumors? You got him fired!" She held her hand over her mouth. That beloved man, brought to his knees by her father's jealousy. She felt sick to her stomach.

"It was easy. The trustees owed me a favor." He looked at her with clinical interest. "Why are you so surprised? Heller was a nonentity."

"Daddy," she whispered, knowing at last that she could never go home again, now that Marva was gone for good, now that the idolatrous image of father had exploded before her eyes. "It's time for you to go."

"Where . . . where do I go?" he demanded, his eyes like cracked blue glass. "I have no place, no one but you."

"You're wrong," she said, and he seemed to be receding already into the smoke-blue haze of an autumn night, her beloved daddy, her knight, her heart's blood. "You don't have me."

When he did walk out, her heart was beating so loud she thought the entire city would hear it, and weep as she did, as she would from this night on, in her dreams of Daddy, and the little girl who had finally died.

———Chapter 10———

I THINK SEMIOTICS is the 'Emperor's New Clothes' of contemporary literature." Geraldine Cutler had actually managed to coin a phrase beneath a blanket of Aden's ardent kisses. Her eyes sparkled up at him like African violets with the dew still on them. Lately, she got impassioned about literary theory at the most inconvenient times.

Of course, he was used to her talking during sex, but it was usually about him, and quite flattering. This talk was different. Aden had decided it had something to do with the article in the *New York Review* touting her as the heir to the Imagist, H.D., and calling her the "Dark Lady of American Poetry."

Aden's authentic British drill trousers, mulberry cotton shirt, and Bushman's fur felt hat lay strewn about the bedroom of Geraldine's light-filled loft on Greene Street. His castoff safari wardrobe (a birthday present from Geraldine; he'd had to wear it. But what *was* he hunting?) seemed out of place in this nun's cloister of a sleeping loft, the latest example of Geraldine's shifting philosophies, with its whitewashed walls, antique ebony prie dieu, and linen sheets, white as tundra snow. Right now, it might be inferred, Geraldine admired simplicity of design. Quotably, she sought to "live her life as a haiku, but in the context of Western tradition."

These days she traveled everywhere with at least one of her three white finches. She kept no frou-frou in her loft, preferring to display instead only one gardenia in a crystal shell, an ancient Tibetan bone, and a broken oyster-shell pocketwatch, inscribed, "We are the hollow men," which she claimed had belonged to T. S. Eliot. A timepiece filled with awe.

These were her numinous totems. With this table as mantra, she could pierce the poetic heavens.

Brisk sales of her books, high-priced lectures, and a hefty parental bequest had kept her tastefully trendy. Aden was beginning to feel like the icing on the cake.

He rolled over on the narrow nun's bed, whose affectedly plain white sheets were stretched drum tight. Something was very wrong.

"There's nothing new about semiotics. It's as old as the Greeks," Aden said. He was usually all set to be delighted by her. But today he felt contentious, troubled.

Defensively, Geraldine now nestled in the crook of his arm. She played with the blond pelt of his chest. Her lovely hair was spread out behind her, a bright lagoon on the bed. God, she was beautiful. Her skin (velvet and bone, like the antlers of a fawn) smelled faintly of crushed lilies; it was the scented water she got from Switzerland. Suddenly, lying there in her pale beauty, she reminded Aden of a cunning eighteenth-century toy, all silver joints and amethyst stones, with a clockwork spring where her heart should be.

Just as he was startled and a little shamed by this thought, Geraldine dropped little kisses, like liquid pearls, along his mouth. Of course, even these days, in her convent way, she hungered for him too. But Aden had always yearned for more than intermittent hunger. It wasn't right to stand like a beggar at the gates of paradise.

"What is it, darling?" Like many city people, Geraldine had never made room for silence in her life. Aden, distracted by the poetry, had never noticed it before.

"Not a thing, darling."

There was still the fun of her saying funny things, and when omens were right, the electrifying way she was in bed. But the breach between dream and fulfillment had widened. For so long he had convinced himself that there was another woman there, behind the artifice, a woman of substance and depth, the woman he needed. He almost had her. He'd worked and worked at it, almost creating her out of whole cloth. But today, for the first time, he was beginning to feel tired, to doubt.

Aden's eyes strayed toward the open window, where a fresh breeze was bellying the curtains, like sails. Surely somewhere out there under that bluest of skies stood a rock of a woman, already capable of loving, of being loved, the way he'd always wanted to love, fiercely, without false barriers of vanity and competition. The need to lavish himself on that woman had become a physical ache. For the first time, he realized it might cause him damage not to.

"Before you," Geraldine murmured, "there was this bisexual short-story writer. I liked him. He had lots of frizzy hair in this poured-steel shade. And then there was the charming modesty of the short-story writer. Not like a novelist, those old windbags. Once they start, you can't stop them, but with a bullet between the teeth . . ."

She was punishing him for the silence. Aden knew this because ever since Gwen Sweet, he'd been almost preternaturally sensitive to women's ways. Afraid to be taken off guard again, he'd become a little bit psychic about them, could read their minds as well as their bodies. But he practiced a kind of spiritual courtesy in this, never using what he'd learned to manipulate or to invade where he wasn't meant to be.

And generally, he loved what he read there: the spaciousness of their psyches, as though they could contain all that a man was—and something gloriously more, a magical connection to all that lived, to the green world, to what the collective race of "men" had lost long ago when they "made" them-selves into false gods.

Aden watched Geraldine jot down a phrase that had winnowed into her mind. It was for an acceptance speech she intended to give at the ALS Awards, months away.

At that moment, he doubted for them both.

As Geraldine lay back down beside him, Aden could feel the bed sag with the weight of all the male mentors—her father, the literary lions, the patriarchs of every stripe—who had shaped the fetching artifice known as Geraldine Cutler.

Could it be that in trying to love her, he was being starved for a woman who wasn't there?

If that were so, imagine how starved Geraldine must be . . .

She ran her hand down his muscular leg. "Hi. I'm back." She licked his mouth like a custard.

Back to what? Aden thought sadly. His body went through the trite motions of love, as he yearned for the witch of a woman on whose starry coattails he might go vaulting free.

In the fall, a solitary Kit Daniels moved back to her now-vacated apartment. Although the place on Third Avenue couldn't compare to Rock's palatial co-op, it was the Elysian Fields to Kit. If the uncleaned windows had been made of pressed diamonds, or the closet-size rooms as commodious as a Versailles salon, she could not have relished them more.

Kit had come to feel that the quiet month before Maddy's defection and her father's visit had only been a short pause between rounds. With the sound of some inner bell, she was off again, head down, hands before her face, fighting for her womanly life on the crowded sidewalks of New York.

Although she still hadn't the heart for a return to the stage, Kit had landed a job at a customized T-shirt boutique on Lexington Avenue where her penchant for pithy new slogans had won her instant popularity. She was now toying with the notion of enrolling in croupier school so that she could work nights in black bow tie and gloves at some nearby Atlantic City casino.

Meanwhile, propelled by guilt and the residue of love, she'd tried to locate Dr. Heller. Kit combed the city theatrical agencies, even went through the YMCAs and low-rent hotels, but to no avail. Dr. Marc seemed to have vanished into thin air. Daily her heart ached for the blow she and her father had dealt the man and his career.

Mallory banged down the last of the packing crates onto the dust-balled floor of his former apartment. "I think that's it." He tipped onto the sofa in exhaustion.

"Want something to drink?" Kit popped her head out of the kitchen. "We have water and"—she peered into the empty refrigerator—"water."

"In that case, I'll take water."

She handed him a jelly glass full of a cloudy suspension, then sat down beside him with her own drink.

He nosed into his suspiciously. "Are you sure you don't want to stay with Rock and me? There's plenty of room, and we love having you."

Kit smiled her thanks. "No, but thanks for everything. I don't know how I would have got through last year, without you."

"Hey, we're brother and sister, remember?"

"I remember . . ."

Mallory clinked down his glass on the coffee table. "Well, I guess I might as well bring the last of your bags into the bedroom and go. Rock and I are off to the Hamptons tonight."

Mallory swung up Kit's duffel bag, sewn out of green parachute silk, and headed for the bedroom. But the bag had not been zippered all across, and the bulk of its contents spilled out onto the floor.

"Oops." He hunkered down to stuff back the oversize panties, appliquéd hosiery, assorted paperbacks, which turned out to be the entire Jane Austen canon, and a sheaf of lined legal paper scrawled all over with Kit's exuberant hand.

"What's this?" Mallory demanded, dangling the pad between his thumb and forefinger.

"That? It's not anything. Just some scribbling I did to get

me through the horror show of last summer . . ." She knelt beside him and hastily rescued the papers.

"Whoa. Wait a minute here. Do you mind if I read it?" Kit was blushing hard. He had a hunch.

"I don't see why you'd want to . . ."

Mallory crossed his arms. "Can I read it?"

Kit shrugged. "If you've got nothing better to do."

He flipped up his hand and she relinquished the pad from where she'd held it, pressed against her chest, like armor. "Now why don't you go inside and take a nice brown shower, while I settle in right here," he indicated the sofa, "to read."

"Have it your way," Kit said, patently unhappy, and Mallory sat down to read.

"Dating Yourself"

When all is said and done, the best person for a woman to date is herself. You're not sure about that? Who else finds your conversation endlessly fascinating, your taste impeccable, your pettiest problems intriguing? Who else understands that you really do look like a young Ann-Margret with your makeup on? Who else will agree to stay home with you and your flu on a Saturday night and not feel the weekend was a total waste.

Consider the alternative: a first date. Now that's enough to put any sensible woman off social intercourse forever.

Approximation of female conversation overheard on every first date since the beginning of time:

1. Tennis? I love tennis.
2. Beethoven? I love Beethoven.
3. Sex? I love tennis.

Yes, there's that bugaboo, sex, to contend with on a first date.

If you do it, you'll lose his respect.

If you don't—he'll lose his patience.

There are, of course, gentle methods of swaying him from his goal. For example, try showing him your new deluxe color-photo coffee table book of *Herpes I*. If that doesn't work, show him the illustrated book of *Herpes*

II. If he's still there when your cherry incense runs out, explain to him firmly that this business about your Uncle Moose from Newark breaking your last boyfriend's fingers was never proven in a court of law and that the charges had to be dropped.

Occasionally, a woman can avoid all this effort by first-dating a man who has just undergone a mind-altering experience: the end of analysis, the end of his marriage, the end of the world. He'll be so busy talking about himself he'll forget what he came for in the first place.

Just remember, when it comes to sex on the first date—even with the above conditions—there are no guarantees.

"TEST QUESTIONS"

MATHEMATICS

1. If a=b and b=c, then there is really no need for the letter c, (or b!).   TRUE or FALSE

SOCIAL STUDIES

1. The Great American wagon trains were known for
   a) elegant smoking cars
   b) braking for small animals
   c) a tendency to stick with a small inner circle

LITERATURE

1. Which of these sentences opens the novel *A Tale of Two Cities* by Charles Dickens?
   a) "It was the best of times, it was the worst of times . . ."
   b) "Although there were many scouts in the pack, we all liked Eddie best because his sandwiches never got caught in the branches."

2. The following sentence is written in the style of which famous writer?
   "Upon being informed that the windows had just been washed, the blithe Lady Emily still felt sure she should watch for germs."

a) Jane Austen
b) Shelley Winters
c) Anonymous
d) None of the above

"Real Women Eat Stones"

In this age of changing sexual roles, it is sometimes difficult to tell the "real woman" from the girls. There are certain hallmarks, however, for the discerning eye.

For example, at a business lunch, the woman with "macha" will never eat fussy tea sandwiches with the crusts hacked off. Instead, she will have, say, a simple plate of stones.

To the delight of her party, she will then pick up the check. It is up to her whether or not to pay it.

Further, a real woman does not use dental floss, even in the privacy of her own locker room. A ratty old toothbrush with very *hard* bristles is more her style.

Role models are very important for the real woman. Thus it is that at no time, under any circumstances, will she show up at a midnight screening of *Gone with the Wind* dressed as Melanie and say her lines back to the screen . . .

"Why I Do Not Like Science Fiction"

SF seems to be the main arena of mythmaking for the late twentieth century—with the possible exception of Calvin Klein TV jean commercials—and I don't think it's doing the job.

What is so great about SF anyway? If you ask me, the genre exhibits a massive failure of imagination at every turn.

Think about it. Here's a novelist or moviemaker looking far into the twenty-fifth century, and all he or she can come up with is to transplant the good guys and the bad guys from the OK Corral into the Galaxy of Baltar 12. There, predictably, mortal combat is going on between the Anorexians and the Corpulets, while Earthlings supply laser-powered arms to both sides, waiting for them to blow each other out of interstellar space, so that they themselves can take over, when the radioactive dust clears.

Now tell me, won't we on earth have moved on to some level of higher consciousness by 5000 years A.V. (after Gore Vidal, first president and founding father of the United States of the World) so that violence will be strictly for squares?

And speaking of a lack of imagination—why is it that aliens are so often depicted as cute creatures with three-foot stalks for necks and liquid Einsteinian eyes?

How do we know aliens don't wear zippered sweaters and old sneakers and talk exactly like Mister Rogers does on PBS?

Come on, Steven Spielberg, get real!

Articles Never Written

1. NIAGARA FALLS: Fact or Fiction?

"List of Ins and Outs"

1. FOR HER:
   It's out to introduce your date as "Bonzo, the Man."
   FOR HIM:
   It's out to introduce your date as "the girl who owes it all to science."
2. It's out to be born rich.
   It's in to be born right.
3. CUISINE:
   ALWAYS OUT: Red wine on a stick.
   ALWAYS IN: Any shellfish beginning with the first letter of the month in which you were born.
   OUT: Being good friends with your ex-husband.
   IN: Being good friends with your ex-husband's accountant.
   FASHION IN: Anything found in your grandmother's attic.

FASHION OUT: Anything found on your grandmother.

"Small Wonders"

People are always harking back to the good old days,
although it happens less and less as the number of people
who can "harken" properly is dwindling.

A clearer picture of the actual merits of today's
civilization as opposed to that of the past may emerge
when broken down into the following lists:

SOME WONDERS OF THE ANCIENT WORLD	SOME WONDERS OF THE MODERN WORLD
1. Library at Alexandria	1. Dry cleaning
2. Babylon's Hanging Gardens	2. McDonald's Golden Arches
3. Colossus of Rhodes	3. Kojack

"Petophilia"

One of the more ominous phenomena of modern
years, is the preference among Americans for pets rather
than people.

Now I have nothing against pets, per se. From an
anthropocentric point of view, I think they can soothe
the savage beast in the worst of us, and we have much to
learn from them and thank them for, but there are limits,
or at least, there should be, for pet owners to observe.
For everyone's sake, including the animals'.

Three Things Pets Should Not Be Allowed to Do:
1.   Ride the New York City subways
   (with all the crime, it's much too dangerous for
   them)
2.   Eat better than I do
3.   Serve as a panelist on a Hollywood game show
   (beneath their dignity, don't you think?)

I suppose I should be grateful that Americans haven't
gone as far in their petomania as the Parisians, who allow
their cherished lapdogs to sit at restaurant tables with
them. In the event this unsavory practice should be

introduced to the States in the near future, I propose we stipulate that a) the pet must be wearing a tie (if male); b) the pet is a good tipper; and c) the pet doesn't mind eating with us.

A half hour later, when Kit emerged, gowned in a mock-silk Chinese robe, she found Mallory beaming at her from the sofa.

"Kit, this is the funniest stuff I've read since my high school yearbook. You've got to get published."

"Don't be ridiculous, Mal." Kit looked hurt. "I'm not a professional writer. And I don't know the first thing about getting published."

"Dear child, you don't have to. Leave it to me." Mallory took off from the pillow couch.

"Mal . . ." She followed him to the door. "Mal, wait! What are you going to do with that?"

"Right now I'm going to meet Rock and we're headed for that staggering traffic on the LIE. But first thing next week . . ." His eyes shone with mysteries.

"Mal!" Kit called after him down the hallway. "I'll never forgive you for this!"

He blew her a kiss, her comic pieces safely tucked away in his shoulder bag. Kit only threw back her head and laughed out loud, unpersuaded.

But true to his word, Mallory had sent the pieces to *Womanhood* magazine, and the very next week, Kit went wandering out of the magazine's offices, a soon-to-be-published author, and dazzled by it.

So pleased had they been that they'd signed her up to do a weekly column.

But buoyed by Kit's success with her first pieces in *Womanhood*, Mallory wasn't about to stop there.

"You're doing a book!" he'd barked into the phone while nodding at the assistant holding up two swatches of watered silk for his approval. He had his own costume company now. He was a star, therefore he barked.

"What?"

"There's interest in your doing a whole book, ever since Rae Jones quoted you in her column in the *Daily News*. They say *Womanhood* is just whistling off the stands since you joined them."

"That's only because they had a full-page beefcake shot of that rock singer, what's-his-name, in the last issue."

"Poppycock! Now you just keep your little fingers busy typing up more pieces. They want to see the whole thing before they'll hand you a check."

"I'll be darned."

"You're going to need an agent too . . . Oops, listen Kit, I've got to run . . . We've got a tech rehearsal in two days, and the male lead just dropped twenty pounds."

"Okay, but Mal?"

"Yeah?"

"Love you, Mal."

"Go write a book." The phone clicked off.

Four months later, around the first day of spring, Kit Daniels lugged her three-hundred-page manuscript into Mallory's factory salon, thumped it onto his desk, and walked out without saying a word.

The very next day, after a sumptuous late breakfast between the sheets—croissants, California strawberries, fresh cream, and café au lait—the now-famous and recently enriched costume designer Mallory Daniels rose from bed with a stately sense of purpose, dressed with care, and presented himself at the offices of Lassiter & Lassiter—the best literary agents in town, according to repeated testimonials by celebrity friends of Rock's, who had chanced to venture into the maze of the literary marketplace.

One of the two best agents in town, a beautiful young man named Aden, was unerringly polite, if distant.

"Mr. Daniels, there's an old but wise publishing saw that goes: humor doesn't sell. I would be wasting our time if I agreed to read your cousin's work. Besides, Lassiter & Lassiter specializes in works of serious literature. Not popular entertainment. A writer for *Womanhood* like your cousin would be more comfortable with another sort of agent, believe me." Aden never enjoyed turning away relatives of would-be writers, who tried to peddle everything from the autobiography of a New York City cabbie ("Remember the blizzard of '84—my brother Joe was stuck in midtown traffic for three hours with an uncle of Art Garfunkel!") or histories of the county fair by small-town librarians ("Imagine, she's been at it for thirty years, personally, last November!"), to sagas poetical, cast handily in heroic couplets by tweed-bound professors who much preferred the wit of Alexander Pope to that of Richard Pryor and were as innocent of the dictates of mass-market taste as Belinda of the plot to rape her lock.

Aden tried to let these civilians down easy.

Even so, Daniels looked as if he'd just sat on a live horned toad.

Aden tried again. "I'm sure that if you took a writer like"—he cast his eyes over the cover sheet, then continued—"Kit Daniels to Lefty Solarz, for example, you could work something out that would . . ."

Kit Daniels? The name capered on his tongue, it chimed through his memory like a carillon! He scanned the biographical material Mallory had provided. "A former Shakespearean actress," it said . . .

Kit Daniels! The deliciously sturdy Desdemona who had stolen the show, and waylaid his playwright's heart, all in one rain-soaked evening on Cape Cod!

God knows the third act of the play was not going well.

Aden had been blocked for months now, stuck in that climactic scene between Germaine and Burt when she leaves him and their child to pursue her career in art. He was desperate for something to break him out—strong emotion, a slight adjustment of the psychological lens . . . Visions of the sugar-plump actress danced in his head, seducing him with the notion that if he could only find her, talk to her, he'd solve the riddle of that damn scene, and for all he knew, that of love and life itself! What wisdom might he hear in the tongue of her laughter? What miracles spark from her witch's fingertips?

Indeed, she had seemed to throw off light that afternoon onstage, his big-bellied Venus, full of anguish and fire. The anguish he knew was there: no actress could have ditched her career for the cheap thrill of stolen laughter unless she was desperate with unhappiness. As for the fire—she surged with the violence of a creature being born.

Her Titian hair had been like a glittering web in which he and his heart would be held fast forever.

Aden gathered up the manuscript, unclasped his briefcase, and slid it in. "Mr. Daniels," he said, looking delighted and incredulous at the same time, "I've changed my mind. I will be taking this manuscript home after all."

"You're doing the right thing, Mr. Lassiter," Mallory said, also delighted.

"I wonder," Aden replied fiercely, as he snapped the briefcase shut. But he really didn't.

—————— *Chapter 11* ——————

Even though Aden Lassiter had stayed up well past midnight reading all three hundred pages of Kit Daniels' manuscript, he was fresh as a daisy by the time the sun rolled up his windowpane in the morning.

He sang through a brisk shower and dabbed on the East Indian cologne he'd picked up on one of his many travels. (Oil of lavender, the old woman in the market had told him—lemon, lime, and oak moss. "For a mun who makes de ladies smile.") Since then he'd never felt really dressed without it. After some calm deliberation, he attired himself in a stylish charcoal jacket with alternating tiny plum and chalk stripes, white open-collared shirt, and soft mohair trousers.

Today, he dressed with a sure sense of occasion.

Today, he would phone Kit Daniels and ask her to come into the office so that he might tell her how completely she'd turned his world around with her sense of cheekiness, her well of passion.

Sometime during that night, he'd fallen madly in love with

the spirit behind the word, with her wit, her gallantry, her irrepressible womanhood.

The obbligato she'd played on his heartstrings that day on the Mashpee stage had been resumed with every phrase she'd turned, every jest she'd crafted.

He broke off a rose floating among the blooms in the hall vase and patted it into his buttonhole.

When he got downstairs, the trees planted along Central Park West were waving their tops and shushing in the breeze. It was a golden morning, just as it should be.

With a light step, he climbed into the sunflower-yellow cab that sped him crosstown. The cabby was an attractive young woman. A good omen?

Aden flirted all the way to the office and tipped her so outrageously well that the laughing driver flipped off her tweed cap and made him a gift of it.

He wore it into the office, to the considerable amusement of the secretaries. Especially his own, the golden-throated Analisa. But even her smiling designs on his job could not dim the luster of his morning.

He wore the cap as he phoned Kit Daniels and set up an appointment for that very day.

He was still wearing it when Kit Daniels was shown into his office—how pleasant it was in here, he really hadn't stopped to notice: the verde-green marble-top desk. The wall-to-wall bookcases. The Crayola-colored posters of his plays.

My God, she was big!

She was covered in some sort of spotted maternity thing. A wrinkled white linen jacket she couldn't even close. And a dreadful silver-spangled beret. All things considered, she reminded him of a float he'd seen in the Macy's Thanksgiving Day Parade.

For her part, beneath the polka-dot camouflage, Kit was edgy. To begin with, she could not quite believe that anyone would seriously consider killing trees to make her book.

Then, on top of everything else, Aden Lassiter had turned out to be, with the possible exception of her own father as a young man, the most casually handsome, chestnut-curled god (wherever did he get that cleft in his chin—from a stone-mason?) she had ever set eyes on.

His eyes were an intelligent, clear gray shade, fringed by dark lashes like a young girl's. Tall and graceful as a Florentine statue, he seemed to have been carved out of a single marble stone, and the word that beat up at her was "integrity." When he looked at you with those loch-colored eyes, he seemed to know exactly who he was—and what you weren't. He smelled of something expensive and wonderful-by-the-ounce.

His clothes looked wonderful on him too. But then he had that attenuated elegance of frame that made it possible for a designer to hang any kind of rag on him and seem damned clever. Mallory, she thought fleetingly, would love him.

Just the sort of preppie prince who had haunted her college years, and yes, caused the humiliation of her debutante ball.

In the midst of all this intimidating beauty, only the worn green bookbag (she later discovered it had accompanied him through postgraduate work, across the Atlantic, and through the snow-capped Alps, which accounted for its kind of worn, talismanic charm) seemed approachable. Kit directed her words to it.

"I've heard you always sleep with your clients." Kit felt so fat and vulnerable and nervy that she had to strike the first blow, and hated herself for it.

"As many of them as possible," Aden retorted without even looking up from the agency contract they'd discussed nicely on the phone and which was now to be signed. At least he'd been right about one thing: her voice was strong magic. It drew him in.

"Men too?"

"What do you think?"

God, had she looked that big onstage? If she were to make personal appearances, he'd have to get that tonnage down . . .

"Doesn't sexual tension make it hard to work with them later on?" Kit's nerves were flapping like butterflies. She wandered around the room, the treasure house of a biblio-phile, fingering the many-colored, stamped, and leather bindings, some antique and obviously expensive, all the while wishing she hadn't been stupid or hopeful enough to come.

"On the contrary. It can be a way of mellowing things out."

Like Kit, Aden was beginning to regret his ever contacting her, but he was much too gracious to let on. "I can always introduce the author in question to an eligible third party, and suddenly we have the warmest regard for one another."

"I see." Kit picked up the slim volume that was displayed face out on the windowsill. "Is she good?"

"Who?"

Kit held up the copy of *Winter Chill* and tapped her fingernail against the photo on the back. "This one, Geraldine Cutler."

"All my authors are good writers."

"That's not what I mean."

Aden paused, suffering. Was this the Titian-haired goddess of his fervent dreams? The actress who would ultimately save his play? "That question is unbecoming to a client. Besides" —he tried to lighten the cloudy atmosphere billowing between them—"I never kiss and tell."

"Now that's unusual. I mean, kissing and telling seems to be a literary staple these days."

"Not in my books. We don't deal in that kind of trash."

"So you'll run your life that way, but you won't talk about it. Very convenient morality."

Aden rustled the papers under her nose. "Do you want to sign the contract or not?" She seemed determined to turn him off—when he wanted so much to like her.

Kit sat down in the Jamaican weave chair across from his desk and lifted off her sequined beret with a slow deliberateness, as though she were trying to make up her mind about something. "All right," she said, at length. "I'll do it."

"Do what?" Aden hadn't meant to be so sharp, but there it was. Open warfare. She had gotten the better of him somehow and he hadn't even noticed her doing it. Not the most felicitous beginning for a business relationship. He was about to tell her so. But now she'd bared her head to him and seemed more vulnerable. Once again, his imagination was ensnared in its coppery glitter.

Kit noticed how he was looking at her, or beyond her to something else more pleasing. She leaned toward his desk and gently tugged the papers out of his grasp. By accident, she brushed his hand with hers, and the world lit up in the blushing colors of Matisse's red room. Amazing how, if left to itself, her body would always choose the wrong partner.

Oh no you don't, she thought fiercely. *I'm not going to play the fool again, falling in love with yet another untouchable prince . . .*

She was desperate to ruin it all now. Before something worse, something beyond her control, took over. For fat girls, she knew, the best defense is a good offense. She would draw first blood.

"I'll go to bed with you," she said.

"How's that?" he asked, only half listening, and increasingly irritated by the painstaking way she scratched her pen across the bottom of the paper. And that hat! Nobody wore a hat like that to a business office. It looked like a Christmas ornament gone wild . . . Why would she want to hide that fabulous head of hair beneath it? "What did you say?"

"I said I'd go to bed with you." Kit continued to stall for time. Should she sign this damn thing? How could she work with a man who weighed her, with a superior smile, and toted up her flaws like chips on a roulette table? What was she getting into?

Aden stared. What was he getting into? "Thank you, but I only require your signature."

When in doubt, forge ahead . . . Kit ended up signing the damn contract, with a flourish. She was allergic to uncertainty and would take action, any action, just to be free of its sting. "Enjoy." She handed him the signed agency agreement. This done, she stood up with more cockiness than she felt, than she'd ever felt—and plopped her beret back on her head. "Later, Aden."

"Oh, please," Aden spoke to her white linen back, no longer resisting the animus he felt for his promising new author. "Call me Mr. Lassiter." She could never be his Germaine now. He was just glad his father and semiretired partner wasn't here to see this—or eavesdrop on it with his glass to the wall.

"Nice hat." Kit fired off a parting shot. With this direct hit, Aden turned fiery red. He whisked the idiot cap off his head and crushed it to his chest in a kind of schoolboy fury.

Kit flounced out of the office, making a point of smiling at Analisa, whom she sensed, correctly, was inimical to Aden Lassiter. The enemy of my enemy . . .

My God, what was she doing? What was she saying? The man had dared to be kind to her, and she was behaving like a harpy! She almost turned on her heel and marched back into the office, but was much too startled with shame.

By the time she'd ridden down to the lobby, Kit was in an agony of remorse.

She retreated to her apartment, and, when she'd fortified herself with a chocolate fudge sundae, rang Aden Lassiter up.

"Hello?"

"Hello, Mr. Lassiter? This is"—she took a breath, tiredly—"Kit Daniels."

There was that magnificent voice again, vibrant and sinewy, which called to Aden, reached up from the layers, to touch him in unexpected ways.

But still angry, he gave no answer.

"I wouldn't blame you if you hung up on me, Mr. Lassiter . . . I behaved like a wild woman in your office today."

"You said it."

She bit her lip, until it bled. "There's no excuse for what I did. I can only try to explain . . . You see, I don't take kindness very well. It's a problem I've had since childhood. I don't trust it, I guess. So I lash out. The best defense and all that."

All of a sudden, she was the maiden in the tower again. "I see."

She spoke quickly to cover the silence she fully expected, and richly deserved. "I don't imagine you'd want to represent me anymore. Believe me, I wouldn't hold you to the agreement I signed, under the circumstances."

"Hold on there. I signed the agreement too."

Kit's voice sang. "Does that mean you'll still take me on?"

On the other end of the line, he smiled at her choice of words. "Yes, I'll take you on."

She let out a deep breath. "Wow, I feel as if I've just been handed a governor's reprieve."

"Listen, I've been trashed by the best. Authors are a skittish breed."

"You can say that again."

"Hey, would you look at this!" Aden seemed amused. "We had a normal moment."

Kit laughed. "Lassiter, would you . . . would you care to have a reconciliation drink with me tonight?"

"Oh, I'm sorry. I've already made plans."

Kit sounded as if she were speaking from a hole beneath the earth's crust. "Oh, okay, I just thought I'd show you how normal *I* can be."

"Uh, wait a minute. I can meet you"—He flipped through his daily calendar—"tomorrow. There's a lunch cancellation." For Kit, a second reprieve.

"Great," she said. "I'm buying. Where'd you like to go?"

"Someplace simple and unchic."

"Do you know Papageno's?"

"Good choice."

"Twelve-thirty?"

"Twelve-thirty's fine."

"It's a date then."

"Yes, I suppose it is."

"See you then." She wanted to get off the phone before he changed his mind.

"Good-bye." So did he.

Papageno's was simple and unchic with white walls, daisies, and blue-checked tablecloths.

Aden Lassiter found Kit Daniels sitting there, staring into her red wine, with a shy, desperate air.

This time she wore no hat.

Her hair glistened, an abundant flow of lights down her

back. As he was seated beside her, he learned that she smelled sweetly, softly, unexpectedly of tea roses. He liked that. She hardly dared look at him with those abashed blue eyes. She seemed almost maidenly.

"What's good?" he asked, after greeting her.

"The gnocchi."

"Gnocchi it is."

"Will you have wine?"

Aden's eyes shifted from hers. "Club soda will be fine."

As he watched her eat, he saw flashes of the goddess onstage. Her eyes glistened when they brought the meal. Her appetite was untrammeled, a marvel. Her talk became happy and bright, especially when Aden toasted her coming success.

Aden poured her more red wine from the carafe. He watched her sparkle, attract the flirtation of the waiter. He was enjoying the energy that poured out of her, like a clear stream of light. He wanted to bask in it.

When they reached dessert, chocolate cannolis and espresso, she stopped to look up at him with wildly blue eyes.

"You know, it's funny, I never eat in front of anybody. I usually try to hide it. But"—she shook her head as if to clear it of some film—"it seems all right with you." Like with Mallory, she thought, only better.

"Yes?" he asked. "I'm glad."

After this, she'd begun noticing details. His hair—worn in a kind of classical bob—thickly curled, close to the head, and how it shone with the high color of a roan stallion she'd once seen. His fine-boned face, with its many points of interest for an artist or lover. Through the filter of wine, she sensed that he was fluid enough, even hurt enough to understand women.

"You know, Lassiter, you're not bad looking. If you'd just put on a little more weight . . ."

Aden let his laughter fly. It filled the small cafe, like sunlight.

"You *are* a wild woman," he said.

"Yes." She nodded in full agreement. "Do you think we can ever work together?"

"I don't see why not. We all have a wild side."

"Even you?"

"Even me."

A glint came into her eyes. "So tell me, Lassiter, now that we're friends. Is Geraldine Cutler any good?"

Aden raised his own gaze to heaven.

────── Chapter 12 ──────

ALMOST FROM THE instant she'd signed on with Aden Lassiter, a glamour had been cast over Kit Daniels' life.

Her collection, *Hot Stuff,* had shortly thereafter been sold to Silver & Silver, a major Manhattan publishing house.

Simultaneously, the mists of depression and failure parted, and beyond lay a New York City that only fortune's elect ever get to see, glittering with a million personal stars. Whatever else he'd done, Aden Lassiter had believed she could be one of them.

For the first time, she felt an open invitation to etch her own individual dance down the dream corridors of Manhattan. She felt blessed, empowered, in a way that the accident of being born into money had never made her feel.

Words streamed from her in great bursts of light. Her soul rang with laughter—the sound of freedom. Ideas grew like a heat in her body, conducted through her fingertips onto the electric pages, which accumulated deliriously, daily . . . And it was just as well she was putting her acting career on hold after the Cape Cod fiasco.

No wonder, then, there would always be a whiff of white magic about Aden Lassiter, for his newest protégée. In her mind, he was a Merlin—his words and actions etched in silver in her memory, as though they'd been outlined by one of those newfangled metallic pens you could buy in the stationery store.

It was, all in all, a lot like being in love. Vibrant with passion, Kit dropped all other occupation and got lost in her writing. Except, perhaps for worrying about Maddy, who was now dutifully pregnant and housebound somewhere in Connecticut. At first Kit wasn't quite sure how to react to this news, having thought of herself as a child for so long, but now she felt that if Maddy Lefkowitz were pleased, then so was she. It would be fun to have a baby around. She loved babies.

During this period, they all seemed to be moving up, and away. Her cousin Mallory's staggering success had led him around the world as costume designer for Metropolitan Opera stars. Kit lost touch with him somewhere in Sweden.

She'd also lost fifty pounds. The energy she had once packed into eating and despairing was now being knit into the creative chemistry of her work.

Until one day, in the icebox of December, she caught the stranger in her mirror.

Fifty pounds lighter, the stranger had an entirely different stance from the old, uneasy Kit—more grounded, it was, feet planted firmly on the ground. This was a woman who could travel light. Her big workshirt and blue jeans floated around her like water. She stripped them off, never taking her eyes from the new bones in her face, her hips, pushing up with a kind of frontier exuberance. She was a brand new beauty, Venus ascending from the waves of fat.

She would never know how long she stood introducing herself to the mirror. For she was thin, like Maddy. And like Maddy, her provisional life might end, and the perfect one begin . . .

Only when the telephone jangled did she realize that her teeth were a-chatter, and there were goosebumps running up and down her bare arms.

It wasn't fear. The room was freezing!

Wrapping the workshirt tightly around her thinned-out frame, she made a lunge for the phone hanging from the kitchen wall.

"Hello?" It came out breathless, as though she knew what blessing was to come.

"Congratulations," said the jubilant voice of Aden Lassiter. "We've just received a copy of next Sunday's *New York Times* best-seller list. And guess who's on it?"

Kit sank down onto her pillow couch. She curled her legs beneath her and tried to stay grounded. "Lassiter, is this a joke, because if it is . . ."

As a writer himself, Aden Lassiter took his authors' work seriously. He knew the tantalizing glow of the perfect phrase, the daily ordeal at the silent typewriter. He himself had been forced to put Germaine and the haunting play she inhabited aside. He was already finishing up another three-act play, *Saul's Thousands,* with much happier result.

"Now Daniels, you know I never make jokes about my clients' careers. *Hot Stuff* is number three. Number three, Daniels! Do you know what that means?"

Every professional writer knows what that means . . . the blast of instant celebrity. A piece of the sky. She would move to a new apartment on Fifth Avenue and lose touch with failure . . .

Kit's heart was on her sleeve. Against all common sense, she began to cry.

"I'm going to have to take you on sartorially, Daniels. New designer clothes, I think. A beauty makeover in some salon . . ." Only gradually did Aden become aware of the tense silence on the other side of the line. "Daniels, are you there?"

"Yes."

"Are you all right?"

"Yes," she lied.

"Good." Aden, who planned his busy weeks by the quarter hour, checked his watch. "Well done, Daniels. Now go out and paint the town. In the meantime, I'll try to get more details on those sales figures, so we'll know how rich you really are. Okay?"

"Okay." She sounded very far away, sunk inside herself.

He hung up the phone, and after a few key calls, she imagined, promptly forgot all about her.

But for the longest time, Kit sat curled up on the pillow couch, with the phone still warm in her hand. Outside, a winter storm was brewing. The apartment quickly filled up with the silence of it.

Success. It was such a big responsibility. It weighed her down like an anchor in deep waters. She didn't know if she were ready for it. And there was no one with whom she could talk. Maddy was up in Connecticut having a baby. Mallory at this very minute was sewing Signor Antonetti into his costumes, in a drafty Stockholm theater. And her parents . . . well, Kit Daniels had no parents.

She was alone.

Kit uncurled herself from the sofa. In a trance, she walked over to the refrigerator and tugged open the door. Multicolored jars of fruit juice tinkled merrily on the shelf. The bald pates of eggs gleamed in their sockets. Her old friend Sara Lee sat in a box marked "cheesecake" and crooned, "Eat me . . ."

"Can I help you with something?" Aden rose from behind his desk, wondering why Analisa had let this beautiful woman into his office without benefit of an appointment. Was his ambitious secretary staging some kind of coup d'état?

In her confusion, Kit did not realize that Aden hadn't set eyes on her for a good six months. He had phoned her from time to time to check up on the progress of her book, and her life, but somehow he'd had no chance since the reconciliation lunch at Papageno's to actually see her in the flesh. And in her case, there was so much less flesh to see! Even now, it was hard to believe she had resisted the siren song of Sara Lee, and the others. In the name of her narrow hips.

"Aden, it's me." Like a patient with bandages she was unwrapping her white wool scarf from around her neck.

"It is?" Aden bent to her. He perused her face. "Daniels? Is that you in there?"

She nodded. Thank God he was too polite to stare.

"Have a seat," he said, eagerly waiting for her to finish peeling.

Kit shrugged off her slouchy black coat, then immediately wished she had it back on. She folded her arms across her chest, feeling dangerously exposed without the wall of adipose to hide behind. "You're sure? I wouldn't want to interrupt you or anything."

"Not at all."

Kit was incandescent. She also looked to be on the point of tears, reminding Aden of his character Germaine in that neither of them felt capable of their own happiness. They simply didn't believe in it. He would have to believe in it for her.

"May I offer you some tea or hot chocolate or something?"

"Only if you're having some." She was quieting down now, looking extravagantly small and pretty in her chair by the window. He felt a poignant sense of promise that he could not readily identify.

"I'm not thirsty."

"Oh, I see."

Aden stood in the middle of the office, feeling his way toward the New Daniels. She was like a new star showing up unexpectedly in some blank curve of space. He didn't know where to place her in the scheme of things—or even if she'd stay put once he'd fixed her there. Probably not. Not Kit Daniels.

He shrugged. "How do you feel about being famous?"

That's a stupid question, Kit thought at first. *He might as well ask how I feel about flying on my own power, or walking upon water, it's just as unreal to me . . .* But then she became aware of the great wave, the inner swell of excitement upon which she rode, perhaps only some of which had to do with sudden fame and fortune. She glanced at Aden Lassiter, then looked away. He was so damn handsome. He was being too kind. This time, she must behave.

"Fine," she replied, uneasily, staring holes into the floor. "Well," she said, after a while. She crossed her long legs, then uncrossed them, and suddenly Aden found he couldn't take his eyes off her. Her pale winter skin glowed with an unearthly light. The air around her vibrated brilliantly as though there were more life concentrated in that twinkling arc than in the rest of the room. Aden had a sharp need to touch, just once, the autumn fire of that hair, then caught himself like a dreamer on the move . . .

"Oh, I almost forgot." He took a few steps across the room to his closet and opened the door, relieved at having something legitimate to do with his hands. He came back with a green bottle of Taittinger's. "This is for you." He handed it to her. "I picked it up after lunch this afternoon."

She was all eyes now, like a schoolgirl at her first dance, as if she'd suddenly had an inkling of the stealthy power that radiated from her core and drew him to her. The atmosphere between them had turned sweet, and musky. Kit nodded at the bottle in her hand, exquisitely aware of his eyes upon her body.

"If I stay—will you drink a toast with me—and have yet another normal moment?" she asked, and watched him watch her, the way Marc Heller used to do. My God! It made her dizzy to be near him. She held on to the sides of her chair, waiting for the carousel to rock its last rock. What was going on? And please don't let it stop . . .

"I don't drink. Alcohol and my family don't mix."

"Oh, I'm sorry." What had Mallory told her about his family history? Was it his father who had the problem with the bottle? Or was it Aden himself?

"My mother was an alcoholic. I wouldn't want to take the chance of falling into that hell."

"Of course." So even the preppie prince had his share of sorrows. She set the bottle down on the beige carpet, willing Aden not to move away. Not yet. But the mood had already been broken.

Aden staked out a spot on one end of the sofa in his bookish office, which turned out to be as far as possible from Kit on the other side. Out of the corner of her eye, Kit caught the cold glint of spectacles in winter light. Behind them, the rapt look was gone.

"Care to talk about it?"

"It?" she asked, extremely irritated at his choice of seating arrangements.

"Your funk."

"I wasn't aware I had one. Doctor."

Aden ignored the jab. "Every author does. It lies in wait, like a battler eagle, until there's one too many rejection slips, a bad review—or a good one. Then it swoops down—pow—and snatches all your good sense away . . ."

"In that case," she admitted, "I have a funk."

"Why do you think that is? No more worlds to conquer?"

"No." Kit leaned forward, her face and hands animated with a fierce beauty. Unconsciously, Aden pressed back against the sofa. "I think for a lot of women—"

"Spare me," Aden interrupted.

"All right—for me—it's more like fear that the truth will come out one day. That I'll be exposed as a hoax, untalented, undeserving of praise."

"As though it were all a mistake?"

"That's right."

"Daniels, we're all on shaky ground."

"Women more than men."

"I never thought of it that way," Aden replied, feeling as he had once before, that day in Mashpee, how vulnerable this woman was beneath the fire-breathing facade, how like a lost little girl. He could see why he liked her after all. The phenomenon of the bright lights—that was just the shock of seeing her so diminished. Wasn't it?

"Men are always questing, aren't they? Sometimes it's for a piece of truth, or for a woman. Their very biology calls for it. It's a beautiful energy, with its own strength, and its own weakness. But a woman has another kind of challenge." Kit raised her eyes to where the storm broke against the twentieth-story window, like a bottle of champagne against a ship's hull. A celebration. Was it time to celebrate then? Her heart leaped. "She must be silent and still, she must not stray too far, be distracted too much. Because what she's after is not anywhere out there."

Behind the glass ovals, Aden leveled his clear gray eyes at

121

her. He said nothing, but she felt comforted that he understood. It was a good feeling. She could see why she'd liked him after all. "See?"

"Damn it! There's happiness here, Daniels. Meet it!" he barked.

"If you'd said 'eat it'—we'd be in business!" she shot back.

They looked at one another from across the sofa, then simultaneously broke up.

"Well," Kit said, almost gaily, "looks like we shooed that old funk away."

"For now," Aden said. "But he'll be back. As long as you look on the down side, thinking you're a hoax, and all that, that's the funk at work."

"Well, on the bright side, I can get my American Express gold card now."

He grinned. "Not exactly what I had in mind. Money doesn't seem to be what you run on. I was thinking more along the lines of a personal challenge." Cleverly, he had used her own word, as if to signal that he had indeed been listening.

"What do you mean?"

"From what you told me at lunch, you've been leading a pretty reclusive life. Well, you're not going to be able to hide away in your room after this, my girl. There will be interviews, parties, television cameras—the works. You're the stuff of celebrity now. And now you're going to have to think about what image you're going to present to the world, God help them."

"I'm an actress," she said with some warmth. "I can do it."

"Ah, but this is different. You're not hiding behind a character anymore."

"Well, actually that sounds like a lot of fun. Let's see . . ." Kit uncurled her legs and got up from her chair, posturing. "I can be Child Kit, Kit the Conscientious . . . Kit the Cursed."

"Why not just be Kit Daniels?" Aden interrupted.

"Who?"

The rain had stopped, and now great flakes of snow were falling, spinning everywhere. The wind blew swathes of cotton gauze across the windowpane, hemming them in with a white stillness.

Kit felt she wanted to get closer to Aden . . . to see him. Aden yearned toward her with his entire body, as though she were a bonfire, and he in need of its warmth.

Just then the buzzer went off on Aden's desk, and both Kit and her agent jumped before the unexpected sound. Aden bounded off the couch to bark into the intercom. "Yes? What is it?" He felt cranky, disoriented, as though he'd just been rushed out of sleep. "All right, thank you, Analisa." Irritated, he lifted his finger from the button. She liked to catch him napping.

Kit was already up from the sofa. "I should be going now anyway. I've taken up enough of your time."

They looked at one another, almost shyly, from across the room.

"You're no hoax, Kit Daniels," Aden said. Then he laughed.

Kit could always tell what a person was like by the freedom of his laughter. Aden's was bright and clear. "May I call for you tomorrow at nine?"

Kit was unreasonably pleased. He desired to see her. Tomorrow. At nine. She was no hoax.

When she turned, there was a giant looming in the doorway. "Kit Daniels?" the giant boomed.

He was Clayburn Lassiter, Aden's father, third and most beloved of Vita Jones's husbands. An Old Testament patriarch of a man at six-feet-three inches, he had desert-sky eyes, a scriptural strength, and a burning-bush tone to his voice that no one could wisely ignore. Among his many achievements, Clayburn Lassiter boasted more National Book Award winners among his roster of writers than any other agent currently in the publishing field. Kit now understood the joke about how his manuscripts came graven in stone.

"Dad? What are you doing here?" This from Aden.

The titan in the cashmere coat bounded in and unwound a coil of what seemed to be miles of peacock-blue and gold-plaid scarf. "Hell's freezing over out there." He grimaced down at Kit. "So I finally get to meet you. I'm the Senior Lassiter of Lassiter & Lassiter, and I just wanted to extend our congratulations . . ." He held out a bottle of Taittinger's identical to his son's.

"Too late, Dad. They've already been extended." Aden waved over to the bottle on the floor.

"Don't you have an appointment with your parole board?" his father shouted, plunking down the champagne on the desk.

The two men exchanged arch glances and Kit felt she was at a sports match, the rules of which she didn't know.

As the steam began hissing in the pipes of the old office building, a muezzin's prayer, Clayburn Lassiter laid his huge hand on Kit's back and guided her out the door to his own office, held in reserve for just such impromptu visitations. "Did Aden ever mention his nickname as a boy? It was Stinky. Yes, Stinky, and there's quite a story behind it . . ."

With a last look at Aden, Kit vanished into the adjacent office.

"I'll see you tomorrow." Aden laughed, leaving Kit to fend for herself. After all, success must have its price . . .

A half hour later, when Kit had been released into the snow, Clayburn Lassiter bounded in from the adjoining office. "You'd be a horse's ass if you didn't go after that one!" Lassiter boomed in his Jehovah-like voice. "She says we can solve the city's housing crisis and the problem of the subways in one fell swoop—by selling individual cars as luxury condominiums! What a rip!"

Aden directed a mild frown at his father, one of those self-mythologizing men who seem to be more vivid, more alive than other people. At times like these it was a burden to be his son. "As of now, that is the front-running candidate for the craziest woman—no, let me amend that, human being— I've ever met."

"Hell, she looks like she'd be a lot more fun in bed than that Cutler woman!"

It was common knowledge that Clayburn Lassiter had taken an implacable dislike to "that Cutler woman" from their first meeting, although Aden noticed that this pose did not in any way prevent Clayburn from trying to lure the author into his giant oak-hewn bed. It was all part of a little game the father liked to play with the son, an ingrained habit by now, this de rigueur seduction of Aden's pretty friends.

Perhaps it came out of a sort of reverse Oedipal complex, defanged, because it was, after all, played out in a spirit of fun. And since he'd never once succeeded with any of Aden's "ladies," who were far too smart for him—and he never really intended to—it was a habit he felt harmed no one, and held a certain innocent entertainment value for everyone involved. Lassiter Sr., like his son, prized the making of fun.

"Dad, you're just being perverse. A symptom of your second childhood." Aden snapped the file cabinet shut. He was secretly surprised by his own reaction. On the question of Kit Daniels he seemed to lose his sense of humor. "If that woman and I ever started up a romance, we'd both end up as headlines, having strangled one another's egos over a late supper."

"Admit it." Clayburn Lassiter relaxed against the rim of the marble-topped desk. "You're interested. Piqued. Strangely aroused. A woman who can make you laugh is a joy forever." Clayburn had to know if Aden were going to pursue this girl, so he could lay the strategy for his own chase . . .

"What's a woman who can make you mad?" Aden was on his way out.

Clayburn Lassiter just laughed. He could wait for the good part, when it came.

And it would.

It was the day after the big snow.

Despite the battleship-gray skies, Kit Daniels awoke to a morning that shivered with promise.

A vitamin supplement and black coffee prepared her for wonderment.

She banded her hair back in a quick ponytail and folded over her arm the baggy black coat with which she'd camouflaged her body for years. Today was D-Day. Today she would be liberated from the beaches of the lovelorn. Aden Lassiter was coming to call.

At nine o'clock, Kit and her great expectations flew to answer the door.

The wind had whipped color into his cheeks. His sable-trimmed coat swept regally around him. He was even more attractive than she'd remembered. And he was all hers to explore.

"Hi," he said. "Brr. We'll have to move fast today. I plan to cover a lot of ground."

"Ground?" she asked, still smiling.

"Uh-huh." He was holding the door open for her. "We've got to dress you like a star."

She stared at him all the way down to the street, where the snow lay melting into slush. This was a business call. He wanted to dress her as if she were a fiberglass mannequin! How had she let herself forget how men managed women's lives! She wanted to strangle him, right there, beneath the icicles weeping from the trees. As her heart cracked, a chunk of ice crashed from the awning to the pavement, narrowly missing their tender heads.

She tried to be civil as together they plunged into the festive whirl of city shops, tied up in red velvet and tinsel, the holiday street Handelian with traffic sounds. It could have been a cheerful morning—it probably was to anyone but Kit Daniels, who'd been betrayed by her friend in the fur coat. He did seem to know precisely what costume Kit would need for her new "role" in life and just where to get your hands on one in the mirrored labyrinths of fine department stores and the chi-chi boutiques that she had always been too large and too embarrassed to enter. But Aden Lassiter obviously knew nothing about women. What's more, he was advancing her the money against her projected earnings for *Hot Stuff*. She couldn't even hate him without guilt.

Nonetheless, it was a heady rush into the world of haute couture, from the instant they'd stepped into the duplex store called Sylvie on level three of the Trump Tower Atrium—a Versailles in miniature, a pale jewel, it seemed, from the pastel banks of flowers perfuming the air, to the "face-powder-colored" sofas where affluent customers could view the latest creations in velvety comfort. There was, further, a waterfall glitter of chandelier and a mirror-paved staircase, perfect for the practice of dramatic entrances and exits. Kit, who with her center of gravity freshly shifted, wasn't yet sure how to move in her new body or how to make it look comfortable to others, was at something of a loss in this tiny palace. More than once, she misjudged the space she would need to occupy on the spindly chairs and dollhouse sofas, her hand coming to rest on the blade of her hips in disbelief. When the fashion show commenced, she oohed and aahed, like a Fourth of July crowd all rolled into one.

Aden, meanwhile, seemed charmed by her fresh reactions. For a millionaire's daughter, she was disarmingly unspoiled.

Oh, there were antique lace confections! An imperial muff of nothing less than purple suede, all trimmed with the sinful lavishness of red and black fox fur! A universe of nacreous sequins, rhinestones asparkle, jet beadings from grandmother's day, and now . . .

A model came out in a floor-length dress of blond-silk lace that bared one shoulder and left the other afloat in parfaitlike layers of Honiton lace; mink, the color of fine champagne; and a cloud of silk tulle, gleamingly edged with satin.

"Four thousand, two hundred," said the neat, dark-haired woman in the Louis XV chair.

Just then, a famous customer came in and the saleswoman excused herself to attend him.

"Four thousand two hundred!" Kit, the former Schrafft's waitress, was impressed.

Aden bent his curly head to whisper something into her ear. For a wild moment she had the impression that he was about to kiss her.

"It's spectacular, and you would, no doubt, do it full justice. So let's get the hell out of here!" He gave a laugh.

Kit felt a pang of disappointment, whether about the kiss or the dress, she wasn't sure. But she had to agree with Aden that she wasn't yet ready for such *ancien régime* extravagance, especially as this was just their first stop of the day.

Reluctantly, they quit Sylvie's *bijouterie* for other palaces of style.

A raid of Maud Frizon turned up a pair of double-strap

kid-skin pumps and blue Napa low boots, which looked like fun to wear although Aden never did talk Kit into overlooking their origins as little sheep and goats.

At Saks Fifth Avenue, where even the floor sweepers seemed hushed and oddly elitist, they fell in love with a polo coat that bore a name to conjure with. It was done in the most eye-boggling shade of fuchsia, and Kit felt compelled to buy the gray flannel menswear pants that went with it.

Around noon, they stepped into Bloomingdale's, on the corner of Lexington and Shangri-la, where they caught a quick vanilla yogurt at the health-food bar Forty Carrots.

Loaded down with packages, Kit collapsed into her seat at the bar.

"I don't care how impatient you are. From here on, we'll have the damn things delivered. By the way, have you thought about moving to a trendier neighborhood?" Aden seemed to be watching Kit's spoon digging into the plain vanilla yogurt, as though he expected her to blow up like a hot-air balloon with the very next bite.

Kit ignored it, for the time being, storing up grievances in her heart. After all, she herself wasn't sure how long this astonishing bout of abstinence would last. Every meal these days was a new gamble, every bite of food a fresh challenge to the household gods.

Imagine: for the first time in her adult life, Kit didn't need the scale to tell her if it would be a good or bad day. She didn't have to shift her weight from the ball of her foot to the heel in order to produce the lowest weight possible at the little glass window. She had often wondered what it portended for her character, to cheat herself daily like that.

Now she no longer needed to wonder. *Hot Stuff* had saved her from the self-imposed slavery of the scale. Sheer busyness had got the weight off in the first place. She suspected it would be up to vanity and willfulness to complete the job.

"I like the East Side . . . maybe a co-op on Fifth Avenue . . ."

He raised one eyebrow. "I said trendy, not impossible." He hoisted his cup and tested the coffee with his tongue. "Hot." He chinked down the cup. "By the way, my father is quite taken with you. He called me this morning to harass me with the news."

"He's a devil. I adore him."

"So I understand. He says he left you at an indecent hour. The neighbors will be buzzing."

"Did he also say"—Kit was amused at the thought of how the father must have boasted to the son—"what we were up to all night?"

A woman in a gray poodle coat took the stool next to them at the blond wood bar and ordered what looked like a whopping bowl of meadow cuttings.

"Well, no," Aden replied. "I try not to encourage him."

"The fact is we played Trivial Pursuit all night. Your father claims I'm the first woman ever to whip his ass . . . three times in a row!" She felt tickled all over again whenever she thought of her wedge-heavy pink pawn slouching toward victory. "But does he always talk so magnificently?" she asked.

"Yes. Imagine being chewed out in that voice? It was like having Jehovah for a father."

She flung back her head and laughed from all the way down. "Don't we all?"

Aden didn't know why it gave him so much pleasure to hear her.

She was beautiful now, yes, even with the plain Jane hairdo and big, black coat, but he could still sense the virago bristling underneath. God, just look at the way she'd kept bucking his choices this morning, making a beeline for the most inappropriate articles of clothing, almost as if to goad him. It was hard to believe that she'd been reared by a fashion-plate mother when she wanted to deck herself out like a cross between St. Joan and Minnie Mouse—all tough-boy leather and pitted studs on the one hand, cutesy miniskirts and baby-girl pink bows on the other!

She smiled at him, in her throttled way, over the coffee cup.

Of course, he could understand her hungering to try radical new styles that had been denied her larger self. But he'd have to make a personal point of checking up on her whenever she was scheduled for a TV interview or book-signing spate, lest she walk out in some outlandish getup and lose whole portions of her public.

Kit Daniels, the poor little rich girl, appeared to have the need to shock, to overturn, to play her own game. His mother had been like that, he remembered, during that vivid time when she glowed with whiskey and old demons. Maybe that was why Kit Daniels' flamboyant brawl of rebellion repelled him as strongly as it attracted.

He'd never understood his actress mother, either, even as he'd continued to love her with a hopeless, heartbroken love . . . Perhaps, if he'd been a better little boy . . .

Of course, Vita had turned herself around, made Clayburn's life a thing of joy for those last ten years before she died, unexpectedly, of complications after minor surgery.

But by then, Aden had become a man. For him, her love had come too late.

"Lassiter?" Kit said.

He looked up to see the white-aproned young girl in a hay-yellow ponytail smiling down at him with her braces. "Anything else, sir?"

"Uh, no. Just the check please."

"What were you thinking about just then? You looked so sad." Kit was taking his measure with her big blue eyes. Oh, success was a wonderful thing, for it provided the luxury of tending to someone else. Through Care for Children, she'd been persuaded to get behind a drive for a new children's wing in a Newport hospital. Now she was getting close to Aden Lassiter. Life was fine and funny.

"I was thinking about a woman I loved very much."

"Did she love you?"

"I think so. Yes, I'm sure she did."

"Who was she?" Kit asked.

"You ask too many questions . . ." His attraction to her brought out the beast in him. It was the thing that worried him most about being around her. Even his amiable father had been shaken by the darkness that spilled out of his mother. Women, especially beloved ones, could destroy men with a fiery breath, a look, a dare.

And yet, they gave life too . . . and a man mustn't back away from giving of his own . . .

For the rest of the biting cold afternoon, as they dodged the melted snow dripping from the canopies of department stores and taxied to and fro, they took care not to converse of anything more weighty than whether to choose black or butterscotch kid gloves to go with the shockingly fuchsia coat.

Aden even dragged his special client to Greene Street in SoHo where they made the most daring purchase of the day: a faux antelope and Italian cotton corduroy greatcoat, with matching vest and mohair sweater. There was a wool scarf, boots, and fur shako hat, as well as nuggets of faux jewels for Kit's ears and shiny bangles for her wrists.

But among their major purchases, Kit's favorite came last.

She'd gone over to touch it as the saleswoman held it up for her inspection, a thing that shivered like diamonds, a fine chain mail, woven of white fire and smoke. It had leaped, this fairy thing, from the hands of an Italian designer.

She tried it on. It rippled over her skin like water. Aden wanted to play his hands in that light-filled stream. Kit was turning and shifting her body this way and that in the mirror. Her skin felt cool and liquid under that dress. She could sense Aden's eyes on her, as every movement she took flashed fire.

"That isn't a dress, it's a piece of magic."

She was in love with her own possibility, Aden thought inwardly, not realizing it was another possibility that had brought the flush into her cheeks and the warmth into her breasts. And to think of that polka-dot rag she'd worn for the contract signing! Looked like a wrapper of Wonder Bread . . . "I should probably have my head examined," he told her, "or at least phone my accountant, but, okay. After all, I brought you into this den of iniquity."

"He's going to let me buy it!" Kit threw her arms around the trim saleswoman. "And to think he also supports a wife and three children on a minister's salary!" She winked. "It's the tips, you know."

Aden glowered at her, but then she condescended to kiss him on the cheek. She smelled of tea roses and spearmint gum, the one flowery soft scent undercut by the snap of the

131

other. Just like Kit Daniels. Aden rather liked the sensation of her being close.

He did not move away.

But there were no more friendly kisses coming his way. Instead, Kit ordered the silver dress from the startled clerk, arranged for fittings, picked up her bundles, and sped off to their next stop with renewed enthusiasm.

When they ducked into Bergdorf-Goodman, stamping off the snow from their boots, an hour before closing, Aden sent Kit to wander the pastel realm of lingerie with wide eyes and a full line of credit.

As Aden had rightly suspected, Kit had never owned beautiful nightclothes. She'd worn old granny gowns and men's pajamas to cover her hugeness, even in sleep.

What a pleasure to buy things right off the racks! And Aden had done this for her! Kit's trip into the closet had turned out to be more fun than she'd anticipated.

If her friends could see her now!

For now, oh now, she could indulge in the silkiest snippets, whispery nothings in shades of coffee and cream. White ostrich feathers and rose bikinis fretted with lace. Things so bare, even the clerk seemed to blush at the sight. She'd died and gone to heaven!

Her sensuous delight spilled over to the people around her. Tired shopgirls were buoyed by her good humor. Indecisive customers listened, rapt, to her opinions on fox-colored robes ("Ruby suits you. Like a Borgia princess.") and cotton slips ("Come on now—let's get that skin breathing again!"). Personally, she sold two black lace camisoles: one to a middle-aged tourist from Cleveland, and the other to a man whose wife had just come home with their new baby. She assured him that it was the perfect gift to make his wife feel loved. And Kit was almost sure she was right.

When all this was done, Kit couldn't wait to get her own parcels home so that she could slide the spaghetti-strapped teddies and satiny camisoles over her bare skin. New senses were coming alive . . . She could still remember the way Aden smelled when she kissed him—like a sunny Caribbean day . . .

"That gong means the store's closing in five minutes, you know." Aden had come up behind her in line. He'd been watching her light up the selling floor for the last fifteen minutes. Whatever else she was, Kit Daniels was one of a kind. "Shall we go?"

Unwittingly, she hugged the package containing her underthings to her chest. She felt wicked and exposed, adolescently glamorous too.

"Sure thing. I'm finished here."

They walked out onto Fifth Avenue where the midtown rush hour was just coming to a boil. Yellow cabs whizzed by. Workers descended into the Hades of the subway system. Steam rose from manhole covers, sulfurous caldrons in the belly of the city. Up top, it was getting chillier by the minute, and people shouldered past with their chins in their chests, all swaddled up in mufflers against the biting wind.

Aden clapped his hands together. "Christ, it's cold!"

On his way out, he had stopped on the first floor to buy her a black cocktail hat with a rhinestone and a feather, soft as a breeze. "This one's on me."

She was modeling it for Aden in the glow of the Christmas windows.

"Not half bad, Daniels," he said softly. "Not half bad." His bright hair flew back in the wind and his eyes shone like Christmas when he looked at her.

"Are we finished?" The salesgirl had packed the hat in a round box covered with holly-red paper, and Kit now laid it back inside the tissue, lovingly.

"Yes, give or take a few things. When you get to California on the first leg of your publicity tour, there are a few places on Rodeo Drive you might find interesting. Then there's your appointment at Georgette Klinger for a beauty makeover and hair styling . . ." He could feel a smile starting up inside, like a battery he'd thought had gone dead. She was so pretty just then, with her cheeks roughed pink by the wind, her eyes brimming with the enthusiasm of the newborn. It was a look he recognized from his own mirror. Variety, money, and taste had been all around her from birth, but he saw now that she'd never really taken part in it. Enclosed as she then was in the "glass box" of fat, staring out at the world of New York glamour. He would never forget the sight of her in that incandescent gown, all shot with silver . . .

Released from her fortress of flesh, Kit Daniels was a vivid, temporarily dazed beauty. If only she were not so mixed up. He hoped he would do right by her.

"So, where are we going for dinner?" Kit asked, swinging her hat box gaily, like a schoolgirl with her books. The air smelled freshly of snow, and the blue haze of twilight cast the buildings in sculptural relief. Aden was forgiven, totally forgiven, for that rebuff in the restaurant. She was finding he was dangerously easy to forgive.

He looked off, into the churning stream of traffic. "Oh Daniels, I'm really sorry. I have an appointment."

Kit was knocked off balance, taken off guard. She tried to cover it up by talking a lot, an old trick she used to employ in the doctor's office, to fend off the hurt of needles . . . "Another client? You're almost making me jealous."

"No, not another client. My fiancée, Geraldine Cutler. You remember, the poet . . ."

"Oh yes, of course," she said recklessly, "that woman in the photo who may or may not be good in bed."

With a pained look, Aden took a few steps to the curb and flagged a cab. When it pulled up, he motioned Kit in.

"Good night, Daniels." He slammed the door.

"Don't worry, Aden," she said from out the window, "I'll see that you get a good return on today's investment."

With a roar of the motor, the cab sped off into the gathering city dusk, its taillights two angry red spots that grew fainter and fainter, and then vanished altogether in the night.

Aden watched it go. All around him, Manhattan seemed adrift in snow, and Aden lost along with it.

Then he saw something bright as fire in the slush piled up against the curb.

It was a little black hat, with a rhinestone, and a feather for luck, that had rolled out of its sodden pasteboard box and been crushed under the wheels of the taxi.

Aden ran his thumb over the blade of feather, then folded the tiny hat into his greatcoat pocket and walked on.

Chapter 13

ONE DAY THE last snows of winter melted away like a dream and the first breath of spring began to flutter in the striped canopies of the outdoor cafes, in the pulses of certain young women soon to be seen all over the city in their pink, lavender, and yellow dresses.

Kit could look down from the rooftop swimming pool of her health club on Fifth Avenue and see them—a bolt of pastels like Japanese paper streamers—rush to meet their young men or stop to sun themselves in the concrete quad of the office building opposite. Some were eating apples and sharing secrets with one another.

Perhaps she saw herself in them, cut down to size by love. Perhaps she wondered when she too would rush to meet a man in breathless disarray.

Like them—she had dreams.

Dreams that made her edgy with shame when she awoke and remembered them in the morning. She claimed not to want those dreams, not to need a man to dust her life with glamour.

But the dreams told her she lied.

He'd seduce her with intimate knowledge that inside she was fat and vulnerable still.

Their hands would clasp, strong together, and he would come upon her like sudden joy in the sun . . .

Even in the dreams, she never spoke his name aloud just in case he might, by some magic, hear her, and laugh at the very thought. She wasn't entirely sure where she ended and he began.

He disliked her, she suspected. And yet . . .

There was that perfect marvel, that jewel of a day they'd spent together, in a city lost in snow. He had seemed to like her well enough then. Something rich and rare she'd glimpsed in his smile . . .

Not that the new, improved Kit Daniels lacked would-be lovers. Every morning, like clockwork, one long-stemmed red rose was delivered, the beads of dew still on it, wrapped in green tissue paper and tucked away in a clean white box. The card read only, "Clayburn," in gold ink.

Since her first publicity tour, she was wanted in thirty-six cities for passionate games of varying intensity and intent.

From one end of the country to another, there was a circus of characters from which to choose. Assorted talk-show hosts. A Texas oil baron. An old cowboy star who offered to give her a foal from the royal line of his famous wonder horse, "Blinkers." Even the mayor of a major city (which one, exactly, Kit could not recall—she'd been to thirty-six) who'd redeemed a boring dinner party with his off-color handkerchief tricks and celebrity anecdotes.

Even now, a full month after the wild publicity run, Kit automatically consulted her neatly typed itinerary the first thing in the morning.

That morning, she'd seated herself with relief at her own mirrored vanity. Everything about the airy bedroom in her new Gramercy Park apartment disarmed her: the peppermint-striped walls, the bleached antique French armoire and forest-green birdcage, the crisp Porthault linens, and the bloom of her bed canopy, cool in Canovas cotton, and lined in fine moiré. It was as refreshing as a peppermint ice-cream soda, and from now on, she intended to spend as much time in here as she could.

Kit picked up the tortoise-backed brush and pulled it through her fashionably shorter hair, parted for drama on one side. Her rose-cotton teddy was embroidered with florets of ribbon: a souvenir of the day with Aden. As usual, her heart's core grew warm and languorous at the thought of him. She would watch him raise his capable writer's hands and lift off the gold ovals of his glasses, making ready for love. More than once on her cross-country sweep, she'd closed her eyes on the challenge of his face . . .

It's a good thing she'd found this apartment in the *Times*. She'd needed a haven like this one after the bedlam of her tour. It all ran together in her mind . . . the TV-station program director with the nerve to ask her publicity escort— an attractive young black woman who had her own hands full keeping his hands off—"Does she have good teeth? They keep sending us authors with lousy teeth, like it's radio or something!"

Then there was the radio host in Chicago who, before Kit went on, forbade her to mention either "religion or naughty underwear" and then, once on the air, proceeded to steer her into discussion of just those topics at every turn!

There were booksellers who had "forgotten" she was "up for today" and couldn't think where to plant her on the ghostly selling floor. ("Erma Bombeck filled the place when she came down last month. Must be the rain kept them home today . . .") The smiling agony of autograph cramp. The interviewers in countless cities, wormy with personal questions. Kit knew in her heart, and sometimes for a fact, that they had never set eyes on her book before.

Many, noting that writing humor was not a particularly feminine occupation, had asked if she were a "libber."

"If you mean, do I carry placards and chant in the streets, no." Kit decoded the question. "If you mean, do I think women have a right to rebel and to howl at the moon, you're damn right!"

Kit was filled with peace when she glimpsed the reflection of roses in the gilded mirror. Even on the road, when she didn't know where she was from one day to the next, by some miracle of lechery, the red roses had found her. No wonder, then, that of all her many new and rejected suitors, Clayburn Lassiter was the sentimental favorite. Apart from his being the very first, there was something endearing about his cartoon courtship. In any case, it was a lot easier to handle than the cool denial of any attraction whatsoever, by which his son kept love at bay.

She stopped brushing, checked by a dangerous thought. Could it be she was using Clayburn as a bridge to Aden?

In the Dutch-tiled bathroom attached to her bedroom suite, she splashed cool water on her cheeks. She needed her wits about her for the day's work. Deadlines, you know. She couldn't be pining over Aden Lassiter all morning, especially as she was sure he never spared her a romantic second thought. Romance was for the birds anyway. Not for a writer.

And she did so like Clayburn for himself!

Kit lifted her pink-awning-striped bathrobe from a peg on the door. She belted it on. Then she gathered up her bottles of shampoo and conditioner for a fierce bout of hair washing.

She had felt a shock of guilt when Maddy's call came through. First Mallory . . . then Maddy . . . ever since her career had taken off, she'd had no time to spare for old friends.

Last she'd heard, her father had put Maregate up for sale and was eyeing a retreat in Palm Beach, as well as a redheaded relic named Margaret Patchworth. But she told herself she didn't care. She'd felt anger at him, and beyond that, love—and beyond that again, a sadness that the two should be so mixed in her. Then too, Mallory was always busy dressing the stars and Marva had been out of touch since Christmas.

As for Maddy—she'd shut herself up in that big house on the hill.

Kit would try to make it up to her as best she could . . . "Where are you, girl? Can I see you?"

"I'm in the hospital. I just woke up, and it's hot in here.

There don't seem to be any windows. The stitches hurt really bad . . ."

"Which hospital? What are you doing in the hospital?"

"New York Hospital. Jared wanted the best, so we've been here all week, waiting." Then as if a thought had just found her, she added, "Kit, I had my baby last night. They did a Cesarean."

"The baby!" In the depths of daily business, Kit had lost track of that precious new life. "How are you doing? Is the baby all right?" Her best friend, the woman she loved most in all the world, had split in two and delivered a baby—without her. And oh, they'd cut her, hurt her . . .

"I'm fine." Maddy tried to sound cheerful. "Samantha is fine."

"Samantha?"

"It's a girl," Maddy said with the patience she would use in speaking to Samantha herself. She hadn't been a mother very long, but she already knew of the abyss that separated the unmarried maiden and the Mother. For the second time since she'd been told it would be a Cesarean delivery, Maddy felt afraid. It was a lonely thing to be a mother.

"Kit, I know you're very busy but if it's not too much trouble, maybe you could stop by to see me . . ."

Kit didn't even wait for the room number.

Dressing quickly, she stopped only to purchase a waving bouquet of seasonal flowers, before she taxied over to the hospital on York Avenue.

The high, carved mahogany door of Maddy's private room was shut tight. She brushed her knuckles against it.

"Come in."

Maddy's voice was angelic as ever.

Inside the room, lavish with flowers, Kit found her best friend propped up in the big bed, looking shaken and bared. Her hair rippled in golden bands against the double pillows. There were gray smudges punched out under what Kit remembered as her angel-blue eyes.

"Kit, you came . . ." Maddy put out a frail hand in greeting.

Kit sat in a chair at the side of the bed, and clasped it warmly. "Of course I came. I stopped to see the baby . . . Samantha. She's perfect. Just like you."

Maddy rolled her face to the window, as though she were in pain. "I'm not so perfect anymore. My stomach . . ."

"The books say that's just temporary, don't they?" Was that what was haunting Maddy, the stretched belly of new motherhood? Postpartum blues?

Kit cast around inside herself for words of comfort, but found none. What did she know of these things? She'd always thought women with young children wanted to be left alone to concentrate on change. As she perused Maddy's face, which seemed subtly altered, broadened and deepened by her direct experience with the life force, it seemed to Kit that her friend had crossed over a mysterious border where she could not yet follow.

"I brought you these . . ." Like a suitor, she held aloft the heavy bouquet.

"They're just lovely. Thank you." Maddy was all eyes. "Kit, you're so skinny!"

Kit snapped off the rubber band from around the bush of flowers and busied herself with filling a vase she'd found under the sink. She could almost wish her old pounds back, with Maddy clearly so anxious about the changes in her own body.

"I knew you'd lost weight. I saw you interviewed on 'Five Alive,' but I never realized how dramatic it was."

"People always look heavier on television." For busy work, Kit arranged the tulips, hyacinths, and roses in the papier-maché vase. "What did you think of the interview?" she asked, seeking to change the subject, for both their sakes.

"I thought it was great fun. Especially when they asked why you thought the ordinary woman would be able to identify with your humor—when you yourself are an 'extraordinary' woman in terms of economic independence. And you said—I remember so clearly, I was so proud of you, Kit—you said, 'There are no ordinary women . . .'"

Kit walked back to her chair and sat down. "I'll tell you a

secret. I was quaking in my boots during that interview. I would have felt a hundred percent better if I'd known you were watching."

"But what about Cheryl St. Gibbons? Is she as rough as they say?"

"I found all the people on 'Five Alive' extremely professional and, well . . . fair. Best of all, Maddy, Cheryl St. Gibbons had actually read the damn book!"

Maddy gave a small smile. "I can't get off a real laugh, Kit. Sorry, the stitches hurt too much."

Kit just sat there, clasping her friend's hand, feeling useless. Something was very wrong with Maddy. Kit could feel it. *Where's your mother?* Kit yearned to ask. *Why isn't she here to comfort you?* It was on the tip of her tongue; she needed to blame someone for Maddy's pain, anyone.

Almost as if Maddy had read her mind, she spoke of her absent family. "Jared will drop by later, after work. My mother and father too. They're walking on air, of course. Their first grandchild."

"But whatever it is that's bothering you, Maddy—no, don't try to throw me off, I can see through you like a pane of glass—whatever it is, wouldn't your mother be the one to help you with it?"

"Kit, my mother and father are so much in love, always have been, they think Jared and I must be as happy as they are."

"Then tell *me*," Kit said firmly, bracing herself for friendship. "What's wrong?"

Tears sparkled in Maddy's eyes. Kit had also read that new mothers cry easily.

"I know this is going to sound crazy, Kit, but . . . Jared's fallen out of love with me."

Poor Maddy! Kit felt lost, as though she'd taken a wrong turn, wandering out of the mists of girlish fantasy into the far more fabulous realms of a woman's life. "Maddy, are you sure? Or are you just tired and imagining all this?"

"Kit, I saw him with a woman. Besides, he told me that I . . ." She sighed, and started again. "He told me that I was too big, too pregnant, to turn him on, and that he was a man who couldn't wait . . ."

Couldn't love, she means. Kit was dazzled by anger.

"Oh my poor Maddy . . ." She knelt on the bed and twined her arms around her friend.

"The worst thing is"—Maddy laughed and cried at the same time—"I still love the bastard."

After a while, Kit spoke into Maddy's hair. "I know it seems like the hurt will always be there, but one day, you'll see him with Samantha, and this part of your life will be over, and you'll forgive him, Maddy, you'll have to. For the baby's sake. He's a man, Maddy, and weak about certain things. You'll just have to be strong enough for the three of you . . . Like a mother."

Later, Kit wasn't sure from where, deep inside her, she had managed to pull out those particular words, but whatever their provenance, they seemed to comfort Maddy, who lay quiet in her arms.

"I'm thirsty," she said at last, with a nervous giggle. "And my feet are both asleep."

Kit disentangled herself, gently, and filled up a paper cup with water. "Here."

Maddy took the cup, then tipped her face up expectantly, as though she wanted to say something more, something about the miraculousness of what had happened to her.

Just then the starched day nurse came bustling into the room. "Time for baby's feeding," she said with brisk authority, and started to draw the beige curtains around Maddy's bed, hemming her in. She looked at Kit. "You'll have to leave now. Visiting hours are over."

Kit reached over to the chair back for her jacket, then swooped down to kiss Maddy on the cheek. "Everything will work out—you'll see. I'll call you tomorrow, just to make sure."

"Kit!"

142

She swung around to look into the burning blue of Maddy's eyes.

"It's a lie," she cried out to Kit, in some private desperation.

"What is?" Kit asked, puzzled.

But the nurse, all business, just ushered her out, and closed the broad wooden door behind her.

———— Chapter 14 ————

IT'S A QUIRKY little island, with floating ribs of rock, set on the cold, blue highways of the Atlantic. It had Vanderbilts and Astors to its credit. The oldest gaslit street in America. The first U.S. tennis championships. With Puritan precedents, its citizens continue to buck the erection of McDonald's on the corner, to believe in early rising and discreet bedding for all.

An uncommon little island, it boasts the venerable chateaux of Bellevue Avenue, the sun-washed estates of Ocean Drive, the refurbished elegance of Historic Hill. Proudly, it plays host to more black-tie dinners and balls than any other American metropolis of its size.

And every four years it has the America's Cup races.

This was, as the world knew, a Cup summer.

Kit Daniels had been beckoned to Newport, not for the races, but to receive an award at a fund-raiser for her favorite charity, the Children's Hospital at Beechwood.

Besides, it was always good to get away from New York—and unruly thoughts of Aden Lassiter.

Behind the granite walls of the private estates on Bellevue Avenue, amid one-hundred-foot copper beeches and flowering pink dogwoods, the Old Guard braced itself for the wave of tourists who were making their restless way over Newport Bridge, snapping instant mementos as they went . . .

Below, the blue sweep of harbor was crammed with yachts. From sunrise to sunset, traffic paralyzed Thames Street, with its storefront restorations. The wharves were flooded with Nikon-wielding families who would practically pay for a peek at the America's Cup sailors, or, the next best thing, the rich in their summer "cottages." They swarmed over green velvet lawns. They packed restaurants to the rafters, until it seemed the whole world had come back to Newport.

An English prince was here for the exclusive show. And a popular ex-Prime Minister who would view the races from the floating privacy of a ninety-one-foot yacht, complete with a Cordon Bleu chef, a galley stocked with crabmeat, and the makings of long, cool drinks.

Kit's black limousine rolled into Newport on an afternoon hung with chilly gray mist. From her car window, the outlines of the houses on Ocean Drive and the shelf of harbor beyond got all blurred together into a silvery gouache. It seemed the only splash of color in that gray cloud of a day was Kit's own aggressively purple jump suit and the spikes of turquoise that swayed from her ears. Although it was summer, she felt chilled to the bone.

"This is nothing." Her hostess's liveried chauffeur shook his head at the fog that poured swiftly across the cold Atlantic, palpably thickening the atmosphere onshore. "You should be out there hauling lobster."

At the mere thought, Kit shivered. Ahead, the backs of the great mansions hulked on the hill. A bad omen?

Maybe she should have refused Mrs. Trewhitt's invitation. After all the traveling she'd done this year, Kit preferred her own timetables, her own bed. It was still a trick to get her head working again after the jolt of all those people and places. Besides, she had Maddy on her mind. Things were not going well with Jared and the baby. Kit had been concerned enough to begin calling every week in support of her friend.

But Mrs. Trewhitt was no mean humanitarian. Kit simply could not refuse the chance to do "her children" some good.

The limo climbed a steep drive. Kit spot-checked her hair in a compact mirror, then felt silly, like a parakeet at tricks. The hair had been braided and waved back by a comb of freshwater pearls in a nod to New York fashion. Now she wished she'd worn it long, as insulation against the damp chill. Vanity be damned!

There was a spit-and-polish line of foreign cars and Rolls Royces parked in the driveway.

In the twilight of fog, Kit could barely make out the house beyond.

Built in the nineteenth century, it seemed carved out of ivy and granite. Kit had heard that it was filled to the rafters with splendid French furniture and paintings. Here Mrs. Trewhitt launched annual Fourth of July spectaculars, myriad teas on the lawn, and fashionably formal dinners.

The limousine crunched over the gravel, then stopped. Kit was let out at the door, her bags taken into the house by a light-footed young porter.

There was nothing but a swoop of spotless green lawn as far as the eye could see, and then she was being shown into the marble foyer—all checkered floor and patriarchal busts. Her hostess, Mrs. Trewhitt, came forward to greet her.

A twelfth-generation Rhode Islander who traced her ancestry back to the state's founder, this commanding figurehead of a lady bore a slight resemblance to the wonderful actress Elsa Lanchester, whom Kit adored for her portrayal of *The Bride of Frankenstein*.

This resemblance immediately put Kit at her ease.

"Welcome to Topsail House." Mrs. Trewhitt, who had granite hair, waved, and cleft like a rock down the middle, was wearing a triple strand of white pearls reminiscent of an Elizabethan ruff about her neck. She spoke with the vaguely British accent of the Newporters that Kit remembered from her debutante days. "You're the last to arrive. The others are already installed in their rooms. Come"—she held out a welcoming hand—"Laurent will show you to yours so that you can refresh yourself before dinner."

Dinner, Kit guessed, would be a serious business, in marble halls. "Thank you." It had been some time since she'd been "installed" in a country place like this. She was reminded that Newport aristocrats had a special disdain for her hometown, Southampton, which was a relative Johnny-come-lately to the world of resorts. Croquet, backgammon, and yachting were the genteel sports of Newport, a far cry from South-ampton's favorite: shopping-for-status at their own Saks Fifth Avenue. The Newport ladies and gentlemen were, in any case, above and beyond status. They were already— she smiled at Mrs. Trewhitt's hickory-cane back—part of history.

At the top of the broad mahogany staircase, slightly to the right, stood Kit's bedroom suite with its parchment-colored walls.

And a gem of a suite it was, too—fitted with such treasures as a Louis XV writing desk on spindly legs and a queen-size bed canopied in écru lace over banana-colored silk. As Mrs. Trewhitt had told her on the way up, it was one of the few suites that overlooked the ever-unwinding, gray silk bolt of ocean below. From off the windy terrace, the seagulls wheeled through their paces, so close one could almost touch them. As the fog burned off, the air turned milky blue and soft, warmer now than when she'd first crossed over Newport Bridge into the holiday town.

After Mrs. Trewhitt left, Kit turned back the heavy antique coverlet and eased onto the bed. If only she could just relax and stop judging in the old way, tacking against the wind, she might actually enjoy this salt-air journey back to the Gilded Age. Imagine: there was even a complimentary bottle of orange water sitting on her dresser . . . and calla lilies lolling in the Ming vase.

For a fiercely romantic interlude, she entertained herself with scenarios of what would happen if Aden Lassiter should suddenly come striding through her bedroom door . . . She'd lay a bet that he could feel the tug of her desire—an itch under the heart, a palmy breeze at the back of the neck, unexplained by natural causes.

What good—she flipped off the uncomfortable sandals he'd

had her buy, onto the Portuguese rug—was this bed, fit for a Medici mistress, when she was so alone?

Oh, why couldn't he have fallen in love with her a little? Just let himself go slightly crazy . . . Even now she could see passionate potential in the care he showed whenever he was around her. He took pains never to be awkward or corny or oversolicitous in his approach to Kit Daniels. He pleased her, by not trying to please.

It was as though she'd taken him by surprise that day in the snowbound city, her heart jumping his. He had, perhaps, never really "seen" her *in toto* before, considered what she might mean to him out of the millions of eligible women in the world. It was always a miraculous moment when a man took time out for that. Inevitably it changed him, or gave his quest a name.

Kit clasped her hands behind her head and stared into space. She wondered what Aden was doing right now. Then wondered why. Now that she'd gotten his attention, he seemed hell-bent on pointing out her flaws. He persisted in acting as though she were trying to bamboozle him with her beauty and tenderness.

When she dared show any tenderness, that is.

Most of the time he didn't even give her the chance. Danced out of the office just before she was scheduled to come in. Broke lunch dates with aplomb and apology, sending his genial father to take his place.

Yes, what did she want with Aden Lassiter, anyway? The bedclothes rustled as Kit turned over. The sea air was making her drowsy by degrees. It always did in Southampton too.

For all his racy reputation, for all his playwright's chic, Aden seemed to fossilize whenever she was around. She could never do anything conservative enough for him. He seemed, in fact, to take negative coloration from her. If Kit said the "moon," then Aden said the "sun." He was bossy, judgmental, stubborn as a politician in the wrong, and a cold fish to boot.

And what's more, when his chestnut hair dipped over his forehead in that boyish way it had, or his silver eyes lit up with a new idea for Germaine—mad with attraction, Kit had begun to envy even his fictional women—that he couldn't wait to get down on the cocktail napkin at lunch, well, she forgot all good sense, she forgot everything but that hollow in her heart that—if they were both very lucky—Aden Lassiter could try to fill . . .

She dreamed on, only this time with her eyes closed.

More than once that spring and summer, Aden Lassiter had been caught dreaming behind his desk.

Today he held a gold-bordered leaf of fancy notepaper in his hand. It had notified him, with all due congratulations, that among the nominees for an "Allie," an award as coveted by serious writers as the Tony by showfolk, were six of his own clients.

Chief among these, perhaps, was Geraldine Cutler, cited for her celebrated book of poems *Radical Grace*.

Unlike years gone by, when the toting-up of Lassiter-bred winners had been a euphoric occasion for father and son, Aden now felt a curious sense of distance, as though he'd been cut loose from familiar moorings and cast adrift in mysterious seas.

The board's felicitations floated to the floor, unnoticed, while Aden stared out the twentieth-story window. Down there—where Aden would rather be—the green tops of trees were swaying in the summer sun. Free publicity and coveted literary awards were as nothing compared to green leaves and soft things, like the lobe of her ear; sparkling things, like the intelligence in her eyes; summer things, like fine auburn hair lifting gently from her neck at the sheerest breeze . . .

He felt one on his own neck. All the windows were closed. And the air duct was nowhere near.

My God! He caught himself on the hook of cynicism. He must be going mad! The woman was a shrew. He couldn't abide her. What man could? He'd thought of little else but her since that bewildering day in the snow when he'd first noticed that she was improbably lovely, and courageous in her struggle to be born.

Analisa, his secretary, buzzed. She was very young, had pin-straight black hair, and kept a picture of DEVO on her desk. Originally, he'd liked her because she was bright and enterprising, and she always took care to enunciate the ultimate consonants of her words on the telephone. Aden had felt this showed rare ambition. No doubt, one day soon, she would have his job.

"Yes, Analisa?"

"Ms. Cutler is here," Analisa said distinctly enough for Professor Higgins' cultured ear. "Shall I send her in?"

"Yes, do that." Geraldine Cutler, the woman he was expected to marry. The woman he would happily marry if he could only stay sane enough to do it. He prayed his perverse attraction to Kit Daniels would pass with the summer. No good would ever come of it.

He could tell from assorted comments his father and his friends had been dropping, that he looked distracted, all right, downright disturbed, lately. It was all he could do to concentrate on his unfinished play, *Plymouth Rocks*.

He actually found himself manufacturing excuses to phone her on the pretext of minute, contractual points—to almost caress her back as he helped her on with her Hermes shawl. He knew it was Hermes, because he made it his business to know everything of even negligible interest about her. By this, Aden could see things were getting out of hand. Daniels herself would be the first to agree.

"Aden." Geraldine was outfitted in a pencil-thin Valentino suit in a sensuous summer fabric. She pressed the heels of her palms against the front of Aden's desk and bent over to imprint his cheek with a chevron of candy-apple lipstick. "Shall I take the day, do you think?"

"The day?"

"The Allie. Don't forget, Maureen Gittings is up for *Bloodroot: A Stalk of Women*. And she's a Yankee."

Aden forced himself back from the dizzy suction of his daydream. "Of course you'll get an Allie. Gittings doesn't have a chance against your book, and everyone knows it."

Geraldine perched upon the lip of Aden's desk, allowing one silkily stockinged leg to swing in a coy little arc. Her almond-shaped eyes narrowed in desire. The violet tongue circled. Then she arched toward Aden, pawing one hand over the other in a distinctly feline ripple, every action flush with sexual promise. A literary soubrette.

Yet Aden knew, for all the red-hot seethe and sizzle of her sensuality, that these days it invariably got short-circuited somewhere in the coils between her fetching body and her forceful mind. Still, where desire had failed, for him inertia had taken over. And there was nothing better out there, anyway . . . was there?

"Aden?" Apparently, Geraldine had been trying to break through the film of his thoughts for some time, for there was now an angry patch of pink at the center of her magnolia-blossom cheeks.

"And they say men don't have monthly cycles!"

"I'm sorry, darling."

"We're supposed to be going to lunch!" She folded her white arms across her chest; at the same time one rather pointed, patent-leathered toe was busy rapping like a woodpecker against the oak-wood front of the desk.

Aden knew it was just a substitute for his tender shin. Or worse.

He was supposed to take Geraldine for pasta at La Colonna, the new hot spot on East Seventeenth Street, where you can see the rock star's wife eat endive with her fingers, or check out whom the princess was wearing these days.

It had totally seeped through his mind . . . There had been a lot of that forgetfulness lately. If this were the fourteenth century, he'd say he was bewitched. But not to anyone else, lest they try to put an end to it.

Just outside his door, Analisa's typewriter was ra-ta-tatting along. She was a super-speed typist, of course, and the smart belling that went up from her machine had an hypnotic effect, not unlike a Gregorian chant. Aden began to envision how her name would look chiseled on the frosted glass door of the former Lassiter & Lassiter offices: "Analisa Aragones . . . " He'd have to give her a mite longer for lunch from now on. Best to stay on her good side. You never know, someday he might be forced to ask her for a loan . . .

It must have been a considerable strain, Aden sensed, for Geraldine to stay civil. "So," she said, as she alighted from the desk onto the bridge of her small, lovely feet, "we'd better get going if we're to make it downtown in time. I assume you had to bribe someone to get those reservations? Most of the time the place is unbookable till ten-thirty at night. Lord, this is such a decadent city. There are no moral responsibilities connecting us, like filaments of soul, one to the other. As Klaraxa says, we are all unbearably slight. I rather fancy myself as one of his heroines . . ."

"Me too," Aden muttered.

"Why, Aden." She flashed him a slice of her sweet muskmelon smile. "So you are."

Only half conscious of Klaraxa's philosophy, he was rummaging through the upper right-hand desk drawer for his wallet. Geraldine, in a move as glittering and quick as a serpent's lunge, snatched a dark object from out of its depths.

A black cocktail hat, with a spray of glitter.

"Oh, Aden," she said archly, "a little polymorphous perversity?"

His gray eyes were steady behind the glasses. "Clearly it's not mine."

Geraldine twirled the little hat around on her manicured index finger. "No? What a pity. I would so like having something to flash on you, Aden. It's sort of like money in the bank. No woman should marry a man who's too perfect. She'll never live it down."

"I'm not sure I like being called perfect."

Aden had circled to the front of his desk. He held out his hand for the hat, as though it were a guilty secret he must lock away.

Instead, smiling her rare smile, Geraldine tipped it onto her raven hair.

"How does it look on *me*, Aden?"

"Charming."

"As charming as it does on her?"

"It belongs to a client, that's all. She left it here in the office. I keep forgetting to give it back."

"Pretty fancy for afternoon wear. What is she—a performing chimp?"

The look in Geraldine's violet eyes had taken a decidedly violent turn.

"You're beautiful when you're vicious," Aden said. He couldn't even explain Kit Daniels and her damn hat to himself. How could he explain them to Geraldine, who was pouting?

Geraldine insisted on affecting the black sphere of hat all during their egregiously expensive lunch of the hearty green and white pasta known as "straw and hay." During which time, Aden Lassiter conceived an irrational hatred of Bolognese sauce, Corinthian columns, and Post-Modern, or, as he later began to call them, Post-Mortem, pastels.

Even hundreds of miles away, Kit Daniels had done him in!

He was desperate to be free of her. He thought of her in Newport, mermaid hair floating like seaweed behind her as she sank into a waveless blue sea . . .

There was an itch, right below his heart.

The breeze, unexplained, blew on.

An hour later, refreshed from her nap, Kit awoke to a room washed in sea light. From the terrace, she could see the cliffs tumble down to a surf wrinkled like fine blue paper, dotted with the white cutouts of sailboats, each stamped with the red foil round of the sun.

Kit was glad she'd have time to acquaint herself with the lofty grandeur of Topsail before mixing with her fellow guests: the sound one's heels made in crossing yellow-marble floors, the precious intimacy of Sèvres porcelain at one's bedside, even the imperious busts staring one down in the hall.

It had been quite a while since she'd nestled in the lap of old money, and while Maregate had been home to a Southampton multimillionaire, its casual beauties paled when compared to this opulence.

Kit dressed her hair with special care, high on her head, daubed a few precious drops of Joy at her pulse points, and clasped on a choke of black Tahitian pearls. She chose a backless stunner of a black dress she'd picked up in Beverly Hills because it had skimmed so neatly down her body, ending in a whisper of a flare at the knee—the whole thing could have been a drawing in pen and ink. Her pale winter skin glowed like liquid pearl against the black.

Thus delicately armored, Kit went down to dinner, which was, in the European manner, at the stroke of eight.

The entire sea-blue and silver dining room, one of two such huge salons at Topsail, was a haze of candles.

There were even tapers bunched on the floor in each bright corner, thin and glittery as Fourth of July sparklers. It was canny magic. A feast of light.

Beneath their feet, the floor was set in a priceless lapis intarsia. Along the back wall, the French doors to the broad-tiled back terrace were flung wide open, inviting in the silky seabreezes and the subtle palette of the Newport moonlight.

Once Kit found her placecard, which rested on a silver scroll, she was introduced by her hostess in Quaker-gray silk to the other honored guests, some of whom Kit already knew from previous hospital fund-raisers.

Among the notables, there was the Hollywood-handsome senator and his equally photogenic wife. A prominent Texas clergyman and a legendary screen star better known for his tropical azure eyes than for his many quiet philanthropies.

Throughout the superb banquet of a leafy gravlax salad with mustard-caper sauce, Shitaki mushrooms and snow peas, medallions of veal, and a nouveau cuisine kiwi tart, Kit, through sheer force of will, kept to the salad, while grumpily noting that only the men ate anything of substance: the privilege of being the dominant sex!

Yet she soon found herself relaxing into the moonlit hedonism of the place. The taut coil of city tensions eased and she felt naked beneath the black dress that first light-filled night at Topsail. The rumble of waves down below became a singularly pleasant dinner music for twelve voices. The air was beating with possibility—a sweet meeting with an exciting stranger? Romance, once again, possessed her city-girl soul. Maybe it was the drinking water . . .

Into the next week of parties, Kit had the impression of fairy-tale largesse, the charm of intimate strangers. Canary diamonds at dinner. Clouds of cotton-candy hair framing the famous faces of famous wives. Yachting caps, and the dazzle of white teeth that could as easily draw out the brilliant nuggets of your supper-party conversation as they could the sweetness within the shell.

And she herself was just as bold, as brilliant, as beautiful . . .

Or so the senator from New York later said, when she met him a few nights later at the awards ball, in the orangery constructed on the Topsail lawn. All smiles, he then went on to compliment others, leaving Kit to enjoy the spectacle on the lawn.

Later, under the rippling black and white tent, there were redwood tubs of iced French champagne, a groaning board that included Nova Scotia salmon and rigatoni salad with pesto sauce; and three hundred guests milling in and out, from Henry Kissinger to the marvelously wealthy—even by Newport standards—Aga Khan, who, it was rumored, planned to watch the Cup races from a helicopter in the blue.

Peter Duchin's popular orchestra serenaded, and later that evening, after the awards had been parceled out, fireworks would be launched from a tugboat and barges on the night-time Atlantic by the retired major of the Queen's own hussars. It was he who had choreographed the fabulous pyrotechnics for the royal wedding of Charles and Diana . . .

Oh what a summer's night this was going to be!

And then Kit was beckoned by Mrs. Trewhitt to the flower-draped dais under the spotlights, to take her place beside the wavy-haired senator, the Texas clergyman, and the star with the azure eyes, as another friend to children. In the diamond-bright gown Aden had helped her choose way back in New York, she received the plaque from the graystone figure of Dahlia Trewhitt. In her excitement, she almost hugged the grande dame of Newport but stopped herself in the nick of time. Then there was a file of congratulators, many with smooth smiles and printable names, just outside the tent in the light-strung orangery.

"I've never shaken hands with such a beautiful philanthropist before."

The speaker of these words was a young man with a finely chiseled smile and a corona of hair the color of old gold. The light in his eyes was cool and blue as a Newport morning. The voice—with its tincture of upper-class English or what passed for such to an American—seemed rich and familiar.

All at once, she looked out on a starry night, in a summer long ago. There'd been a canopy of balloons, the sorry spectacle of an obese girl falling madly in love with the heartstopping perfection of a man who could never be hers . . . Jonathan Cantwell.

Kit put her hand over her heart, as though she would press it back. My God, she'd forgotten the Cantwells were a Newport clan. Dear Lord, don't let him recognize her! She could never bear those heaven-colored eyes on her again, kind enough to give pardon. Even now, she could sense the shadow of the bloated, unhappy girl she'd been, in some ways still was, beating behind her . . . If she turned, just so, in the light of the colored bulbs strung along the orangery trees, she might even catch it . . .

He introduced himself. "I'm afraid I didn't catch your name in all the excitement, Miss . . . ?"

"Kit," she replied, hardly daring to look him in the eye. She held her breath.

"Would you like to dance, Kit?"

So he didn't remember her! She felt the distance one instinctively feels from those one has deceived.

"I'd rather stay out here."

"I can't say I blame you." He tucked her arm beneath his. "The air is like champagne tonight. Here, come this way."

He led her away from the tent to a copse of beechwoods at the green rim of the lawn. Not more than twenty yards away, there rose a wall of pale-hued stones in the darkness, and below that, the nickel-colored sea tossing through the night in its timeless cadence.

The moon was slung in a low yellow arc. Strains of dance music, a cluster of blue notes, shimmied down to them from the party tent. In counterpoint, the waves hurled themselves against the rocks with the sound of distant thunder.

Kit placed her hands on the smooth stones of the wall and looked out to sea. "When I was a little girl, I used to think that the world switched off at night. Niagara Falls, the surf at Malibu—everything, even the moon, right after I went to sleep. Like a city street blacked out, the plug pulled by some mighty hand.

"Once, I even tried to stay up all night long, just to prove it to myself. I slipped down to the beach and kept my vigil over the moon and waves. My father found me the next morning, huddled in my sweetgrass blanket, with my favorite rag doll, Annie Laurie, clasped in my arms . . . I had fallen asleep at my post. Only Annie knew what went on while I dreamed in the sand."

"And what was it she saw?"

"She never did say."

Jonathan moved closer. "I like that story. I like you." His hair smelled of bayberry and his narrow face and hands seemed ringed with supernatural fire in the moonlight. Perhaps, what she'd puzzled over as a child—the silent, indomitable pulsebeat of mother earth, beyond the powers of men and machines, alien to all restriction, to time itself—was true of people's lives as well. Perhaps there was no such thing as a personal past, complete in itself, and set in the amber of memory. Wouldn't it be fine if that which we most love, that which is rooted in our hearts so firmly that it can never be ripped away, has an existence parallel to what we call the present, and never comes to an end at all?

Had she ever stopped loving the dream of Jonathan Cantwell?

Could she ever stop wanting him . . . the golden trophy, the prize of her blighted, bloated girlhood?

Could she change that past—now?

"What do you think about it?" she asked him, without looking at his face, a deferred pleasure.

"I think you were a very thoughtful little girl."

"And you . . . what kind of a little boy were you?" Suddenly, she needed to know everything.

"I didn't think much about those kinds of things. For me, tradition took the place of wondering. Control got all mixed up with love. I guess money can do that sometimes."

"I know what you mean."

"You do?" He looked into her eyes. "What did you say your name was?"

"Kit Daniels."

"For a moment, I thought . . ."

"That you knew me?"

"That I've always known you . . . or someone like you."

And then a terrible thing took place. Kit felt a giggle working its way with her. She was finicky about romance. Perhaps because she longed for it so badly, she mistrusted it, couldn't write herself into the clinch scene, without making mischief, cracking a joke.

Besides, look what happened the last time she had let herself go. Jonathan had seen her imperfections.

She could never forgive him—or herself—for that.

"I think we'd better get back to the party. Mrs. Trewhitt may be looking for me." She just had to get away from him or the laughter would break over her, and she would go wild with it. She was as out of control as a teenage girl at a pajama party. He was tender and beautiful. He wanted her. Why was she doing this?

Mouth set, she headed for the bright lights of the tent.

His face was no longer shining. With a few short strides, he caught up to her. "Will I see you again?"

"I'm sorry, Jonathan. I don't know." What if she blew up again? What if she looked to the world like what she really was inside—a hot-air balloon in designer clothes? Would Jonathan Cantwell want her then?

And yet, for the sake of her alter ego, overweight, underloved, shouldn't she find out, once and for all, if what she'd felt for Jonathan Cantwell III had been a tremulous puppy love, easily dismissed with a sharp slap of humor? Then she would be able to relax and move on to another life, another love—or at least the abortive, baffling relationship she had with Aden Lassiter—*sans* regret. It was a good goal for a woman: to make herself whole.

"Kit, wait! Come to my yacht tomorrow. We can watch the races from there."

Kit had begun to make her way across the dark stretch of lawn through the thick tracery of trees, and he followed at her heels like a beautiful blond stallion, with his long, graceful step. She'd handled being alone with him tonight, but on a yacht tomorrow, in the full light of day, mightn't she trip all over her tongue, be a clown?

"All right, Jonathan," she heard herself saying. "It's a date."

"Tomorrow then." He kissed her hand with an old-fashioned grace, like a figure in a drawing-room play, a Newporter down to his fingernails. With alarm, Kit realized he reminded her of her father. "For the races."

"Tomorrow," she said, suddenly not feeling like laughter at all.

She stepped into the stream of guests, and to Jonathan Cantwell III she seemed to float along, the brightest among them.

———Chapter 15———

Aden Lassiter paced his book-stocked office, once, twice, three times, his fine nostrils flaring, stoked like a horse at the starting gate.

He was supposed to be putting the finishing touches on *Plymouth Rocks* for tonight's first read-through at a famous Broadway theater. But he'd been hung on one line by the seat of his intellectual pants all morning long.

With her usual solicitude, Analisa had also plied him all morning with coffee and buns, crême fraiche, fruit, and soft smiles. Hah. He suspected she practiced talking with marbles in her mouth, like Demosthenes by the sea . . .

The sea! That's what had been undoing him all morning. Images of a long-legged, insensitive beauty stretched out on the deck of some canvas-winged behemoth of a yacht, her sinuous, oiled body lulled into slumber by sun and sea . . .

In his head, the beauty peered over her sunglasses.

Kit Daniels, damn her! Wanting her was like having a low-grade fever, a crick in the soul. He felt reckless and easily bested. Twice this week he'd been seated near the kitchen in his favorite restaurant. And Master Card kept charging him for five hundred dollars worth of Beluga caviar he'd never tasted.

This was all so new to him, this business of being out of joint with the world-at-large. He'd always had an intuitive sense of the next right move, a built-in radar for getting from here to there in life, with no superfluous stops.

These days he had a fiancée to whom he was honorably if dubiously committed, as well as a prospective inamorata he couldn't stand to be with for more than ten minutes straight . . .

He stared with suspicion at the plateful of fruit. Maybe he should change his diet. All that exotic stuff Analisa insisted on feeding him. It was probably spiked with some hallucinogen from out of the pages of Castaneda . . .

To the belling of Analisa's typewriter, he jotted down a note on his red-bordered calendar: get Spanish cassettes. He'd have to learn the darkly fertile language of Cervantes, Marquez, Fuentes, sooner or later, as, sooner or later, it would become the official language of the United States, and he wanted to be able to communicate with Analisa, his new boss, who wore her dark hair like an inquisitorial hood . . .

"Hey—" His father filled the doorway, like a pillar of stone. "Ready for lunch?"

For some reason, Clayburn seemed to be "just dropping in" quite a lot these days. Whatever happened to semiretirement?

Aden flung down his number-two pencil. "Yeah. Let's go. I can't seem to squeeze out anything worth a damn today."

"What's the matter, son?" Clayburn thundered from the doorway. "Cut yourself on the Cutler woman's bones?" Fresh from Antigua, Clayburn was sunned to the shade of teak and exuded even higher-than-usual animal spirits.

"I'm in no mood."

His father leaned over to slap him on the back as Aden rounded the desk.

"I have a piece of good news that might just lift you out of the slough of despond."

Aden set the soft felt hat onto his head. "Must you talk like that, Dad?"

"Sorry. Don't you want to hear my news?"

"Dad, please . . ."

"I was going to save it for '21,' but I think you need a spoonful of sugar right now."

He paused to hike the level of drama.

"So?" Aden could barely contain his irritability.

"So. I'm getting married."

"What the hell are you talking about?"

"I'm talking about putting a period to my golden bachelorhood and taking a wife."

"My God. Why?"

"Why?" Clayburn hesitated as though he hadn't anticipated such a question. "There are myriad good reasons."

"Name three."

"All right, all right," he trumpeted like a bull elephant. "One, she'll keep me warm in the winter. Two, she'll grace my old age. Three, with her, I'll always be younger."

"Younger than what?"

Now it was Clayburn who was getting impatient with his son. He shrugged. "Just younger."

"Who?"

"Well, I haven't asked her yet, but as soon as she comes back . . ."

"Goddamn it, who?" Aden held open the frosted-pane door to the outer office. His father strode through like a biblical king.

"Who else? Kit Daniels."

Aden stopped in his tracks. "What did you say?"

"Ah, Analisa." Clayburn stopped to chuck her under the chin. Analisa held up a plate of green objects. "Papaya? Mano? Kiwi fruit?" she asked in a crystal tone.

Aden groaned.

That year, the morning of the first America's Cup heat dawned bright and hot. Kit Daniels chose pale almond silk sprinkled with orchids in pink, white, and gray, and a broad-brimmed picture hat rigged with satin ribbons. She carried a swimsuit and a few cosmetics in a pink canvas bag.

As a favor, she was driven down to the dock by Mrs. Trewhitt's limo. She felt very la-di-da, and it was fun.

Jonathan, in navy-blue blazer and white slacks, handed her into the soft rock of the boat.

His eyes were blameless blue and earnest. "You look delicious."

"So do you."

He laughed. "You'd better hold on to your hat. The winds are rowdy out there." He pointed to the horizon where white sails tacked to and fro in the wind.

She put her hands on either side of the brim.

"It was really only for Mrs. Trewhitt. She seemed so downcast when I told her I didn't have a hat to wear today. She lent me this one." Kit pulled out the pearl-knobbed hat pin and lifted off the chapeau. She shook out her softly waving hair. "I would much rather go natural."

He moved his hand through her hair in an oddly intimate gesture. "Today, we'll do only what comes natural."

"What a beautiful boat," Kit said quickly, as a salty seabreeze washed over her, cool and clean as a wave. If only she could be as straightforward, as clear with her life . . . and just get on with it.

"Come here, I want to show you something." He pulled her by the hand to the tip of the port bow. "See that yacht out there with the red pennant? That's the *Triumph.*"

Kit knew that the town had been crawling with blue-eyed Aussies for weeks now and that this was one of their boats, heavily favored to win among the cognoscenti.

"She looks fast."

"She is. And what's more, she's manned by a topflight crew. That's the winner. I can tell just by the way she sits in the water." He kissed her hand. She never moved her eyes from where the *Triumph* rose and fell on the waves.

"Would you like to see the cabin? I had the wood for the ceiling flown in from the Atlas mountains."

Kit nodded then. She followed him down to the cabin.

Once her eyes had adjusted to the dim light, there was the gleam of precious metals and polished woods. A chandelier like a tiny golden mosque overhung the place where Jonathan slept. Lozenge-shaped, the bed had been spread with cashmere that glittered with thousands of gold threads. Throw pillows in brilliant Moroccan hues were scattered upon it. Matching tie-dyed fabrics ballooned from the navel of the ceiling where a rosewood fan gently whirled, creating the effect of a tent in the desert.

The ceiling itself was traditionally Moroccan, fashioned out of slim cedar trunks. Hand-rubbed to a high sheen by no fewer than twelve artisans, the walls had been set with a Koran-like intricacy of ocean-and-sky-toned tilework. The air hung drowsily, perfumed with bouquets of bougainvillea and the unexpected tang of oranges and mint.

On a low, rough wood table, a bronze plate held a Moroccan breakfast, fit for a desert prince and his sloe-eyed bride.

"I have a retreat just outside of Marrakesh," Jonathan explained. "Morocco is the last paradise left on earth."

"I'd hate to think that."

"It's true. Except for wherever people are making love." He turned the blue light of his eyes on her. She wished they were Aden's eyes, then censured the thought.

The air in the cabin was indolent, musky, rife with sensual promise. Kit moved away from him, struggling to get things clear in her mind. The past kept rushing in, full-tilt.

"Excuse me a moment," Jonathan said tactfully. "I want to shove off. There's a little island where I like to anchor. We can breakfast there, until the races start. If you like, you can change into your swimsuit and meet me on deck."

As soon as he was gone, Kit sank down on the bed, feeling curiously weak and dizzy in the perfumed heat of the tent, which seemed to partake of nothing of the present, but bore her back, relentlessly, to the past, the fat girl she had been. It was "her" fault Kit was here!

She imagined that the spirit of the "old" Kit had split off and lived a desire life of her own. The weight she'd dropped was certainly enough to compose a whole other woman. She was beginning to think that this was the real Kit Daniels, and the one entangled here was the counterfeit, the splinter, the spook. To be sure, she had not yet dared to dispose of the late great Kit's clothes. They haunted her bedchamber, a ghostly flutter at the back of the closet.

But, if all this were true, which of the "Kits" was it who sat here patiently waiting for her first love?

Then there was no more time to think. Jonathan Cantwell reentered the cabin, his jacket slung over his shoulder, his white cotton shirt parting to show the vulnerable gold of his chest.

It happened in the dense, florid atmosphere of dream. Although she didn't actually see him move, he was suddenly hungry on the bed, beside her. And now they gave way in one another's arms. The miniature golden mosque was a weave of fire above their heads, and all at once she knew it didn't matter how love came about.

The old, heavy-footed Kit didn't care. This was her sexual politics. Her revenge. For all the kicks-in-the-stomach rejection, the patriarchs, the useless, angry mothers, for all the playboys, and the perfect "tens," who'd helped to make psychic pain and self-contempt a woman's second nature, her own true nature, denied the nourishment of self-love . . .

There was tenderness in Jonathan's eyes, and puzzlement, when he made love to her. Kit felt passion slide over her like a raiment of fire. She surged with female power. She marveled—having never before been the one to love less.

"I knew when I first saw you"—he laid his head at the warm parting of her breasts—"that we would be lovers . . ."

"Shh . . ." She reached down with her cool hands and stroked his sun-colored hair. She could be kind. It was up to the more powerful to be kind.

His beauty glowed under her hand. She wanted to be filled by it, by him, to the heart. She thought she could never get enough.

"I know who you are, Kit Daniels," he said, afterwards, when she lay quiet in his arms. "That first night by the ocean. I recognized your eyes. You see, they never change."

"Oh Jonathan, why didn't you tell me?" She made as if to

get up from where she'd been resting the length of her body against him. She felt a little ashamed.

"No, Kit." He put a restraining hand on her arm. "Please stay. I didn't mean to embarrass you."

She laid her head back down in the crook of his arm. "I don't know what to say. I feel so silly."

"Don't say anything. It's not necessary. In answer to your question, I guess I didn't show that I knew you because . . . well, I felt you must have had your reasons for not saying anything."

Of course. How simple. He had trusted her. And she, in her anger against men, had thought him incapable of such a thing.

"You don't care about my weight problem?"

"You're beautiful now. That's all that counts." He turned her in his arms and kissed the hollow of her neck. "God, I want you again."

"Yes . . ." She caught her breath, because it was true . . . because she was beautiful now.

Making love on a yacht anchored off a deserted Newport cove, Kit Daniels never did get to see the races that day. Later she heard that the blue-eyed Aussies and their *Triumph* had sailed into Newport history and taken the golden prize.

As had she.

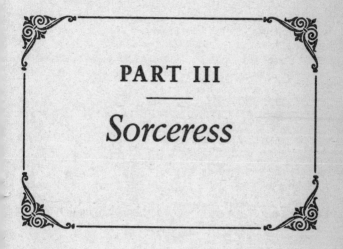

PART III

Sorceress

────── *Chapter 16* ──────

WITH HER INDEX finger Maddy worked at the pink tuft on the fringe of the heavy chenille spread.

What day was this . . . Saturday? Monday? They were all the same to her. They began with no sun and ended with no sun. All she heard was Samantha's cry from dawn to dusk, inside sleep and out. Sometimes she even heard the baby howl before she'd made a sound . . .

No one had told her that a baby would cry so much, filling up her mother's shrunken world with her scream, always hungry, it seemed, always searching for you with her mouth. All they told you about was pink rattles and burping, and "Congratulations, isn't that nice."

It wasn't Maddy's fault she couldn't nurse Samantha. Her breasts had gone angry and red and hard. Stubbornly, they'd refused to give milk to that puckered little hole, that pink cavern that would never be satisfied no matter how many times Maddy got up during the night, as quiet as a mouse so as not to disturb Jared, who dreamed of having another woman asleep beside him.

Maddy cuddled and cooed and cursed the baby for leaving her life a dried-out desert, where nothing bloomed.

Still Samantha would cry. And then Jared would storm at her, and call her bad names, and threaten to leave the house for some peace.

He paid the bills. It was right he should have peace. But what about her . . . what about *her* peace?

The nurse was taking care of the baby now. And she did seem to have a surer touch than Maddy herself. Maybe because the baby knew that mother was always sad, always straying back into the past when there was no baby, no black hole to feed with her body and her soul . . .

Sometimes Maddy could smell the musk of the other woman on him and had to sleep with the windows flung open. It was a high, dirty odor that reminded her of a captive fox she'd once seen as a child. The vixen had fine, sharp teeth and a glaze over its eyes. It may have been dying . . . or giving birth.

Maddy rubbed her temples with her fingers. Inside her head, the clamor never stopped. Maybe because when she gave birth, something had broken loose up there and now it would never be set to rights, because nobody could see it.

She crept out of bed. In her bare feet she stood before the wall-length mirror. With the air of a martyr, she inched the lace-fretted gown up her thighs, over her breasts. She studied the new map of her belly with fascination. It had gone down quickly, the doctor said; she looked like a young girl again.

But Maddy knew better. She knew all the secret places where her skin had been stretched to bursting, where the baby had left its footprints. Her once-lovely stomach sagged. The scar was like a zipper on an old pouch. She couldn't bear to see herself anymore.

She let the gown fall, hiding her scarred nakedness.

The pills that put her to sleep had a strawberry-pink color that reminded Maddy of the pretty dress she'd worn to her "Sweet Sixteen" party. Mother had helped her pick it out.

"You don't look too heavy in that one," she'd observed, standing just inside the curtained stall of the dressing room for critical distance. "But if you're not sure—I saw such a cute little girl before in a lacy white thing you might want to try. On her it was stunning."

How nice that must have seemed to passersby. A mother and daughter close enough to spend a day shopping together. But now Maddy saw through it.

A mother who can't love will criticize, as if the best she can do is teach her daughter to submit to male requirements. To the inevitable. To her own unfaced rage.

Maddy didn't bother to count pills as she placed them on her tongue and swallowed them one by one, with a drink of water, until the plastic bottle was empty. And there were already so many shadows on the wall, she just slipped quietly away into the darkness that swallowed up her room, to become another.

Kit's visit to Newport had extended well beyond the original two weeks. She and Jonathan had become inseparable companions, getting away on the yacht for long lazy hours in the sun, for lovemaking in the sand of private beaches.

As was their custom over the past month, it had been arranged that Kit should meet Jonathan on the dock for breakfast.

Instead, Jonathan found Kit, bags packed, huddled in the Trewhitts' limousine, and bound for home.

"But why?" he asked, frowning. The strong column of his neck rose from the open-collared blue cotton shirt. It made her hands greedy to touch him.

She swung out of the limousine, anxious and white as narcissus. "I have to. An old friend is very ill. Her parents cabled me this morning."

He took her by the hand. The beard on his face was nothing but golden down as he brushed a kiss across her mouth. "Kit, please tell me. Are you leaving because of us?"

She knew she shouldn't mislead him, but she was too tender, too confused herself, in the light of their passionate explorations these past weeks, to have much control over the situation. "John, what we had was a gift."

"But do you still want to see me?"

She'd always wanted to be in this position, had dreamed of

it. But there was no pleasure in giving pain to him, no pleasure at all. "I don't know how to say this, John. But I want this love business so much I can't trust myself at all. I guess I need time."

"I don't really understand." He looked out to where his yacht rode the gentle green swells, no doubt thinking of the first time they'd made love. "But in any case, I think I'll let you come back to me." The kiss he gave her almost broke her resolve to leave him. Then he held open the car door and handed her in.

In her heart, she thanked him for everything. Especially for letting her go.

Aden had finally knocked off work on his newest comedy and packed it downtown to the venerable old playhouse on MacDougal Street, where it played to full houses for its limited three-month run.

The reviews were strongly enthusiastic, but all agreed on one point: the character of Germaine was unfinished, its outlines foggy in a disturbing way. Was she a comic or a tragic figure? they asked. Light or dark? Should you love her, hate her—or laugh at her? The playwright didn't seem to know, and neither, it turned out, did the audiences. This unresolved ambiguity dragged on the play as a whole, and gave an inertial stamp to Germaine's individual scenes, the kiss of death to comedy.

Aden had long sensed that Germaine's fragmentation reflected some essential division within his own beleaguered heart.

But it had taken Kit Daniels' sojourn in Newport to help him find where the emotional fault line lay . . .

In his study at home, at rehearsal, over teetotalers' drinks at writers' bars, in bed at night, his mind ran on the jagged peaks of her character like a nimble creature of the Tibetan peaks. She was quarrelsome, ambitious, immature. She was generous of heart, gallant, exciting, a spur to his romantic soul.

There she perched, avian and elegant, in the forked branch

of his psyche, unwilling to come down and be anatomized, stuffed with words, mounted in print. If she were willing, he could dismiss her then, get back to Geraldine. Once he resolved the eternal ambiguities Kit Daniels represented, he would be able to "finish" his unfinishable play.

The theater in Shubert's Alley was triumphantly booked and the cast was ready to go.

He didn't have much time . . . either way . . . to make his move.

It was Kit's first visit to the Londons' oak-shaded home in Ridgefield, Connecticut. The house turned out to be an 1818 Colonial with a pond and paddock and three-point-eight pastoral acres.

When Kit had been let in by the Haitian housekeeper, there was no one else in the house but a nurse who was gobbling up a romance magazine in the parlor. The nurse was for Maddy. Samantha had been packed off to her grandparents for the month of her mother's recuperation.

On the phone, the Lefkowitzes had spoken shrilly of stomach pumps and psychiatric wards. It was Kit who had persuaded them to let Maddy go home.

"She's out back," the nurse said in a flat, unromantic voice.

Kit found Maddy sunning herself on the back terrace. She had her own eyes on. With a welcoming smile, she tried to rise from the peppermint-striped chaise longue but fell back weakly. Despite the smile, her eyes were wary.

Kit kissed her friend's cheek. In the late summer sun, there was the distant blue glitter of an in-ground swimming pool. "Adventures in paradise." Kit gestured toward the pool.

"Did they tell you to bring your bathing suit?"

"I wish they had."

"You can use one of mine."

"Sure. Thanks."

Kit looked around for a place to sit.

"The pink chair wobbles. Try the gray."

"Oh, okay." Kit pulled up the gray chair that stood on white PVC pipes. It made a scraping noise over the slate tiles.

Remote and mysterious, Maddy adjusted her sun visor and looked out over the sprawl of yard to a distant green line of trees. Kit clasped her hands over her knees. She'd intended to speak with cool reserve and noble purpose, to save her friend from herself.

"They tell me you tried to kill yourself." It had just come out, and she was glad, relieved really.

"I told you. He's sleeping with another woman."

"Then leave him."

"I can't."

Kit could see that Maddy's marriage was a stake at which she was determined to burn. What's more, she loved her martyrdom. Maybe because as a fat girl she'd always been in pain, she now found life hollow without it.

"It's not Jared's fault," Maddy said, rubbing some suntan lotion into the palm of her hand. "It's Samantha. She cries all day, all night. She keeps him away."

"Maddy, that's crazy! You don't really blame the baby; she's the victim here. She needs your love."

"I don't have any to give. I'm a spook. I'm not here."

Kit felt chilled. Maddy's flat, expressionless voice seemed cut off from the engine of her feelings. She floated on that lounge as though some fundamental connection between the world and herself had been severed. Or perhaps it had never been there. Perhaps she lacked some essential ground on which to stand as a woman. Was that why she twisted this way and that, only as others exerted their emotional force upon her? And now she didn't even have the comfort of food.

Just the ecstasy of the stake.

"I don't understand you, Maddy. What do you want?"

She looked exhausted. "I just want some peace."

"I'm sorry then. You can't think of yourself first anymore, because, Maddy, you brought a daughter into this world, and you've got to see her through."

Maddy looked up with such bitterness shining in her face that for a moment Kit thought she might ask her to leave. "Why? Who did that for me?"

Kit reached for her friend's cool hand. "Maddy, you don't mean that. You're just tired and sick."

174

"Oh, am I? That's lovely. What do you know about these things? Where's the center to your life, the passion?"

"It's not my life that's at issue here." Kit was shaken by the hint of rage in Maddy, buried so long beneath the sweetness, until today, when it erupted like sulfur and black ash.

Maybe that was why women's chemistry was more acidic than men's. The corrosiveness of their anger, eating away secretly at the heart, the worm in the female rose. What's more, the face of that primal anger seemed to mirror her own.

"Oh yes, it is your life that's at issue. Come on, you don't fool me, Kit. I can see how you pity me. But it's you who should be pitied. I hear you talk about men, like fashions you can put on and take off, at whim. But you've never really given yourself to any one of them. You've never been ravished by anything greater than your own ego, as I have . . . It's not the man, you see, it's the ravishing."

At first, Kit said nothing. It was true. Even as she'd taken up Jonathan's offer of love, she'd held the best part of herself apart. She was yet untouched. A virgin island. But was that bad?

"I have my work." She rushed to defend herself. "I'm passionate about that."

"*Male* passion. Ambition. Don't you see it yet, Kit? All that has nothing to do with women. Get out of your head where your father put you—and your mother left you. I mean, they teach us what to say, how to act around men in order to get the glittering prizes, but no one, no one in this whole damn world ever tells us how to be women."

Kit felt a tug of panic. Could this be true? But she wasn't like Maddy . . . Maddy had a feeling for the floor, like certain modern dancers, hurling herself down, down. Kit was a creature of the higher regions. She loved the airy leaps, the pretty turns of mind. She was in love with the light, while Maddy courted the darkness.

The housekeeper appeared at the sliding doors to the terrace. "Will your guest be staying for lunch?"

Maddy looked at Kit. "Will she?"

Kit struggled with herself for a moment. She was angry.

She was hurt. Then she relented. Maddy needed her. She couldn't abandon her friend now. "Yes," she said, "I would like that."

"Why don't you stay the night?"

"All right."

"Mrs. Portman," Maddy addressed the housekeeper, "would you please bring us out a cool pitcher of lemonade? It's getting hot out here."

"Of course." The woman slipped back inside.

"Would you like to read something to me?" Maddy reached over to a lacy white-steel table beside the chaise, and then handed Kit a book with a familiar cover. *"Hot Stuff,"* she said. "My favorite."

Kit was moved. Here was another surprise. Maddy had collected her books, following her career with all her generous heart, while Kit had lost touch with all but the rudimentary facts of her friend's existence.

As she opened the book, she vowed that Maddy would never be far from her mind.

———Chapter 17———

By TEN O'CLOCK the next morning, when the air fairly bubbled in the heat of the August sun, Kit Daniels gratefully arrived at her one-bedroom nest in Gramercy Park. With its high French window leading onto the jewel of a terrace and its seductive southern light, it seemed to be welcoming her home.

And a good thing too.

She was exhausted by the emotional events of the past weeks and none too happy with herself. The Jonathan Cantwell episode had taken place in a sensual trance, and when she awakened from it, the doubts had come crowding in.

For her, the idea of loving Jonathan was full of unstable charms. Like a New Testament angel, he offered straightforward beauty and a simple, sentimental dogma. She could be loved more, giving him less. It was safe.

The problem was, Kit was afraid that if she pushed him to the wall, Jonathan Cantwell III would never push back, but would give way, that he was soft and crumbly inside, and would be no match for the dragon—the one inside every woman—who, every once in a while, raised its golden head and snorted fire.

If only there were a man alive who could stand up to that dragon, without either wilting and giving in—or roaring back with a dragon's breath of his own!

Such a man probably didn't exist. And if he did, with her luck, she wouldn't recognize him.

Maddy thought she'd recognized him.

She'd let herself be ravished by love for her husband—but she couldn't seem to do the same for her child, their daughter. Kit couldn't bear to think about it anymore.

All she wanted right now was a cool shower and an easy drift to sleep.

The shower was cool, but the sleep would not come.

She sat on the edge of her bed with a princess phone in her lap. She dialed the Rhode Island exchange. Halfway through, she snapped the phone down in its cradle.

Still unsure, she dialed again, all the way this time.

Jonathan picked up on the second ring as though he'd been waiting there by the phone.

"Hello?"

"John, it's Kit."

His voice went soft and rich. "Kit. I was just thinking about you. Where are you?"

"Home." She hesitated, feeling a bit foolish now that she had him on the line. "John, I have to ask you something."

"Ask away."

"If I were to get obese again, tomorrow, would you still feel the same about me?"

Jonathan paused. "What is this, Kit? Some kind of game?"

"Jonathan, I'm very serious."

He thought a moment. "All I can say is you wouldn't be the same person if you were obese."

"You're not answering the question."

"It's unanswerable."

"Would you feel the same about me?" Kit kept at it.

"Well, Kit, I know we would always be good friends. But to

be frank, I'd find it a turnoff if you let yourself go like that. Heavy women are just not my cup of tea. Okay?"

"Okay." Kit shifted the phone to her other ear. What Jonathan said was what millions of other men would have said. It made perfect sense. But not to her woman's heart. She felt betrayed.

"Just say the word, Kit, and I'll be down on the next flight."

"No, John, I'm not ready for you yet."

"You should be. I love you, and I think you love me." There was a note of pettishness in his voice. "What about Sunday?"

"What about it?" She was now sure she shouldn't have called.

"Shall I come and get you then?"

"No, no. I'll call you."

"On Sunday."

"Yes, on Sunday."

Just then the doorbell sounded. "John, there's someone at the door, I've got to run."

"But, Kit."

"Good-bye, darling . . ." She was more than happy to cut the conversation short, not much caring who was at the door to help her do it.

When she answered the buzzer, there was Clayburn Lassiter, of all people, with a lone white rose in his hand.

"Clay!"

"I thought I'd deliver this one in person."

Delighted, she gave him a lusty hug. "It's so good to see you. Come in." She led him into the living room, spun from a palette of soft peach, aqua, and rose, which had been admiringly described by Mallory as "an abalone shell opened up to a floor plan."

Clayburn stood there, with his larger-than-life smile. "You look terrible. But irresistible just the same."

"I know. I just got in this morning. Traffic into New York is a circle of hell Dante never wrote about."

"Serves you right for fleeing the city."

"Everybody flees the city in summer."

"Why be like everybody?"

Rose in hand, she sank down onto her chintz-covered sofa. She closed her eyes and inhaled the scent of the rose. Suddenly, she knew she would probably not be able to rise again until she'd had her sleep.

"How's lunch sound?"

"Oh Clay, I don't think I can make it today. I'm exhausted."

The blazing sun in his face was suddenly dimmed. "I guess I'm the public nuisance my son is always telling me I am."

"Not at all." Kit waved airily at an armchair. "There's no one in the world I'd rather have watch me fall unconscious than you. Come and sit down."

"You really are done in, aren't you, Kit?" Before she had a chance to protest, Clayburn had cupped one of her flats, then the other in his giant paw, so that they looked like doll's shoes, and eased them off her feet.

He swung her legs up to the sofa.

"Now what?" Yawning, Kit tilted her head so that she could see him kneeling there beside the couch.

"Now sleep!"

"Clay"—she laughed—"I can't very well fall asleep with someone watching me. It's unnerving! It's indecent. It's weird."

"But you said . . ."

"I was only teasing."

"Oh." His big face crumpled like a brown paper bag. Kit wondered if every man in midlife crisis caught that same cockeyed romanticism. She felt maternal toward him. She sat up again and patted the sofa beside her. Obediently, he sat. "Now, tell me, what's been going on here while I've been away . . . Is Aden"—there, she'd said it, the name—"happy with the way his play has been received?"

"Aden?" He cracked a bearish smile. "Who wants to talk about Aden?"

"I do," Kit said peevishly. She was dog-tired, the air conditioner wasn't doing its job, and she felt guilty as ever for using Clay to talk about Aden.

"Well, I don't." He looked grouchy, like a honey bear

drawn out too early from the spell of hibernation. "Will you marry me?"

"My God," Kit said. "You'd never forgive me if I did." She lay back down, wearily. "Now go home. I'll talk to you tomorrow."

"Now wait a minute." Clayburn slapped his knees. He heaved up from the sofa like a tame whale in an aquatic park. "Since you won't be my wife, then how about being my date for the Allied Literary Society Awards on Saturday night?"

Kit's eyelids were closing fast. "Anything you say, Aden," she mumbled.

Clayburn pulled the draperies in the living room before he left, debating, meanwhile, whether or not to tell his son that Kit Daniels was in love with him.

With an eye to mischief, he decided it would be much more fun to watch them groping toward love, like drunkards to their beds, and, in the end, more rewarding for them both to have discovered the truth themselves.

He pressed a kiss to her forehead and hurried out with a light step. For Clayburn Lassiter, literary agent and bon vivant, was, although he didn't know it then, greatly pleased at the way things were turning out.

The clap of flashbulbs. A line of smoky-paned limousines moving through the late sunlight. The din of celebrity.

From Mrs. Onassis to Lefty Solarz, the literary world had turned out for tonight's presentation of the Allies. They milled about with their cocktails, under the glittering Grand Rotunda of the New York Public Library.

That evening Kit had worn a strapless white Lanvin, unfolding in a series of petals down her slim body. Her hair was brushed in shining waves over her bare shoulders.

"There's Mailer and Styron, Beattie and Walker." Kit ran on with recognitions. "I've never been so close to genius before."

"They're just writers," Clayburn interjected.

"That's like saying 'it's just a volcano.'" Lefty Solarz stopped to exchange polite greetings with Clayburn, then moved on.

"Lefty Solarz! He's become more famous than his authors!"

Clayburn sniffed. "Lovely man. But I'm a better agent."

Kit patted his hand. "Of course you are."

After cocktails in the rotunda, they moved on to another echoing cavern of a room, where a sea of tables had been set up. The tables were dressed with furbelows of fall: lady apples, grapevines, Shaker boxes . . .

Miniature blackboards were appropriately used as placecards.

The bill of fare was hearty. Cerviche followed by a chicken pot pie, sizzling on a large oval copper pan on each table and fit for a Tom Jones.

The centerpieces were two-tone cakes, laced with chocolate marzipan and decorated with names of glory from the pages of American literature. Kit and Clayburn had Ishmael and Queequeg on theirs, which struck Kit as a possibly bad omen, considering the fate of the *Pequod* and its crew. She realized she hadn't thought to ask Clayburn who their fellow diners were apt to be . . . Award nominees, presumably.

Geraldine Cutler, turning heads in a low-cut bodice of green taffeta and bell skirt, swept into the cane-and-wicker chair directly across from Kit Daniels. She exhibited no flashes of "despair" as her poetry might suggest, but blazed whitely, like the diamonds around her neck.

Aden Lassiter came up behind her, in black tie. There was surprise in his smile.

"Oh, hello, Daniels. Dad." He treated his father to a bruising look. If Kit were here, did that mean she'd agreed to be his father's bride?

As uncomfortable introductions were being made, it was Kit's turn to shoot a glance over at Clayburn, who seemed beside himself with glee. He'd known all along his son was coming with Geraldine. He'd plotted this Gotterdämmerung of a table arrangement and told no one.

It was the first time Aden and Kit had been thrown together since her return from Newport. Somehow, Kit had imagined a warmer welcome home than this.

Unconscious of her danger, she began to pick at the warm,

freshly baked French bread on the table. With every breath she felt more ravenous . . .

"How was your trip, then?" Aden was determined to be as pleasant as possible. Kit Daniels could, after all, end up as his stepmother. Besides, she was surpassingly lovely in her white camellia of a gown. He wanted to catch her like an armful of flowers to his heart.

"How is your new play coming?" Kit asked, as Geraldine, who was obviously prepared to win an Allie tonight, memorized her acceptance speech off a sheet of blue notepaper.

"We're in production," Aden said. "But I still can't get *Plymouth Rocks* out of my mind. That play deserves a second chance—if I could just get it right."

Kit was distracted by Geraldine's presence. "Your fiancée's beautiful. In an albino sort of way."

"Eat something and be quiet, Kit. By the way, you're getting too skinny to show your shoulders in that dress."

"What about *her?*" Kit hissed, stung to the quick.

"Thinness suits her. It's part of her style, like her Kabuki-mask skin. On you, it's, I don't know, overdone."

Kit felt her face grow hot. "In case you hadn't noticed, I'm dressing as I please these days. I've been from one end of this country to the other, and I'm a big girl now."

"You mean you *were* a big girl." Aden was put off by his own churlish response, comforted only by the dishonest thought that he seemed to have no control over it.

There was something about Kit Daniels that never failed to frighten Aden Lassiter, even as it fascinated. It was a little bit witchy the way she took him over, and he'd better watch his step tonight or find himself completely in her power.

But what kind of magic would it be? Geomancy, divining from the configurations of the earth itself, a science of crevices and mountain chains? Aeromancy, reading signs in the air? Hydromancy, sharing the secrets of tides and ebbs, piercing the water of whirlpools, springs, lakes, or smooth brilliant surfaces of all kinds, like a shaft of sunlight, then talking to the sprites within?

Or, pyromancy, divination by means of fire or flames?

Yes, he could imagine the miracles sparking from her

fingertips. It would be by fire that she would cast her potent spells.

As always, he found this thought exciting. She was hot underneath that cool white dress. She gave off the humid scent of wildflowers after summer rain . . . What was happening to him?

"Aden, honey," Geraldine laid her hand on Aden's arm. (Didn't couples know that their endearments sounded false, Kit wondered, when spoken in that self-absorbed tone?) "I'm still worried about Maureen Gittings. Do you think they'll go with her? She won the UBA. Could it be her year?"

"The UBA was a sympathy vote because she never wins anything. No need to worry. Tonight's your night," Aden said, with just a tinge of weariness, in which Kit found inordinate gratification. Evidently, they'd had this discussion before.

"She has on the same dress she wore that night." A southerner, Geraldine was superstitious.

"She only has one," Clayburn said kindly.

Geraldine blinked her violet eyes at him. Her psychic vibrissa stirred. Kit was sure she had only just become aware of his presence at their table. Any port in a storm.

Traitor! Kit was quite put out with Clayburn for the duration of the evening. She should have married him and shown him a thing or two . . .

"Kit is a writer." With this, Aden tried to divert Geraldine from the topic that caused her such unendurable anxiety.

"Isn't everyone?" Geraldine asked brightly.

"No, I mean she's a published writer. One of our clients, in fact."

Clayburn looked merry. The chemicals he'd thrown together in this literary crucible were churning! What fun!

Suddenly, Geraldine seemed to be trying to gauge Kit Daniels' hat size.

Clayburn picked up the lagging conversation. "Unfortunately, Kit's book didn't qualify for this year's awards because of the pub date. But next year, she'll be a winner in her category, I'm sure."

"Which is?" Geraldine sounded bored. Her eyes wandered over the room of glitterati.

Kit concentrated all the force of her will on bringing down the chandelier on Geraldine Cutler's head. Then, Stephen King could write a novel about her, *Chandelier-Chucker*.

"Humor," Clayburn said.

"Of course."

And Kit knew that this was an insult from the heart.

The chandelier seemed to sway gently over Geraldine's black-silk head.

Then, mercifully, the ceremonies began, throughout which Kit ardently rooted for the much-maligned Maureen Gittings and her book.

Aden sat stiffly between the two women as though he'd been strung through the head and backbone with a golden surgical wire. He watched Kit out of the corner of his eye.

She, in turn, was very, very aware of the heat that seemed to rise from his muscular body, the sweet warmth of his breath on the back of her neck. She shifted in her chair, a hundred times.

She felt mean and jumpy, full of unruly longings.

Then, halfway through the ceremony, the moment came for the poetry prize.

A distinguished European poet in a full beard attained the podium. "The poetry prize," he purred in a flavorsome accent, "has been given to a relative newcomer in the field, better known for her short stories than her poems. We will, no doubt, be hearing of her for many years to come."

There was a polite murmur in the tense audience. They all knew what he meant.

The bruin-shouldered poet unpocketed his spectacles and clipped them onto his wandering nose. "For her splendid work in the volume called 'Radix Malorum' the prize for poetry goes to . . . Mary O'Me-a-li-a." He pronounced her surname as though it were a five syllable word, giving each vowel the European value and prolonging Geraldine Cutler's agony.

The blue square of speech came loose from Geraldine's

hand. She let out a sound, halfway between a gurgle and a "hmm," of which the latter was, Kit supposed, the more acceptable sound for a good loser to make. Kit felt sorry for the woman, despite the man in whose arms she sheltered. Aden Lassiter was purring words of encouragement and demurral into her pretty ear. He stroked her arm (Kit could almost feel it on her own skin). Admirable man! Lucky lady to be so well loved! Maybe it was Kit Daniels she should feel sorry for.

Although none of their party had the heart for it, they sat through the remainder of the presentations. This done, they filed out of the museum and into the rainswept summer night, for the skies had begun to rumble and pour while they were inside. Limousines whooshed out of the wet darkness to take up their gowned and tuxedoed passengers, then darted away again into the gloom.

When their own chauffeur, Max, beckoned, they climbed into the car without a word. He was a bright young man with penny-colored hair who had lost all his savings in a pyramid scheme. Any day now, he often sanguinely assured them, he would be back in the chips, the proud owner of his own cab company.

But tonight, even Max was morose and taciturn behind the wheel.

The four passengers sat in the special silence that rain makes. At Kit's request, one window was rolled down a crack to let in the gusty coolness of the storm. She darted a glance at Geraldine, trying not to be too obvious about it. The other woman looked wilted and diminished, like a prom corsage at the end of the dance.

Aden had Geraldine's hand clasped in his own, but he was looking at Kit. She met his eyes.

Kit held her breath, crazy to read the expression on Aden's bright triangle of a face . . . one part tenderness, one part defiance, as though he would not let her upset the delicate balance of his inner feelings. Men were, she knew, quite fragile when it came to emotions, and even though she wanted him to want her, to look at her the way she looked at him, with seriousness and desire, she felt soberly responsible for him in a way that romance could not explain.

Maybe this time she was really in love. A bad break. Because on the surface, he was brick and stone against her. Kit felt wily and dangerous. She blushed at the role she'd been dealt in the evening's drama. Finally, the femme fatale.

At this point, Clayburn, who had drunk too much champagne back at the museum, began to hum "Oh Shenandoah," at Kit's elbow. Geraldine looked limp as a kitten in Aden's arms. The shadows of passing cars fell in bands across the backseat, and Kit's mind whirled, under a cloud of desires.

The pop of the car door.

Aden was bearing his defeated fiancée home. Kit watched from the window, rejoicing at her fall, hating herself but unable to stop.

She could just make out Geraldine's parting words to her lover. "No, darling, not tonight. Tonight, 'hell is other people,'" she quoted Sartre. "Now be a good boy. I'll be all right, really. It's just a silly prize."

Aden cupped her small, exquisite face in his hands and pressed a kiss to her lips. Watching, Kit felt as though she'd been hit by a car. What did she expect? Aden owed Kit Daniels nothing but good contracts and fair treatment. He'd already extended himself beyond the call of duty to outfit her like a celebrity and set her toward stardom. By his own admission, he found her exasperating. She irked him into shows of distemper that usually erupted only after many years of wedded stress. Besides, he was an honorable man who'd already made his choice of woman.

Tomorrow, she would call Jonathan and tell him to come for her: Jonathan, who worshiped her. There was nothing for her here.

With reluctance, or so it seemed to his anxious observer, Aden got back into the car. "Do you think she'll be all right?" He pitched the question over Kit's head to Clayburn, who was no longer singing, but looked rather more sober in the light from Geraldine's luxury co-op apartment building just off Greene Street.

"She'll be just fine, son," Clayburn assured him kindly. "Sometimes a woman needs to be alone. That's all. Drive on, Max."

At that moment, Kit forgot her unsisterly envy in the thrilling spectacle of Aden's kindness to Geraldine Cutler. He was really shaken and had to be persuaded several times by his father not to return to her apartment. For Kit there was a matter of tenderness toward him, yes, and regret that the two of them could never share anything more than royalty checks and stolen looks in the backseat of a Rolls. She wished she could tell him about the things she'd discovered tonight.

Instead, she clasped her hands in her lap and stared stonily ahead at the plastic shield that protected Max from his rich clients, unaccountably angry at Aden for lacking the foresight to know that she would, sooner or later, have come along— and for falling in love with an anorexic poetess with a silicon chip of a heart.

Clayburn, forgotten in the internal storm of feeling, was the next to be dropped off. Just before slamming the car door, he turned and remarked over his shoulder to his son: "She said no."

Aden looked as though he'd just been handed a reprieve from the gallows.

By the time the limo zoomed away from the curb, the rain had stopped. The air seemed washed clean and the car made a faint swooshing sound as it rolled, as if on velvet, toward Kit's Gramercy Park apartment.

Kit would always remember the moment she first felt the brush of Aden's hand against the cup of her shoulder . . . heard his voice saying, "Maybe this is the only way to get you out of my system . . . I'm not even sure I like you, Kit Daniels."

"I know." She moved against him, while his lips played upon her mouth, the hollow of her throat, a wild tactile music. "I've never liked you much either."

He smiled, a clear, intelligent smile; his whole being seemed to radiate with that smile. And she knew, at that moment at least, they "liked" each other very much.

Somehow, still touching as much as possible, they moved

out of the limo and rode up to Aden's duplex apartment where there was hand-stenciling on the hardwood floors, café au lait suede on the walls, and a blaze of constellations that turned out to be the skyline of Manhattan, twinkling just beyond the panoramic window.

Once in, Aden threw his keys onto a hall table and went straight to a drawer in his study desk. He took out a small object and handed it to Kit.

She picked up the black cup of a cocktail hat glittering with rhinestones. "You've kept this? All this time?"

He nodded, never taking his eyes from her face.

It was cool and dark and delicious as they sank down on the platform bed made of black marble and blond wood. Saffron-dyed gauze had been slung in an arc above the bed, and the well-traveled Aden had followed an old New Orleans custom, swathing his bedroom furniture in white muslin sheeting, rolling up the rugs to bare the bleached wood floors against the summer heat. With the flutter of gauze above and Aden's heart beating a hard rhythm against her own, Kit would almost believe they were sailing some tropical sea together, naked to the waist, their skin flashing in the darkness.

Their excitement was almost unbearable as they caressed one another. The most delicate contacts set them both shivering with erotic heat.

Aden drew himself up so that he could look into her eyes. "I've waited so long for this. I want to see how you look when we make love."

Kit felt herself go weak, even as she took fire from his words.

Then, he seemed to hesitate. "But I have to know." His fingers played through the shining flow of her hair. "Will you *let* me love you, Kit Daniels?"

How wonderful! How natural and right for him to ask this question of her! It was part of his magic, this easy communion with time, this sure sense of cycle, place, and season. It gave him a window on the ever-shifting landscape of a woman's soul. Now all he needed was the permission to look through . . .

And she had the wisdom and courage to give it. In answer,

she clasped him to her with her long, lovely legs. Her white dress peeled down, floated about her on the round bed like a blossom in a rain barrel.

He pored over her face hungrily, as though there were something he needed to find there.

What is it, Aden? What do you want from me, need more than ever to find?

Then the gunfire of the buzzer sounded, so insistently that Aden had to respond. In the light pouring through the doorway, Kit could see him talking to someone. "Come on up," he said with a grim expression. Then he stepped back into the bedroom and began hurriedly to button his clothes. "It's my father. Something's happened."

Kit climbed out of bed and put her own clothes on, fumbling at the glide of zipper along the back of her dress. His face softening, Aden came over without a word and moved his hand up the metal track. Kit had never felt so thoroughly caressed. His hand burned where it moved gently up her back. From behind, his arms slipped around her waist, and he put his mouth to the side of her throat, where it was most sensitive.

She captured one hand, turned up the palm, and kissed it.

They stood there, content for a moment, just like that, and it was in Kit's mind to ask him what it was he'd been looking for in her eyes when Clayburn Lassiter burst into their sensual dream, and Aden was taken from her by the news that a distraught Geraldine Cutler had overdosed on sleeping pills and was lying in a coma at Lenox Hill Hospital. Clayburn had come to pick him up, on the way there.

As his father spoke, Aden squared his shoulders and lifted his chin, as if to take a blow.

Kit's heart brimmed with tenderness and sorrow for him. And for herself, because Geraldine's weakness would bind Aden to her as no mere seduction ever could.

All this because he was a kind man, who loved women.

That old line came to mind: Enemies are friends who would have been . . . After tonight, would they go back to being enemies?

Kit wasn't sure how she knew about these things; the other,

incomplete men in her life hadn't prepared her for an Aden Lassiter. But she accepted the knowledge of love with a new humility which had been born in the charmed circle of Aden's black marble bed. After tonight, it would be hard to go back to the old ways.

Walking between father and son, she moved out to the wide, brightly lit street.

They saw her off in a cab, then headed for the hospital where Geraldine lay tonight, more powerful than ever.

Kit turned the little hat between her fingers, over and over, like her thoughts.

Had she finally climbed down from her rational perch? With Jonathan, she'd been coolly in control, from beginning to end. Not a victim, but not a lover either.

Tonight, in Aden's arms, she'd made friends with love. With this sudden blessing, her relationship to the world could hardly stay the same.

A place was being prepared, and she'd be made welcome there. Even if she never saw Aden Lassiter—a man who was already bound by the same mysterious force to another woman—again.

——————— *Chapter 18* ———————

Aᶠᵀᵉᴿ ᵀᴴᴱ ꜰᴵᴿˢᵀ flurry of schoolbells, turning leaves, and rows of pedestaled pumpkin pies in bake-shop windows, the season of autumn just barely hung on in the smoky haze over the city. But before long the Atlantic's cold breath swept in and blew it all away. To New Yorkers, that signaled the arrival of snug woolens, holiday galas, and new Broadway shows.

Aden Lassiter's, however wasn't among them. *Saul's Thousands* had opened to acclaim at a first-rate repertory theater, but the hoped-for move to Broadway of *Plymouth Rocks* had been beset by one problem after another. Costly backstage accidents. A flu epidemic that laid up a good third of the cast.

And then, there was the trouble with Germaine.

Aden had become a positive maneater on the issue, pestering the director to fire his original choice for the role and then displaying a seeming inability to settle on any other of the umpteen perfectly capable actresses who were lining up to play the part. It was irrational, pigheaded—not at all like the suave Aden Lassiter theater people knew and loved.

Rumors flew like dockside confetti. "Writer's block." "Too

much partying." He'd been "seen" last spring at the Tony Awards, "trailing clouds of coke . . ."

Or maybe it was that fiancée of his, the poet, they gossiped backstage.

Still reeling from the news of Geraldine's suicide attempt, Aden had entered her hospital suite that rainy night, half buried under his load of flowers and old-fashioned guilt. As Clayburn Lassiter later commented, Geraldine had seemed more like Scarlett O'Hara at a barbecue than a desperate, death-courting woman.

The angel hair was arranged just so. By the next day the hospital gown had been replaced by a delicate gown of honey-colored lace that played about her ankles like a fairy's garb.

She was basking in the attention—too much so for the father's liking.

But the son didn't seem to notice.

What they both noticed was Lefty Solarz's card on Geraldine's night table.

Trouble was curling up the edges, eating toward the paper heart of the hardbound world of Lassiter & Lassiter, and Clayburn was beginning to think he might have overdone it this time.

As soon as Clayburn and Aden left, Geraldine sat back in bed with a smile.

She found this all so amusing, in a macabre sort of way.

The plain truth was: there had been no "suicide attempt" by the newspapers' "Dark Lady of American Poetry." No, she had only fumbled in the dark with her sleeping pills. Absentminded about dosage to the point of danger, she had made a ghastly mistake, but with certain advantages.

Aden was eating out of her palm. They all were.

She dialed the telephone on her night table, referring to the white card Lefty Solarz had given her earlier.

She had taken a backseat to the Yankee establishment long enough. It was time for a change.

And so it was that Aden Lassiter, caught between a ruse and a hard place, had danced attendance on his lady love, keeping a round-the-clock vigil at her hospital sickbed (visiting-hours-cum-phone-calls), in a minuet of contrition over wanting another woman.

At home, he watered her posies and had her laundry done just right. He fluffed her pillows and smoothed her brow. He read large Russian novels to her for hours at a time and gossiped of rival poets.

Geraldine said little and looked frayed and frail as a feather boa in an antique clothes stall. She ate only the meals prepared for her by her lover's own hand.

Meanwhile, Aden himself was losing too much weight, and his Broadway cast, still in rehearsal, danced on the razor's edge of mutiny.

Then one night, made careless by weeks of successful anonymity, a man with a familiar voice answered Aden's twelve o'clock call to Geraldine.

Lefty Solarz.

He huffed and hawed.

At last, he put Geraldine on.

"Aden, Honey," she said, "you really can't claim to be surprised."

"Lefty Solarz?" Aden asked, incredulous.

"Yes, indeed. We're planning to be engaged."

He felt light-headed, as though he'd shot up too quickly from a deep-sea dive. "Have you thought what the children will look like?"

"Don't begrudge me this, Aden. Believe me, it's killing me to let you go, but Lefty is a very nice old gentleman. And what's more, he loves me. Which is more than I can say for you."

"In that case, I wish you all the best." Aden got off the phone, whistling a happy tune—he could swear, to the clanging accompaniment of his chains being struck off.

Kit Daniels hadn't seen Aden Lassiter for weeks, not since the night Geraldine had wanted to die. Her own life had been on hold. And there was nothing she could do about it. Aden would have to come to her, out of pure strength, out of male conviction.

Trying to keep her mind off the man she might love, she was closeted with her overdue manuscript, swilling black coffee and munching on carrot sticks. While burning up the keyboard of her new IBM word processor, she barely took time for personal conveniences, like fresh air and human companionship, lost track of whole seasons, like fall.

She did make room to write to Mallory Daniels, who had just embarked on a triumphant sweep of the new Western-style theaters of Japan.

And, of course, she phoned Maddy every week, to tell her of this and that, and to make vague plans for lunches that never panned out, due to Maddy's frequent bouts of agoraphobia. She consistently found reasons not to stir from the old white house, leaving Kit frantic with worry for her friend and her child.

As soon as the book was finished, Kit promised herself, a pencil clenched between her teeth as she pored over the penultimate chapter of the third draft, she was off to Connecticut.

Two hours later, around ten, Kit leaned back in her fake Windsor chair, lifting her arms above her head in a luxurious stretch.

Still one of the great pleasures of life, the stretch.

And no calories.

She rubbed her eyes, which were rabbit pink (having lived with Mallory, she'd never be able to think in basic colors again) almost all the time now, from staring at the double-time march of little emerald letters on a computer screen.

Automation, thy name is eyestrain!

She gazed with longing to the window where clear winter sunlight was pouring in. Maybe a walk outside would do her good, clear her head of cobwebs and clichés.

She buttoned on her leather jacket and walked down the one flight to the front door of her townhouse.

On the street, the icy wind bit at her cheeks and blew her hair around. It breathed down her neck, so that she was in a hurry to pull on her gloves. To think it had only just been blue summer on the gentle sea, the last time she looked! She wasn't prepared for this tightening band of winter cold cinching the city, the swaybacked arch and groan of the great trees along Gramercy Park. She passed the locked, speared-iron gates of the exclusive park, still not sure where her steps were leading her.

The late morning streets were pleasantly deserted. Writers soon found that "real" people vanished on Monday morning and only reappeared again, in brightly lit, crowded eateries on Friday night. For the rest, these were the disenfranchised, the children, the retired, the freelancers of every stripe, unemployed models, artists, actors—and, of course, the tourists, who, unlike blasé New Yorkers, could be seen craning up, with their heads in the clouds, anchored to earth only, it seemed, by exotic necklaces of Nikons and Minoltas.

Kit walked briskly into the teeth of the wind, for a cleansing. On solitary days such as these, with a cold sun putting a pewter shine on the city, she felt she owned the place.

She strolled across to Twentieth Street and down Fifth Avenue.

Then she noticed a tall, melancholy figure in a cashmere coat, with a flare of lion's mane around the collar. He was moving toward her.

She glanced away, observing the urban taboo against eye contact with a stranger. Then, something told her to look again.

The young man's face reflected the same surprise as her own. For a moment, it appeared as if he were going to try to ignore the mutual recognition, then thought the better of it.

He approached her with reluctance as though he were being prodded by a long, sharp stick between the shoulder blades.

"Daniels, how are you?"

"Lassiter! What are you doing here?"

He looked furtive and off balance. "I . . . come here."

Kit tried to help him out. "It's a pretty neighborhood."

"Yes, it is." Tension churned in the air around them like the wings of sparrows. "Very pretty," he said tersely. His face was closed.

"How's Geraldine?"

He was looking at her funny again, as though there were something he needed to find. "She's completely recovered. There's not even a sign of depression." He paused, as if he intended to deliver an important message to Kit, but the moment passed without words. "The damnedest thing happened. She's left Lassiter & Lassiter. For Lefty Solarz."

Kit arched one eyebrow. "Lefty Solarz? God, your father must be chewing bullets!"

"He runs around muttering darkly to himself all day about the bite of ungrateful women being sharper than a serpent's tooth. I fear for his sanity."

"Don't." Kit smiled. "Your father is an old trickster. He always comes out on top."

"I suppose so." Aden had that stranded look in his eye again. He couldn't seem to catch his bearings. "He even fooled me. I thought you were actually going to marry him."

"No, I wouldn't be so cruel. To him, I mean," she added quickly.

They'd begun walking uptown. Neither looked straight at the other but darted sidelong glances at safe moments when they wouldn't be noticed. Their timing was consistently off, for the glances were always noticed.

Kit's cheeks turned pink, whether from the sting of the wind, or from excitement about what she imagined Aden was turning over in his mind, she couldn't tell. "I'm not even sure I like you," he'd said that night in the cab, when he'd dissolved their divisions, temporarily, with a kiss . . .

A young woman with a bookbag slung over her shoulder edged by. She had a green chiffon kerchief over her head and looked fiercely independent.

Kit wondered if she'd ever looked like that in her college days. Staring down the world, over squared shoulders, so terrified that she would be found out and exposed as a frightened little daddy's girl.

"Wait, Kit!" Aden stopped. He seized her by the arm. "I don't know how it happened, but it seems that I'm falling in love with you."

Kit gave him a hard look, then pulled away and resumed walking at a steady pace. Inside she was reeling. She'd thought she wanted this to happen, had woven daydreams on nothing else since that fiercely beautiful night in his bed . . . But something had gone haywire. She'd begun to detect it in the way Aden was looking at her, speaking to her, touching her. It was shy and fiery all at once. Gone were the bandying of insults, the unpredictable, almost-come-to-blows quality of their relationship that had kept her on the tip of her emotional toes. From here, romance looked like a prison.

Why did he have to spoil everything by falling in love with her? Why couldn't things just stay the same?

"What about Geraldine?" she asked him, uneasy.

"There is no Geraldine. There never was."

"Oh."

"I'm sorry," he said then.

"So am I . . ."

"What kind of a cockamamie thing is that to say?" he burst out, swinging her around to look him in the eye.

"Well, what kind of a cockamamie thing is that for you to say: 'I'm sorry!' " she mimicked his cool voice. "How can you be sorry for such a sign of favor from the gods as to fall in love?" Even she knew she sounded crazy. She was so tangled up in contradictions, she needed someone to tell her what she was feeling.

"My God, you're crying," he said more softly. "I didn't know you could cry." He touched a fingertip to her cheek.

"Well, so I am," she said with wonder. She used to cry all the time. Now it was an occasion for wonder.

They stood staring at one another, unhappily, at a standoff. Some sort of bargaining was going on, negotiations of the heart, that neither one fully understood.

"Now what?" Kit broke the impasse.

"I think you're supposed to tell me whether you're falling in love with me."

"Oh, Aden"—now she searched his face—"how can I tell you what I don't even know myself."

"I knew it! I told myself not to come here today, I knew you weren't ready. God, you're no woman, you're a child, a precocious child! You can't even take responsibility for your own passion."

"Maybe that's because I don't even know who lives inside this body yet." She heard herself saying things to him she'd never imagined were in her to be said. "It's all so new to me. You of all people should understand that . . . you saw what I was before."

Aden drew her to him. "None of this means a damn thing, Kit . . . when we want each other like this."

She twisted away. "It does to me," she retorted, desperate for his understanding. He was her friend. She had a sudden selfish insight. He should know her by now. "It's as if I've been locked up in prison for years, staring out through the bars at all the wonderful things that can happen to a woman—the love of a man, marriage, children, acceptance. I need to believe that I can be that woman, that I want to be that woman, before I can love you."

"God, I was right. You're incapable of your own happiness," he said. His gray eyes flashed with anger. "It's true—only you can accept the good things that are coming to you—but you won't, Kit, as long as you're trying to psych out life with the logic of your head, instead of flying blind, with the soul. You lack faith, Kit."

"You don't know what the hell you're talking about, Aden. You've always been beautiful! And you're a man. You've had time to identify with the best things in life."

"What about that night? Didn't that mean anything to you?" They'd begun to head for Kit's apartment, Aden sticking close to her side.

"I was a kid in a candy shop, that's all." She couldn't bear to look at him anymore. She pulled ahead and continued walking, her eyes round and blank. It had suddenly become very important to get away, more important than to help Aden understand her or to understand herself. Through the grillwork spears, she saw an old man in a salt-and-pepper cap look up briefly from his newspaper. He was sitting all alone on a bench inside the neat green rectangle of Gramercy Park. The great mothering trees, the gravel paths, the flower beds looked comforting and broad.

In a haze of doubts, Kit used her key to open the gate and darted through into the almost deserted park. She backed herself into a tree, with a wild feeling that it might give her strength. Then Aden caught up with her.

This time he wisely said nothing. Instead, he leaned over, laid his hands on either side of her face, and touched his lips to hers. She trembled, and he felt it.

"Now," he said, "tell me you want me to go away." The old man folded his paper in neat squares and drifted out of the park. Kit threw her head up, defiantly. She kept her eyes on the burning blue of the sky as she spoke under her breath.

"I want you to go away," she said, hating the lie and blaming Aden even more for making her say things she didn't mean.

The soft radiance that Aden gave off whenever he looked at her seemed to waver and go dim, as though some inner flame had been extinguished. He looked diminished in her eyes, when only a moment before he'd been filled by mysterious lights, a motion of spirits. She wanted to see those colors again, wanted to evoke them in her lover once more. But she was afraid—of being "ravished," Maddy would say. She would say of being ruled.

"Aden . . ." She put her hand out to touch his arm, but he had withdrawn from her to some inner recess where she could not hurt him further.

"Your publisher asked me to tell you—" he had become all business, to her relief, to her sorrow—"that you're scheduled for an important television interview."

"Just give me the place and the date," Kit replied with a sense of unreality. How could she be talking like this with the man she loved plainly hurting in front of her? "I'll be there." *Don't let me do this to you, Aden—to us.*

Inside the woollen gloves, Kit's hands were numb.

She only gradually realized her entire body was chilled to the core. As the rising wind rattled the bare branches above her head, Kit feared she would never be warm again.

So this was love.

——————— *Chapter 19* ———————

K IT WAS NEVER quite sure what had made her do it, but she was outrageous enough on the "Jack Cornwall Show" to merit a reprimand from both Lassiters hard on the heels of the early morning taping.

It could be she'd needed the voluptuous release of irrationality that compulsive eating used to afford her. It could be that now she had to be crazy in other ways, give vent to the jumble of feeling inside her or go mad with it.

It had been hard enough to work up the enthusiasm to disport herself before hundreds of thousands of people so soon after her bitter break with Aden. For a solid month after, she'd attempted a sort of cerebral shutdown, in which she'd done nothing but bathe in the green glow of the word-processor, play old Jim Croce records, and reminisce with Maddy for long hours on the phone. She also reread Jonathan Cantwell's letters, which had arrived in a heavy, vellum stream, ever since the summer.

Like his frequent phone calls, they were filled with sweet

exhortations to come back to Newport and resume their interrupted affair.

Time and time again, Kit cast up the same elusive answers: "I'm not ready"; "I'm not sure"; "I'm too busy with my career." But after Aden, blue-eyed Jonathan seemed softly appealing and infinitely more safe.

Jonathan didn't poke around inside her heart or try to change her style. He liked her just the way she was.

Because he didn't know just who she was.

For the first time, in one of her letters, she hinted at returning to Newport. She slid open a desk drawer and tore off a stamp from a roll she kept there.

"How could you, Daniels?" She could still see Aden spitting fire in the studio, after the taping. Clayburn had already left in a huff. "Who the hell do you think you are?"

"Come on, Lassiter. It wasn't that bad." She picked her way over the television cables.

"Not that bad! God! When Cornwall asked you why people should read your book instead of all the others on the stands, you said what made him think people should watch his soporific show instead of early morning cartoons!"

"He deserved that," Kit said, unrepentant.

Still in heated debate, they made for the studio exit.

"He was the host. You don't say things like that to a host, deserved or not! I had a hell of a time fixing it all up afterwards. And you're jeopardizing the careers of our other authors too, Kit. Did you ever think of that?"

"Lassiter, I wouldn't worry if I were you. Most Cornwall fans won't even know what 'soporific' means. They'll assume I was complimenting the man—a marvel of taxidermy, by the way."

Shrugging, Aden had slung his suede jacket over his shoulders. "You just don't take anything seriously, do you, laughing girl? I mean, the way you run around trampling over people's egos, it's as if you think this is all a dress rehearsal or something, not real life. Well, my dear, this is it! Prime time. Your future takes root in the present. And from the looks of it, someday you're going to be one hell of a lonely lady."

They pushed out the exit and went their separate ways.

Seated at her desk, before her sunny terrace, she sealed the envelope. Kit could still feel the reverberations of his tirade that morning. One hell of a lonely lady . . .

But free.

Was it true? Had she become, since her miraculous transformation into a beauty, a marvel of selfishness and cynicism about love, making up pretty romantic stories she didn't believe in, laughing away the authentic challenges and traditional joys of a woman's life?

She moved out from behind her desk on the way to the kitchen, where she filled the copper watering can. Out on the terrace she began watering the herbs in her windowbox garden. Ah, Sunday, blessed Sunday! No day for self-recriminations . . .

Her herb garden was her pride and joy. Kit loved the taste of fresh basil on her homemade pasta dishes and often experimented with herbal remedies for minor ills. She'd become quite the earth mother since moving to her terrace apartment, sending off chamomile flowers for Samantha's teething problems, or the European herb borage for Maddy's chronic stomach ills. Grandmother Ilona would have been proud of her luminous collection of sunstone and moonstone, cat's eye and black opal.

But was she a lonely lady?

The thing of it was . . . anything Aden Lassiter said about her was suspect. Setting down her watering can, she eased herself into the wicker garden chair, the better to think it all through.

After all, wasn't he thinking of himself when he spoke about her "trampling" on egos? It was perfectly natural for him to feel bitterness toward her.

And then too, he was a man, and no man wants a woman to have the upper hand. He wants her pliant, at the end of his leash. Like her own father.

No, she had to go as far as she could go, push to the outer limits of her character and talents, stand, shrewishly, shrewdly, on her own, without reference to Aden's or any other man's good opinion . . . It was her job to be inflammatory.

Kit was just pushing back the French doors with the

peacock-figured lace panels, warmly reminiscent of her grandmother's old bedroom, when the downstairs buzzer went off.

Aden? Her heart, unimpressed by philosophy, jumped.

"Hello?" She spoke, breathless, into the intercom.

"Get down here this instant, darling. I'm carrying you off to Sunday brunch at one of those ridiculous cafes with the strawberry daiquiris. It's time to be a New Yorker again."

"Mallory!"

Kit considered her costume for a moment. It consisted of old cotton khaki trousers spattered with white-out and a man-tailored shirt the color of a rotten tomato. Her hair was pulled back, for expediency, in a ponytail. She just knew she conjured up the tomboyish "Kitten" on "Father Knows Best." "But I'm not dressed."

"Come as you are. And hurry up! There are hundreds of people on Houston Street alone who would give their health-club memberships for a brunch date with me."

Happy again, Kit threw on her denim jacket, snatched her black-and-white-striped sling, and hurried down to the street.

Mallory was tanned to within an inch of his life, his hair slicked back and gleaming like yellow marble, in the Italian way. As usual, he was dressed in a dandified manner, rather like Maurice Chevalier. He also looked more seasoned, and very, very dear. She flew into his arms.

"Oh Mal! What a surprise to see you! I was afraid you'd gone international on me."

"Ah yes, I must say the Roman men were a powerful temptation to stay . . . but I got homesick for Egg McMuffin and you."

"Roman? I thought you were in Japan."

"I was. Detoured to Rome on the way back. For some R&R."

"Oh." They linked arms and strolled downtown in the late morning sunlight.

"I know a place in the teens, down here somewhere." He twisted his hand vaguely in front of his duckling face. "They have a trio that plays chamber music, and hot rolls with raisins."

"Sounds like a diversified band." Kit felt all warm inside. Wasn't it something how Mallory turned up whenever she needed him? Maybe it had some connection with love.

Somewhere in the teens, the popular old restaurant did indeed present itself. A converted brownstone, filled with greenery and cool mirrors, it was hopping with Sunday brunchers in jump suits and expensive jogging clothes.

Two women and a man sat weaving baroque and ragtime melodies in a sunny corner as Mallory and Kit were shown into a glassed-in annex by a young man in an overly tight suit.

After Mallory had made a great show of ordering a strawberry daiquiri with two straws and had secured an expensive bottle of Swedish water for Kit, they sat, cockeyed with familial pleasure, across the table from one another.

"You were in all the trade papers here," Kit offered. "They say you really knocked them out in Tokyo."

"All of Nippon was at my feet. By the way, I didn't get a chance to tell you in my last letter, but I made an extraordinary find in a Bloomsbury bookstore when I was in London. Take a guess."

"A signed edition of Virginia Woolf?"

"No. A copy of *Hot Stuff.*"

Kit was completely won over by his delight.

"I put it right up front where everybody could see it."

"Good for you!"

The frizzle-haired waitress came and they ordered eggy things on English muffins. Then Mallory spoke again, without his usual ebullience.

"Rock and I aren't together anymore."

"I'm sorry to hear that."

"It's all right. You see, in America no one noticed how dull he was, but in Europe and Japan, he became a distinct liability." Now he cracked a smile. "As I remember, my French colleagues refused to acknowledge his presence at the dinner table at all. In Japan, he was a danger to himself and others! He actually walked through a paper wall. *Très outré.*"

"Oh my." Kit let out a giggle. "But I know you, Mallory. You liked to tease Rock but you know as well as I do that he was one of the most generous souls you'd ever hope to meet."

"It's true. I miss him more than I'd hoped."

The waitress laid the hot platters before them and they dug in.

"What about you, Kit?" Mallory casually leaned his arm against the back of his chair and waited to be regaled.

"What about me?" Ever since her publicity tour she'd resented any questions about her personal life. Even Mallory was no exception.

"Jonathan Cantwell, for one thing. Leaping lizards, Sandy, I could hardly believe *he* turned up! And what about Aden Lassiter? I saw him first, as you remember. Your letters were full of names, but no wedding dates. Are we talking joint accounts here, or what?"

"Should we be?" Kit's eyes flickered away from Mallory's.

"Isn't that how most of God's creatures are supposed to go, male and female, two by two, unto the ark . . ."

"I'm not on an ark."

"Aren't you afraid of drowning? The well of loneliness and all that?"

Silence was a wedge between them.

"Good eggs," Kit murmured.

"Why are you so unhappy, Kit?"

"I don't know what you're talking about."

"Stop it. I may have been six thousand miles away, but I could still hear your heart skip a beat. And now that I see you, I know I was right to think you're in utter misery about something. Now spit it out, girl."

"Does everyone have to marry?"

"Come on, Kit, this is Mallory you're talking to. I'd be the last to say that. But you do need to love someone. Desperately."

"Why?"

"Because you're only half a person when you're born into this world."

"Mal, I think you've been talking to the French too long. You speak yet say nothing."

"All you think about is what and who has hurt you, Kit, not how you can best love. Believe me, you won't be yourself until you love someone more than yourself."

"Maddy did that. She wanted to be ravished," Kit said, coldly eyeing him. "And look what's happened to her."

Mallory shook his head. "Maddy's spirit was raped—not ravished—by her idea of men. She thinks they're gods. You don't think that."

"Don't you understand? I don't need any of them, Mal. For the first time in my life, I'm without stigma. I'm free. I'm strong. I'm out from under."

"You know, not every man is like Uncle Whit."

He'd struck at the heart of the matter; her eyes were full of shadows now. "What's that supposed to mean?" Lately, it seemed, everyone was ganging up against her, rocking here, testing there, trying to spread chaos on the emotional waters . . . because she dared to be free?

"You think a man will consume a woman, leech energy from her, try to be her son. Isn't that so?"

"All right," she said with rising heat. "I guess I do believe that, yes. A man will consume a woman, if she lets him . . ."

"Oh, Kit, it makes a big difference who the man—and the woman—are. You're not your mother. You don't have to make the same choices she did." He reached over to pat her hand. "It's time to forgive your parents, Kit. Remember what you are. You really like people. You have the gift of laughter."

Kit was infuriated. "Who the hell do you think you are to come dropping into my life whenever you feel like it, dispensing pennies from heaven! You're a man, and I'm a woman now! God, you don't even know me anymore!" Kit was busy gathering up her things. She didn't have to listen to this; she pushed back her chair. "I have work to do, Mal. Deadlines to keep. Thanks for the brunch."

Mallory was still sitting over his coffee at the table, a pensive figure in a straw hat, as she walked past the restaurant.

Chapter 20

WITH THE HIGHLY touted publication of her next book, Kit Daniels succeeded beyond her wildest dreams.

In time, *Gucci Go Home* scored an even bigger hit in the bookstores than *Hot Stuff*, and Kit was now more or less a regular at the firecracker string of media parties detonating with famous names.

Once having declared her freedom not to love, her whole life turned on that declaration. Loving Aden, she'd reasoned, would make her soft. She couldn't take the chance of ever turning soft. Instead, she grew hard—and professional at it. Sexuality was something she put on before a mirror, dangled at a party.

In apparel, she was drawn to spacy metallics and leather. Clinging carapacelike fabrics, in which to avoid herself. She'd had her hair shaped in a sculptural, almost geishalike style. Her movements were lacquered and precise, as a ritual knife in motion. Her smile was controlled, even challenging across a dinner table, at a gala. And there were many of those. Too many, without any real celebration.

It was at one of these parties—this time thrown in a private house on North Sutton Place, next door to the residence of the UN secretary-general—where the trouble began. There 350 "intimate friends" of Kit's publisher had gathered to wish him a rousing seventy-fifth birthday.

Collie and Dana Silver had closed off a part of the area to make an outdoor kitchen for their caterers. A girl in a swing pricked out with spring flowers soared in graceful arcs above the grass. Striped tents had been set up in the waterfront garden, and each guest was given a flashlight in the shape of a writing quill to help them find their way to the small public park where drinks were served by golden boys who all looked like out-of-work actors.

Like any good New York party, this one had kicked up the dust of controversy. Patrician neighbors, irritated at being barred from taking their evening strolls, had actually staged a mini-demonstration against the Silvers, who, they claimed, had no damn right, thank you very much, to close off a park for private purposes.

In the city, Kit Daniels knew, a green space is worth its square feet in gold.

When Kit arrived with Aden Lassiter—the Lassiters had watched over her with insulting solicitude ever since the episode on the "Cornwall Show"—guests in turn-of-the-century costumes were gliding this way and that under the sparkle of fireworks.

Aden, in white tie and tails, was wrapped in silence. Kit was his enchantress in her cinched gown of black mousseline, a black aigrette with a diamond clip twinkling in the upturned bell of her hair. (She'd been all set to wear men's evening clothes when she'd come upon this striking antique.) It was going to be sheer torment to have her here beside him and not be able to touch her, to dance with her till dawn, and then to love her. He had never really recovered from her turnabout that day in the park, or from the bad joke of their timing. He'd known she was the right one before she did. He would never fully understand her. But hadn't that been part of her charm for him—the mystery of her moods, the heart's dizzy leap from moment to moment—which woman would she be?

For her part, Kit was driven to hurt Aden, again and again, as though she would stamp out of his heart, once and for all, the last spark of goodfeeling he might harbor for her.

Anything else would drive her crazy with guilt, doubt, and her own unrecognized longing for him, or someone like him, to love.

As such, she found herself commenting on every good-looking young man who turned up.

"Who is that striking man? Over there by the musicians." Kit's plume shivered.

Aden cast a glance over the costumed crowd. Then he eyed a glass of champagne on a passing tray. Tonight, he was going to need it. "Judson Gold," he said, in a voice of loving hopelessness. The diamond in the aigret seemed like a cold, bright eye. Tonight, she was like a marvelous feathered thing, hurtling through the wind, away from him.

"Of course."

Judson Gold was, as Kit and everyone else in the literary establishment knew, a fierce intellectual, up from the meanest parts of L.A., and his presence here was the evening's social coup.

A five-time divorcé, he'd been a street brawler before he'd been a Pulitzer Prize winner, and it showed. In scars and scandal. As a result of many tantalizing rumors, every unattached female at the party was primed to be swept away by the writer, who, it had been claimed in several celebrity biographies, could come over a woman like a storm in the desert, all passionate energy and dust in the eyes.

He was, by conflicting accounts, either the most charming or the most obnoxious man in New York City, depending on your political affiliations, or whether you were a woman on whom he'd set the indelible mark of his desire.

"Introduce me, Lassiter."

"Damn you, Daniels." He hated himself when he was like this. "What belongs to you, comes to you. You don't have to force the issue."

Kit reflected once again how all the fun had gone out of Aden since he'd fallen in love with her. He was wan and defensive, relying on philosophy, like an old man. She did not like to see him like this.

She shrugged. "Fine. I'll introduce myself."

"You're headed for a fall, laughing girl. He'll put you in a book, with a pin stuck through your navel."

"I'm not afraid of him."

"Oh, you're a real firebreather, aren't you, Kit Daniels? Well, watch out, Little-Girl-in-the-Candy-Shop, because this time the candy might just bite back . . . hard."

"I can handle him."

"You think so!" Aden grabbed a drink off a proffered tray. He'd been trying for the longest time to get her to figure out how she'd got from there to here. Point A to Point B in her dizzy life. Maybe it would take a sacred monster like Judson Gold to pull her to a standstill for a little while. He just couldn't bear for her to be hurt.

"Just watch me."

She waited just long enough for two celebrated novelists to wander away from their conversation with Gold, then made her approach. "Hello, Mr. Gold."

As he didn't bother to look up from the pile of olives and drained martini glasses on the squat square of table in front of him, Kit wasn't sure whether he'd heard her.

She stood her ground. "Mr. Gold," she tried again, "you write damn good books."

Again, nothing, but the soft pop of fireworks in the night sky.

Kit took this opportunity to study the legend-in-the-flesh. Unlike Aden Lassiter, he was not built to be a very elegant creature, but ran to stockiness. She could imagine his formidable muscles punching through the air when he was in motion, walking or making love. Over his eyes spread a starry patchwork of scars. His skin was hummocky, and coarse as a miner's. His eyebrows bristled together, as though fired by the immense energy swirling inside his rather large and noble skull. The face would have to be strong to bear those keenest of hawk's eyes.

As she swayed before him, Kit felt her body tingle beneath

the black silks, the way one feels when one passes too close to a switched-on television set. A sexual static clouded her mind and made her want to get closer to him. She had the strangest desire to mother him, bake him sweet rolls for Sunday breakfast, and furiously nurse his genius to the light. He could probably make love for two days straight . . .

"I know I write good books, little girl," came Gold's reply, sometime after Kit had given up hope of hearing one. "But how the hell would you?"

He knocked back his drink with a hammy fist, swiped another from a passing tray. "Why do they feel the need to pickle these miniature olives in all this good rotgut? Seems a damn waste." With infinite care, he added the offending green olive to his pyramid. He sat astride his chair, as if it were a woman.

"I know because I've read your novels," Kit said quickly. "All of them. From *A Dark Glass* to *American Beauty*."

It was then, and only then, that Gold levered up his great head and regarded her with a flare of interest in his sleepy gold-flecked leonine eyes. "An American beauty who reads books? You must be gay." His voice was low and lazy and had a hint of sandpaper about it.

"No. I'm just a writer, like you."

"What's your name?"

"Kit Daniels."

"Never heard of you." He set down his latest ravaged glass in rude punctuation.

"I'm just starting out. I'm a humorist."

"Oh yeah?" He braced his broad chest against the folding chair, with some difficulty, and held his hands behind the great shagginess of his head.

With a lazy stare, he denuded her. "All right. You have my undivided attention. Say something funny."

"I beg your pardon?"

"You said you're a humorist. Say something funny, or get out of my face."

Kit thought fast. "Since I've read all your books—even the less successful—I think it's only fair that you should read all of mine."

212

He snorted. "God, that is funny. You've got balls to say that to me. A beautiful hetero woman who reads *littrachoor* and has balls." He moved his magnificent head up and down, like a Chinese street dragon in his dance. "I like that too. And I suppose you'd want a quote from me touting you as the heir to what's her name, Jane Nisewitz, and boosting your sales a hundredfold?"

"Why not."

A pause. Kit felt pleasantly uncomfortable as he once again took her in from head to toe.

His golden eyes seemed to shutter. Had she been dismissed?

Skirts rustling, she turned to go.

"Hey, American Beauty." The legend grabbed her hand and she was thrilled, beyond words. "Where do you think you're going?"

"Home, I guess. There's nothing here. The same people. The same drivel. Spring flowers in September."

Gusts of laughter went up along the river. Strains of Mozart came floating by, like golden birds on the wing.

"I'll go with you," he said in his deep, supple voice. "This lionizing business is a bloody bore. The surest way to burn out any spark of genius you might once have had. Whom the gods would destroy, they first invite . . ."

Gold dismounted the chair. "Before I leave, I've gotta kiss a few key asses. I'll meet you out front. My limo's the one that looks like a Toyota with its lights punched out."

And with that, he strutted away, as glitteringly dressed guests parted for him like a Cecil B. De Mille sea. For the first time, Kit realized that the genius was wearing a pair of faded jeans, a workshirt, and decidedly eccentric running shoes adorned with "Star Trek" decals.

Now that she'd captured the lion's attention, Kit put the question to herself: who had "captured" whom? Maybe she should just turn tail and run while she still had the chance?

"Just what do you think you're doing?" Aden had glided up behind her. She caught the flare of alcohol on his breath, which alarmed her. He held his glass low, at his side, as though he would hide the fact of his drinking from Kit.

"You've been drinking!"

"Never mind. Just what do you think you're doing with Mr. Wonderful?"

She assumed her most sophisticated pose, which was, in fact, a copy of a 1958 *Harper's Bazaar* cover her mother had done. "Seducing, darling."

"Hah!" Aden ripped off his glasses in an excess of feeling. "That's what you think, Daniels! Don't you know that Judson Gold is the most notorious womanizer on the literary circuit? He grinds up females like you for his chapter headings. You don't realize what this kind of sexual vampire can do, Kit. He'll take your heart and your passion, mix them up with his ambitions, and bake them into whatever novel he's writing at the moment. Then he'll be bored and you'll be bleeding."

"Sounds like Every Man. Besides, we're just going out for an innocent drink."

"With Judson Gold, there are no innocent drinks, there is no innocence. Besides, you can do that here. This place is awash in drinks! Here, take my drink!" He held out his tinkling glass, unsteadily.

Kit's patience cracked. "I'm a grown woman, Lassiter. I don't want to hear any more of this."

"Oh, is that so?" Aden whisked his glasses back on in a sweep of frustration. "Come on, Daniels, be honest. You may like to play at the liberated woman, with the hostile couture and the tough-cookie talk, but I happen to know that inside there, there's still the self-doubter who's susceptible to the diseases of romance and male idealization. She'll do you dirt, Daniels, every time."

"I know who I am."

He shook his head no. "You're rejecting who you are—in order to be fifteen again. Or should I say for the first time? You don't seem to understand that you can't live a life without heart, play at these empty poses. If you did, we wouldn't be standing here cutting each other to shreds. We'd be in bed somewhere, making life worthwhile for both of us!"

Kit felt breathless, as if she'd taken a blow to the solar plexus. And yet for him to lay such hurtful, intimate, loving blame on her, Aden must, in his own male way, care fiercely what happened to Kit Daniels tonight.

She liked very much to be cared for. Especially by him.

She caved in to a momentary sweetness. Then too, for once, maybe Aden was right. Maybe she was still riddled by romanticism. In danger from her fat former self.

Then out of the corner of her eye, she caught a glimpse of Judson Gold, headed their way.

"Wonderful," Aden said, in maudlin intoxication. "The man looks like one of the three bears. And you can be Goldilocks."

In a reflex action, Kit was about to fire back at him when she was seized by another, mischievous idea. "What do you mean Judson Gold is a pseudo-intellect with more in the way of ex-wives than IQ points?" she said in a stage whisper.

"Excuse me." Gold politely pushed past Kit, then walked up to an embarrassed, speechless Aden and popped him on the nose.

Taken unawares by the blow, Aden pitched backward and tumbled onto the grass.

"Shall we go?" Judson asked a horrified Kit.

"Aden!" she cried out to him as Judson shepherded her away from the curious throng. The host and hostess, she later learned, were delighted. Their party was made.

"Aden!" Kit cried again.

"Oh, so that was his name," Judson growled. "Nice guy."

The next day was Saturday and the sky outside Aden's apartment was full of scudding clouds. A major storm—of biblical proportions—would suit Aden's mood just fine.

He lay stiffly in his marble bed, as though it were a tomb and he an effigy carved upon it. Tenderly, he touched the many colorful swellings on his face.

Damn that Judson Gold! If he hadn't sprung at him from out of nowhere, Aden was sure he could have taken him in a fair fight! Wasn't he superbly toned from the daily five laps around the health club swimming pool, and from his jogging?

That man was a monster!

But Aden had only himself to blame, for getting mixed up with a New Age crazy woman like Kit Daniels, and her life of deliberate delirium. She was a dragon who could scorch a man to cinders, claw his male ego to tatters, if he got too close.

But he might as well look on the bright side. Since today was Saturday, he didn't have to go into the office and display his fatal weakness to Analisa. No telling what she would do if she scented blood . . .

He swung up off the bed. He had some editing to do, hanging fire for weeks now. A new art book by a talented friend who recast old children's fairy tales.

Listlessly, he picked up the manuscript, that accusation gathering dust on his night table.

The telephone rang. It was at times like these Aden wished he had succumbed to the electronic age and bought himself an answering machine. He'd thought he was being so unpretentious, so Emersonian to respond to calls with his own naked voice.

"This is a recording." He sounded cross and he knew it, and for once, he didn't care.

"Aden? It's Kit."

"So it is. Called to give me a blow-by-blow description of last night's bacchanalia, choreographed by Disney? Or did you perhaps assume I had expired from loss of blood and juvenile embarrassment, and decided to find out if I left you anything in my will?"

"No, Aden," she said in a small voice. "I called to ask about your nose."

"What about it? It's still there, if that's what you mean."

"Is it broken?"

"Hardly. Just sort of . . . insulted."

"Oh Aden, it was all my fault. This time, I'm really sorry."

"Go and sin no more." Aden waited for her to get off the line. "You're absolved," he said when she didn't. "See you around."

"Wait, Aden . . ."

His foot tapped on the wood floor with a staccato life of its own.

"For the record . . . nothing happened between me and Judson Gold last night. He was so drunk I had to drive him home and tuck him in."

"So?"

"So I spent the night alone."

"Frankly, my dear, I have fifty other authors to deal with. What makes you think I lose sleep over your nocturnal arrangements?"

"But last night you said—"

"Last night, I was only trying to protect my investment. It was clear to me that your friend Gold would love you and then leave you an emotional ruin, unable to dredge up one feeble word of cheer, much less salable humor."

There was a block of time during which Kit sat there, hurting, waiting for his extempore speech to sink in.

In their hearts, neither of them really believed his explanation, but neither was willing to know the reason why.

"That's a disgusting thing to say, Aden. I'm not a machine, you know, grinding out pages like homemade lasagna. I have feelings. My nose gets out of joint too."

"Try asking Judson Gold to reset it for you. He's got a great left."

"Aden, for once, I'm trying to be serious. I want to be straight with you."

"So am I being serious. I'm finished with you, Kit Daniels, on anything but the most superficial, business-card level. I am passionately interested in your royalty clauses, but the rest of you leaves me cold."

"Well, that much is true! You *are* cold! You're the most arid, unfeeling, impenetrable man I've ever known!"

"Thank you. If you can say that, I know I'm on the road to recovery. It seems I lost my mind for a while back there, thinking you were a woman who understood that emotion is power, not weakness, that someone to love is a necessity, not a luxury. But I was wrong. Dead wrong. You're some kind of modern-day firebreather, picking men off one by one. You only want us around to show how much you don't need us. Well, Daniels, I'm tired of not being needed. And I'm not going to apologize anymore for wanting to be loved—by you or anyone else. Good-bye, Kit. Make sure you get your manuscript in by next week. It's due."

His phone crashed down.

Kit sat with hers for the longest time and keened in her hands.

Unlikely relationships between men and women may be pursued for myriad reasons—boredom, fecklessness, inspiration. But among the worst of these putative "reasons" (reason after all has nothing to do with it) is pure spite.

It was, perhaps, this latter impulse that brought the angry Kit Daniels to the grand and slightly tarnished portal of Judson Gold's five-story brick house on Chelsea's Seminary Block.

He had phoned her, barely an hour earlier, on one of those sodden midsummer evenings when even the pigeons have lost their appetites and the air is blue with unshed rain.

Ordinarily, on a Sunday night such as this, Kit would have turned up the air conditioner full blast, bared herself to a teddy, fixed a pitcher of iced tea, and plowed through the *New York Times* until the words began to swim on the page or she became too jealous of some other writer's rave reviews. But when she once again came upon the rock candy of his voice—guttural, insinuating—the familiar points and lines on the map of her evening dissolved and reassembled themselves into a configuration both rich and strange.

Who was Aden Lassiter anyway?

She'd brushed her hair with such ferocity that her scalp began to sting. How dare he try to dictate the terms of her involvements? She was tired of playing Galatea to a pygmy Pygmalion. She deserved some excitement, some Mad Manhattan romance.

Kit ransacked her closet for the outfit that would strike just the right sophisticated note. They would have perfectly dry martinis. Talk books. She would come away from this night with a lifetime of anecdotes. Whenever her name was mentioned, it would later be reported by literary gossips, Judson Gold would flash an enigmatic smile and lay his hand over his lion's heart . . .

Kit settled on a sun dress, a white cotton field, confetti-strewn with black and pink microdots. She pinned her shoulder-length hair high above her ears, for coolness, and twisted the back into a silky chignon, for effect.

Aden had taught her to play the game well, she thought, as she grabbed for her keys and her straw envelope purse. She no longer needed him or anyone else, if it came to that, to hold her by the hand and swaddle her in male approval. She had her own place to stand on now, could take the Emerald City by storm with her own brains, her own heart, her own nerve. Like all wonderful wizards, her mentor, Aden Lassiter, was a fake, riding on borrowed power.

So saying, she hailed a cab.

Ten minutes later, they pulled up in front of Judson Gold's house. The street was deserted, and the row of houses had a distinctly secretive air. Why *had* he asked her to come here? At the time, she hadn't thought to argue with genius.

For an instant of prescience, Kit considered not getting out of the cab. Then she thought of Aden Lassiter wagging his bony, schoolmaster's finger at her, forbidding her ever to have fun, and she paid her fare and went forth to whatever fate awaited behind those fanlighted white doors.

Sighing, Aden switched off the green-shaded library lamp in his study. He leaned back in his tufted leather chair.

These were the absolute final rewrites for the show.

There had to be a time, as with a painting, that even one more stroke, the merest breath of paint, would turn the piece into something other than what it was meant to be.

And yet, somewhere in the far reaches of his mind, he knew despite his weariness with the project, his danger level of frustration, that it was not really time to quit on this one.

If only he could push Kit Daniels out of his head, he might have room for other, saner affairs.

Most likely, he didn't want *her* anymore. He just wanted to make peace with her or at least the supercharged image of her, which had fastened on to his imagination like something pincered and shelled that grabs you underwater.

Come to think of it, this whole Kit Daniels/Germaine business had a murky, underwater feel.

Aden unrolled his exercise mat and began a series of fifty push-ups. All the while, the problem of Kit Daniels came swimming in at him from strange angles: he couldn't see her face quite clearly, as though her image were refracted by submarine light. Her very existence touched shadowy, unfathomed places inside him he hadn't thought a man possessed.

Sometimes it felt as though his elegantly simple universe had been shattered and strung back together by a madwoman. He often asked himself why he'd continued to care about her, when it had long ago ceased to be fun. One or another of his actresses was always falling in love with him. Geraldine had wanted to marry him. He could have his pick.

It was like his play. There was no proper ending. No active solution. In the end, he supposed, there was just patience. And waiting.

For what, he didn't know.

He flattened down against the mat and stared up at the blankness of ceiling.

Should he call her? Tell her he was sorry for the way he'd swung out at her the other night? Had he been trying to turn her into the very kind of woman Geraldine Cutler was? A man's creature. A cunning doll.

He made for the phone, then took a step back in a tangle of uncertainty.

If he didn't care about her anymore, why was he trying to make it up?

Good breeding.

He picked up the phone. He set it down again.

That was a lie. There was more to it than that.

Germaine. She could help him with Germaine.

But she hadn't been able to illuminate anything for him before. In fact, she just kept casting more shadows in his direction. He was better off without her.

He dialed the phone. She'd said she would be home all

weekend, cutting and polishing her manuscript in time for the deadline.

He wondered and waited for her to pick up.

Like any idolator, Kit Daniels had long cherished a sentimental picture of how the home of a master American novelist should be fitted. Tasteful antiques. Glassed letters of Nathaniel Hawthorne. Bourgeois comfort, vaguely nineteenth century. A wife who gardens.

She was not prepared for the stark black walls and white Styrofoam sculptures, the funerary masks and Persian erotic art that embellished room after room of Judson Gold's Chelsea townhouse. The drug paraphernalia set out like communion on the marble slab of a coffee table. The what-looked-like a macramé footbridge, spider-strung from wall to wall in his booklined, grape-colored study, above which he lay coiled in a wooden aerie, two red eyes staring down, aglow from too much coke and too many apocalyptic visions.

"So, there you are," he said, in that lazy way she remembered so well.

She could barely make him out through the thick haze of marijuana smoke.

"Come on up."

Kit regarded the rope ladder with suspicion.

"Is it safe?"

"Probably."

"Can't you come down?" Her cool was slipping.

"Did you know that by looking upward with your eyes you immediately shake your consciousness? It has a hypnotic effect. That's why the Sieg Heil motion . . ." He punched his hand straight up to demonstrate.

Down below, Kit was feeling more and more that she'd taken a wrong turn somewhere and stumbled upon a block of brownstone asylums that nobody else in Manhattan knew about. She had never enjoyed talking to a person who was stoned. It put the unstoned person at such a disadvantage, like one person trying to pedal a bicycle built for two.

In the background, Varèse compositions binged and

bonged their percussive hearts out, punched through a hidden stereo speaker.

She was about to run for her life when Judson, once he'd got unraveled, began his descent. He scrambled down nimbly, like a young boy—evidence of having had years of practice in the dark.

"Usually, I make everyone walk across the plank. Drives editors crazy. But with you—I'll make an exception."

He trailed a finger down her bared back, and she felt chills. Then he hooked his thumbs onto the straps in front and pulled her to him. "Nice dress," he growled. "Take it off."

Kit laughed uneasily. The man was a Pulitzer Prize winner. A genius. This couldn't be happening to her.

How many wives did they say he'd had? And what had happened to them? She had disquieting visions of pastel ladies sailing off the cableway, one by one . . .

"How about a drink?"

Kit relaxed into her shoes a bit. Now they were getting into more familiar territory. Having been a pariah of the youth culture in her "fat girl" days, she was suspicious of drugs and easy sex. For all her outer brass, she really sometimes craved champagne and courtship, as her mother had.

"Sit down." He shambled over to a black lacquer chest, where he tinkled glasses and stirred drinks, with as much of a racket as possible.

Kit looked around, in vain, for a chair. There were only gargantuan pillows, imprinted with erotic positions from the *Kama Sutra*. She hesitated, then sank down onto one, feeling compromised and not knowing what to do about it.

By the third shot of scotch, she was lolling with her shoes off and the pots-and-pans crashes of the Varèse seemed to be taking off from the closed studio of her own head.

The scotch had been what she did about it.

All in all, she felt much more mellow.

So relaxed, in fact, that when she woke up, she was stretched out on the Persian rug in the author's aerie. She could, if she held out her hand, touch the ceiling.

She could not, however, hold up her hand.

"Was there something in that drink?" she drawled like a southerner, and tittered at the sound of it.

"A little black magic." He poured smiles over her, genially, like a clergyman at Sunday services. "Have some more?"

"No, thank you." Kit's eyes attempted to focus, on their own, as she really couldn't do much to help them. It was fascinating. Judson looked about twelve feet tall, but that may have been because she was flat on her back on the floor. Or was it the ceiling? The room was spinning now, like the ballerina in the bubblegum-pink tutu who tiptoed on the top of her jewelry box in her baby-doll room at Maregate . . . "Sumberla . . . Somewhere my love . . ." she tried to sing, but the right sounds didn't float out. "Daddy?" Kit asked, from inside an aquarium. "Is that you?"

"Yes, kitten." Judson Gold let fly a laugh and the floor rocked with the vibrations. "I'm your daddy. I'm just going to phone some of your mommies to come over and play with us tonight. More is better, don't you think, kitten?"

Kit smiled to herself, with lips that slid all over her face. Mommy was coming. All would be well.

──────── *Chapter 21* ────────

WHEN THERE CONTINUED to be no answer at Kit's end, Aden became by turns fractious, relieved—and then, vaguely alarmed.

No matter what he might personally think of Kit Daniels, she was a hard worker. If she promised to have her manuscript in by Monday, she would have it in. And he knew there was enough last-minute work to keep her busy at home all evening.

He felt sure she would not have gone out for any extended period tonight, unless there was some emergency.

Suddenly, Aden's head was full of thoughts of Gold and his five wives, who were not only excellent friends, but who also occasionally liked to get together for a cozy ménage. Everyone in the industry knew about the chic orgies they staged in that quiet townhouse in Chelsea.

Everyone but that lamb chop, Kit Daniels!

Aden was up like a shot. He grabbed his wallet and his keys.

As a writer, Judson Gold was a magnificent phenomenon. As a man, he was an amoral omnivore.

Aden rushed from the apartment, fearing for Kit, not sure why he even cared.

Once again, Kit's fantasies had failed her.

Certainly, she had expected to be a *femme* on her feet, flirting, *fatale,* and more or less awake when the time came for dancing on ceilings and other forms of romantic ecstasy.

In the end, she was to be drugged and forced onto the Procrustean bed of one man's (and five other women's) erotic imaginations.

Kit's head felt big as a toy balloon and just as light.

She wondered what was keeping her pinned down to the floor of the treehouse. A dull thudding of mallets that had originated in her vertebrae now inched its way up to her temples and settled behind the ears.

Sour notes of alarm came rushing in with it.

She wanted her body back. She wanted the floor, solid ground bumping up against her feet. Her head floated up on its string. She forced her eyes down, toward the tiny, faraway patch of floor. Her eyes hurt, but she was rewarded.

For there she saw Aden—could it be Aden?—bursting into the room and crying out a challenge to her father.

Her father laughed again, a laugh that reverberated through her skull and set her teeth on edge.

Aden was climbing up the shaky ladder. A soft beigey arrow shot out from his body. Her father was toppling back. She was hanging on to Aden as he brought her down, down to earth.

Later, in her own bed, she'd curled up in Aden's arms and cried and cried because she was only a naive, father-loving little girl, after all.

She told him about her family, about Mallory and Maddy. He said he understood. Then left her to cry alone.

Straggling up above the Gramercy Park rooftops the next morning, the sun looked as bloodshot and ragged as Kit Daniels felt.

Afraid to look, she'd half expected to find Aden Lassiter beautifically asleep on the pillow beside her.

She half hoped he would be.

But of course, he was too smart for that: she was volatile, out of control. Once he'd opened himself to her and she'd refused the gift. He would never trust his heart with her now . . . Nor should he.

She checked the calendar, blooming with summer fields, on her bedroom door. She was expected at a literary brunch at the Crystal Room at Tavern on the Green.

Kit groaned from the heart. All she wanted was to curl up into a sheepish ball and sleep the summer—and its fevers—away.

Then she remembered: she had to go; Aden would be there, waiting for signs of a change. She owed him. She caught a glimpse of her manuscript on the night table and groaned again. She'd be late with it after all.

In a somber mood, she dressed in black, hoping it would convey her new sobriety.

When she felt reasonably ready to face the world (she was sure everyone knew about her sulfurous night with Judson Gold) she went downstairs. She poked around in her mailbox and came up with a yellow mailgram.

With a sense of foreboding, she inserted her nail under the flap, tore the paper, and read. Whereupon she was kicked in the metaphorical head.

Kit Daniels arrived half an hour later at the six-million-dollar sheepcote turned dazzler in Central Park. Outside, the rustic tavern was adrift in greenery. Its chic insides sparkled with crystal and brass.

In an emotional blur, Kit was shown to a room where the cocktail party was already in full swing. Lois Shoor Mallon, heiress and literary groupie, was playing hostess.

"Darling, we thought you would never get here. Tootie Helfmayer was playing the piano with her eyes closed. As our dear Dee-a-na Vreeland might say, it was just too divine!"

Kit felt she had fallen down the rabbit hole once again. She regarded Lois calmly, while in fact, she was a hair's breadth away from grabbing her by her tanned, ultrathin, rich-lady's arm—breadsticks, overtoasted, came to mind—and shake her until some sort of sense rattled up through her neurons to her lacquered head . . . *Judson Gold, your literary God, is a wolf in lion's clothing. What have male writers to do with us anyway? Either their heroes are in flight from suffocating mothers—or in pursuit of mysterious mistresses, between whose thighs lie the answers to the existential questions . . . Well, where do we find the answers to our questions? Who will bear our emptiness? No one, because in the end, we all believe a woman's lot is misery, self-sacrifice, the love that consumes . . .*

She caught herself just in time, haunted by the sense that life meant to tell her something important—between Maddy's breakdown, Mallory's unasked-for advice, the Judson Gold nightmare—Aden—and now the bombshell of a letter this very morning. But like a child who hasn't yet learned her ABCs, she pored over the signs to no avail.

"The spinach quiche is fine, darling, but don't touch the tortellini." Lois's fishbone face swam into view. "Oh, listen to me! You can tell I eat like a horse." She patted her concave tummy.

A horse indeed! Kit's stout inner voice rose up in outraged femininity, in anguish.

Since she'd given up the sulfurous sizzle of French fries, the sharp pitch of salt, the red devils of pepperpot, wine sauce, chili con carne, for the moral beatitudes of dieting—what had she left?

Kit felt the old glass wall come crashing down between her and the other woman, the familiar split in consciousness she used to suffer when she was still a "fat girl" trying to pass among "normal" people.

She made a last-ditch effort to pull herself together for the party.

Meek now, she let Lois Shoor Mallon lead her to the buffet table, while Tootie Helfmayer played Michael Jackson's "Beat It" with her eyes closed. All around her, there were ice sculptures in the shapes of swans and geese. There were carved roasts, Cornish hens, smoked hams drifting in Hawaiian pineapples. Here, a dip into condiments, neon-bright in

227

Christmas reds and greens. There, a celebration of silver serving dishes heaped high with wild rice, and gilded bowls full of Chinese vegetables!

All the while, guests were buzzing around the white-clothed table like bees around a hive, and suddenly, Kit felt dizzy in the presence of so much food. The table seemed to exert a heavy, gravitational pull, like a high-density planet in outer space. Kit flashed to the letter she'd received this morning. *You can't leave me in the dark like this, Mommy. We haven't finished, you and I . . .*

Then, as if her mother's news were not upsetting enough, Kit spotted Aden Lassiter, with his steady hand barely touching the small of a female back. She looked again, just to make sure she'd got it right. There they were at the bank of high windows. Kit stood very still, watching, branding into memory.

She was a precious brunette, with a curve of sugary white shoulders and endless neck. Geraldine Cutler, of course.

Good for Aden, Kit thought with a self-effacing shock. He was finally doing something smart for himself! She broke away from Lois and the tidal pull of the lunch buffet and wandered down toward the file of windows. She just wanted to thank Aden for showing up last night before she veered off into oblivion. Due to her arch stupidity, her impoverished romantic fantasies, she could kiss Aden Lassiter good-bye.

Kit watched Geraldine touch Aden as she spoke, flitting expertly with her darting, butterfly hands. Anyone could see they were lovers again. Kit looked away . . .

It would have been so easy for Aden to exploit her terrible need, her dire confusion last night. Almost any other man might have tried—even though she was not ready to be touched. Instead, he had championed her female cause without asking for anything important in return.

Kit felt surprised by Aden, regarded him with new respect.

"Lassiter?" She stepped forward in her imagination. "I love you." He stood at attention in his French-gray midsummer-weight suit, a subtly colored peach shirt, and silver flash of tie. His hair flamed with energy. The ridiculously long lashes behind the gold frames gave a demure look to the spare architecture of his face.

Had he always been that vulnerable around the eyes?

Did he always dish out such an eager, unruly smile when she was near?

Standing in front of that sunny window, he seemed to blaze with male beauties she'd never really caught sight of before. She remembered with her muscles, on her skin, the animal feel of his arms around her last night, and wanted to howl for all the lost chances at love.

But if her heart ached with gratitude for him, she was furious too!

Furious that he had shown her up for what she was: a clown, and not at all the sophisticated lady who never lost her cool. Face it, she'd always been a clown. By definition, a "fat woman" is a figure of fun, sexless, cut off from all hope of romance. That was why she'd always laughed it out of her system, heckled it away, before she forgot herself and started to hope too much.

But there was still time to do something fine and unselfish for once in her life. To play the clown no more. She had not yet been spotted by Aden and his lover.

Quietly, Kit slipped out of the busy Crystal Room.

The cable this morning had invited her to Marva's wedding in Rome.

She'd always wanted to revisit Rome.

PART IV

Daughter

─────── *Chapter 22* ───────

IT WAS AN untried tenet of Kit Daniels' that overseas travel should, ideally, only be undertaken after sufficient rest and psychological preparation. As it turned out, she'd enjoyed neither of these things when she boarded her TWA night flight to Rome, en route to Marva's wedding.

Her attempts at slumber were consistently blocked by the image of Aden Lassiter caressing his lover the day before.

And then there was the Medusa's head of her mother, waiting to turn her to stone at the end of her flight.

An abyss of childhood memories opened up in her head. She knew she would spend the rest of her journey—perhaps her life—trying not to fall in.

As the motors hummed, the stale air wafted around her seat, bearing the unmistakable smell of an airline cabin.

Before long, the flight attendants brought artificial morning into the hushed first-class cabin, snapping up the stunted window shades, serving out glasses of orange juice and cheery matutinal greetings.

Kit observed her fellow passengers with some envy, as,

one-by-one, they awoke from sleep, their eyes pooling in bewilderment at first and then relaxing into recognition of their whereabouts. She envied them their yawns, their low blood sugar, even their momentary disorientation.

Anyone could tell she hadn't slept all night. Her hair felt gritty, her clothes unkempt, as though she'd been rolling across gravel all night along.

With an effort of will, she rose to go to the rest room, where she splashed cold water over her face and brushed her teeth until the gums shone pink and bled. Feeling a bit better, she faced out the remainder of the trip by boning up on her Italian, which was poor.

Then the plane rumbled into its touchdown, smack in the middle of a Roman candle of a day. Marva *would* choose the sweltering height of summer to wed her count . . . Kit's matriphobia was coming to a boil.

The noonday sun was like a great Augustan coin suspended in the sky, as she ducked into the air-conditioned terminal at Leonardo da Vinci Airport.

There was the usual bureaucratic quagmire at customs, and then she was nervously riding an air-washed Mercedes to her mother's house in the pastoral Monte Mario section of Rome.

Predictably stalled in the madcap Roman traffic, Kit removed the straw hat from her head to place it in her lap. She always wore straw hats in Europe. Her mother had favored them, and like Mrs. Trewhitt, believed a woman wasn't properly dressed unless she wore a hat. As the fluid, orchid-colored halter dress pooled around her knees, she wished it were cool water.

From the window, Kit saw the golden churches rising like rock-crystal caverns in the distance. The last time she was here she'd been ten years old and accompanied by both her parents. It was also the last time she'd remembered their behaving like a normal family.

Kit rapped on the plexiglass divider. She signaled to the rakishly mustached driver that she'd like the air conditioner turned up.

He shrugged. *"Non posso, non posso, signorina."*

She slumped back into her seat, finding it increasingly hard to pull in breath. The same thing had happened to the ten-year-old Kit. Of course then she hadn't been able to put a name to it. But the thing that oppressed her, that lay on her lungs like a stone, was the sheer weight of the centuries. This decadent city was crowded to bursting with the living and the dead. For beneath the modern Rome lay the ruins of the Baroque. Under the Baroque, the Medieval Rome. Even deeper, Classical Rome. And under that again, the bones of some pagan realm as old as earth itself.

With all this layered karma pressing in upon the car, Kit was almost relieved to pull up in front of her mother's melon-colored house.

At least there would be a kind of rest, and something cool to drink, if not a warm, maternal welcome.

A trim figure in a yellow cotton dress met Kit on the steps. One of those smooth-faced European women of a certain age, she introduced herself as the housekeeper, Signora Gruccio. Her hair was the iridescent blue black of folded wings, parted severely down the middle and tucked into a bun. Her eyes were carved and deep-set like a Greek mask.

"*Benvenuto*, Signorina Daniels," she said, without feeling the necessity to smile. "Your mama is"—she hesitated, testing the words—"at the shops. She asked me to welcome you."

The chauffeur was already coming around with Kit's bags and chugging up the steps.

Signora Gruccio waved her hand. "This way, Signorina."

They moved from the intensity of the Roman sunlight into the cool mysteries of her mother's house.

There was black and marble everywhere. A black lacquer living room. Black marble dining table. A sculptural bowl holding herbs straight from the garden.

Even the bathroom, with its sunken tub flanked by wonderful eighteenth-century French terra-cotta sphinxes, was done in black marble.

For what, Kit wondered, was her mother in mourning?

It was not expected. She had always imagined her mother moving in sunlight, freely, like a bird of paradise.

Kit followed Signora Gruccio upstairs, where the stark

contemporary drama of the downstairs rooms gave way to more traditional colors and decor. The bedroom assigned to Kit was Second Empire, its bed hung with specially designed trophies of ribbon-threaded lace over azure brocade. The needlework carpets that covered the floor were laid one upon another for luxury. There were carved stone swags over the door, which led to the rooftop terrace.

Imagine, with the housing mania in Rome, Marva had outdone everyone by acquiring both a garden *and* a terrace!

Typical. And exquisite.

Cream-colored damask from Venice swathed the walls. Multiple sofas stood richly dressed in their nineteenth-century Turkish brocade, embroidered with white silk. A rare Regency *bureau plat* in black shone with gilded decoration. Each flawless detail served to create an atmosphere of tasteful elegance: the hallmark of Marva Chance Daniels. Kit was drawn back to the past. She was ten years old again, in love with her mother.

As she walked through a white coffered door into the sky-blue sitting room, decorated with old valentines and blue glass that broke the sunlight into prisms, Kit thought how pleasant it might be to stay here. Pleasant, that is, had she been invited for any other reason than her mother's second marriage . . .

She'd already promised herself to leave the instant the wedding took place. It was only a week away. Where she would go from there—seeing as how the mere thought of Manhattan cast up haunting images of Aden Lassiter—Kit couldn't tell.

Before the Regency wall mirror, Kit removed her hat and placed it on the gilded bureau.

A face came into the mirror, a long, positively elegant face, with the Dietrich eyebrows and the fairy pouf of silver-blond waves.

Marva was carrying a French blue-mesh shopping bag filled with fresh vegetables and fruits. She put it down at her feet, turning even that homely act into a marvel of grace.

"I came up as soon as I heard you were here." Her arms went out.

Kit moved into them with a will grown stiff with the years.

Her mother, as always, was cool to the touch, scented with Violetta di Parma water. It was one of Marva's many affectations—all primed to give off an aura of intense fragility. Young Kit had concluded from this that Marva had been too fragile to be a mother, and that it was somehow Kit's fault.

Marva held her at arm's length. "My God, Kit, I hardly recognized you. I had no idea."

"And she does her own marketing too." Kit assumed the bright malice of the gossip columnist. She hated being a prop in Marva's self-mythologizing. "What happened—did the cook quit?" As usual, she wanted to sting the bird of paradise into a show of feeling, any feeling for her daughter.

"No, of course not. I wanted to do the marketing myself today. I'm making all your favorite foods. Eggplant parmigian, you always loved eggplant parmigian . . ."

"That was when I was ten years old, Marva. I'm not ten years old anymore."

"Darling, I'd hoped you'd gotten over this 'Marva' business."

"I will if you will."

Marva's face wore a look of pain. "You're still trying to break my heart, Kit. When is that going to be over?"

Kit faced the bureau and picked up one of the cobalt-blue vases, turning it over in her hands as though she would study it in detail. But she only wanted to hide the tears that had rushed up from some secret childhood well to stand in her eyes. Marva didn't deserve to see them; not a drop. She'd forfeited that right a long time ago. "You spoke to Daddy?"

"Yes—we're very good friends."

"Isn't it amazing what a little divorce can do."

"Your father is well." Marva picked up her mesh bag and held it, as if it were a baby, to her chest, with two hands crossed over the bundle. "He's remarried, you know, and living in Palm Beach. Maregate's been sold."

"I'm not interested, Marva. He cut me out of his life a long time ago."

"I know he did. I was sorry to hear that. But I understand

you've done quite well for yourself. As it turned out, you didn't need that money . . ."

Kit turned to her mother, her hands behind her back, resting, for strength, on the *bureau plat*. "My God, you don't know me at all, do you, Marva?"

"You're tired, Kit." She pushed back a wisp of bright hair, managing to make the effects of fatigue and humid weather on a woman into a physical poem. In spite of herself, Kit was full of fierce admiration. "Why don't you freshen up, and we'll meet for dinner? It'll be just the two of us tonight. And then tomorrow, you can meet Paolo."

"Your chauffeur? I've met him already."

"My fiancé, the Count di Rispoli."

"Are you sure he's not a chauffeur?"

"He comes from a very old family, Kit. I've been to their palazzo in Pisaro."

"Which he's opened to tourists . . ." A warning bell went off in Kit's head. Despite the long, bitter years, the stubborn, rooted resentments that had grown up between them, this was still her mother, and she could see the shadow of danger cast by this gigolo so clearly, as though it were a fin cutting through the crystal-blue water of a reef.

"I can't say I understand why you're choosing to be childish about my marriage, Kit. But since you are choosing it, I suggest we cut this conversation short and prepare for dinner." Her withdrawal left an emotional vacuum in the room.

Kit's nerve turned. Made weak by the barrage of childhood conflicts that hung in the air of her mother's house, she sank onto the magnificent bed. She wanted to fly right back home.

An hour later, when Kit reluctantly went down to dinner, she expected stilted conversation and Marva's rabbit-food inventions.

What she found was a mother who, almost from the moment she'd caught sight of her newly defleshed daughter, had begun, unconsciously, trying to feed her.

That night, it was only cold antipasto, shrimp scampi, and zabaglione with fresh strawberries for dessert. But for the entire, frantic week before the wedding, Kit could expect to be plied with dishes fit for a Holy Roman empress. For lunch the chef would come up with one of his impeccably simple pizzas—flavored with rock salt and heaps of fresh rosemary. Homemade apricot gelati, wreathed with mint, turned up for a midafternoon cooler. Panzeroni, a crisp, butterfly pastry filled with a creamy mixture of mozzarella, basil, and tomato haunted the rooms in Monte Mario with its delirious aroma.

Despite her rigorous schedule of fittings and powwows with the florist and the chef, the bride was somehow never too busy to stop by the kitchen and have some celestial cream pastry or succulent sausage and pepper collation sent to her daughter's room for a late-night snack.

And Kit, who had little to fill her time, was now besieged by expertly prepared, exotically tempting Italian food. She woke up every morning in terror that today would be the day the black hole would open up again, and pull her, helpless, in . . .

As if this weren't enough to send Kit Daniels' weight spiraling, all her uncharitable fears about Paolo di Rispoli were soon confirmed. Marva's "friends" were all too eager to gossip about the young di Rispoli—possessed of a blindingly white, three-story Renaissance palazzo, and very little else. The family coffers were as empty as his words of love.

Kit was lounging on her mother's terrace, the future site of the wedding reception, amid the pots of vivid pink petunias and faded mauve hydrangeas. She poured another glass of Chianti. It was her second day in the Eternal City, and still much too hot for sightseeing.

Suddenly, she felt something soft brush against her lips. She tipped up her sun visor, leveling into the liquid gaze of a young man dressed, poetically, in white.

He was intent on brushing the petals of a long-stemmed red rose against her mouth.

"Sweets for the sweet," he said in a soft-as-roses accent. "A line from an English play. Everyone think it means, how do you say it, bonbons? But in the play, the character is talking about *fiori*, flowers, no?"

239

"Yes." Feeling disadvantaged by her position, she sat bolt upright. She gave her hand to the young man. "You must be Paolo?"

He displeased her by kissing it. *"Sì.* And you are the *bella ragazza* I have heard so much about."

"My mother told you about me?"

"Certo. She talks of little else."

The man was an outrageous flatterer. He had a double-stitch row of pearl-button teeth that showed more or less continuously as he talked. His hair was slicked back, a dramatic black lacquer, to match Marva's decor, no doubt. His lines were quite limpid and quite correct, like a fine showhorse. He was very nervous.

After ensconcing himself in a fretted pink metal chair beside Kit's chaise longue, he leaned over to trail the corolla of the rose down one of her tan, bare legs.

"Why is it, *che cosa,* that American women always have these extraordinary long legs? You are made like a designer's first, most exquisite draft."

"You're marrying my mother for her money." Kit gave him a blunt stare, meant to intimidate.

He looked genuinely puzzled. "Yes, of course. But I hope that will not keep you and me from being friends."

Marva swept out from the house loaded down with last-minute bundles. She stood radiant as any first-time bride in the sunshine.

Kit was still mesmerized by her every movement.

She glanced over to the young man who had just been toying with the seduction of his future stepdaughter. He too seemed genuinely captivated by Marva. But how long would that state of affairs last? She was twice his age, and very tired . . .

Marva leaned forward to caress Paolo's handsome face. Her mother glittered like something left over from Eden. And why not? Her heart, at least, was as hard as a diamond. Perhaps only one just like it could scratch its surface. Now she would spend the rest of her life in a crumbling Italian villa with only a gigolo husband and the illusion of passion to keep her.

Kit hardened her heart. It was, after all, what Marva so richly deserved: a woman who had peddled those very illusions on glossy paper, the male-made distractions of romantic love, of heartless sensuality, of ideal "womanhood." It was on such cheap, papery images that Kit Daniels had been nourished, and left starving for more, oh God, so much more . . .

Now and then, when the brutal Roman winter shouldered through the drafty chimneys and she was stalled between the distractions of titled houseguests and trips abroad, somewhere in the cold place between sleeplessness and dawn, Marva Chance Daniels di Rispoli might feel the true gravity of her emptiness and go seeking release in her lonely, only daughter, way out at the far corners of tribal memory and desperate hope.

But by then it would be too late to reclaim Kit, who'd already been taught by experts just how to escape from those she most loved.

"Aren't you cold like that, Kit? The air may be humid but it's very breezy out here on the terrace . . ." Her mother raised her hands to her narrow hips.

Kit turned pink in the face. As though she were a dirty little girl, like all other little girls, plotting to attract Paolo's attention—just because she had on her raggy old shorts!

For the rest of the endless week, Kit tried to stay out of the bride and groom's way. She volunteered for trips to the shops of the Via Condotti and took her meals, when possible, in the sharply lit, noisy cafes, where she met other American tourists and exchanged pieces of homey nostalgia over glasses of anisette and espresso.

For hours on end, she would dream of Aden Lassiter and what might have been if he'd been less patient with love—and she more.

She concluded, those warm Roman nights, that, for better or for worse, she was trapped in her dance of otherness, always different from the rest, always the odd woman out.

She used to think her relationships with men had failed because she was fat, unlovable, out of touch with the world and its wonder. But then why hadn't she and Aden Lassiter

241

worked it out—now that she was thin? She ran her hand over the curve of thigh beneath her silk jacquard dress as though to reassure herself of its size. Sometimes she still gave herself twice the room she needed to pass another pedestrian on a narrow street. The fleshy woman was always there; Kit carried her on her back, in her mirror, angry and unredeemed by her physical body's transfiguration.

How to release her, and be free at last to embrace her life, the exiled princess no more?

────Chapter 23────

Tʜᴇ sᴋʏ ᴡᴀs a sharp Mediterranean blue. The wedding guests were an intimate few, milling about on Marva's storybook terrace with its irregularly-shaped swimming pool at the foot of a sloping green lawn.

Knee-deep in billows of pink roses and Parma violets, servants in starched white jackets served a saturnalian menu. To begin with: fresh oysters (oysters, Paolo had said, are always very, very good for you) shucked on the spot, a huge straw basket piled high with fried shrimp, fish, and breaded olives stuffed with meat and balls of cream.

Then pasta tagliatelli and meat-filled cappelletti in a sauce of mushrooms, cheese, and butter, were lifted hot from a giant, scooped-out chunk of Parmesan. Steaks, sausages, giant mushrooms, meat and seafood brochettes, as well as piadina—those flaky rounds of bread—were being grilled on the barbecue, to be washed down with toasts of fruity sangría and Italian champagne.

For the finale—Kit knew the caloric litany by heart, as the chef had been preparing it for days—there was crème brulée, chocolate custard puffs, and homemade gelati in five flavors —watermelon, canteloupe, fig, strawberry, and raspberry— to supplement the star dessert, *bostrengo,* a wedding cake from Pisaro with polenta on the outside and the soft glow of fresh fruit on the inside.

After the civil ceremony, during cocktails, the guests sat upon cushioned straw mats, sipping from enormous Venetian-glass tumblers and breathing in the fragrance of the marjoram, mint, basil, and oregano planted along the edge of the patio. For them, the wedding was a Roman dream.

For the daughter of the bride, it was a nightmare.

From the moment Kit stepped onto the terrace in her straw hat and eyelet chemise, she'd come under siege on two fronts. From within, by dint of the sheer variety and volume of the wedding feast—from without, by young Paolo di Rispoli, her new stepfather.

In self-defense, Kit tried to fill up on carrot sticks and, when she thought Paolo wasn't looking, finally stole off, as unobtrusively as possible, toward the glassy blue shimmer of the swimming pool at the garden's edge.

But the Conti di Rispoli was not far behind.

He was resplendent in tropical linen, with a white fedora, encircled by a slim silk band, on his head. With his swarthy skin and chocolate eyes, he was a classic figure of seduction, a mockery to Kit of her mother's wedding day.

He came up behind her and touched her shoulder with cool fingers.

She turned with a start. "What are you doing here?"

"What are you?" He spoke with his soft vowels and sinuous consonants, trying to wrap her up, take her away.

She held her hat with one hand against the brisk breeze that rose to where the sun-washed terrace clung on the ancient heights of the city. "Congratulations on your wedding day." She said this knowing he was impervious to irony. She felt ridiculous because he was.

"Cara," he sang into her ear, with warm, champagne-sweet breath, "have you considered what delight, what unimaginable bliss it would be for me to have both the mother and the daughter?"

Once Kit might have responded to him with utter outrage, or even a burst of laughter, but she had only to look at the young man—his viperish handsomeness, his greedy eyes, to feel nothing but loss and sadness for them all.

The wind ran through the line of yew trees with the sound of crashing surf.

Maybe she could be tolerant of the man because she was old friends with the greedy child inside herself. It was the stubborn child, after all, who'd brought her to Judson Gold. "My mother will be looking for you," Kit said.

"Kit!" He held out his long, lovely hands in supplication. "Are you sure? If you are concerned about your mother . . . I know she wouldn't mind."

"What did you say?" Kit didn't know if the rushing sound in her ears was from the high wind or the blood come to pound in her temples.

She recalled then what Maddy had said to her in the hospital after Samantha was born. "It's a lie." She hadn't understood it then, it was still too big to be fully understood, but part of the lie that entangled millions and millions of women every day was the notion that there is an easy answer for what goes on between men and women. That any perfected image of yourself is protection from the pain. Here she'd kept the pounds off for two whole years, and all her furies were still with her!

She still didn't know how to be loved. Still attracted Judson Golds and Paolo di Rispolis instead of men.

She still hadn't learned how to live.

In fact, being so small only made her feel more vulnerable to the plots of men, to sexual demands, to emotional baitings and buffetings. She had no girth to cushion her from devastating blows, from little men like these . . .

Kit began to run, she needed to run, toward the tall bank of swaying trees. Her skirts whipped against her legs in the wind.

When she couldn't run anymore—she was shaking so—the ground rose to meet her, and the tears overflowed from the dark childhood well; she wouldn't dam them anymore. The hunger came upon her, in the old way, multiplied like yeast cells inside her, and she began to crave, with the rage of body and soul, the cream cakes, the juice-ladled sides of beef, the aromatic breads with which the kitchen had been filling up for days. They'd been rising in a carnal ascension, pushing out the walls of the house, seeking her black mouth . . .

Oh my God, what was happening to her! Panic stopped up her heart. She knew it was a dead end, knew in advance the stale taste that would be left in the soul after the orgy. She knew the dense, dull thingness of whole boxes of crackers gobbled down, their cellophane sustenance a disappointment every time. The sugared nausea of Napoleons and eclairs. The bloated retreat after the binge. She knew all this and yet . . .

She cast about in a frenzy for berries on the bushes, nuts on the ground, anything she could cram into the volcano's mouth . . .

In the end, she pulled up the grass of the lawn in clumpfuls and swallowed them down. She lay facedown on the earth, her hands curled into the grass, like the hair of a woman. As always, her emotional instincts had been right: to be nurtured by the mother, by the earth. As always, her body had chosen the wrong food, the indigestible, the poisonous . . . The old disharmony within her left Kit sick to her stomach on her mother's manicured lawn.

"*Sta bene*, Paolino." Marva caressed her husband's hand, where a gold band had been newly placed. She seemed incapable of being anywhere near him without touching him. "I'll explain everything to her. You must go back to our guests."

Kit overheard the tender exchange as if from across a stretch of ocean. For her, the words had the kind of heightened clarity of sounds borne across the water.

Marva's soft footfalls came toward her.

Her mother was wearing a white brocade chemise from the twenties, a long rope of white pearls, and a cloche hat with a gilt fan of rose pinned to one side.

She was unearthly, white and gold like an archangel in the old illuminations. Her face was unbearably bright . . . She

246

knelt down to the ground and lifted Kit into her arms. "Hush, my darling, my baby girl, there is nothing to cry about . . . you are safe here with me." On her knees, she rocked Kit, until she'd stopped weeping.

"Marva . . . Mother . . . you've made a terrible mistake."

"Shh." Her mother's voice floated on the wind above Kit's head, a sound sweet and clear as the song of a flute. "I know what Paolo has said to you. Is it really so bad to be desired by a beautiful young man?"

Kit sat up so that she could stare into her mother's eyes. "You don't understand. He is disloyal to you."

"He is not disloyal. He is young, Kit, and we have . . . an agreement."

Kit felt a wave of dizziness. She let it pass, digging her nails into the earth to ground herself. "Do you mean to say that to hold a man here you would give him your daughter?"

"Kit, you are such a child! You or another, what matter, as long as he returns to me? In fact, it is better if you are the object of his desire. This way, he will never stray very far."

Kit struggled out of her mother's embrace; she felt filthy. "Marva, he's using you."

Her mother turned her exquisite face in profile. "Yes. But it can't be helped. I want him, you see." Now she was pleading for understanding, pleading with those famous eyes.

Kit felt a serpentine fire shoot up her spine—fury, it was, fury and bereavement for all women who worshiped men. She and Marva, they were not so different after all. "You want to be used? Is that what you're saying? You want to be used?"

"Perhaps." Marva brushed off her immaculate skirt and came to her feet. In the rawness of the sun's glare, Kit was surprised to notice that her mother was no longer young. "I don't put a name to it. I only know that when he loves me, I feel alive. The rest of the time I'm like someone who's been buried up to the neck in sand. I feel nothing."

Kit raised her knees and folded her arms over them, in a protective circle. She leaned into her hand, almost dreamily. "Why don't you let me take you home to Daddy?"

"This is my home. And your father and I live better—more sanely—without each other. Kit, you don't understand. Paolo makes things hard for me . . . interesting. It's what I need."

A confused, frightened child again, Kit listened to her mother. What had Aden said the night she'd met Judson Gold? "What belongs to you, comes to you." No wonder she was terrified by Marva's harsh self-portrait: buried up to the neck. She was her mother's daughter. She would be buried too.

"I don't know why I'm so surprised," Kit cried out against the fear. "You were never a mother to me. Why should you start acting like one now?"

"Oh no, you're not going to do this to me." Her mother spoke with the first anger she'd shown since Kit's arrival in Rome. Kit's own anger was driven out by her need to understand. What woman is glad to leave her own girlhood behind? What woman is ready for the shock of a child—a daughter—on her system, her secret plans? A daughter drains a mother of her vitality. She takes her youth and mars her beauty. And then, later on, when a mother is most vulnerable, in middle age, a daughter bests her—younger, more beautiful than she ever was. No wonder they must learn not to hate where they love . . .

Still Kit was up on her feet now, hands clenched at her sides. "You criticized, you cut at me, you never made me feel welcome in this world."

"For the love of God, Kit!" Her mother cast her eyes down. "Let me go!"

Kit stared at her mother, as if for the first time. The single shocking fact was that her mother was as needy as she.

This changed everything.

Kit stood quietly, face-to-face with her mother, watching, waiting for certain things to come clear, like the light moving on the water after a violent storm; in the hunger that had gripped her, she was just carrying out her mother's unconscious wish. As long as Kit was weak, her mother could be strong. As long as she was imperfect, her mother could breathe perfection. With sheer force of will, Kit pushed back the ravenous thing inside her, one more time.

In the clear sunlight of a wedding day, the daughter saw the mother: with a new understanding that passed beyond old grudges, old disappointments, old competition, old pain.

Awkwardly, slowly, Kit closed her arms around her mother, sealing their passionate connection as women, and thus as mutual tormenters. She could probably never forgive the mother for not loving the daughter enough. But she could let her go.

"It's all right, Mother. You can go." She thought she'd said it to herself, deep inside, where no one could hear. But Marva did.

"I knew that," Marva said. "Yes."

They broke the embrace.

---------- *Chapter 24* ----------

ADEN LASSITER SAT alone in a rehearsal room littered with paper coffee cups. His olive wool fedora was slanted over one eye, leaving his bright face in eclipse. His long legs were propped up before him along the varnish-smelling wood floor, as though he would hold off a critical world. Although he was stock still, the air around his head rippled with waves of tension.

Plymouth Rocks was going to be a flop. They weren't ready for Broadway.

"We'll go back and try her out of town." The producer, Thomas Wyeth Gregory, a beefy man with a straw-colored cloud of hair floating above a face of midwestern calm, came back in, brandishing a notebook. "We'll tell the papers it's for rewrites."

"Oh boy, now that's original! It *is* for rewrites."

"And for recasting. Germaine isn't working, Aden. Germaine never works."

Aden threw up his hands. "Damn it, Tom, don't you think I know?"

A few of the actors straggled back across the highly glossed floor, to pick up an article of clothing here, a plastic hairbrush there. Swilling half-finished cans of Diet Coke, they conversed in low, mournful voices, as though they were at the wake of a distant acquaintance. They raised their hands in farewell salutes and left, discreetly, for lunch.

"Aden, Germaine's got to go."

"No!" Aden jumped up with such ferocious energy that he toppled his folding chair. "She's the heart of the play. That's like a surgeon saying, 'Let's tear the patient's heart out.'"

"Okay, okay, there's no need to snarl!" Tom sighed. Aden, who had started out so easygoing for a playwright, had turned into a tantrum-throwing tyrant over the last few months. It had to be a woman. That poet he was always curled around?

He snapped his notebook shut. "I hate to be the one to tell you, but the patient's heart ain't beating." He clapped Aden on the back, cordially. "So sleep on it. I'll book another out-of-town run. Newport maybe."

Aden glared—but made no protest. Postponement was breath. Time was life.

It was a supernaturally bright afternoon outside the rehearsal hall. The time was early fall when the mind is supposed to be clear as glass. His was more like glue.

As usual, Aden had plans with a lady for lunch. Having renounced Kit Daniels and all her wiles, he was so emotionally well disciplined now. Disillusion ran through him like electricity and gave him the charisma of indifference. Women had been flocking to him, even more than usual. There was no more talk of marriage.

In his shaving mirror, he didn't like what he saw.

He headed for the phone booth in the lobby. The quarter chimed. The call went through.

"Hello? Hold on a sec. I've got to turn off the damn computer."

He heard the rumble of a chair being dragged back.

She got back on, breathily. "Sorry. Hi, again. By the way, who is this?"

"It's Aden. How about lunch?"

Kit's heart stammered. "Yes. All right. Fine." She'd been

home from Rome for three months now, had purposely been giving Aden Lassiter a wide berth. Sent her work downtown by messenger. Discussed any textual changes with the father, instead of the son. She was miserable, because for Aden and Kit, it was too late.

Or was it?

"Where are we going?"

"To the park. Do you know where the statue of Hans Christian Andersen is?"

"Yes."

"Meet me there."

"But what about Geraldine?"

"Geraldine?"

"Will she be coming?"

"Of course not. I haven't seen Geraldine since Tootie Helfmayer played Michael Jackson on the piano. With her eyes closed."

Steady, girl, Kit warned herself. This doesn't mean a thing. He would still be better off with almost any other female on earth than he would be with you. Together, you're like cherry bombs on the Fourth of July—at any moment one of you might blow.

"But what about food?" Kit bit her lip. She could never be casual about mealtimes, especially after her breakdown at Marva's wedding.

"I'll take care of it. Just be there."

She dressed in a nubby-textured overshirt of olive chambray, layered over a cardigan sweater and a buttondown cotton blouse in graph-paper squares. Her swoop of pants were linen and cotton with a side slash of pockets and full-sail legs. The fedora in "driftwood," as Mallory might call it, and a coral knit necktie completed the funky picture. She'd gone in heavily for the menswear look this fall. Until now, she hadn't realized how heavily! She felt unwieldy, like a moon-walker.

By the time she arrived at the foot of the statue, Aden was already waiting. An old white willow picnic hamper was slung over his arm. He was tapping his foot. He was decked out in an outfit almost identical to hers. As the afternoon blazed crisp green, orange, and gold around them, she had the feeling that something extraordinary was about to happen.

"You took your sweet time," he said, out of sorts. "What were you doing—shearing the sheep?"

"Five minutes is not considered advance notice in polite circles," she snapped back, "for anyone over twelve."

"Well, damn it, Kit, you still *dress* like a child." He glared at her.

"You liked it well enough when you bought it!"

He glanced down at his costume and colored red.

"Let's go," he said through gritted teeth. He tramped over the grass and she, after a moment's hesitation, clambered after him.

Aden seemed headed away from the radio-hefting teens and the skaters gliding by on plastic wheels.

At length, he settled on a reasonably sunny place beside a gnarled old maple tree. Without looking at her, he lifted a blue-and-white-checked bistro tablecloth from the hamper, snapped it open, and let it float down onto the grass. Other wonders soon appeared from inside the depths of that basket: matching blue-checked napkins, a chilled California Sauterne, long-stemmed glasses and white plates, cold chicken, a long crusty French bread wrapped in a cloth. There were jewel-colored pineapple and cherries in a white ceramic bowl. Droste chocolate for dessert and, to top it all off, a thermos of hot coffee.

He sank down, cross-legged, on the tablecloth.

She stood staring at him with a mixture of affection and uneasiness.

The breeze whooshed through the trees and ruffled his hair until he looked like an unruly boy who needed either a kiss or a slap on the wrist.

"Do you intend to stand all afternoon?" he asked in that tone of intimate irritation that he often adopted with her.

"I'm deciding whether or not you asked me here to do me in among the trees and then dump the goods in Conservatory Pond."

"For God's sake, sit down." He produced a corkscrew and soon the cork leaped out with a pop. He poured the Sauterne, still foaming, into the glasses, licked his finger where the wine had trickled down, and handed one glass to her. "Drink up and shut up." She noticed he poured one for himself, too.

She picked a spot across from him and leaned back into the palm of one hand. Sipping the wine, she shut her eyes. The air was sweet smelling, the sun warm on her back.

Sleepily, she watched the motion of shadows winnowing on the grass, like an underwater current. Aden made up a plate for her and cut the bread. She took the opportunity to study him, through slitted eyes, as he worked the blade.

These were always her best moments with Aden: when he'd cut through the husk of abstractions she threw up around her, with a laugh, with a word, as smoothly as he sliced through the crust of bread.

When they were at peace, she saw him as part of her chorus. They had music to learn together. All at once, she understood why she had yet to meet his gaze for too long. It was like holding a dialogue with the murmurous voices of her deepest soul. It exhausted her.

She used to catch a little of the same curious sensation with Mallory and Maddy before they drifted away from her . . . as though the three of them were fragments of the same entity, as though, alone, each was incomplete—unreadable pieces of a human jigsaw puzzle, a whole person only when they were fitted together.

When he held out a plate, she accepted it with a polite thank-you. They turned the chicken legs daintily between their fingers. They popped cubes of pineapple into their mouths. Out of nervousness, between them, they polished off the bottle of wine.

"I never did congratulate you on your mother's marriage." Aden's tie was unknotted, his hat upended on the blanket. He was pouring the coffee from the thermos into a Dixie cup.

"Thanks."

"Was it very difficult for you? Those things usually are for the children."

"Not in the way you'd expect. I'm used to my parents going off on their own and doing exotic things. I was always third on the list, anyway, sometimes dropping down to fourth or fifth, if there were a pretty new friend, a new car, a new horse . . ."

"I'm sorry." He had a surgical glint in his eyes that Kit remembered from therapy. But right now in the sun with him, it didn't put her off.

"Don't be. I learned a good lesson. About lust."

"Between a man and a woman?"

"No. The lust of a woman for her own life. The need to know how she got from here to there. The lust for female roots."

"Yes. I see." The look faded away and he relaxed again.

"Which brings me to the question . . ." She blew on her coffee then sipped it. "Why am I here with you today?"

"All right, Daniels. Here it is." He paused. "What do you think about coming back to the theater?"

Kit felt a pang of disappointment. Perhaps she'd hoped for some detonation of heat and light.

"Theater? But I've been blackballed from Maine to Juneau by now. My friend with the Mickey Mouse watch will see to that!"

"I'm talking about my own show, *Plymouth Rocks*. We're recasting the part of Germaine."

She watched the sunlight play in his hair, the brilliance of his eyes as he talked to her of his one, his truest love . . . Suddenly, she saw his aura flashing out, a neon yellow. She'd never seen one before, wasn't quite sure she even believed in auras. But she saw Aden's aura.

Aden paused. It had come to him as he'd watched, wincing, that last, deadly rehearsal of *Plymouth Rocks*. It was Kit Daniels he'd craved for the part all along. If she were around, shedding her wild light, he would have a chance to resolve the play. And she could use some of her stark energy to create something fine for herself. "Well, what do you think?"

"You have gray eyes," Kit said suddenly. "Did you know that?"

"Uh, vaguely, yes. But, Daniels, will you do it?"

She closed her eyes again; her back and shoulders felt cool against the tree bark. Broadway, how terrifying! Still, there was something safe about the theater. It was a place to try on psychic disguises, put reality on and off with the flick of a lightboard. She could shelter there in that floodlit lagoon and try to forget how out of control she was, how lost, how much in need of the kind of love she'd once flung back at Aden— what a fool, when you think of it, to be so scandalously proud as that!

He was picking up his picnic things. "We'd better get back. I'm expected at rehearsal this afternoon."

Kit smiled to herself, against the tree. If she wasn't to have his loving friendship, she would take his character, Germaine.

"I don't want any money for this," she told him. "I'll pledge my salary to the children's hospital at Beechwood."

"In that case"—he was grinning at her, quite unexpectedly to both of them—"I'll kick in my royalties from the play. As a kind of good-faith bargain with you."

Each seemed to be listing toward the other in a warm pool of sun, charmed with themselves, at peace for a change.

Aden held out his hand to her, and she, smiling, took it.

To universal delight, the first rehearsal went along splendidly.

The new actress (where had she popped up from? she was almost eerily good) Kit Daniels seemed to breathe life into the sleeping role of Germaine, as none before her had even come close to doing. With some artistic license, she'd shaped the built-in ambivalence of the character into a species of personal charm. Even the costumes seemed to have been lifted from her own private closet.

As for the playwright, if this were the fourteenth century, people might say he'd been bewitched. He danced around Kit Daniels, speaking softly to all, the roaring beast of his ego seemingly tamed by the talented beauty.

Then too, the daily firing off of rewrites became less frenetic and bitter, until one day, they ceased altogether, like cannon salvos on a battlefield, leaving the cast to do their work in an atmosphere of sunlit peace.

For the cast and crew of *Plymouth Rocks,* things had turned around at last, and they faced their Newport run with confidence.

During that charmed period of her life, Kit Daniels woke up every morning with a sense of revelation. As she downed her orange juice and black coffee, she asked herself each day if she could trust this absence of pain, this simple pleasure in life that settled into her spirit like a songbird in a tree.

How could she have foreseen when she said yes in the park that afternoon (was it only a short month ago!) that being so close to Aden Lassiter would be like opening up her front door every day and stepping out into blue space! All her life she'd wanted wings. But whenever she'd tried to launch herself, some new crack in the undercarriage would show up, a stalling of the heart would take place. Again and again she'd come in for a forced landing.

If she pushed off this time, let her feet kick at the highest clouds, would she have to surrender to the dull pull of the earth again?

Maybe her star would shine out from Germaine's depths.

"Beautiful," Gary the director said, bobbing his head, bald at the dome, swagged in gray all the way around. He smiled from stage left. "That was perfect, Kit."

Afterwards, she and Aden had gone to lunch at a Japanese restaurant (the salt comfort of the sea, rice paper, and the rustle of silks) because it had, only a day ago, been consigned to the "outs" column in a major glitter publication and because they always lunched together these days.

"You're the lifeblood of the production," Aden told her, with unabashed admiration. "I can't thank you enough for taking the part."

That was when—if she could date it with any precision— Kit had her crisis of faith. She would not serve him as muse. She would not give her blood. She would speak her mind.

When rehearsals resumed that afternoon, it all began falling apart between them.

Kit picked fights with Aden Lassiter over mostly nothing. She fell back on her old tricks to goad him to anger.

Aden was, by turns, hurt, infuriated, homicidal. He thanked his lucky stars he was not still desperately in love with her, as his foolish old father seemed to believe. But it was only at the technical rehearsal that the magnitude of his problem sank in.

Kit hurried over to the lip of the stage and flung down her script, like a gauntlet in an old movie. "God, that's a stupid line for a woman to say! Nobody talks like that except writing students in the green hills of Vermont!"

"All right now, Kit, we've been over this before." The director took pains to be patient, as did most of the other actors. After all the wrong casting choices, they were glad to have Kit Daniels, bad-girl bitchiness and all. They watched, bewildered, from the sidelines, their minds leaping to the next job.

At first, Aden looked as though he'd been bitten by a rattlesnake. Then, with his play as hostage, he seemed to think the better of it.

"No, wait, Gary, let's ask Ms. Daniels here how she would say it. After all, the theater is a democratic institution."

Kit knew—in that infinitesimal fragment of time it takes to snatch the next thought out of the air—that she'd gone too far. But it was too late to pull back. She'd have to stand her ground.

"As it happens," she said, "I do have some alternatives to this . . . maple syrup, that might be of some use."

Kit went to her saddlebag, backstage, and brought out a raft of rewrites. She handed them to Aden across the proscenium.

Aden pivoted on his heel and stalked out of the rehearsal hall. Newport was only a week away and he could sense the whole glittering superstructure of his young career shiver and sway, in danger of imminent collapse. What had made him believe he could—or should—control Kit Daniels anyway? The woman was a crucible of contradictions! With her, he'd entered the zone of paradox. Working with her was like living with a live volcano in one's own backyard.

He walked through the gray heart of town, without seeing or hearing much of the traffic, the steaming manholes, the clangor of construction around him.

It began to rain in great gusts. He turned up his collar, then ducked into the Gotham Book Mart to dry off.

The Gotham was an old favorite. It invariably soothed him with its dusty smell of university libraries and its quaint sign, WISE MEN FISH HERE. It was just about the best of its kind in New York City.

Automatically, Aden scanned the shelves for the works of his own authors.

Aha, there was one. *The Medieval Bestiary for Children* that he'd helped edit.

His hand reached out to the blue spine. He lifted it from the shelf and thumbed through the shining pages, chock full of capering griffins, snow-white unicorns, and many other beasts of yore.

Because of the storm, there were few customers to disturb him in the sleepy shop. Aden felt his inner peace restored.

Which is when his eye happened to fall on an engraving of a dragon. And a magnificent beast it was too, winged and fiercely beaked, dripping with scarlet and gold scales, like plates of precious metal. One captive maiden stood in the charmed circle of its crimson breath, curled and billowed like the sea.

As portrayed, the dragon, bejeweled, enameled, was a thing of exquisite beauty, and Aden began to notice a kind of family resemblance between the monster and the captivated maiden, traditionally enclawed.

The lady and the dragon were one.

Existentially speaking, she was in no real danger, in no real need of being rescued. In fact, the deeper into the cave she followed her dragon, the deeper into the gauzy layers of Self she would step.

The prince was unnecessary. A mere appendage to the story. A cruel, age-old joke was being played at his expense.

When Aden emerged from the shop, the sun was shining again and he was carrying a brown paper package under his arm.

It was a book about dragons. For he needed to know the nature of the magical beast, whom all men must confront in love.

———— *Chapter 25* ————

O PENING NIGHT IN Newport. Palmy. Swellegant. The dress rehearsal had flowed smooth as new milk that afternoon. Tonight, Kit Daniels' dressing room was a mysterious clutter of glass bottles and jars out of which would come the colors of Germaine. Emulsions of palm—oil of almond, peppermint oil—softened Kit up for the masquerade.

Her wall-length mirror was studded with bulbs and telegrams stuck out at crazy angles, all around it.

One was actually from the playwright.

"Baby, you're the greatest," it read in bold blocks of print, taking a cue from Ralph Cramdon's tenement honeymoon. "Break a leg. Break two."

Kit had read it over and over, as though by doing so she'd penetrate to the heart of the man who'd written the words. She'd been beastly to him.

Then she'd broken down and cried, which was what she needed to do before a major performance anyway.

Now that the yogurt foundation had set into her face, bringing down the swelling that emotion had made, she was busy outlining her eyes with kohl pencil. She mouthed her lines.

The woman in the mirror, topknotted, with one eye ringed in black and face creamed white, looked hieratic and half sunk in the past, like some onyx-gazed priestess in a faded Cretan mural.

Aptly, when Aden had burst into her dressing room, high with boyish spirits, she'd had the distinct feeling she was also seeing an Aden of mutable fires, caught in transition, and really didn't know what to make of him. This, she'd decided on the spot, was only fair as she'd been confounding him for ages now. She'd been on the point of telling him so when he'd begun his wild talk about dragons.

"Do you know," he'd inquired, with what seemed to Kit eyes limpid with fever and a dance of raw nerves, "that there are in the Bible the following references to the dragon: Daniel xiv, 22,27; Micah i, 8; Jeremiah xiv, 6; Revelation xii, 3,7; Isaiah xxxiv, 13, and xliii, 20. Or that in mythology the dragon has been depicted as a ravishingly beautiful woman with long, flowing hair?"

"My God, Aden. What are you talking about?"

He'd swept her up in his arms, into a giddy revolution. "Hey, lady, you should know."

He'd been up all night with the dragon book, immersing himself in its ornate mythology. He'd finally come to the understanding that he'd been behaving no better than Judson Gold: thinking to tap into Kit Daniels' subterranean currents of energy for his own creative use! She'd been right to resist him, to layer her own wonderful suggestions for Germaine over his own. Now that he'd read them through objectively, her rewrites were all being used. And Aden could clearly see he'd been out of touch with the woman within—or he wouldn't have been driven to control the one without.

"But what really intrigues me," Aden went on, "is that in alchemy the dragon's fire-breathing properties refer to an image of burning thirst or hunger. Böhme says it's a will which desires yet has nothing capable of satisfying it except its own self." He looked at her expectantly. "Now do you understand?"

"It sounds a lot like a definition of woman."

"Yes, doesn't it!" he'd come back, eyes twinkling like a madman. "But right now, my talented cowriter, you just go out there and let our daughter dance!"

Which is what the critics later agreed, more or less, Kit had done.

From curtain to curtain, the cast, headed by Kit Daniels as Germaine, had set the play on its toes, given Aden's speeches mercurial wings. The audience howled with laughter at all the right places, even at some Aden hadn't thought of. Sighed as the characters sighed. Seemed to draw their very breath with Germaine, who lit up the stage with her eager beauty, her plainsong of female hunger and hope.

They knew, supercharged as they were from the first step into the stagelight, that they'd scored a direct, dramaturgical hit, the retort of which would reverberate from this provincial house all the way to Broadway.

With some difficulty, Aden managed to elbow his way into Kit's dressing room immediately after the performance.

"Dinner?" he'd called over the bobbing sea of congratulations spilling into her closet of a dressing room.

She was tall in her Chinese scarlet robe. She rose above the rest with sudden majesty.

He couldn't believe his eyes. She was shaking her head no.

But he understood her so well! He was the man to help her finally merge the dragon and the maiden. He was the perfect lover.

When he looked again, a blond man with a delicate face and Newport hauteur was enveloping Kit in his arms.

"This is Jonathan Cantwell, an old friend."

She'd introduced them offhandedly, when he'd finally made his way to her side. She gave off the syrupy smell of theatrical makeup. Aden was close enough to see where the fault line of her pancake stopped at the throat, and where her own creamy color flowed, mysteriously white and luminous. He smudged the line with his finger. She looked at him, startled.

"A pleasure to meet you." Cantwell stuck out his arm,

which to Aden seemed unnaturally long, like a prop. Were he to shake it, might it not come off in his hand? His rival would be exposed as a marvel of robotics, and Kit would turn to him.

Didn't Cantwell know that it was Aden Lassiter who had done battle for this woman, courted the dragon? What were these two thinking of?

"John, meet the playwright Aden Lassiter."

"Bravo, Mr. Lassiter. I think you're the best thing to come along since Frayn in England. Your comic sensibility is a tonic."

This is turning into a Newport tea party, Aden thought, mad with impatience to be alone with Kit. He had so much to tell her . . . about dragons and other things. *I don't want a freaking tea party. I want Germaine . . .*

But Germaine was going to dinner with Jonathan Cantwell, and tonight, for once, Aden was going to forget his childhood vows and get riproaring drunk. Then he'd either rethink the whole impossible situation with Kit Daniels (this time, he'd really thought he'd solved her) or write another ending to their damn, wonderful play.

"Thank you," he said. "Have a good time."

Kit and Jonathan would be up till the crack of dawn, talking and kissing, and drinking fine wines.

The next morning, Kit swung her legs out of bed and ended up flat on her back, staring up at the faraway ceiling. Her limbs had crumpled like cheap cardboard in the rain.

If she were to put it into words, it felt as though her skull had been cloven in two by some invisible blade, like a coconut with a machete. Elusive aches in her body gave rise to the suspicion that she had been pummeled all over by tiny rubber mallets. The muscles of her arms, the joints of her fingers, especially, throbbed in syncopated rhythm.

"A summer cold," said one Newport doctor. Another, more credibly, diagnosed complete exhaustion and pumped her full of Vitamin C, supplemented by baleful warnings to "stay in bed."

There would be no more performances out of Kit Daniels for the rest of the summer.

With the exception of Kit's understudy, the cast of *Plymouth Rocks* was stricken. Kit was doubly stricken. Forevermore, Aden would think she was malingering, spoiling his finest play. Now they'd never grope their way back together!

He did come, once, officially loaded down with hothouse flowers and good wishes from the entire cast. But seated gravely at her bedside, he looked hot, sullen and off-center as the ache in her head. He wouldn't even meet her eyes. If he had, he'd have seen they were full of apology.

All the same, their show went on to a brilliant reception and more packed houses. Broadway gleamed at the end of the painted pilgrims' progress, a golden city on a hill.

Dahlia Trewhitt, upon hearing of Kit's illness, and after finally identifying the actress as "that Hamptons girl," put her echoingly empty mansion at Kit's disposal.

Then Jonathan Cantwell dropped into the bubbling brew of Kit's life, like sugar into tea, and it all took a fairy-tale turn.

Under Mrs. Trewhitt's very nose, he lost no time in whisking Kit off to his twenty-room family "cottage" for convalescence among apple blossoms and the sea chants of gulls.

Day after day he commanded the sun to show for her and wheeled her down to where the green lawn sloped off to the sea in shining vistas of freedom.

He courted her with fresh pineapples, flown in from Hawaiian isles, a tonic orange water out of old England, Cantwell family stories about beautiful yachts and the Newport sea.

She dressed in tropical whites, to match his own, as though they would be brother and sister together, innocents in the sun.

In turn, she told him of life's crossroads, of a playboy father who'd abandoned his daughter, and a tragic mother who had abandoned herself.

On the lighter side, she confessed a weakness for strawberry daiquiris in tall glasses and books by English spinsters with several, smart-sounding names.

Bit by bit, she'd relaxed into the placid blue circle of his world. Unlike Aden, there were no devils in John, no calls to sexual arms.

Sickness and its stillness, then, had become a useful thing. A brilliant piece of timing. For self-reflection. For finding the structural weaknesses within . . . She hadn't been ready to fly.

Days passed. And then Kit was well enough to walk about. One day she discovered the hot jets of the Jacuzzi that was set into the center of the glass-walled solarium. With its brushed chrome and cobalt-blue tiles, it soon became her favorite spot on the Cantwell estate.

Head tilted back, eyes closed, she felt with her toes the fine medallion of raised tile on the floor of the bubbling pool. A nautilus-shell motif, familiar now.

On bare feet, Jonathan walked over to her, swooped down, and gave her a sweet hot rush on the lips.

It was the first time he'd touched her with passion since she'd fallen ill and come under his care.

Although it did not excite her as Aden's mere presence in a room could do, Jonathan's caress gave her a radiant fullness, a soft glow of well-being. Her eyes came open to see how his body flowed in smooth, tanned symmetry. Droplets of water clung to his golden chest hair as he lowered himself into the soft lap of the pool.

"You look ecstatic. Like a holy picture."

She smiled across at him. "This place is conducive to ecstasy."

"That's why I fought so hard for my family to keep it a few years back. They have so many houses, they didn't care about one more or less. So I hit them with sentimental arguments. But it was really for my own selfish pleasure."

"Umm, selfish pleasure sounds very good right now." In fact, for all her love of food, Kit had yet to feel at ease with the good things of the world, as though she didn't yet deserve them. With seeming irrelevance, she had a flash of her father, standing for hours at his mirror, angling his hat until it would break at the right slant across his face.

"Kit . . ." Jonathan rested his elbows back on the stoop of the tub. "Will you marry me? I think it's about time."

"John, I adore you." She was surprised into truthfulness. "But I don't—"

"—love me. I know. That's all right too."

She was about to object, but he held his finger to her lips. "I'm really kind of bored, you see. Always have been. There's nothing I do, nowhere I go that compels me to surrender myself."

"You mean you're looking for wings."

"No, nothing so grand as transcendence. Just involvement. It's as though I've been living in a house made of nothing but highly polished mirrors. Smooth, silvery, dead surfaces. No matter where I look, I see only my own face. I can't punch through my own image, to the core where life burns. But you, Kit, you make me laugh. You get my attention. When you're around, I see you. It's a kind of freedom from myself, I guess."

To Kit, the world had gone giddy. Maybe it was the Jacuzzi. Weren't they always warning you to get out before your heart went wild?

"You'd better know what you're getting into. I'm a dragon, John." She regarded him through the watery pink glow of the solarium and the euphoria of her recovery, of which he was so great a part.

"I don't believe it."

Kit studied his face, unbelieving, afraid she'd find herself on the verge of laughter at his proposal. It was what she'd fled from all through life—and what she'd most wanted: a guarantee for love.

The laughter didn't come as she'd thought.

And then, surrendering to her exhaustion, she thought nothing at all.

"Yes, John," she said. "My answer is yes."

Aden heard the bad news about Kit Daniels from the velvet-throated Analisa. It was his first day back from the out-of-town run, a blue Monday.

After a brief phone call placed to a car service, Aden had vanished from sight, so that all his clients, and even, in the end, his father, had become alarmed at the terminal memo he'd left Analisa: "I'm going to jump off a cliff. Love, Aden."

Two weeks later, with Analisa's help (she'd located the car service that had taken him to the end of Long Island) Clayburn had found his son on the windy dunes of Montauk, where, true to his word, he was leaping off a cliff.

Needing a more elegant alternative to the "good cry," Aden had opted for a clean, beautiful bout of windsurfing among the beach plum and scrub pine of the Montauk dunes.

That first day, he'd floated out on borrowed wings, against a horizon that looked like the Japanese flag: a red disk of sun rampant on a field of clouded white. In general the sky seemed baggy and hospitable, as the weeks went on, a blue peace. Here for hours at a time, he could swing between earth and nonordinary reality, piecing together the lovely riddles of his earthbound life.

It was near sunset when Clayburn's old black Mercedes rolled onto the spongy flat of private beach.

The drone of the engine gave way to the sound of crying gulls. He got out to scan the sky for the cut and glide of his only son. Then he spotted him, hanging fifty feet in the air from a flimsy batlike contraption while the waves below washed a dozen different shades of green, and the hurdy-gurdy of the wind played weird tunes around him.

Coming to rest at the foot of the flat-topped ridge, Aden lifted off his lucky helmet and laid it down on the firm sand. When he'd first started surfing, he'd piled on the gear—kneepads, goggles, gloves. Now he was stripped down for action to his black-nylon jump suit and helmet. These days, he also broke the cardinal rule of never going up alone.

Untouched by his father's exclamations, a kind of Zen calm belled down over him, as it did whenever he performed the rituals of skysurfing. He stood back from the "kite," mentally checking the cables for wear, the tubing for cracks, the bolts for signs of bending. With care, he studied the overall balance and the general condition of the rigging. All seemed to be well. There would, of course, be a preflight inspection the next time he surfed. He'd take his chances, but he was no fool.

One of the nice things about his "Apollo" was the speed and ease with which it could be packed away. The red flag he'd attached to each end fluttered in the wind, as he handled the kite he'd made with his own hands (a weekend hobby), as if it were a living creature, with intimate concentration, and even love. For weeks, he'd been holed up in his beachhouse bedroom with things like prebent tubing, drill, wrench, and hacksaw, putting finishing touches on his glorious bird of plastic and nylon, under which he now so proudly soared.

She was beautiful, brightly colored as any bird of paradise for easy retrieval in the sand.

Quiet now, Clayburn watched Aden go about the silent task of disconnecting and rotating the cross bar, bringing the leading edge bars to the center along the side of the keel, rolling the sail, coiling the cables, and stowing it all in a long, small-diameter bag, in which it seemed it would never fit.

Once collapsed, it was stowed atop his car on a jerry-built rack that put Clayburn in mind of some sacred Indian funerary pyre.

It had taken all of five minutes. During which time, Clayburn tried to gather his thoughts.

Today, Aden had been in the air, rocking back and forth, delirious with his blue freedom, for three hours. He'd cruised to the bottom of the ridge, dragged the gear back up, launched himself into space all over again.

Now he looked exhausted.

"Come on home now, son. You've been at it long enough."

Aden shook his head. "I like it out here."

"We'll talk over dinner."

"I'm not hungry."

"Then we'll go for a drink."

"I'm not thirsty."

"Kit Daniels?"

Aden looked away.

"Get into your car," Clayburn said. "Drop your stuff off and I'll drive you to the Yacht Club for dinner."

Fifteen minutes later, on the way to the Montauk Yacht Club, Clayburn aimed an anxious glance at his son, from behind the wheel of his Mercedes.

The blue peace was already wearing off.

"She outrages me, Dad. She twists me up inside like a pretzel. Just when I think I have her all figured out, she goes and does something totally out of whack with whatever came before."

Clayburn shook his head and made a turn off the highway. "Maybe you shouldn't try so hard to figure her out. She's not a thing that's all finished and polished to a turn, wrapped up with a ribbon. Kit's not one of your characters, Aden. She's always new. She invents herself afresh every day."

"I know what you mean." Aden shifted in his bucket seat. He was quiet for a while, staring out at the ocean flashing by his window. "I've always meant to ask you, Dad . . ." Now Aden kept his eyes straight ahead, on the ribbon of road. "Did you ever feel like giving up with Mother? I mean, those years when she was really bad, when every morning the whole world stunk of booze."

"Of course I did, Aden. I wouldn't be human if it were otherwise."

"How did you keep going?" Aden shrugged.

Clayburn took a moment to think. "I guess I just kept focusing on how much it hurt her to do those things to me. I don't believe I thought of myself at all," he said with a kind of wonder, as though he were speaking about a stranger from the past. "I couldn't afford to."

Aden was silent the rest of the way. Only when they'd come to a stop in front of the restaurant did he speak again.

"Dinner's on me, Dad," he said.

Clayburn smiled. His boy was coming home.

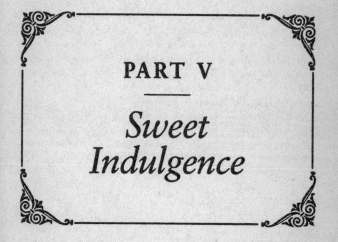

PART V

Sweet Indulgence

Chapter 26

MALLORY HAD FLOWN in to do Kit's trousseau. Maddy was still too "ill" to attend the wedding. Jared sent some vague excuse, as well as a rare Sèvres porcelain dog, which Kit hated. As for her parents, Marva and Paolo couldn't be reached on their perpetual around-the-world honeymoon cruise. And Whitney Daniels III had willingly consented to give the bride away.

In a sentimental mood one night, Kit had phoned him in Palm Beach and asked the favor.

Much was made of the fact that a thunderstorm had ripped apart the nuptial morning, but that afterwards a gauzy bridge of rainbow had arched itself over the palatial turrets of the Cantwell cottage.

Summer had indeed never smelled so pretty and green as in Kit's cantaloupe-colored sitting room, where cumulus clouds of day lilies and white orchids in clay pots had been brought in to cushion the bride in a veritable fortress of blossoms.

Someone must have understood that she needed to be cushioned.

Mallory Daniels buzzed around Kit, brushing a cheekbone here, pinning a tress there, doing anything to keep from saying what was on the tip of his tongue.

And Kit knew it. She sat in her black bell of silk taffeta with the lapping of Caen lace at the bodice, and looked like stone. "I can use some more Queen Anne's lace here." She jabbed her finger into the mess of auburn curls Mallory had so artfully arranged.

"You don't want to look like Ophelia *after* the brook," Mallory snapped. "Weedy trophies and all that."

"Just do it."

"Pushy broad." Mallory tinkered with the coiffure, then threw down his rattail comb. "At least *I* know when to quit. I can do no more."

Kit could see in the glass that she was already taking on that incandescent glow of archetype. She hadn't been able to get a square meal down for two days . . .

"Ready, Kit?"

"Mallory?" She sounded sick, like when they were kids and used to binge all night on popcorn wheedled from the servants. He came in closer for a better look.

Well, maybe it was Kit's wedding day but it was the first time he'd ever seen his cousin look truly ghastly, and he was going back to when she was big enough to be the entire road company of *A Chorus Line*. To Mallory, she'd had a special kind of beauty then, with her woolgatherer's dream of a head of hair, trailing wistfully down her back, her sweetly goofy earth-mother smile. She was herself then, even if she did need to lose fifty pounds. Now she was a mannequin who looked to have blood as thin as her upper arms.

Of course, Kit didn't look ghastly in the conventional sense. Kit rarely gave way to the conventional. It was what Mallory called the "emotional body-electric" of a person, hovering just outside the physical body, pulsations of light, a rainbow envelope. And while her physical body looked glamorous enough to the naked eye, this other body was almost certainly collapsing in despair. Mallory could always see into Kit, whom he loved in his own nervous way. She never fooled him the way she fooled herself and just about all the other men in her life. Except maybe Aden Lassiter.

Her hands were cold in his. "You dog," he said, striving to be bluff. "I'm green with envy. You finally got our man. Of course, I would have given him my all, if he'd had the imagination to ask me for it. But our Johnnie is the straightest arrow that ever flew!"

"I know," Kit replied. Mallory had to look again to make sure that she was actually crying . . .

He handed her his handkerchief, a Hapsburg antique. "I'm sorry, baby. I can't help you with this one. Out of my depth." They'd been black lambs together, which accounted for their lifelong bond. But with this marriage, Kit Daniels was being welcomed back into her family and by extension into the clubbiest of worlds—in a way he, with his sexual "waywardness," could never be. Why wasn't she ecstatic? After all, Jonathan Cantwell was It. He had an archbishop of Canterbury somewhere in his background and a sacerdotal odor still accompanied him whenever he entered a roomful of worshipers. As for his looks, they were a cross between Scott Fitzgerald and Superman.

Kit squeezed his hand and wouldn't let go. "I hope someday you'll find someone to love you, too."

His heart was cleft in two. But he wouldn't show it. It was not the way he was with her. "From your mouth to Rock Danforth's ears." Today, he missed his ex-flame. Mallory had loved bringing him around to artsy East Side parties and watch him deaden conversation. Of course there were drawbacks to this. Once Rock made up his mind—it was like poured concrete—there was no breaking through.

He scrutinized Kit, who seemed to be trying to avoid eye contact at all costs. "Want to talk anyway?"

She shook her bewreathed head, managing to look bridal and funereal all at once.

"There, there." Mallory patted her on the back, gingerly. "All brides feel sick to their stomachs. It's nothing to be ashamed of." Then, knowing that somehow he'd failed her, he took this opportunity to escape the bridal room.

A fraction of a second later, Whitney Daniels knocked at the bedroom door. His new wife, Margaret, was a shapeless drift of rose chiffon behind him. Kit thought of her as Mrs. Potato Head. "Darling, you look divine. Just like your mother."

"Thank you." Kit wished she could ask someone if every bride felt this drowsiness, this paralysis of will and desire in which she was simply a puppet of mysterious forces from beyond. But she didn't dare.

"Jonathan is a prince. You've made a good choice."

"Yes, Daddy."

She tried to rise from behind her vanity table but found that her wobbly legs would not support the weight of her ensemble and its attendant symbolism. Whitney Daniels came forward to take her arm.

"All right, Princess," he said. "It's time."

Aden Lassiter would always remember the day Kit Daniels was to become Mrs. Jonathan Cantwell III.

In despair, he tried to fill the twenty-four-hour period with motions and shifts. Lunch with friends. An exhibit of Japanese lacquerware. Arranging an elaborate date at the trendiest new disco in Tribeca.

None of it worked. Lunch fell flat. The Japanese exhibit, with dragons rampant, showed a wedding gown. That night, he stepped out of his apartment with a fanatical sense of possibility—and the germ of disillusionment that nestles inside it.

The hedonistic disco was, at best, mildly diverting. But the night was haunted for him. The girl (she was all of nineteen) never came quite into focus. He could have predicted this when his date showed up with plastic earrings in the guise of sushi. "Futomaki," she explained. "It's a raw statement."

Struggling for sense beneath the aggressive lights and musical blare of the disco, he knew that without Kit Daniels, the world would never be a truly wild or sad or happy-as-hell place again.

* * *

From every modern romance she'd ever read, Kit Daniels had ascertained that beneath the cloud of orange blossom and incense, a bride always looks giddily forward to ecstatic wholeness with the other side of her soul.

Try as she might, she felt no such thing. A panic settled into her bones, and she was marched, unsteadily, into the church on the arm of her father.

From then on Kit was paralyzed in her cloud of black taffeta. The flower-filled air was cloying and sweet in her mouth, as the organ bellowed sanctity in the choir loft. She was beginning to understand the uses of ritual: it distracted you, in an orderly way, from what was really going on.

All of Newport society stood at her approach. Half a million dollars had been lavished on this wedding. A half million more if the finery of the guests and the gifts were counted in. And out of all this extravaganza, the only comforting sight that presented itself to Kit was the face of her confused cousin, Mallory.

All of a sudden, Jonathan smiled at her from the top of the flower-banked aisle. It was a blind, smug, self-congratulatory smile.

It was all Kit Daniels needed. She took one step forward. Then gathered up her skirts.

Twisting away from that blind of a smile, she tossed her bouquet of stephanotis over her shoulder, in a final nod at tradition, and bolted from the church.

"Go, Kit!" Mallory called triumphantly from the pews, as though he were at a hockey game.

With eccentric elegance, Whitney Daniels began to laugh.

In the wake of the truncated wedding ceremony, the fortune in fabulous gifts was returned. The guests apologized to. The caterers recompensed. Jonathan went into hiding, in Gstaad. Whitney Daniels flew home to Palm Beach with Margaret, and Mallory, after several fruitless days of investigation as to Kit's whereabouts, left for New York.

The bride seemed to have dropped off the face of the earth.

It was a weeklong binge, a super binge, in which she

indulged at a little hotel in an unfashionable neighborhood. With syrup, wheat cereal, sacks of brown sugar, fresh cream, baked goods of every description . . . anything sweet, with ruth baked in, to stave off the darkness, the shadow hulk of her self that threatened to devour her with every heartbeat. She'd done a terrible, sacrilegious thing in the world of our fathers. His laugh had been terrible, wild, cruel!

Oh and Jonathan, Jonathan, her man of substance, of society, of security! How she'd humiliated him, broken her bond as a lover! She was a traitress, a cruel, greedy pig . . . She must be punished. She was being punished.

Just by being who she was, here in this hotel room, eating herself into narcosis, clouding her eyes with sugar.

Two weeks later, Kit Daniels had gotten her personal "death wish." She'd regained fifteen of her "fat girl" pounds.

There she stood, at the center of all that angry flesh, packed dense as a good Droste chocolate, mute, sullen, and unforgiving of life and all its works.

If she were lucky, no one would ever find her.

She opened the box of chocolate-cherry donuts and shook . . .

Mallory Daniels stopped at Aden's office before flying off on the Concorde for a show in Bonn. He had come to tell Aden of his reprieve.

"She doesn't want me," Aden said through his hands, torn between a wild exultation and a sweet despair.

"Don't be a ninny. Of course she does. Only she doesn't know yet."

"But how in the world am I supposed to find her? Witchcraft?"

"I don't know. This isn't my story." Mallory looked around the office. "What happened to your old secretary?"

"She's not here anymore."

"Oh, what a shame," Mal murmured. "She had such a beautiful voice."

"Yes, she did." Aden was already on the phone, undoing dates so that he could be free to pursue Kit. "She still does."

He didn't tell Mallory that Analisa had forsaken Lassiter &
Lassiter for a partnership with Lefty Solarz. It was the one
bright spot in his world. He wished them well.

"Good luck." Mallory paused dramatically at the door.
"And don't be afraid to give it back to her when she kicks up.
She needs that, you know."

"No, I don't know." Aden looked up absently. "But
thanks."

Mallory raised his hand. "No need. I love the woman too,
you see, in my own way. Always have. And if you can't make
her reasonably happy at last, I'm just going to have to scout
around for another 'Prince Karma,' the prospect of which I
find utterly exhausting. I'm getting much too old for all this."

"I know what you mean," Aden replied. "I know just what
you mean."

Drugged with shame, Kit Daniels got in touch with no one.
She wanted only to crawl into bed, dragging the heft of her
fifteen pounds like a ball and chain, and die.

Now that her instincts had overpowered her will, the last
few illusions had fallen away. She felt as though she'd been
bared to the nerve, her back broken in this great confronta-
tion.

And to think she'd aspired to be that rare accomplishment:
the fully feminized woman! Thrilling to her own rhythms!
Narcissistic in an acceptable way! She'd fancied herself a far
cry from that little girl who'd been seduced by her father's
spirit, by Dr. Marc, by Judson Gold—fully confident she
would never grow heavy with love, would stay light on her
toes, playing the golden fish in the water for all it was worth.

She shifted her face to the wall, one arm thrown over her
eyes, so that she could not see her shame rippling under the
bedclothes. The behemoth, the thing that reared up from
behind her glib, slickly polished intellect, had devoured her
chances for happiness, for a normal life, devoured her very
chances for a soul of her own in a mellifluous storm of sugary
goo.

Damn it all, this wasn't fair! All she'd wanted was to be

loved. To love like a woman of feeling. The sham of a society marriage would have destroyed her in the end. Like her mother, her beautiful, broken mother . . .

Of course, she should have anticipated pulling something serpentlike out of the hat, just like this! After all, she'd come from a family of traitresses. The rootstock, the tuber, the bulb were rotten. Marva was a jewel-naveled Jezebel who seduced millions of her sisters into buying the glossy packages. And now she herself had destroyed the finest man in the world. Now that she thought of it, it was funny. For all his riches, his air of finesse, sweetly blond Jonathan Cantwell had always seemed vulnerable, as though he might, one day, attract catastrophe.

How shocking to find out: she was the catastrophe!

She lay in her bloated bed and looked down the length of the green chenille coverlet. A veritable hillock rose where her stomach should be, plunged to a wide valley of pelvis, then ballooned out to a green promontory: her two thighs coming together.

All week she'd been in a rage of despair, traversing the creases and folds of this big country. Lost in the wilderness of her own soul, reaching for food was not enough. It never tasted as good as it looked.

Jonathan was not enough. Almost pointlessly handsome, even his passion was polished: the passion of a limited lover.

Like a jazz musician who never changes his licks, Jonathan had exhibited the same emotional phrases over and over again. Why didn't she see it right away? The quality of his loving was too tame, too timid for her vibrant needs.

Yes, she'd had to do what she did, but oh, the callousness of it, the degradation for her fiancé and his family. She was an evil witch of a thing . . . a poison.

She couldn't even take comfort in shared blame.

After God, who had made her weak and needy, who was there to blame but her mother, who'd been left starving by her own mother and so on, all the way back to Mother Eve? Conceivably there could have existed some mighty race of women, lost in the mists of time, who had never been part of that sorrowful chain. But they were too remote, too elusive a presence to do Kit Daniels much good.

Kit didn't even know how long she'd been locked in this prison of defection and despair.

The rusty curtains lay hunched against the windows of the hotel room. She couldn't tell if it were night or day, sunshine or storm, beyond that pane. Gorging, dreaming of gorging, dreaming of the deli down the street, the bakery twelve blocks away. A phantasmagoria of food. She was too embarrassed to go in alone and ask for those six chocolate eclairs. She would inquire of the clerk as to whether he thought it was enough for ten people.

She was flying apart at the seams. The other day—was it Wednesday?—she had "woken up" in a strange part of town, hadn't known where she was or how to get back to the hotel. All she knew was that she had to eat day and night, or something horrible, unspeakable, would happen to her.

She had to eat—or die.

After Mallory had gone, Aden Lassiter had hastily packed his green bookbag and set off on a quest of the heart. He would find Kit Daniels and bring her back to the world of the living. If she wanted to come . . .

He'd bribed just about every luxury hotel clerk in the city. Then he'd hired a detective to poke into the seedier places, the places Kit might think no one would know about.

That's how he found her, a month later, huddled in misery. Pounds and pounds greater than when he'd last seen her.

He was waiting by her door as she made her way back from a raid on the all-night deli around the corner.

For the last month, he'd been in a rage of frustration. But as soon as he saw her, everything else flew out of his head, but his love for her. Even so, he would have to be more dextrously in love with her if he were to survive the rococo turns to come.

Kit flung her arms over her face and slumped over in grief, attempting to hide her "ugliness." The groceries tumbled to the carpeted floor.

Tender but unsure, Aden went to take her into his arms.

As he'd half expected, Kit pushed him away.

"I'm glad I found you, Kit."

"Kit isn't here. This is It, the Beast. Kit is dead, so you might as well go away!"

Aden stood firm. He would not hazard losing her to this ravening self-hatred, this wild mood of despair. "No," he said levelly. "You're getting out of here. You're going home."

"Why can't you leave me alone, goddamn it, just let me eat my heart out." She fumbled with the keys and pushed into the door, intending to shake him then and there.

Throwing himself bodily, he wedged himself between the door and frame, then pushed his way into the sitting room.

"I'll have the manager throw you out!"

He was about to grab her by the shoulders, then caught himself. He had no right. "Stop it, Kit!" He'd have to wake her, break through to her some other way. The face of his own mother, remote, boozy, jazzed up with gin, pushed into his mind, and he faltered.

Kit took the opportunity to slip into the bedroom and lock the door against him, against a love that might recall her from the dark place.

Aden stood, crucified, on the other side of the cheap pine door. "Kit, we've got to love being human too."

"I don't know . . . I don't care anymore about any of it. I just want to die."

"Well, goddamn you, I want you to live!"

There was a silence that seemed to stretch on for hours, when it could, in reality, only have been a few minutes' passage. Then Aden heard the click of a lock. The door fell ajar. He walked into the room where Kit had staged her anguish.

And she pierced his heart with her question.

"Why, Aden? Why do you want me to live? I'm of no use to anyone, never have been. Fat, ugly, a big disappointment to my parents. I never really lived. My life just never started. I mean, I kept waiting and hoping for it to, but it never did. I lived in my head, denied my hands, my heart: I wasn't even whole. I just lurched from one crisis to another, congratulating myself for pulling through another boring day, another depressing hour, without exposing what a great big nothing I was, without screaming out my rage. I never lived. And Aden"—her eyes were big and brilliant with tears—"what I'm most ashamed of is—I still don't know how . . ."

Aden felt chilled to the heart. He had never seen female suffering up this close before. His mother's suffering had unfolded behind childhood's closed doors and was really more of his father's sorrow. He'd watched it from afar, a little boy in love with the woman who'd given him birth, who then tried, over a decade, to take her own unfathomable life.

What could he say to his Kit? What could he do for her?

"Kit, you're ill. You don't know what you're saying."

"No, Aden. Inside this cave of blubber, there's just a vast, empty zero. There's nobody here for you to save, Aden, for you to love . . . that's why I couldn't let you get too close to me. I didn't want you to wake up one day and realize there was no one lying beside you. Just a cipher, a blank, a nothing."

The woman he loved was weeping beside him on the bed with the cheap green coverlet, and there was nothing for him to do but let her cry out her pain, in his arms, until the emotion cutting through her had run its course.

His mind raced. He played for time. He'd have to strike the right nerve, say the right thing, or lose her forever. He knew one thing from living with his alcoholic mother, and that was that male ego had no place where a woman is drowning herself. He was no champion.

He could offer his love, but only after Kit decided that there was room for it in the mansion of her soul, that she wanted the stake in life this might give her.

He must be clear with her, and help her see that she had created this swollen body, this antilife for herself as a kind of symbol, yes, and that once having read it, she would no longer need to incarnate it. He would fight through the layers to the woman in agony, but that woman, he now clearly understood, must find her own reasons for wanting to be great, protected by a husk of flesh, for assigning power to fat and usurping it from her essence as a woman, in the end, for desexualizing herself. Mightn't that woman learn not to judge the fat, as good or bad, but see that it held certain qualities within it? A metaphor, perhaps, for some other billowing hunger . . .

He reached down into himself, to the place where the woman dwelt within him, as it does in all men, unacknowledged or not.

He stroked her flowing hair with a light hand. When she did not object but moved closer to him, he spoke to her softly. "My darling, that spirit of fire in you, that sulfurous dragon, that brimstone—did it ever occur to you that those are the energies, the desires of your soul? God, maybe you should just feel them. Rejoice in them. Let the real hunger come, and name itself. Dance with those images cast up in the psychic firelight, on the walls of your soul, and you will probably never mistake the hunger for life, as the hunger for food again."

"But the rage, the selfishness."

"You've got to let yourself feel the longings, Kit, not anesthetize them by gorging food."

"It's almost as if I've been blown up with my fantasies of life, never really daring to perform an act of love." She looked up into his seriously beautiful face.

"How could you love, Kit, when no one had ever shown you how?"

"But Aden," she said, "this was an act of love, wasn't it? Just now."

"An act of love. Yes. That's what all of life is." The sweet warmth he had felt since taking Kit into his arms had become an almost unbearable heat that throbbed in every part of his being. Could he prove right now, once and for all, that he could love without fear of rejection?

The way she felt in his arms, there was no reason not to think so.

They moved together so easily for once.

She gave no thought to shame, to lifelong prohibitions about naked imperfections.

She was celebrating the fire that moved within them,

danced into his embrace, her clothes shed like so many blossoms from a springtime tree.

He touched her reverently, patiently, his eyes half closed in concentration, learning her, the heft of her breasts, the contour of her belly, the smoothness of her thighs.

She sighed and dropped wild kisses down his chest. She stroked the plane of his flanks with her hands and spoke a sensual language with her tongue until he moaned out loud with pleasure.

"I've waited so long for this, Kit . . ." Aden spoke with all the pent-up tenderness of his male life.

"I've always loved you," she said. "I was just afraid, that's all."

"And now?"

"Now, I want you inside me, where you belong."

Her words excited him, and the pace of their lovemaking became more urgent and hungry.

He pulled her up so that she was facing him, and she wrapped her limbs around him. The place where their bellies touched was burning up with heat that radiated from the carnal core.

They were content to look into each other's eyes, as they merged, filled with love and ecstasies of fire.

Kit's heart cried out with unimaginable joy each time they burned to incandescence, that night of sweet redemption and celebratory love.

It seemed natural for the two lovers to hide away in Montauk at Aden's borrowed beachhouse, where he'd recently spent so many long, lonely weekends by the sea.

It was a redwood and glass construction with multilevel decks and a sublime view of the rugged Atlantic shore. Inside, it shone with whitewashed walls and Delft tiles. There was a ladder that led through a trapdoor to a summer bedroom, built high up for cool breezes and bright, lazy afternoons of love. A Singhalese mosquito net, dyed a pale peach, was draped over the bed. Indian pelmets were hung over the windows, and delicate Art Nouveau lamps shivered from the oak-beamed ceiling.

The kitchen boasted a flagstone floor and a battery of copper pans and baskets pegged onto the wall. Here Aden prepared simple, healthy meals for them both.

Day by day, with the fiery strength of their mutual passion, Kit began to pull herself back from the brink of the black hole.

In the cool of the morning, they were sitting at the dining table in the courtyard. The table was covered with a gaily embroidered Greek tablecloth and set with their simple breakfast of fruit and cheese. (Kit was no longer afraid of food. She respected it and its magical properties and selected carefully what it was she hungered for. She could now eat and be satisfied with small portions—even of her favorite dishes.) In the midst of tubs of lilies, ficus, and flowering plants, they clasped hands across the table. It had been another sweet, silent session of lovemaking and they were smiling at one another.

Aden stroked her hand. "God, I love you." He pushed back the chair and came around the wooden rectangle of table so that he could touch her and kiss her again.

Kit pressed a kiss into his palm. "You used to hate me."

"Never."

"Liar!" The seabreeze was heavy with the tang of salt as it moved invisibly through the garden court. That year of Kit's great love, it seemed to be perennial summer.

"All right, there may have been something in that Molotov cocktail of feelings that appeared to be hatred, but it was just desire turned on its head, believe me. Secretly, I loved your feistiness." He thought for a minute. "In fact, do you know when I first started to love you?"

"No. Tell me."

"It was onstage, in a little playhouse on the Cape."

"You were there? I don't believe it!"

"Oh yes, I was there. You were so original, so much yourself: I was overwhelmed."

"But I was crazy, selfish."

"Selfish according to whom? Crazy according to what? For God's sake, Kit, you were the most magnificent creature I'd ever seen, making up your own standards, your own rules."

She laughed.

"Don't ever lose that, Kit. Hold on to it. It's what children have until about seven, when they become their parents and the people around them, when they let go of their drunken delight in life and forget that, for the most part, it's supposed to be fun. Believe me, that's what made me love you in the first place."

"I do believe you," she said, still intoxicated by his nearness. "Go sit down, or I'm going to have to seduce you right on this table."

"What's wrong with that?"

"What will your friend's neighbors say?"

"Probably that you've lost your chance to be Miss America."

"Oh, Aden, I feel so free here with you! For the first time, I can breathe." Privately, she thought the wonder of the place was the sun. Feelings you had in the sun were different from any others. More clear, piercing, intense. Feelings with wings . . .

She loved the way he touched her in the moonlight, too. The way they tangled in their bed, so that she no longer knew where her body ended and his began. She even loved the harried way he looked when salt spray filmed his glasses and blew his hair around as they stood on the low rise, looking down at the churning green sea, the featherbedded clouds piled up high above.

In opening up their hearts, Aden had blown the roof off the world! Even though Kit hadn't slimmed down yet to her "ideal" size, her life had finally begun. The last illusion, that thinness was all, that it would solve every one of life's great puzzles, end each petty grief, had begun to melt away in the sunny, fragrant garden of their love.

He sank back down on his chair with the blue and white canvas pillows. "You know, I've been thinking about what you told me last night. About why the weight didn't stay off the first time."

"And?"

"As you said, the first time it was vanity and will. This time it's out of love for your female nature and its needs. You're owning up to your instincts—your darkness, if you want. That's why, this time, it'll work."

"I think so too."

"Come on." He threw down his napkin. "I feel like a walk on the beach."

The sandpipers were pitching their way across the sand on their crazy-tilt legs. Kit rolled up the cuffs of her pink cotton jump suit so that she could splash in and out of the cold surf.

Aden watched her with love shining like a glory in his face.

"Know what I'd really like to do?" she asked, after a while, hooking her arm through his.

"Go back inside and make bliss again?" he asked in a soft, conspiratorial tone.

"Yes, that, but . . . what I dream about doing lately is marching into Serendipity on Sixtieth Street—were you ever there?"

"Uh-huh."

"Strutting my stuff into Serendipity and sitting myself down right by the door where I can be seen in plain view. Then order and consume, quite slowly, very ostentatiously, a mother of a banana split—you know the way they make them, with the four scoops of ice cream, topped with real hot fudge sauce, butterscotch syrup, strawberry preserves, crushed pineapple, chopped walnuts, slivered almonds, mighty ziggurats of whipped cream . . ." She sculpted an imaginary mountain in midair. "And, need we say it, a banana! Consume without apology, you understand, without tears, in front of all those celebrity wraiths, Jackie and Gloria, et al. And then . . ."

"There's more?"

"Don't interrupt! And then, when I have duly polished off the banana split, I long to go into that boutique they have, glowing under Tiffany lamps, and purchase the most outrageously trendy outfit in the microminiest size they carry!" Her eyes were full of stars.

"Okay, my turn . . ." Aden reached out to tug on a lock of chestnut hair.

Mischief gleamed in her eyes. "Oh no, you don't!" She pushed him aside and bolted down the strand. Aden followed with long, easy strides. He caught her around the waist and pulled her down into the rippling surf.

They tussled in the water. Laughing. In love.

Then he carried her to the dunes and laid her down on their blanket in the sun.

Aden's tongue and the slant of sunlight seemed to be invading every part of her. He came to his knees and pulled his midnight-blue knit shirt over his head, exposing the tanned triangle of his upper torso. Her wet clothes clung to her skin and somehow added to her delirium. Every breath she took caused an even more intense sensation.

He brought her to her knees, peeling the clingy, wet fabric from her body until she was nude and longing in the sun.

To the tambour roar of the surf, she gave in to the overwhelming sensations of pleasure—the smell of the sun on Aden's skin, the breeze playing in her long, sea-tangled hair . . .

She curled around him like a rare shell around the glow of pearl inside. She filled herself with him.

Passion broke upon them once again, and they cried out together with what seemed to be the very breath of the sea.

Their summer simmered on into late September, and then autumn with its pale golds and shimmering bronzes blew into the coast on a fresh nautical breeze.

Every day, Kit ran along the dunes, until her skin was copper-colored by the sun. She windsurfed with Aden, finally getting her wings. Everything that belonged to her, came to her. The sensible diet and exercise regimen she knew was a process, that most female of things, so that the hike of a few pounds or a weekend's happy backsliding were no longer the occasion of deep despair. Kit believed in a morality of the body now. She considered herself beauteous and beloved, dark side and all. The female hunger was finally being satisfied.

Although Aden's life rotated around Kit and their beach-house hideaway, he did drop in, now and then, on rehearsals for *Plymouth Rocks*.

It was at one of these rehearsals that he got the idea for the perfect gift for Kit. Germaine—her old role back. And he had a new attitude about the changes she'd made in the script. He was going to give her an acknowledgment in the Broadway playbill. He wanted to tell her about his plans, today. If he could just get her down from the sky, that is!

She was, by now, deep into the arcana of tangs, standoffs, and saddles.

Originally, she'd taken to the skies as part of their lovers' pact to do at least one impossible new thing before breakfast —which could range from the first taste of a truffle, to the spotting of a new word in Webster, to taking your life in your hands at the trapeze bar of a hang glider.

A novice, Kit was really only ground-bouncing on low terrain, but she coveted Aden's easy glide off sheer cliffs, his lazy eagle spins in midair, his masterful drive into a wall of wind. She was working up to it though, daily.

"Nose down, nose down," Aden would cry up to her through the leather trumpet of his gloves. Hang gliders who went below fifteen miles an hour and stalled had been known to bump and bruise, and sometimes, when high expectation met solid ground, even break their adventurous limbs. And Kit's limbs, Kit's life, were daily becoming more precious to Aden Lassiter.

Kit shifted her weight and managed to start up her glide again. She brought herself safely down.

Aden bounded over to her. "Beautiful! You're really getting good!"

The wind on the dunes was always blowing and cold this autumn. She doffed her helmet and shook her hair out in the wind. After helping Kit to close up the kite, Aden poured hot coffee from a thermos for them both. Then he lazed back against a rock, letting the rays of the fading sun bathe his face.

"Umm, this coffee hits the spot." She sat cross-legged on the sand, cradling the cup in her hands.

"The wind's getting rough out there. We're going to have to call it quits for a while."

"Oh no! I'm just getting the hang of it."

"The 'hang'? I'll let that go."

"No, really, what will I do with all this libidinal energy?"

"There must be something we can think of. Golly." From under his tweed cap, he watched her body move. The ends of his muffler fluttered out in the stiff wind that would soon come roaring in from the sea. Kit came to her feet.

She laid her length upon his, placing a hand on either side of his curly head. "Who says the male of the species has a one-track mind?"

"I do. Sex is the most sensible thing to think of when a woman like you is flinging her compact and incredibly sensuous body upon yours on a dune in the October sun."

They did not speak very much after that, being occupied with more interesting things about each other than small talk.

When at last they'd broken from their embrace, Aden straightened his clothing. "I've got to check out the rehearsal today. I thought maybe you'd want to come along for the ride."

"Why should I?" Kit still wasn't sure she was ready for the bright light of curiosity that would be trained on her when she returned to the city.

"Well." Aden picked up a pebble and skimmed it into the surf. "I thought—since you were looking so damn good and feeling so fit—you might like to get back into the theater."

"You mean—play Germaine in the Broadway production?" Kit was touched by his show of faith, yet terrified of letting him down yet again. She threw her arms around his neck. "Oh Aden, why can't I just stay here and wait for you?"

"Kit, the part was written for you. No, it was written *by* you. Will you do it?"

"I'm not sure about this, Aden." She studied the light in his steady gray eyes.

"I am."

She played her fingers through his curly hair. "I guess I've got to get back to the real world again sometime. This is as good a way as any to do it."

"There you go."

Nostalgic already, she looked around at the familiar, naked roll of dune, the wild stretch of sea, the sliding blue cyclorama of sky against which they'd played out their lovers' story. "I'll miss this place."

"We can come back." He kissed her behind the ear. "For anniversaries. We'll romp naked over the bonfire-lit beach."

"Race you back to the car," she called over her shoulder.

"Race you to the moon." Aden smiled, and pulled her close.

───── *Chapter 27* ─────

BACKSTAGE, THE AIR in Kit's Broadway dressing room was thick with tea roses and the fume of boxed chocolates.

Here and there lay a band of sequins, a flash of feathers, the sensuous artifacts of a stage life: a feminine eruption in reaction to Kit's personal life. She had, to everyone's surprise, lived like a temple ascetic since rejoining the cast of *Plymouth Rocks.*

All through the rehearsals, she'd been the model ensemble player, learning her new lines for the first day, showing up bright and early, throwing in the sponge only after all the rest had given up on a tricky scene, stubbornly working and reworking her character until it gleamed with definition from the surrounding text.

The director was amazed. The battle-wise cast kept waiting for the honeymoon to thud to an end—but, miraculously, it never did.

The result was dazzling. The show had never been better. She'd been acknowledged as a contributor in the playbill.

Kit was sporting Germaine's "bad boy" coif—smooth on top, teased at the sides. Her cheeks were painted a strong watermelon shade, her mouth lacquered in deepest scarlet, brazenly spread beyond the natural lip line. The eyes showed rich and suggestive with colored lids, brushed in red, canary, and stone gray.

Tonight was one of the most important nights of her life.

Tonight she would prove to Aden that she'd taken responsibility for love.

She would let him in on the secret that she was as much an intrinsic part of him as Germaine, and that the betrayals of the past were over and done.

Loving them both was like learning to walk all over again, with a new stance, a new style. She felt dazed and happy, and frightened it would end, all at the same time. She tried not to hope for permanence, moved away from the mirror lest she see too much in her eyes.

Then Aden came in to embrace her. It was time to go on.

In the end, the stage was littered with bouquets of roses. The house rafters shook with cheers. After tonight's performance, the world of Aden's play would be spoken of as Pulitzer Prize territory.

Kit was drawn into a deep curtsy, again and again, by the pull of audience applause. She blinked back tears in the lights.

In between curtain calls, she ran out to Aden and kissed him. At one point, the other cast members broke into enthusiastic applause, which brought the tears back to her eyes. They'd played a long way together.

At the cast party at Studio 54, the dance floor was a hot jumble of balloons. Aden vented his first-night exhilaration in a ruckus sale of anecdotes.

Kit wore her molten silver lamé, slit savagely down the side. Her hair was a roil of curls over a fevered brow.

She was a Broadway star. What's more, she was in love.

It had never occurred to her that being a whole person might be so much fun.

East Coast celebrities passed in and out of the flashing

lights, kissing the air around her cheeks and purring congratulations.

Clayburn Lassiter showed up with Geraldine Cutler, and the four of them had a good laugh over the ALS Book Awards, the sting of which had been blunted with the reshuffling of affections and the slow passage of time.

Critics fawned and champagne flowed.

Aden exhibited some of the delirium of his former days, acting the playboy in his white wool jacket with the pink tea-rose boutonniere.

He fooled no one. With Kit Daniels in the room, Aden Lassiter was so obviously in love.

They saved each other for last. A slow dance for lovers.

"I love you," Kit said.

Aden looked out on the sea of brightly colored dancers.

"Just like that?"

"Just like that."

"Then marry me," Aden said suddenly, ardently. "I can't stand the suspense. You're driving me to write."

Kit stopped dancing, her eyes sparkled with excitement. "If you didn't ask me tonight, I was going to ask you."

They embraced and he swung her around the dance floor in his arms. The other dancers applauded.

"Let's do it now!"

"You're crazy!" She laughed.

"My father can perform the ceremony—he'd be the perfect Jehovah."

"I think we need a blood test first."

He turned his back on her. "You're no fun."

"Oh yes I am!"

"She's going to marry me!" Aden was informing passersby. "You did say you were going to marry me?" he asked Kit.

She smiled. "Yes, I did."

"God, we're going to be so good together! Our children will have red hair and fabulous chins photographers will beg to see."

The disco rumbled with a beat like the heart of a behemoth. It struck at Kit's nerves.

"What children?"

"You know, they're those short people who don't have credit cards?"

"Aden, I'm not ready for motherhood."

"Hey, it wouldn't be right away. I'm not ready for that either."

She was walking on eggshells as it was. Mightn't the ground break under the passionate weight of a third person to love? "I'm not interested in having babies, Aden. Ever." She could see his gray eyes grow cloudy. She was going to lose him if she couldn't convince him of her fears, convert him to her lack of faith.

"Well?"

"This isn't the time or place."

He caught her by the arm, suddenly serious. "Now, Kit, I want to hear it now."

To their observers, they seemed to be embracing again, but Kit meant to break away from the man she loved. She indicated the gallery of tables above the dance floor where sequined celebrities sparkled in the darkness, coiled in various tête-à-têtes, and, it was rumored, coked up for the long evening of partying ahead.

She was being earnest with him across the table.

"I don't understand, Aden. Why is having children so important to you? Why isn't loving me enough? Is it because you want some kind of immortality?"

"No, it's not that at all. I have my writing for a shot at that. It's just that I've always known there's a rightness to certain things, a suitableness, and for me, fatherhood is one of them." His eyes were a soft plea, his words fiery.

"Aden, I have so many things to do," she said desperately, to those eyes. "If I want to get into some serious writing of my own—a novel, I've got to be so careful with my new life, with you. I can't risk betraying my female self again."

"Does this have to do with Maddy and her daughter? Because I promise you our experience would be different. I *love* you."

"It has nothing to do with Maddy." Kit shook her head. "Think of the tedium. The interminable nine months. The delivery. I'd probably gain a hundred pounds. And afterwards, I don't know—I just can't see myself as the little angel in the house. It won't work."

"Kit, at least say it's possible."

"No. It's not possible. Too many women have been worn out before they ever reached their creativity. I don't want to be one of them. As I said, it won't work."

"No," Aden said, and her heart stopped. "I can see that."

"What's that supposed to mean?"

"I suppose it means good-bye." He unfolded his legs and backed off from the table.

"Aden, stop. You're frightening me." She leaned toward him.

"I'm sorry, Kit. I don't have any control over how I feel about this."

"How can you say that—after we've come such a long way?"

"I don't know, Kit—I don't see that we've come such a long way. Here you are, still worrying about putting on weight. Here I am, still trying to change you."

She reached for his hand. "At least give it some time. We'll talk about it again."

"There really isn't much point, is there?" He rose and gently moved his hand out of her grasp.

She was stung to the core. "Aden, you can't mean to leave me."

"Kit, I love you more than anyone could have told me I'd love a woman. You're in deep, a part of me now, and in that sense, I could never leave you. But after what you said here tonight, I'm afraid I don't believe in you—in us—anymore. The way I used to. The way I need to. Good-bye, Kit. This time you're going to have to stand alone."

Later, when she was running over and over in her mind what had happened that night, she tried to remember why she'd let him go. Finally, in a dream of loneliness, she remembered. She let him go because he was right to want more love in his life, because she was inspired by her own love. She let Aden Lassiter go because she must, this once, stand alone.

* * *

In the year that followed the brilliant Broadway debut of *Plymouth Rocks*, Aden Lassiter did win a Pulitzer. Clayburn bedded Geraldine. Analisa's new agency (she'd left Solarz too) had signed up the president's million-dollar memoirs. And Kit Daniels had resumed her writing career when *Rocks* hit its three-hundredth performance.

She ran with the New York night life, numbered sheikhs and political savants as her intimates, wore the kind of sexy black rags and loads of talismanic jewelry that only a self-proclaimed witch would wear.

Contrary to the expectation of his many friends, Aden did not throw himself into a playtime round of parties and bedrooms when he and Kit Daniels abruptly parted company. Instead, he became rigorous and monastic in his search for the perfect Montauk sky, the perfect phrases for his new drama.

Although he was careful never to say anything crude about his former leading lady/client in public, associates guessed that to invite them to the same party would be the height of social negligence.

That Broadway dancer with the pomegranate lips and the sculpted eyes began to show up at all his favorite hangouts around town. Only Aden Lassiter knew who populated his dreams. And he wasn't telling . . .

But Germaine-like characters kept weaving in and out of his works-in-progress, towering female figures harboring all the wisdom, all the madness of the universe in their savage breasts.

Kit yearned for him every day they were apart.

She was tempted to wait at the stage door after his rehearsals, like any love-struck, purple-haired groupie. She telephoned doggedly every Sunday night when Aden himself was most likely to pick up the phone. She'd bogged down in her novel.

At last, on the anniversary of *Plymouth Rocks*, sometime in midfall, she ran out of hope.

There were men during this time, slick, hungry, Manhattan men. But none of them brought her the thrill of the ropeway, the lure of possibility if she could just cross to the other side of her self—as Aden Lassiter had done.

The closest she got to Aden in the year following their breakup, was at Geraldine's publication party, to which Clayburn had urged her to come.

"Aha!" Clayburn had cried in stertorous tones at her entrance. "Come to eat wormwood and ashes, I see!" He staggered her with a mammoth hug. "All this manhood could have been yours!"

"I know. Sometimes I think I made a major mistake in turning you down."

"You did, you did!" he crowed exuberantly. He then gathered her closer to speak soft conspiracy into her ear. "Have you seen Aden lately?" He shook his great head. "You'd better get him back fast. That's all I have to say."

The Dave Brubeck Trio was playing "Night and Day" on the stereo system, and drinks were flowing. A rumble of laughter went up behind them. All the world seemed to be having a jolly old time.

"He doesn't want me this way, Clayburn. He says he doesn't believe in me anymore."

"Poppycock. The boy's a fool with love for you. Just you wait and see."

"You're very dear." She cast her eyes over the roomful of chic guests. "Has he come yet?"

"Not yet." He went to pick up Alison What's-her-name, the dancing queen."

"Oh no."

"Hey, you're not going to give up that easily, are you?"

A drink later, he'd walked into the party, with Alison McAllister on his arm. She had a Parisian street-style haircut stained the color of fresh orange juice. Her body in motion was a series of perfect curves. The red chiffon bustier dress zigzagged down her body, screeching to a halt at various places, just for effect. A pink diamond pin glittered at each place. Her legs were infinite, sculpted by dance. They glided in with a raucous life of their own.

And all Kit could focus on was the costume Aden wore—a

casually constructed autumn stripe blazer, narrow-width hickory-nut tie, and sharkskin, retro-look pants. It was so silly, really. But he hadn't owned any of those items of clothing when they were together, and it suddenly seemed heartbreaking that his life had gone on, in its daily minutiae, without her. It was as though he'd shed his summer skin, to become something intricate and gorgeous, and unknown to her.

She thought of the gold frames carefully folded and encased on the night table by the side of her bed. The green bookbag in which he carried his youthful memories, was as much a part of her image of Aden as his smoky almond-shaped eyes and schoolboy grin.

The full sense of her loss was too much to bear. She put down her glass and slipped away from the scene that cut through her like a knife.

It was the first cold day of winter, and dusty clouds blew around the sky. The city gave off the damp smell of snow. Kit wanted it to storm, to rage. Happiness had eluded her, like the skyline half sunk in mist. It wasn't that she didn't trust happiness, but it was just something that happened to other people, like winning the lottery. The thing others were rewarded with for a life well lived.

She hadn't even had a life to speak of, until Aden.

How could she expect any reward?

Kit hugged her slouchy red coat to her. It was going to be a long, lonely winter.

And maybe, this time, for her, the summer would never come.

By spring Kit still hadn't moved on with her new book, and the deadline bore down on her with ferocious inevitability.

In the past, when she had been stuck for a fresh slant on things, she'd escaped into conversation with Maddy, up in her white house in Connecticut.

But Kit hadn't received any answers to her last few letters, and Maddy wasn't returning her calls. Of course, that wasn't unusual, considering the demands of caring for a baby. On top of that, Maddy was never really well.

Around the last week of May, on a Tuesday, Kit received a phone call from Jared London, informing her that his wife Madeleine was dead.

Kit left for Connecticut in a rented limousine.

The lawn was just pushing up green, and the house gleamed white in the sun that dipped behind the steeple of the town church.

Kit breathed in the sweetness of the summer air as she came up the walk. In vain, she searched for signs that Maddy was gone, experiencing only a deep peacefulness she hadn't known in months.

Kit was shown into the solarium where the family was in mourning. There was a dull buzz of voices; nutted homemade cakes were being offered around. Jared came up looking frail and shaken. He grasped her hand. "I'm so glad you could come."

It was funny how families turned to outsiders in times of crisis. Maybe because they made events cooler, less apocalyptic. Jared seemed all curled in on himself. *Guilt,* thought Kit bitterly. *He's feeling guilt now for not loving Maddy enough . . .*

"God, Jared, what happened?"

"They said it was anorexia. She just stopped eating. At first, she made up her own crazy diets, a quarter of a pear for lunch, a transparent slice of cheese for dinner. No one could live on it. And she was obsessed with weighing everything, claimed she was fat, and had to diet for a while longer. We tried intravenous feeding, but in the end it seemed she was intent on dying."

Kit had only to close her eyes to see the progress of the adolescent disease. The imaginary bulge of phantom pounds. The sharpening military discipline. The slash of Maddy's will upon her martyred body. Turning knock-kneed. Goiter-eyed. The hair falling in clumps. A perfect skull staring out with serene eyes. The skeleton in every woman's closet. "Feed me," it cried. "Feed me, Mother, for I am weary and near to death."

Kit swayed and held out her hand to the wall in order to steady herself. In a cold flash, she saw herself lying on

Maddy's bed. She felt the closure of her own windpipe. The rattle of her own bones against her own skin. She had lived as Maddy had lived. Undernourished. Unanswered. Unloved.

She would die, as Maddy had died, from starvation, succumb like her poor love-starved sister, unless . . .

"Why didn't you call me sooner?" Kit demanded, warding off the panic with another, more easily handled emotion.

"I was away when it happened, on a business trip."

Suspicion flashed in her eyes.

"You don't believe me."

"It's not my place to believe you or not. You have only Maddy to answer to." She started to move away.

"Wait." He studied Kit's face. "Did Maddy tell you that I was seeing another woman?"

Kit's gaze was steady, accusing. "Weren't you?"

"Kit, you may have no reason to believe me. You've never liked me, I know that. But it was the disease that made her turn against everyone around her, everyone who loved her. She made up fantastic stories about us all—her mother, her father, even you, Kit. She forbade us to call you. Got hysterical if we mentioned your name. Said you were a psychic vampire, draining her soul."

"I'm not going to listen to this." Kit broke away. He was just trying to separate them, as he'd always done. Kit went deeper into the room, where Maddy's mother was sitting and rocking back and forth, her eyes cloudy with grief. Her granddaughter, Samantha, was sitting on her lap.

The old woman didn't say anything but nodded at the seat opposite. Kit, her heart still pounding, sat down.

"She looked so beautiful," the old woman said, entranced with pain. "In her flowing white robes, like a newborn baby. Her skull was smooth and transparent as fine parchment. She did not breathe."

"Mrs. Lefkowitz?"

A low moan came out of the woman, a psalm of grieving and loss.

Suddenly, Kit hoped Maddy had forgiven her mother before she died, before she'd won her battle to the death with her hated female body. She hoped and prayed that Maddy had sensed that a new life had begun.

Maybe in the euphoria of her starvation, she had glimpsed a way of being for women—no longer boxed in by the flesh, no longer split by her own self-hatred—but fiercely free and potent with her love of life, all of life, the world, the flesh, the devil-woman.

Maddy had found her life only in death. She'd made an awful sacrifice so that other women would see the truth before it was too late. But was it too late?

Kit was gripped by a terrible urgency.

Maddy's mother could not be reached. But there were others . . .

She looked into the brilliant eyes of Maddy's child. The little girl raised her arms to be picked up. Without a word, Kit took her from her grandmother and moved out the sliding doors to the terrace outside.

The hot summer sun was slipping quietly away, into the gold-decked horizon. Shadows banded the patio. Kit's mind circled back to her past with Maddy: sharing "bug juice" on hot summer blankets, magazine photos of "hunks," big dreams of the big city. The love of men had seemed such a remote, exotic possibility then. But as it turned out, her friend Maddy had never really believed it was one of her own.

"My mommy is all gone," Samantha said, breaking Kit's heart. She smelled just like a little girl: chocolate milk and Johnson's powder. Her lovely hair was golden, like her mother's. Kit took Samantha onto her lap.

This was the real tragedy. Here.

The daughter who would never know her mother, who would suffer through the same journey, alone, with no hand inside hers.

Kit hugged her tight. "I will be the voice of your mother," she whispered. "I will tell you stories of her. I will show you such glories . . ."

Samantha put her arms around Kit's neck and kissed her cheek.

"You will never be alone," Kit sang. "Now listen. Do you hear the wind blowing through the trees?"

Samantha listened.

"That is the song of your mother in the leaves."

"And there . . ." She set Samantha down, took her by the hand and walked onto the grassy plot behind the house. "This earth, beneath your feet. This is the back of your mother, holding you up, blessing your steps. And do you see that big, shiny ball up there in the sky?"

Samantha looked up solemnly, with a child's love of the magic, the mysterious, and nodded yes.

"That is the face of your mother, shining her light upon your face." Kit dropped down to her knees. She pressed the softness of the child into her arms. "Do you understand, Samantha?" The little girl gave a big smile.

"Are you my mommy now?"

Maddy, you should have waited, Kit said to herself. Tears rolled down her cheeks. *There are omens and signs. But you kept waiting for a savior man. Samantha was the savior. She was the champion. Unto us a child is born. You could have lived and loved Samantha, if you'd only known . . .*

She rose up and took the child in her arms. "Good-bye, my dear friend," she whispered, rising, with the child in her arms. "And thank you."

As it was a weekend, it was easy to find him.

The dunes tumbled and crashed down like siena-colored surf. The sky was a molten blue. Mist-feathered seabirds cut parabolas in the clouds.

Kit's car rolled into the curve of private beach. She shut off the humming motor. Except for the charge of the sea, there was no sound. The car door popped as she slid her legs over and alighted on the sand.

She shaded her face with her hand.

He was high up on a cliff, wings spread like some giant mythological sunbird, his hair a flaming torch in the wind. He stood shining and beautiful on that sandy hill.

Funny. You could search and search, but until you loved, you couldn't see that winged man, the shining hill, only dust and air, shadows on the ground.

She moved forward.

He glided to a perfect landing at the foot of the hill as though pulled by an invisible golden chord. He shed his wings and took off his helmet, looking like nothing so much as a visitor from another world. Kit's hair streamed back in the wind.

"Yes," she said, when he had, at length, noticed her standing there. "I will."

"You will what?" Aden hunkered down, examining the wear and tear on his Apollo, patiently telling each bolt like a believer at a string of rosary beads.

"I will marry you." Had the sun ever been this bright? Kit had to look away. "And we'll see about the rest."

He was silent, going about his business. He did not look up.

When he'd finished, he stood up to his full height in his black jump suit and stretched lazily. "What makes you think I still want to?"

"This . . ." In answer, she moved firmly into his arms, curved her hands around his neck, and brought his mouth down the slight distance to hers. In their excitement, they knocked cheeks and foreheads. They gasped for breath.

"So you've finally made friends with the dragon," he murmured, between kisses. "I was hoping you would."

"What?"

"Just something I saw in a book somewhere."

"I've got to tell you. It won't be easy. I'm not easy."

"I know."

"I can't really afford you, Aden. Or the distractions of love. Too many women have been drained by marriage and children so that they never get to that spark of divine fire inside. But I guess you'll just have to be my sweet indulgence."

"I'd rather be your man."

"Maybe the man I want hasn't been invented yet."

"We'll invent him together."

"The world will hate you. They'll call you a fool."

"It doesn't matter a hoot—if you love me."

"I do."

He looked at her from beneath his long lashes. His curly chestnut hair blew around in the wind. "So does this mean the courting of Kit Daniels is finally over?"

"You never had to court me!" Kit smiled. "Only love me."

"You're a witch."

"Thank you."

He raised her in his arms and swung her around in a dizzying arc. "God, I do love you!"

Kit threw back her head and gave a lusty laugh. "I take it you like the idea of a wedding?"

"You're quick."

"You're wonderful." She hesitated. "Will we fight an awful lot, do you think?"

"Of course." He thought again. "Hell, yes."

Kit looked out around her, at the windy dun-colored dunes, the sea pooling and sucking in at the shore, and she couldn't stop smiling. "Have you noticed how much summer there is this year?"

He let her down and looked deep into her eyes, like the lover he was. "Oh yes, I've noticed."

She put her hand in his, and together they faced into the sun.

From the Unpublished Journal of Mallory Daniels

Kit Daniels and Aden Lassiter finally did get married on a muggy morning in the dog days of August, and I for one was positively ecstatic.

They decided for some vague, crackpot reason to move out of the city and are living somewhere on Montauk. Kit's come full circle—both writing furiously and rearing their spitfire daughter, Darcy, who can outlast any five adults on any given night. I know, because I am the dimwitted Cousin Mallory, Emergency Baby-sitter. (Listen, I may complain a lot, but Darcy is the apple of my eye, and I would give up my shiny new "Oscar" for Best Costume Design if she wanted it to keep her "Cabbage Patch Kid," one Nadine Fredericka, quiet.)

Needless to say, Kit and Aden give out that they are disgustingly happy. They fight all the time.

As for Geraldine and Clayburn, they went on to

become the Ferdinand and Isabella of the publishing industry. After Clay's burst of semiretirement, the two of them managed to pull off a National Book Award. Although no one can understand it, businesswise they are good for each other. *Chacon à son gout.*

Finally, there's me. Well, Rock and I did get back together. After the big push for my Oscar, I felt kind of empty inside, and he seemed the logical antidote to my loneliness. Not to get sloppy or anything, but I haven't regretted it a moment since.

This journal is giving me a headache, so I'm going to close now. I just hope I can sell it, fast, for a zillion dollars, because there's this cute little villa in Rome that Rock and I have had our eye on for a while now.

It belongs to Kit's stepfather, Paolo, and has oodles of closet space. So, do me a favor, and tell your friends about my book.